She had seen the murderer, but it looked as if she might take the fall herself…

"Oh, my God. He's dead."

Emmeline craned her neck around to find herself in the crosshairs of several horrified stares. She caught a whisper of movement out of the corner of her eye. She turned and saw the woman in white crossing the lobby. She broke her stride for only a second, long enough to cast a quick glance over her shoulder. Instinct told Emmeline that the woman had to be stopped.

With little grace, she prized her hand from the dead man's hold. If she could just prevent the woman from leaving the hotel.

She found her way blocked by several patrons. "Where do you think you're going?"

Emmeline's back stiffened. "Would you please get out of my way? I have to stop that woman. It's very important."

A portly gentleman with a smug, craggy face clamped his sausage-like fingers around her upper arm. "So that you can scarper to Argentina or wherever it is criminals go these days? I don't think so. I was not born yesterday, you know. You're staying right here until the police arrive."

She struggled against his grasp. "Criminal? You don't understand."

If the answer is a lie...the truth is murder

Journalist Emmeline Kirby is reeling from the recent discovery that her parents were murdered while on assignment, when she was five. She flirts with danger as she sets off on the long-cold trail to find their killer. At the same time, her probing questions about the suspicious death of Russian national Pavel Melnikov gain her a coterie of enemies. To complicate matters, her path crosses with prominent industrialist Victor Royce, who turns her world upside down.

Gregory Longdon, her dashing fiancé and jewel-thief-cum-insurance-investigator, has grave problems of his own. His past has caught up with him. Alastair Swanbeck, a ruthless entrepreneur with ties to Putin and the underworld, is alive and intent on revenge. Swanbeck's cat-and-mouse taunts reveal that he can get to Gregory—and Emmeline—anytime he desires. When evil's poison lurks in things that are better left alone, the quest for justice could prove fatal for Emmeline and Gregory.

Critical Praise for Daniela Bernett

Lead Me Into Danger

"Adventure from Venice to London with an engaging cast of characters in this fresh, fast-paced mystery filled with jewel thefts, international intrigue, unexpected twists, and a lovely touch of romance." ~ Tracy Grant, bestselling author of *The Mayfair Affair*

Deadly Legacy

"Stolen diamonds, revenge, and murder are served up at a cracking pace as Emmeline unites with Gregory once again in this intriguing second installment of Daniella Bernett's mystery series." ~ Tessa Arlen, author of the Lady Montfort series and Agatha Award finalist

"Daniella Bernett weaves a complex and engaging tale of suspense and mystery in *Deadly Legacy*...The story [has a] Hitchcockian feel...[and a] shocker of a twist ending that took me completely by surprise." ~ Debbi Mack, *New York Times* bestselling author

"Emmeline and Gregory's new adventure is a delightful blend of mystery and romance, filled with dazzling twists and turns, unexpected dangers, and old and new tensions in their relationship." ~ Tracy Grant, author of *London Gambit*

From Beyond the Grave

"Dark secrets, deceit, and murder threaten Emmeline and Gregory's future along the scenic Devon coast...A story sure to please fans of romantic suspense." ~ D. E. Ireland, authors of the Agatha-nominated Eliza Doolittle and Henry Higgins Mysteries

"Escape to Torquay with Emmeline and Gregory for a seaside whirlwind of mystery, romance, and unexpected secrets that will leave you eagerly anticipating the next book in the series!" ~ Tracy Grant, author of *Gilded Deceit*

"*From Beyond The Grave* is a tense thriller that had me hooked from the first page, and kept my attention until the last; it has even made me go and buy the previous two books in the series. The attention to detail, the layers of deceit and lies between the characters, and the plot combine to make this an enjoyable read." ~ Bookliterati Book Reviews

A Checkered Past

"Daniella Bernett delivers up another masterful tale of suspense, this time involving family betrayals, government intrigue, and insidious wartime crimes, that will have readers clamoring for justice. Prepare for a brisk ride with plenty of twists to keep you reading late into the night!" ~ Alyssa Maxwell, author of *The Gilded Newport Mysteries*

"Stolen art, memories of the French Resistance, and a charming man of dubious integrity make *A Checkered Past* a delightful read. A wonderful installment in Daniella Bernett's Emmeline Kirby-Gregory Longdon series!" ~ Tasha Alexander, *New York Times* bestselling author of *Death in St. Petersburg*

"Emmeline and Gregory are back in another fast-paced adventure as they unravel a mystery that stretches back to World War II—and touches on the secrets of Gregory's shadowy past. An enchanting blend of adventure, mystery, and romance that makes for the perfect late summer escape." ~Tracy Grant, author of *The Duke's Gambit*

Other Books in the Emmeline Kirby/Gregory Longdon Series

Lead Me Into Danger
Deadly Legacy
From Beyond the Grave
A Checkered Past

ACKNOWLEDGMENTS

I would like to thank Acquisitions Editor Lauri Wellington, who continues to have confidence in my work; editor Faith C., who gives my books the extra polish they need; and Jack Jackson, a master designer, who creates the beautiful covers for my books.

My continued gratitude to the Mystery Writers of America New York Chapter for its support.

I would like to thank bestselling author Tracy Grant, who has been on this journey with me from the beginning. My deepest thanks also go to Alyssa Maxwell, Emma Jameson, Meg Mims, Sharon Piscareta, and Tasha Alexander, with whom I became friends via Facebook and exchange lively ideas about writing and life.

WHEN BLOOD RUNS COLD

An Emmeline Kirby/Gregory Longdon Mystery

Daniella Bernett

A Black Opal Books Publication

GENRE: MYSTERY-DETECTIVE/WOMEN SLEUTHS

This is a work of fiction. Names, places, characters and incidents are either the product of the author's imagination or are used fictitiously, and any resemblance to any actual persons, living or dead, businesses, organizations, events or locales is entirely coincidental. All trademarks, service marks, registered trademarks, and registered service marks are the property of their respective owners and are used herein for identification purposes only. The publisher does not have any control over or assume any responsibility for author or third-party websites or their contents.

To my parents and my sister Vivian with love,
I am so lucky to have you.

CHAPTER 1

London, July 2010:

*M**y parents were murdered. Murdered.* This torment-
ing thought careened around Emmeline's head for
the millionth time in the two weeks since Yoav
Zielinski, the Israeli cultural attaché, had sent her that damned
letter and file. She pulled them out of her desk drawer and
slowly read through them once again, although she could re-
cite every word in her sleep—that is, when she had been able
to sleep.

Zielinski was a kind man who sincerely believed she
should know the truth. After all, wasn't the search for truth
and justice the very tenet by which she lived and breathed as a
journalist and now as editorial director of *The Clarion*? Yes, of
course it was and it always would be. And yet...and yet this
was different. These were her parents. This disturbing new
knowledge had shaken her more than she was willing to admit.
She was drowning, plunging deeper and deeper below the water's surface. She was being suffocated by her utter helpless-
ness. She had to find her parents' murderer. But how? It had
all happened twenty-five years ago when they had been on
assignment in Lebanon.

Emmeline shoved the file away from her and fingered the
photo of her parents, which sat on her desk next to the ones of
Gran and Gregory. All the important people in her life. Where
should she start? If there had been any clues, the trail had gone
cold by now. So very cold. Who would want to kill her parents
and, above all, *why*? She rested her chin on her hand. Her gaze
strayed across her office to the window. However, she saw

nothing of the lovely London skyline. Her mind was trapped in the past. A past she was ignorant of because she had been a mere child of five. At that time, her world had been filled with happiness because she had been secure in the knowledge of her parents' unconditional love. She didn't need anything else. They were everything anyone could ever want and more. Then one day, her world was shattered and they were gone. Just like that in a blink of an eye. But they didn't simply die, they were *murdered*.

Emmeline stiffened. This terrible weight on her shoulders didn't affect her alone. She knew Gran had a right to know, painful as it was. She had reached for the telephone a dozen times in the past week, but her courage had deserted her at the last second on each occasion. She had to find the right words. She couldn't keep it from Gran. But how did one tell a mother that her daughter and son-in-law had their lives snatched away?

Emmeline shook her head. A long sigh escaped her lips. With a trembling hand, she picked up the receiver and punched in the number. Her heart was in her mouth when her grandmother's voice came on the line. "Hello, Gran. It's me."

"Well, hello, Emmy." Helen Davis's voice was laced with love and warmth. "What a pleasant surprise. MacTavish and I just this instant returned from a long, lovely ramble. Didn't we?" There's a muffled *woof, woof* in the background.

Tears stung Emmeline's eyelids. She could picture her grandmother and that rascal of a Scottish terrier tramping about the woods in the Kentish countryside. "That sounds nice." She hoped Gran couldn't hear the tremor in her voice. She sat up straighter in her chair and said in a rush, "Look, Gran, the reason why I rang is because…well, I need talk to you about something. Something important."

"So talk. I have all the time in world, love."

Emmeline cleared her throat. "It's…it's a bit involved. I was wondering if it would be all right to come down to Swaley this weekend. I know it's all last minute, but—"

Helen cut her off. "Silly girl, since when did you have to ask? You know that you're welcome any time of the day or night." She paused and then excitement tickled her voice. "Wait a minute. I know what this is all about."

"You do? But you can't have found out," Emmeline stammered.

"When are you going to learn that there's not much that gets past me? You and that devilishly attractive scoundrel have finally come to your senses and set a date. Haven't you? It took you long enough. I don't know what you were waiting for—"

Emmeline had to nip this in the bid before it got out of control. "No, Gran. Gregory and I haven't set a date yet."

She could hear the irritation creeping into Helen's tone. "Sometimes I despair of you. I really do. Why are you holding that poor boy at arm's length? He's proved his love to you a thousand times over. The past is the past, Emmy. You have to let go. Otherwise, it's going to eat away at you until there's nothing left."

This was too much. Her eyes were swimming and a lump had lodged itself firmly in her throat. "That's just it, Gran," she whispered hoarsely. "The past doesn't want to let go of me. It keeps coming back to haunt me with a vengeance."

There was silence at the other end of the line for a long moment. Then, Helen said softly, "Come whenever you like. Don't worry. There's nothing we can't sort out together. You'll see." She paused. "But I'm warning you that if you don't bring Gregory, MacTavish will not allow you to cross the threshold. Do I make myself clear?"

For the first time in a week, laughter bubbled up to Emmeline's lips. "Yes, Gran. Message received and understood."

"I'm glad to hear it. By the way, I'm not going to allow the two of you to leave until we settle on a date for your wedding."

"*We*?"

"Of course, *we*. Much as I love you, I'm sad to say that the two of you have been a complete and utter disappointment. You have proven that you're quite incapable of accomplishing this simple little task. I blame myself. I left you to your own devices for far too long. But no more. You need a firm hand to guide you. Someone has to show you the error of your ways. Maggie thoroughly agrees with me."

Emmeline bit her lip. She was certain that Maggie, her best friend, and her grandmother were on the phone plotting round the clock. Seeing her and Gregory married had become their sole mission in life. And heaven help the person who stood in their way. They made a formidable pair. "I see. Do you really need me and Gregory? It sounds as if you and Maggie have already set the date and arranged the honeymoon."

"That's quite enough of that. I'll have none of your cheek, my girl," Helen replied. Although the words were stern, there was an undercurrent of amusement in her tone. "I'll expect you and you-know-who on Saturday for lunch."

Emmeline's mouth curled into a smile. "I love you, Gran. I'm the luckiest girl in the world because I have you."

Helen chuckled in her ear. "Indeed you are. And you know how much I love you, my precious darling girl. However, you will feel my wrath if—"

"Yes, yes. I know. A date."

"Good. I'm glad to see that we understand each other. Cheery bye until Saturday."

There was a soft click as her grandmother severed the connection. Emmeline's mood sobered. Until Saturday. She had three days to find the right words. But murder was so vile and sinister. Were there any *right* words?

ℰ∽ℰ∽

The minute Gregory stepped into his sumptuous two-bedroom flat in the sleek 1920s Art Deco building on Albert Road in Primrose Hill, the hairs on the back of his neck prickled with the unsettling certainty that somebody had been there. Or still *was* there. He quietly dumped his keys on the Queen Anne console table.

His body tense, every nerve tingling and straining, he crossed the entrance hall on the balls of his feet. His not-so-old *métier* as a jewel thief stood him in good stead. His tread was so light that his footfalls barely disturbed the air. The only one who would be taken by surprise would be his hapless intruder.

His fingers curled around the doorknob. He took a deep breath before he flung open the door to the spacious living room, which had a picturesque view of Regent's Park.

No one. He made a slow circuit of the room. Not a single piece of furniture or painting escaped that shrewd cinnamon gaze. Nothing was out of place, not even the *objets d'art* on the mantelpiece.

He repeated the same exercise in the study, the dining room, kitchen, the guest bedroom, and the bathroom. Nothing. And yet he couldn't shake the nagging feeling that someone had been there.

He stood in front of the master bedroom and pushed the door open with his foot. It creaked slightly on its hinges making him cringe inside.

His gaze locked on it instantly. A single, perfect coral rose nestled on his pillow.

He was across the room in two strides. He stared down at the delicate bloom. His fingers reached out and grazed its velvety petals just as the telephone on his night table began to ring. He fumbled for the receiver.

"Hello."

No one responded. His back stiffened. He could hear someone's steady breathing.

He gritted his teeth. "Swanbeck." It wasn't a question. "I got your present." He held the rose out in front of him and twirled it between his thumb and forefinger. "You can't hide forever."

The silence was broken by a deep-throated huff of smug laughter and then the line went dead.

Gregory slammed the receiver back in the cradle, making the crystal glass on his night table jump. *Damn and blast*, he thought. *Why couldn't the bloody bastard have remained dead? Things were finally falling into place with Emmy. Why did Swanbeck have to surface from the mire again?*

The strident peal of the telephone interrupted these unsettling ruminations. Right.

He snatched up the receiver. "I'm not impressed by your

little games. In fact, they're rather childish. Only a coward clings to the shadows."

"What are you on about, Gregory?"

The unexpected sound of Emmeline's voice unbalanced him for a minute. "E—Emmy? Is that you, d—darling?" he stammered.

"Yes, it's me. Are you quite all right? You sound distinctly...odd."

He recovered his equanimity and said smoothly, "Do I, darling? It must be the connection. You know what modern technology is like. The more sophisticated it is, the more prone to problems. I'm perfectly fine. Better than fine actually, since you've agreed to become my wife. Why would you think otherwise? I was simply sitting here daydreaming about you."

"Uh, huh," she replied skeptically. "I don't believe you. You're up to something. I can hear it in your voice, but I don't have time right now to worm it out of you. I have to run into a meeting. I wanted to thank you for the roses. They were a lovely surprise. They just arrived."

The smile vanished from Gregory's lips. His fingers tensed around the phone. "Roses? What roses?"

"What do you mean what roses? The enormous bouquet of coral roses, which you know are my favorites. They came with a card. 'To the love of my life. I am nothing without you.'"

Long, tapered fingers of cold fear wrapped themselves around Gregory's heart and his mouth went dry.

Emmeline continued to chatter on, but he had no idea what she was saying.

"You aren't listening, are you? I can feel it."

He cleared his throat. "Of course, I am, darling. Every word is etched in my mind." He hoped he sounded lighthearted. "It simply slipped my mind about the roses. I'm glad they brightened your afternoon. Remember, the reservations are at eight. I'll collect you at seven-thirty."

"I haven't forgotten. This is my last meeting of the day and then I'm going straight home to change. There's just one thing I wanted to tell you. We're going down to Gran's this weekend. It's a command performance I'm afraid."

Gregory's body relaxed a little. "Ah, Helen. The other great love in my life. How can a man be so lucky?"

"Dearest, you can turn off the charm. This is me you're talking to. You don't have to extoll *my* grandmother's virtues. Just listen. I've put it off too long. I have to tell her about...well, about Mummy and Daddy. But I have to do it in person."

"Of course you do. I'll be there by your side. I won't let you do this alone." His voice was gentle and full of affection.

"Yes, I know. And I love you very much for it," she replied shakily. "I've never needed you more. I feel like I'm stumbling around in the dark." She paused and then went on in a stronger voice, "However, prepare yourself for battle. Gran has plans with a capital P. Apparently, she is going to keep us prisoner—under the watchful eye of that brute of a guard dog MacTavish—until we set a date for our wedding."

The laughter rumbled forth from Gregory's throat. "Is she now? A woman after my own heart. I should have enlisted her services long ago. Perhaps if I had, we would have been an old married couple by now."

"Ha. Ha. You know very well that Gran and Maggie are putty in your hands. They've been in your corner since the Ice Age. They don't need any encouragement to enthusiastically take up your cause."

"What can I say, my love? They are two extremely discerning women and recognize quality when they see it."

Emmeline groaned. "Right. I've had quite enough of your ego for one afternoon. I've got to run. I'll see you later."

"I'll be counting the minutes," he replied, but she had already rung off.

Gregory sank down heavily onto his bed. He frowned as he stared malevolently at the rose.

"Touch one hair on her head, Swanbeck," he said aloud, "and I'll kill you."

He squeezed the rose so hard that a thorn pricked his thumb and drew blood.

CHAPTER 2

Emmeline was surprised—although she shouldn't have been—at how calmly her grandmother had taken the news about her parents' murder. After the initial shock had passed, Gran had been very matter-of-fact, the perfect embodiment of stiff upper lip. And extremely infuriating.

"Well, Emmy," she had said. "It's quite a disturbing turn of events, isn't it? But it doesn't alter the fact that Jacqueline and Aaron are dead and nothing will bring them back."

"What are you saying, Gran?" Emmeline had asked incredulously. "Don't you *want* to find out who murdered them? Don't you want to see that justice is done?"

Gran had taken her face between her hands at that point and pressed a kiss to her forehead. "How will that help? It was all so long ago."

"But—"

"Shh." Another soft kiss. "It won't bring them back. And I, for one—" There was a tremor in Gran's voice just then. "—am too old to go through that heartache all over again. It's best to let sleeping dogs lie."

Emmeline had jumped up, incensed. "I can't believe my ears. We—I—*must* find out the truth. Mummy and Daddy's murderer has been roaming free for twenty-five years. Doesn't that bother you?"

Helen shook her head sadly and sank down into the overstuffed armchair. "Oh, Emmy."

Gregory had intervened—to his regret—at that point. "Darling, perhaps Helen is right."

She impaled him with what she hoped was the darkest glacial stare imaginable. "*Et tu, Brute*? I thought you were on my side."

Gregory had sighed and gotten to his feet. He attempted to draw her into his arms, but she took a step backward and mulishly crossed her arms over her chest.

He threw his hands up in the air. "Fine," he snapped, his voice laced with annoyance. "Wallow in your righteousness, if it makes you feel better. But don't take your frustration and fear out on those who love you. Everyone is on *your* side. It's just that you're not thinking clearly at the moment."

Emmeline had felt like the wind had been knocked out of her. She was well and duly chastened. "I'm sorry. I've been rather childish, haven't I?"

She slipped her arms around Gregory's waist and pressed her cheek against his chest.

He had rested his chin on top of her head. "Not childish. Just you." He pulled away and gazed down at her, an indulgent gleam in his eyes. "You can't help being who you are. God help the rest of us mere mortals who get in your way."

A faint smile tugged at the corners of his mouth as she swatted his arm and her heart melted. Everything was all right between them. For the first time since he had come back into her life, she truly believed they had a chance.

After that, Gran had taken charge. And true to her word, she was relentless. It was no wonder that in the end she had gotten her way, as always, and they had agreed that October would be a lovely month for their wedding. Three months was not a lot of time to make preparations, but as she and Gregory both wanted an intimate affair—just family and a few close friends—Gran assured them that she and Maggie would see to it that it was a day to remember. After all, they had been discussing their ideas for *such* a long time that it was merely the moment to put their plan into action.

✦✦✦

Emmeline leaned back in her chair and chuckled as the picture of Helen's face, all glowing and flushed with excitement, floated before her eyes.

"Dear, dear, Gran," Emmeline said aloud to her office on

Monday morning. "I would have been lost without you."

A light tapping on her door brought her back to the present. It was Desmond, the senior political correspondent. He wanted to go over something with her for a series he had in mind.

They settled matters very quickly and then it was time for Emmeline to go out to do her interview with Victor Royce for her new series on influential men and women in British society, who had come from humble backgrounds and worked hard to overcome the odds.

Royce had long intrigued her. He was far from a recluse. It was common knowledge that he was the son of Jewish immigrants who had fled France to escape the Nazis. He was first-generation British, but so much about his past was shrouded in secrecy. Was this merely a case of an extremely wealthy man wanting to safeguard his privacy or did he have something to hide? There had been whispers in recent years that he was a spy. For the British? The Russians? The Israelis? Who knew? There also were spiteful rumblings that he had made his money through illegal means.

The questions only seemed to multiply. One thing was certain, though. Emmeline was going to take a damn good crack at finding out the truth. Her instincts told her that there was a fascinating story lying just beneath the surface.

෴

A tall, slim woman in her late forties dressed in a crisply tailored beige suit was waiting for Emmeline as she stepped off the lift.

"Miss Kirby?" she asked politely in a low husky voice.

"Yes."

The woman smiled and extended a manicured hand. "I'm Mr. Royce's secretary. He asked me to keep an eye out for your arrival. I'm afraid he's running slightly behind schedule today. He had to attend to an unexpected problem that cropped up with one of Royce Shipping's tankers in Aberdeen."

Emmeline pursed her lips. "I see," she replied stiffly. "So Mr. Royce is canceling our interview, is that what you're telling me?" *Who does the arrogant bugger think he is wasting my time?* she fumed silently.

"Good gracious, no. Mr. Royce is a man of his word. He promised you an interview and you shall have it. However, he suggested that I give you a tour of the office first. I can provide a brief overview of the company and its different divisions while he takes care of the Aberdeen matter. He hopes to meet with you—" She checked her watch. "—in about half an hour, if that's all right? I'll do my best to answer any questions that you may have."

"Oh...well, yes. Yes, that would be fine." *Perhaps I judged the man too hastily*, Emmeline thought. *I must learn to give people the benefit of the doubt...at first.* "That would be splendid. It would give me better insight into the inner workings of Royce Global Holdings. I've done a little research and I already have a few questions."

The secretary smiled, the lines crinkling at the corners of her blue eyes. "Excellent." She extended an arm to her right. "Will you please follow me this way? I think we'll start with the Mining division."

A little over half an hour later, the secretary was leading Emmeline down a corridor toward Royce's office. It had been a highly illuminating tour. She had scribbled away in her notebook the entire time.

The secretary rapped her knuckles lightly on her boss's door and paused for a second before she reached for the doorknob. She poked her head round the door. "Mr. Royce?" The office was empty.

"Hmm. Not back yet." She opened the door wider and stepped aside to allow Emmeline to pass. "Why don't you have a seat, Miss Kirby? I'll just go see what's detaining Mr. Royce. In the interim, would you like a cup of tea while you wait?"

"That would be lovely. Thank you."

The secretary nodded. "I'll only be a few minutes." She softly closed the door behind her.

Emmeline crossed the room. There was a caramel leather sofa and two matching high-back armchairs clustered around a low coffee table on her right, but she chose the chair opposite Royce's magnificently carved mahogany desk. She was certain that it was an antique. Perched on the edge of her seat, her back straight, she allowed her gaze to drift over the office for a moment or two to try to get a feel for the man who ruled his empire from this inner sanctum. Victor Royce had excellent taste, indeed. She was looking forward to meeting the man in person.

However, the minutes ticked by and still there was no sign of him. Emmeline used her time alone to go over the questions she had prepared for Royce. She jotted down a couple more based on the tour she had just been given.

She jumped when the door suddenly flew open behind her. "Please forgive me, Miss Kirby," a deep male voice intoned.

He was by the desk in two strides. Emmeline started to get up but he waved her back down. "Please don't get up."

She got a quick glimpse of a tall man with a bit of a paunch and a thick head of straight hair that once must have been a rich brown, but was now turning gray, as he scooted around the desk and settled into his own chair. "There, that's better."

He extended his hand across the desk and looked her directly in the eye for the first time since entering the room. "It's a pleasure to meet you, Miss Kirb—" The smile froze on his lips and his breath caught in his throat. "Good God, Jacqui."

It was a stunned whisper.

CHAPTER 3

The strange look in those deep brown eyes made Emmeline shiver. "Jacqui," he said again. His gaze was fixed and yet she didn't think he was seeing her. She craned her neck around, but the door was closed.

"Are you all right, Mr. Royce? Shall I get your secretary for you?"

He blinked twice. It was an uncomfortable moment before he responded. "What?"

"I said shall I get Jacqui, your secretary, for you."

He cocked his head to one side. "Jacqui? My secretary?"

"Yes. You were just calling for her. Perhaps she can help."

He leaned back in his chair, dazed. "I don't understand."

"That makes two of us," Emmeline said *sotto voce.*

The door opened at this point and the secretary came in carrying a tray laden with a teapot and delicate cups and saucers decorated with tiny red rosebuds.

Emmeline stood and hurried over to relieve her of the tray. "Ah, thank goodness. Mr. Royce appears to be in some sort of distress. He was calling for you a moment ago."

The secretary shot a concerned glance at her boss. She took a half-step forward. "Mr. Royce, is there anything you ne—"

He flapped a hand at her impatiently as he rose to join them. "It was nothing, Delia."

Delia? If she's Delia, who the devil is Jacqui? Emmeline thought as she stared at Royce.

"Put it down to an old man's mental lapse," he was saying, as he took his secretary's elbow and led her to the door. "Now, go about your business and leave us."

Delia hesitated, her gaze flickered toward Emmeline before settling on her boss's face.

He jerked his chin. "Go on. I'm fine. Nothing that a lovely cup of tea won't cure."

She shrugged. "If you're sure, Mr. Royce?"

"I am. Please see to it that I'm not disturbed for an hour." He slid a sideways glance at Emmeline. "I've kept Miss Kirby waiting far too long already."

"Yes, Mr. Royce." And with that, she was gone and they were alone again.

Royce slipped a hand in one pocket and turned to face Emmeline. He gave her a sheepish grin.

She felt rather foolish standing in the middle of the office holding the tea tray.

"Where are my manners? Let me take that." Before she realized what was happening, he had relieved her of the tray and was walking toward the coffee table. "It's cozier over here. More conducive to talking."

Emmeline stood rooted to the spot. She didn't know what to make of this man. "Come on," he urged as he placed the tray carefully on the table and settled himself in the middle of the sofa. He picked up the pot. "I'll be mother, shall I?"

The smile he flashed was infectious and she found herself returning it as she went to join him. "It's your office, after all, Mr. Royce. I'd say that you have the right to do whatever you like." She lowered herself into the armchair across from him.

His brow furrowed slightly. "That rather makes me sound like I'm an ogre and I assure you, I'm not. Milk? Sugar?"

She shook her head. "No, thank you. A slice of lemon, please. And you don't strike me as an ogre. Rather, a man who likes things just so."

He pierced a slice of lemon with a tiny fork and dropped it into her cup. "Hmm. Well, I suppose you're correct to certain extent."

He proffered her the cup and then busied himself splashing milk into his own. He stirred and lifted the cup to his lips to take a sip. Satisfied, he leaned back in his chair and crossed one long leg over the other. He was silently appraising her over the rim of his cup.

Emmeline shifted her body and took a sip of tea to cover

the fact that his steady brown gaze was unnerving. *Damn it. Why is he staring at me like that?*

She took another swig of tea and put the cup down on the table. She cleared her throat, becoming brisk and business-like. "Now then," she said as she flipped open her notebook. "As I told your secretary over the phone when we arranged this interview, I'm doing a series on influential British men and women whose wealth and positions were not handed to them on the proverbial silver platter, but rather who drove themselves to achieve their dreams through sheer will and hard work."

"And you think your readers would be interested in me? The son of Russian and French Jews who had to flee not once, not twice, but three times because the Nazis were baying at their heels and wanted blood. It was not enough that the bastards stole everything they could get their filthy hands on." His jaw tightened and there was a harsh edge to his voice. "Everything."

"Yes, indeed. It makes for an even more compelling story. The story of survival. The drive and determination to push forward even when faced with insurmountable odds. That's true courage."

"You think so? With anti-Semitism rearing its ugly head more and more these days, you don't think it would give those with hate in their hearts another excuse to spew their vile rants about Jews and money. Ahh, forget it." He threw his hands up in the air in disgust. "Not being a Jew, you wouldn't understand, Miss Kirby."

"But you're wrong. I do understand because I *am* Jewish. I was fortunate to have been born here in England, and so were my parents and grandparents. But I *know* the stories. They're part of the fabric of my life and my family's history. I've been on the receiving end of some subtle and not-so-subtle insults over the years." Her head tilted back and her chin jutted forward. "What you have to do is to stand up to those types of people because they are nothing but bullies...and envious cowards. You must never let them get away with it. Never."

"Hmph," was Royce's only response. He stirred his tea

slowly, the tiny spoon tinkling as it brushed against the side of the cup.

Emmeline held her breath. Perhaps she had gone too far. Sometimes her tongue had a tendency to run away of its own accord when she was in a lather about a subject on which she had strong feelings.

Royce simply stared at her. The thoughts behind those mesmerizing eyes were well and truly veiled.

She cleared her throat. "Forgive me, Mr. Royce. I shouldn't have been so outspoken."

He leaned forward in his chair. "Nonsense. It's quite refreshing to meet someone who knows her own mind and is not afraid to speak out against injustice. And for those too weak to be able to do it for themselves. I'm very impressed. You remind me of—" He broke off and sat up, back ramrod straight.

That same odd look crept onto his face again. "Yes, Mr. Royce?" she ventured anxiously.

"What? Oh. You remind me of...someone I used to know. A long time ago..." His voice trailed off in a whisper. He tore his eyes away and took another of sip of tea.

Emmeline studied his profile over the rim of her cup. She could see that he was trying to master himself once more. Whoever this woman had been that she reminded him of—and it had to be a woman to roil his emotions to such an extent— she must have been very special. The one who got away.

She heard a faint sigh escape his lips. Regret at what might have been? She could have been watching herself two years ago when Gregory had left her. And then shortly afterward, she had lost the baby. She felt tears prick her eyelids. How well she recognized that look of longing mingled with a deep and wretched sadness.

"Are you all right, Mr. Royce?" she asked. Her tone was gentle. "Would you rather reschedule the interview?"

His gaze met hers. In that instant, they understood each other without a word passing between them. He shook his head emphatically. "Certainly not. Fire away with your questions."

"Well, if you're sure." Her cup and saucer clinked softly as she set them down on the table and pulled out her notebook. "Family always exerts a strong influence and helps to shape one as a person. So, I'd like to start with your parents. I'd like you to tell me a little about them. You said that they were Russian and French Jews. How did they meet?"

"In the Resistance. My father had been studying to become a doctor in Vienna. He saw the writing on the wall when the Austrians welcomed Hitler with open arms. He abandoned his studies and fled one night with a single suitcase. He tried to get back to Russia to his parents, but he got trapped…in Berlin. The heart of the devil's lair. If he wasn't killed, his only chance was to try to get to Switzerland."

Emmeline perched on the edge of her seat and leaned in closer, all her attention fixed on this man. "How terrifying."

"Indeed. Out of the frying pan and into the fire. He lived in hiding for two months. He found an abandoned house on the outskirts of the city and managed to loosen one of the boards so that he could enter and leave. He didn't dare wander the streets during the day. Only at night he would venture out to try to find some food to calm his terrible hunger pangs. Of course, this couldn't go on indefinitely. Someone must have seen him coming or going and betrayed him. One night, two Nazi soldiers were lying in wait for him. They beat him badly. Then they dragged him out by his heels and dumped him into the back of a foul-smelling lorry. He heard one of them mumble something about the train and camp. My father didn't need to hear more. He knew what that meant. Every part of his body was twisted in pain. One eye was swollen shut. He had three broken ribs, one of which had punctured a lung. But he knew he had to get away. Somehow. Once they reached the train station, it would be too late. All would be lost.

"But it was not his time to go that night. You know what saved my father?"

Emmeline shook her head.

"A pothole. Bloody great pothole. The lorry hit it and overturned. The soldier driving was knocked unconscious and his mate was dazed. My father tried to wrest his gun from him, but he was too weak. The solider knocked him to the ground, gave him another vicious kick to his ribs, and stood there laughing as he aimed his rifle at my father's chest. For an instant, time froze and they simply stared at one another. Then the solider spat at my father and pulled the trigger."

Emmeline shuddered and drew in a ragged breath into her lungs. Her heart quickened. But she waited for Royce to continue his tale.

"A fraction of a second before the shot went off, my father summoned all his strength to roll to his left. The bullet hit him in the thigh with a fiery vengeance. Blind with pain and rage, he lashed out with his other foot, catching the solider on the ankle and knocking him off balance. My father's fingers scrabbled wildly until they clamped around the cold, hard metal of the trigger. He pulled it before the soldier could recover his wits. The horror of killing a man paralyzed him, but then the primal instinct for survival took control. My father managed to crawl the hundred feet into the woods by the side of the road. For five days and five nights, that's where he remained hidden under some leaves, delirious with pain and fever, too terrified to move."

"Dear God. I can't even imagine what your father went through. How did he get out?"

Royce paused and took a long swallow of tea. "That part was always fuzzy in my father's mind. He had vague images. Men's voices heard as if through a fog. The fact of the matter is, he was smuggled out of Berlin and into France. His first clear recollection was of waking up in a safe house. The first person he clapped eyes on was my mother. And what a lovely sight she was. Thick chestnut hair falling in waves to her shoulders and intelligent brown eyes flecked with gold." A fond smile touched his lips. "He told me he fell in love with her even before he knew her name or heard her speak."

Emmeline couldn't help but return his smile. "A true *coup de foudre*."

"Indeed. Anyway, by now you've probably guessed that this was a Resistance cell. They nursed my father back to health. In exchange for saving his life, he joined the fight against the Nazi bastards. Working together in such stressful circumstances, the little band became close. A family. Everyone in the group had lost someone to the bloody war. In my mother's case, her mother, father, and brother were rousted late one night from their flat in Paris and sent to Dachau. My mother escaped the Nazis' clutches because she had been staying with a sick aunt that night. She never saw her parents or brother again."

Royce became silent for a long moment. Sorrow and anger etched in the lines of his face. He shook his head.

Emmeline's heart ached for what his parents and the millions of others like them had suffered and lost because of a mad man.

Royce pulled himself together and sat up straighter in his chair. "Well, look at me getting all maudlin. My parents would not have liked that one bit. Despite everything they had gone through, they didn't become embittered by what they had experienced. On the contrary, they always lived each day to the fullest and were grateful that God had spared them. In March 1943, they managed to escape to London. They married in May. It was not easy as refugees, but they were blissfully happy. They were eager to become citizens. My father changed his name from Mayer Rutkovsky to Martin Royce to become a true Englishman. My mother had seen the name Royce in the paper and liked the way it rolled off her tongue. Sandrine Royce.

"My parents were both fluent in several languages, among them German, and then there was their Resistance experience, which made them doubly valuable to Britain's war effort. They never told me *exactly* what they did, but from certain things I was able to glean as I was growing up—a slip of the tongue here and there—I think they were spies and were sent back into Germany to carry out more elaborate sabotage missions and to rescue our wounded airmen." He saw Emmeline's eyebrows shoot up. "But then it could just be a boy's romantic fantasy. In any case, it was all before my time. I was born in October 1946. My parents were so proud. I was the first generation. I represented hope for the future. And so, they settled into life in their adopted country. My father became a chemistry professor at King's College and my mother gave piano and voice lessons."

Royce sat back and grinned. "She had a lovely voice. As a boy, I would sit entranced, listening to her sing. She should have become a professional opera singer, but she was content as she was. And so the years passed until they retired to a little cottage in Oxfordshire. My parents taught me to work hard and, above all, to learn in school because education is the key that opens all doors."

"Yes, for Jews education is all important. My grandmother instilled that in me."

"Your grandmother? Not your parents?"

Emmeline put her notebook and pen down in her lap. "My grandmother is the one who raised me. My parents died when I was five, nearly six. They were journalists like me. My father was a correspondent and my mother was a photojournalist. They were a team. They died in 1985...while on assignment in Lebanon." Her voice faltered for an instant and she had to swallow the bile rising to her throat. She clasped her hands together so tightly that her knuckles turned white. *They were murdered*, her mind screamed silently.

His face took on a grayish pallor. "Journalists...Lebanon...Five years old. How...tragic."

She managed to regain her composure. "It was. But I have the best grandmother in the entire world and she saw that I wanted for nothing."

His mouth broke into a smile. "I'm glad to hear it. From what I see today, your grandmother has done a superb job."

Emmeline felt her cheeks grow warm. "If she were here right now, she would be preening. You would become a friend for life." She tilted her head to one side and rested it on one finger. "Yes, I believe you would get on tremendously. Gran is very, very dear. She would talk your ear off. I'm afraid her favorite topic is me. So stand warned, you may get bored after the first ten minutes."

His smile grew wider. "Not a bit of it. It would be an honor to meet your grandmother one day and have her regale me with the family history of the intriguing Emmeline Kirby."

She chuckled. "You'll be sadly disappointed. I'm very far from intriguing. I'm just a journalist doing my job. Actually if I think about it, our family histories are not all that different."

He took a sip of tea and an eyebrow quirked upward. "Oh, no?"

"No. My great-great grandfather changed his name when he came to England from Russia—well Bessarabia, really, which like many other areas in the region was gobbled up by Russia—in the late nineteenth century. His 'maiden' name— as the saying goes among Jews—before he changed it was Abraham Haimovic and he was a boy of twelve, when his parents sent him away because of the pogroms. They hoped he would find a better life, even if it meant never seeing him again. He had no money. He didn't know a soul. He was utterly alone, but he somehow managed to make it all the way to London. At the beginning, Abraham spoke only Yiddish. But he learned English. He had to, otherwise he wouldn't have survived. He found a job in a tailor's shop and worked and worked. His dream was to have a shop of his own one day. He scrimped and saved, until finally he made his dream a reality.

"First, he bought himself a flat. This was a major accomplishment. Up until then, he had been living in a cramped room in a boardinghouse. When the business started prospering, Abraham decided to change his surname. He bought himself a house. Now that he had something to offer, it was time to find a wife. And he did. Her name was Rebecca, a petite beauty with long, raven hair and almond-shaped blue eyes, whom he met at the synagogue. After six months of courting, they were married. Abraham and Rebecca had six sons. The last of which was my great grandfather, who, in turn, had four sons. The baby was my grandfather, Simon Kirby, who became a barrister and eventually a QC." She sat up straighter and beamed at him. "My grandfather was awarded the Order of the British Empire by the Queen for his distinguished career."

"Yes, of course. Silly of me not to make the connection with your name immediately. Who hasn't heard of the great Simon Kirby? He was highly revered in Jewish circles. The world lost a brilliant legal mind when he died." He shook his head. "Only sixty-one."

Emmeline felt a tear sting her eyelid. "Thank you for saying that. I have vague memories of my grandfather. From what Gran has told me, he never really recovered from my father's death."

There was a pained expression in his eyes. "I'm sorry. I can well understand that. As a parent, you never expect your children to die before you."

Her chest tightened and her breath caught in her throat as she remembered the baby she had lost. That empty ache never left her. Never. Not even now that she and Gregory were back together. "No," she replied in a hoarse whisper. "You never expect your children to die before you."

She took a gulp of tea to try to regain her equilibrium. She hoped he hadn't noticed that her hand was trembling slightly.

"And your mother's family? What about them?" Royce asked.

She took another long swallow of tea and cleared her throat. "Well, Gran is my mother's mother. That side of the family came to England centuries earlier from Portugal to escape the Inquisition."

"Really? How fascinating and—"

He broke off as the door suddenly burst open and a tall, good-looking man with reddish gold hair who must have been about forty walked in. "Dad, I've had Muldair on the phone again and he—"

Royce's eyes narrowed and two vertical lines formed between his brows. "Jason, you can see that I'm busy. I told Delia that I was not to be disturbed. Muldair can wait. Tell him I'll ring him back later," he said with barely disguised irritation.

His son flicked a cool, green-gray gaze in Emmeline's direction and replied, "Delia said you had some hack of a journalist with you. They're just busybodies with nothing better to do than to pry into other people's business. They don't deserve the time of day. On the other hand, Muldair and Aberdeen *can't* wait. He needs a decision on—"

The chink of Royce's cup and saucer slamming down on the table reverberated on the air. He shot to his feet. "That's enough. You don't run the company, and if you continue to exhibit such crass behavior you never will. *I* still make the decisions around here. Miss Kirby is not some 'hack' as you so disparagingly put it. She is the editorial director of investigative features at *The Clarion*. Now, apologize to her for your rudeness."

The younger man snorted. "You must be joking."

Emmeline's eyes locked on Royce the younger, as her mind devised several *very* painful ways to wipe that sneer off of his smug face. She pressed her tongue against her cheek to keep it from giving him the lashing of his life. After all, she was a professional, and it wouldn't do to sink to his level. She was better than that. Well, she hoped she was better than that. But she didn't know how long she could keep her temper in check. The man was living on borrowed time.

An ugly crimson stain colored Royce's cheeks and his nostrils flared. "Get out. *Now*. I'll deal with Muldair shortly."

"But, Dad—"

He grabbed his son by the arm. "Jason, just go. We'll discuss this *later*."

Father and son eyed one another with mutual contempt without uttering a word for an uncomfortable moment.

Then Jason shook off his father's grasp. "Fine."

He turned on his heel without acknowledging Emmeline and flung open the door. The room became quiet once again after he had left, but the air still crackled with tension.

Royce thrust his hands deep in his pockets and exhaled a long breath as he fumed silently.

"Perhaps I should go, Mr. Royce," Emmeline suggested quietly.

He looked up, startled. It was almost as if he had forgotten that she was there. "What? No. I'm so terribly sorry, Miss Kirby, for my son's unforgivable behavior. Unfortunately, he and my daughter are their mother's creatures." His jaw clenched. "I've tried—God knows I've tried with them—but sadly it's a lost cause." This was said more to himself than to her. "The only one I'm truly close to is Adam, my younger son. The middle child. He's the only one of my three children who is anything like me. In disposition and appearance." He shook his head. "Forgive me. I should not be airing the family laundry in public. What you must think of me—of us—I don't know."

She stood and gave him a smile that she hoped was full of sympathy. "It's all right. Sometimes it's just easier to talk to a stranger."

His brown eyes raked her face. "A stranger. Yes, perhaps. But now, I'm afraid I'm going to have to cut our interview short."

"Of course, I understand. Aberdeen demands your attention," she said as she gathered up her handbag.

He gave her a wry smile. "Not everyone would have been so tolerant and understanding. Especially with my son."

She extended her hand. "Things beyond our control happen. Thank you for agreeing to meet with me today. Perhaps I can ring your secretary tomorrow to arrange a convenient time to continue the interview. Another day this week?"

They shook hands, and then he took her by the elbow and guided her to the door. "I feel absolutely awful about how everything turned out today. Look, I've just had an idea. We're having a party at the house on Friday. Our big summer bash. It's a family tradition. It's a black-tie affair. Why don't you come? Bring someone, if you like. Give me a chance to redeem myself."

"That's not really necessary, Mr. Royce. I couldn't intrude on a family gathering."

He shook his head. "Nonsense. You wouldn't be intruding at all. We have dozens of friends. Frankly, the thing has grown so much over the years that I don't even know half the people my wife invites these days. She assures me that they're from the 'best circles' and I should be seen among them. It's all rot, of course. I could care less whether someone is from best circles or not. If someone's pleasant and can carry on an interesting conversation, that's good enough for me. So please say you'll come. Why not humor an old man? You'll still have your interview, I promise. Come on, what do you say?"

Emmeline hesitated a moment and then nodded, her mouth breaking into a smile. "All right. That would be lovely. Thank you. I'll bring my fiancé."

"Splendid. Splendid, Emmeline. May I call you Emmeline? The name has always been a particular favorite of mine. It has a mellifluous ring to it."

She felt her cheeks flaming. "Thank you. And yes, you may call me Emmeline."

He gave the knob a twist of his wrist and held the door open for her. "Wonderful. Speak to Delia." He nodded his chin at his secretary, who had looked up from her computer. "She'll arrange the interview. Until Friday. I look forward to seeing you again and meeting your fiancé. It's Cheyne Walk. Delia will give you the address."

They shook hands once more. "Right. Thank you, Mr. Royce."

He lingered there on the threshold for a second and then quietly closed the door. He leaned his back against it, feeling its solidness. He pursed his lips and became thoughtful.

Emmeline Kirby was an intelligent young woman. But she was wrong. She was most definitely intriguing. He pushed himself away from the door and crossed to his desk. In fact, there was something about her that was very...unsettling. The hairs on the back of his neck tingled. Perhaps Jason was right about journalists prying into people's lives. Maybe the interview was a mistake.

He tapped his fingers on the desk and snatched up the receiver. He punched in a number. The call was answered almost immediately.

"Hello, it's Victor. I have a little job for you. I want you to find out everything you can about Emmeline Kirby, the editorial director of *The Clarion*. I want to know her political leanings, what books she reads, what music she listens to, where she shops, her fiancé, her friends, where she went to school, her entire family history—on both sides. *Everything*. Drop whatever you're working on and make this a top priority." With that, he rang off.

He replaced the receiver in the cradle and shivered involuntarily as a cold dread seized his chest. Emmeline Kirby was trouble. For all their sakes, he hoped to God what he suspected wasn't true.

CHAPTER 4

Superintendent Oliver Burnell whistled a tune of his own composition as he pushed open the door of the Dacre Street entrance to New Scotland Yard. At once, he was assailed by the vibrant thrum of activity all around him as the Metropolitan Police—affectionately known as the Met—went about its daily business.

He felt refreshed after his fishing holiday up in the Scottish Highlands with his cousin. It was just the tonic he needed. His last case—the hunt for a ruthless former IRA commander named Doyle and the shocking arrest of a senior officer—had drained all his energies over the last fortnight. More than he was willing to admit, even to himself. However, the brisk clean air, the icy waters of the river and the stark beauty of the Highland landscape had chased the cobwebs from his mind and helped him to put things into perspective. He was eager to get back to work, especially since Assistant Commissioner Fenton would no longer be breathing down his neck and making his life intolerable. He wondered who would replace the supercilious bugger. He shrugged his shoulders. *Ah, well, no use speculating. Whoever the new assistant commissioner is, he or she has to be better than Fenton,* he reasoned.

Two young constables stared after Burnell with their jaws wide open. Never, *never* since they had joined the Met had they ever seen the heavy-set superintendent look anything but stern or utter anything but an impatient command. They really couldn't understand how Sergeant Finch could work with the man. Now, however, old Burnell was smiling, nodding his head, and bidding everyone he passed a cheery "Good morning" as he made his way to the lift. There was a definite spring in his ponderous step and a twinkle of amusement in those deep blue eyes. The constables exchanged an astonished look. Well, wonders never cease.

Burnell started whistling again as he punched the button for the lift. He rocked back on his heels as he waited. When the doors slid open, his smile grew quite broad.

"Why, Sally, how lovely to see you," he said as he stepped aside to allow her to get out.

Sally Harper, devoted secretary to the now tarnished and forever tainted former Assistant Commissioner Fenton, impaled him with her hard hazel gaze. "What's that supposed to mean, Superintendent Burnell?" she asked him suspiciously.

To say that they had never gotten on would be an understatement. They wore their mutual dislike like a badge of honor. Much of their antipathy was an outgrowth of Fenton's condescending and patronizing attitude toward Burnell. The assistant commissioner, who had rapidly risen through ranks because of his connections, attempted to undermine Burnell at every opportunity. Now, the superintendent understood why. The man felt threatened. And with good reason, it turned out. Like a conjurer, Fenton blustered to deflect attention from all his dirty little secrets. But in the end, they came back to haunt him and he was plunged into the blackest depths of ignominy.

It couldn't have happened to a nicer chap, Burnell thought. *After all, what goes around comes around.* He started to chuckle, but turned it into a cough as Sally gave him the evil eye.

"Forgive me. I must have caught a bit of a cold while fishing up in the Highlands."

"If you're not careful, it will develop into full-blown bronchitis. And then where will you be?" The icy glint in her eyes belied the saccharine tone of her words and the phony smile plastered on her lips.

"Why, Sally, you do care. I'm touched. But there's no need for you to worry. I'm as strong as an ox."

She patted a stray strand of chestnut hair into place. "You're certainly as large as one," she murmured.

"Eh? What was that?" But he had heard her quite clearly.

"Nothing. Now, did you want something specifically, Superintendent Burnell? Otherwise, I don't have time to chat. I'm rather busy."

Burnell's eyes widened. "Really? I must say I find that odd. What work could you *possibly* have to do now that Fenton is banged up in the nick where he belongs?"

He was gratified to hear her sharp intake of breath.

She bent her head closer and hissed, "Why you odious little man. How dare you say such a thing about Assistant Commissioner Fenton—"

"Ex-Assistant Commissioner Fenton."

She sniffed. "—such a fine man. There will never again be a man of his professional caliber and stature."

"Thank God for that. The Met can do without murderers and corrupt officers muddying its ranks."

Her voice was barely a whisper. "Insecure that's what you are. You've always been consumed with jealousy. It's just gnawed at you all these years."

Burnell snorted. "Insecure? Jealous of Fenton? You've gone round the twist. What other fairy tales are you concocting in that unhinged mind of yours?"

Sally straightened up and tossed her chin in the air. "Unhinged, am I? We'll see. Those who don't toe the line usually fall behind...or are shoved aside," she replied smugly.

He rubbed the back of his neck. "Very cryptic, indeed. Any other pearls of wisdom you'd like to impart? I could collect them and write a book."

"You will have your little jokes, Superintendent Burnell. One of these days you're going to go too far, and then you'll be tossed out on your ear."

"Ha. I'd like to see them try. My record speaks for itself. I'm one of the Met's best detectives and well you know it."

She smirked. "Such conceit. I know nothing of the kind. Assistant Commissioner Fenton was at his wits end. He despaired of you."

Burnell clenched his fists at his side. "Don't make me the villain in all this. It's not my fault that your hero was knocked off his pedestal. A pedestal, I might add, he never should have occupied in the first place because he was the blackest of criminals."

Sally's back stiffened and her eyes narrowed. "You are beyond contempt. I hope you have a thoroughly rotten day."

She pushed past him and stalked off down the corridor, her heels clicking angrily against the polished floor.

A malevolent smile tugged at the corners of his mouth as he stood there watching her retreating figure. "And I hope," he said *sotto voce*, "that the earth opens up and the Good Lord has the sense to toss you into the fiery depths of hell. The Devil will rue his misfortune, but the rest of us mortals will live out our days in peace and contentment. If a situation ever called for divine intervention, surely the moment has arrived." He tilted his head back and stared at the ceiling. "Lord, what are you waiting for?"

Reply came there none.

Burnell threw his hands up in disgust. "Fine. Have it your own way. It was a perfectly reasonable request."

"What was a perfectly reasonable request, sir?"

The superintendent snapped his head around so quickly, he heard a tiny crack in his neck. As he rubbed the spot vigorously, he said, "Finch, what are you doing creeping up on people like that?"

He saw his sergeant's brown eyes twinkling with what appeared to be amusement. "I wasn't creeping, sir. I walked perfectly normally down the corridor and when I reached your side I heard you muttering—"

Burnell waved a hand dismissively. "All right, all right. Never mind."

A smile curled around Finch's lips. "Welcome back, sir. Did you enjoy your holiday?" he asked as they stepped into the lift.

Burnell beamed. "I did indeed. I hadn't seen my cousin in five years. A born and bred Londoner, I thought he was crackers to retire to the Highlands. But how wrong I was. It was delightful. No stress. No rushing about. Just the sky, the river, and good company. The fishing was marvelous. What more could a man ask for, eh?"

"I'm glad to hear it, sir. You're looking well. No, robust. That's the word. You're looking positively robust."

Burnell clapped Finch on the shoulder as the doors slid open and they got off the car. "Thank you, Finch. Very kind of you to say so. But perhaps a little too robust." He cast a downward glance and sighed when he saw how snugly his suit jacket clung to his midsection. He undid the buttons. Maybe it wouldn't be as noticeable? Another sigh escaped his lips. "I start the diet tomorrow." He crossed his heart with two fingers. "Otherwise, I'll have to sit through another lecture from my GP on the evils of gluttony. I tell you that man's single joy in life is telling his hapless patients—in minute detail, I might add—that they will die from a favored list of diseases unless they radically change their lifestyles. I ask you, how can a grown man survive on a rabbit's diet? Leafy greens, carrots, and other vegetables. It's simply not human."

The sergeant bit back a smile and said in a grave tone, "Certainly not, sir. What kind of sustenance is that?"

Burnell stopped in front of his office door and smiled at him. "Exactly. I knew you were a sensible chap. Too bad you're not my doctor. These men of science have been locked up in their laboratories for far too long." He was warming to this theme as he fumbled with the key in the lock. "It would do them good to get out into the real world from time to time. Then they would gain a better understanding of how man truly lives."

Finch started to cough to cover up his laughter. "Sorry, sir. A bit of a tickle." He pounded his chest with his open palm and cleared his throat noisily. "There, all better."

"Mmm" was the superintendent's only comment. He was not deceived. However, the good mood from his holiday still lingered so he was going to let it go.

He unlocked the door and ushered the sergeant inside his office. As he removed his suit jacket and hung it neatly on the hanger on the back of the door, he asked, "So tell me what's been happening while I've been away."

Finch lowered himself into the chair opposite his boss's desk. "Quite a lot, really."

Burnell's eyes widened. "Oh yes?" He rolled up his sleeves as he crossed to his desk. "Do tell," he said eagerly, trying to ignore the groan of protest made by his chair as he sat down.

"Where to start? The day after you left on holiday, Mrs. Fenton hired a very expensive solicitor and filed for divorce. She's put the Hampstead house up for sale and has gone into self-imposed exile in their villa in Monaco 'to try to put the shattered pieces of my life back together.'" Finch touched the back of one wrist to his forehead and sighed dramatically.

The superintendent let out a low whistle. "My, my. The poor dear."

The sergeant grinned. "Indeed. She has vowed not to set foot back in England until her nerves have quite recovered from the humiliation."

"One almost feels sorry for Fenton. Almost. She's left him to flap in the wind alone. Now that's what I call wifely affection."

The detectives had a good laugh at Fenton's expense, but the bitter taste of outrage hovered just beneath the surface. Their ingrained sense of morality, duty, and justice was utterly appalled by the abuse of power, the cover-up, and the ultimate sin, *murder*.

When their mirth had dissipated, Finch asked, "Sir, do you think Mrs. Fenton knew about her uncle and her husband? She *says* that she was completely taken unawares by the revelation."

Burnell leaned back in his chair and interlaced his fingers behind his head to create a pillow. He pursed his lips together and exhaled a long, slow breath. "We'll never know for certain, but between you, me, and these walls, how is it possible that she didn't know? I think that our Mrs. Fenton is far more clever than anyone gives her credit. She turned a blind eye and made sure not to sully her hands. And now, she's living it up in Monaco while her husband will rot in jail for the rest of his life." He tapped his knuckles on his desk. "Knock on wood. By the way, has Fenton's trial been scheduled yet?"

"Yes. September thirtieth."

Burnell nodded. "Well, well. The Crown's prosecutor has

been busy. I suppose we all want to put this behind us as quickly as possible."

"Best that way."

"Yes. So anything else to report?"

Finch hesitated.

Burnell gave him a sharp look. "Out with it, man," he prompted.

"The brass has hired Fenton's replacement. He started last week."

The superintendent's eyebrows shot up. "What, already? They certainly didn't waste any time. Who is it? Is it someone I know? Someone within the Met?"

"No," Finch replied carefully, "you don't know him. The brass wanted a clean slate."

"I don't blame them after all the embarrassment. So who is it?" Burnell rested his elbows on the desk and leaned toward the sergeant. "Why are you drawing this out?"

"I'm not. Honestly, sir. The new assistant commissioner is Keith Cruickshank. He's from the Midlands."

"There, that wasn't so hard."

Finch swallowed. "No, sir."

Now, why did his ulcer suddenly give a flutter? "What's wrong with Cruickshank?"

"I didn't say anything was wrong with him."

"You didn't have to. It's written all over your face."

A slight flush colored Finch's cheeks. "You'll have a chance to form your own opinion of the new guv'nor. You have a meeting with him in half an hour."

CHAPTER 5

Burnell frowned at his office door, through which Finch had just scuttled with the alacrity of a nervous rabbit before he could ask another question about their new leader. It did not inspire confidence. Burnell's ulcer concurred. Bang went his holiday good cheer out the window. It was back to reality. His ulcer emitted another grave rumble in sympathy.

His agile mind spent a few minutes trying to conjure up a portrait of the new assistant commissioner. Keith Cruickshank. The name told him nothing. He had never heard of the man. Was he a good police officer? Or merely another Fenton who was kicked up the ladder because of his connections?

The superintendent shrugged his shoulders in frustration. "Bah," he said aloud in disgust. How he hated stumbling around in the dark without any information to go on.

He glanced at his watch. The time for speculation was over. He pushed himself to his feet and rolled down his sleeves. The appointed hour had arrived for him to meet Assistant Commissioner Cruickshank.

Cruickshank could be a perfectly agreeable chap with a keen mind. In fact, a joy to work with, he told himself reasonably as he slipped on his jacket and straightened his tie. *Of course, he could.*

And yet, that look on Finch's face had spoken volumes.

Burnell thrust his hands deep into his pockets. He tucked his chin into his chest and pursed his lips as he made his way down the corridor. By rote, he took the lift up one floor. When the doors slid open, his feet followed the well-trod path to the assistant commissioner's office.

There he was confronted for the second time that day by

Sally's stony countenance. Her features were set in severe lines, but a spiteful smile played about her mouth.

"Ah, there you are, Superintendent Burnell." She made a show of glancing at her watch. "And almost on time."

He clenched his jaw. "A delight to see you again, Sally. But I think you'll find that your watch is a teeny bit fast. I'm exactly on time. As always."

She snorted. "Well, you managed to waddle up here. I suppose that's a feat in itself."

He drew in a deep breath through his nostrils. *Lord, why do you put temptation in my path? Is it some sort of a test? Do you really want me to throttle this irksome woman? I'm quite willing to do so, if that's your master plan.*

However, aloud he said, "If you're not careful, one of these days that loose tongue of yours is going to wrap itself around your neck and give you whiplash."

"Very droll. I'm blinded by your wit, Superintendent. Now, if you're quite finished, Assistant Commissioner Cruickshank is waiting to see you. He's not at your beck and call."

An acerbic retort danced on the tip of his tongue, but he choked it back at the last second.

He waited in silence the few seconds it took Sally to tap on Cruickshank's door and heard a muffled "Come in" in response.

She opened the door and stood aside to allow him to pass. He could have sworn he heard her chuckling under her breath as the door closed behind him.

He squared his shoulders and cleared his throat. "Good morning, Assistant Commissioner Cruickshank," he said as he crossed to the desk.

He stiffened as his new boss rose to shake his extended hand.

Bloody hell, he thought. This *is the new assistant commissioner. The chap's barely out of nappies. This must be someone's idea of a joke.*

If he had to hazard a guess, he'd have to say that Cruickshank couldn't be more than forty, although he looked younger. He was tall and lean, and if the muscles rippling under his crisply tailored suit were anything to go by, he was the sporty type. The man was probably proficient at everything he tried. How revolting.

Meanwhile, not a strand of his thick ginger hair was out of place on Cruickshank's head and his bright brown eyes held an eager, impatient gleam in them. *Just like a puppy*, Burnell snorted silently. The man looked like the type who had *ideas*. He sighed. Extremely tiresome.

Cruickshank resumed his seat and Burnell lowered himself into the chair opposite him.

"I'm glad that we finally have an opportunity to speak. I like to get to know my officers. I understand that you've been on holiday. Pleasant time, was it?"

"Yes, it was, sir. My cousin and I went fishing in the Highlands."

Cruickshank folded his hands on the desk. "Indeed. How nice. However, I would like to emphasize something from the outset. I insist on punctuality. I realize that you have been under some pressure with your cases in recent weeks, but I will not have my officers rolling in at whatever time pleases them. Do I make myself clear? It's rather bad form and sets a poor example for the younger chaps."

Burnell stared at him in confusion. "Of course, sir. I heartily agree. Being punctual is a sign of professionalism."

"Good. I'm glad that we understand each other. I'll chalk up today as a one-off."

"Today, sir? I'm not following you."

Cruickshank tapped his watch. "I make it just eleven. I was informed that you didn't arrive at the office until ten-fifteen this morning. Very disappointing. In future, you will make sure that you are on time."

Burnell's fingers dug into his knees, hard. "Sir, didn't Sergeant Finch tell you? I was at a security conference this morning. It's been on the calendar for months."

"Finch? I didn't speak to the sergeant. I asked Sally. She told me that you were returning from holiday today, but she didn't mention anything about a conference. If that's the case, I apologize for the miscommunication."

Burnell pursed his lips. *No, of course our dear Sally didn't tell you. The devious little schemer wanted me in your bad books from the start.*

"Pardon, sir," he asked. He had been so absorbed in coming up with a way to teach Sally a lesson that he had missed what Cruickshank had been chuntering on about.

The assistant commissioner gave a disapproving shake of his head. "Do try to concentrate, Burnell. Remember that your holiday is over and it's time to focus on work again."

Don't I know it. He sat up straighter and plastered a smile on his face. "Right. My record speaks for itself, sir."

Cruickshank opened a folder in front of him and tapped the sheaf of papers. "Ye—es," he replied carefully. A thoughtful expression flitted across his face. He appeared to be choosing his words. "As you say, your record speaks for itself. I see that Assistant Commissioner Fenton has made countless notes in your file. It makes for extremely enlightening reading I can assure you." He raised his head and met Burnell's eye. "I must say it is *not* a flattering impression."

The superintendent gritted his teeth. One hand curled into a tight ball. "Sir, may I remind you that *former* Assistant Commissioner Fenton was arrested for murder and other crimes. He was afraid that I was getting too close to the truth—as indeed I was—and sought to deflect attention from himself by discrediting me."

"I find it rather distasteful that you would resort to blaming Fenton for your…deficiencies simply because he is no longer here to defend himself."

What? Are you stark raving mad? Fenton's the criminal not *me.*

Burnell drew a deep breath through his nostrils and cleared his throat. "Sir, I meant no disrespect. I was merely attempting to point out—"

Cruickshank cut him off with an impatient wave of his hand. "Yes, yes. That's quite enough. I believe that man has the capacity for change. Therefore, today we start with a clean slate. I hope you'll seriously try to mend your ways, Burnell. You'll find that I'm a reasonable man and quite broad-minded too. But I warn you—" He wagged his forefinger at him. "—I will not put up with the same nonsense that Fenton did."

Burnell's ulcer roiled with indignation and bile rose to his throat. *The more things change, the more they remain the same.*

CHAPTER 6

Philip Acheson's golden head was trapped among the strands of noonday sunlight tumbling from the sky the minute he emerged from the shadows of the Corinthian columns of the Foreign Office, the elegant Italianate building designed by architect Sir George Gilbert Scott in the late 1800s.

At last. Gregory had been waiting for Acheson for the last hour at the top of the steps that led from King Charles Street to Horse Guards Road. They couldn't be considered friends, but he had reached a sort of détente with the diplomat. He chuckled. *Diplomat.* How amusing. He was bound by the Official Secrets Act now, as was Emmeline, Burnell, and Finch, and therefore his lips would be forever sealed because only a very small circle knew that Acheson was a diplomat in name only. He really worked for MI5, Britain's counterintelligence agency, and not the Foreign Office's Directorate of Defence and Intelligence as everyone believed. Even Maggie Roth, Acheson's wife and Emmeline's best friend, was ignorant of the truth.

I suppose a spy does require a modicum of diplomacy to extricate himself from sticky situations, Gregory mused.

He waved a rolled up newspaper in the air. "Acheson," he called.

Acheson's head whirled round, and he stopped short a few feet away from Gregory. Disbelief and suspicion were reflected in his blue eyes. "Longdon, what are you doing here?"

"I was out for a stroll and suddenly I found myself in the neighborhood. Then I said to myself—we're on intimate terms, you understand—I said, 'Self, will you look at that?

We're practically on Acheson's doorstep. It would be frightfully bad manners if we didn't pop in to say hello.' And so, here I am." He flashed a cheeky grin at the other man.

Philip rolled his eyes. "What a load of rubbish. What do you want?"

Gregory's demeanor became serious and he took a step closer. "I'd like a word with you. A *professional* word."

"Make an appointment with Pamela. I'm rather busy at the moment. I'm off to a meeting." He turned away and started to walk down the steps.

Gregory put a hand on the other's man's sleeve to check him. "Please, Acheson. Off the record. This is important."

Philip sighed. "What could a jewel thief-cum-insurance investigator for Symington's possibly have to discuss with me that you couldn't do so in the normal manner?"

"You, of all people, should know that walls have ears, even in the rarified corridors of the Foreign Office. I'm not being melodramatic when I say that this is a matter of life and death. I can take care of myself, but this concerns Emmy."

That caught Philip's attention. He stiffened and a shadow passed over his face. He gave a curt nod. "Right. That's a different story altogether." He gestured with one arm at St. James's Park across the road. "Let's take a stroll, shall we?"

Gregory fell in step next to him. "But your meeting?"

"So I'll be a little late. Haven't you heard? London traffic is murder at midday."

Gregory smiled. "You don't say."

They remained silent as they crossed the road and entered the park. Gregory slipped his hands into his pockets and casually cast a glance over his surroundings. There were a scattering of civil servants on their lunch break sitting on the benches along the path enjoying a sandwich and the *Times* crossword or a chat in the sunshine. Tourists and residents also were out and about feeding the ducks and other water fowl, or merely strolling.

There was a small group clustered around a pair of enormous pelicans snapping photos or simply staring in amazement.

Gregory relaxed slightly. They weren't being watched, *at the moment.*

"I wouldn't have troubled you. But there was no one else I could turn to. I tried to contact Villiers, but he's *incommunicado.* I suppose such a serious wound will take time to heal."

Philip halted and turned to face Gregory. He searched the other man's handsome features. There was nothing reflected in those cinnamon eyes to indicate that he suspected the truth about Villiers and the connection between them.

Philip's mind drifted back to the conversation he had had only two weeks earlier with Laurence Villiers, the deputy director of MI5, as the man lay in his hospital bed with two folders at his fingertips, one marked TOBY CRENSHAW and the other GREGORY LONGDON.

Villiers twisted the sheet between his fingers and stared at the ceiling.

"Sir, Longdon is not one of my most favorite people in this world, but don't you think he has a right to know?"

Villiers's head snapped round. "Know? Know what? How would knowing help? He's better off this way."

"Is he, sir? How can you know that for sure?"

"I—I did what I thought was best for him and Clarissa." His voice caught in his throat. *"There's no room for a wife and child in a spy's life. I—I made the mistake of thinking it was possible to have both. I was wrong. It was all a dream. A lovely dream for a time, but a dream all the same. Dreams can't last. It was a tissue of lies from the start. Two people can't make a life together based on a lie."*

No, Philip thought as he stared at Gregory now, *two people who truly love each other need to be able to trust one another without question. It's not my place and I gave Villiers my word, but surely even Longdon deserves to know that one of his parents is alive?*

He shook his head. It was not right, but there was nothing he could do about the situation.

"Are you quite all right, Acheson?" Gregory's body tensed. "Look, if you don't want to help because of your feelings toward me, just say so now and we can both stop wasting time."

"Don't be ridiculous," Philip shot back, his tone laced with irritation. "I'm a professional. Personal feelings don't enter into it. Besides, I can't say that you're a reformed character—and I certainly would never be foolish enough to leave you alone in a room with a fortune in jewels—but you've redeemed yourself somewhat over the past few months. Mind you—" He wagged a finger at Gregory. "—you still have a *very* long way to go."

Gregory's eyes danced with mischief. "I didn't realize that you feared for my soul, Acheson. I'm touched that you care. I can assure you that my soul is quite intact. No fears there."

Philip threw his hands up in the air and walked toward a bench, muttering under his breath, "Give the man an inch. I should have known better."

Gregory chuckled as he followed on his heels. He lowered himself beside Philip, who folded his arms over his chest.

Gregory crossed one leg over the other. To the outside observer, the move was casual but only he knew how tightly coiled his nerves were. His smile had vanished almost instantly. The time for laughing was at an end. "Have you ever heard of a man named Walter Swanbeck?"

Philip sat up straighter, his gaze probing and intent. "No. Who is he?"

"You mean who *was* he. He is no longer among the living. He died in 2005."

"I take it he was not a pillar of the community."

Gregory gave a solemn shake of his head. "He was not. Swanbeck was a ruthless billionaire, who made his money in oil and shipping. He could buy anything he wanted. But he was greedy and not very particular about the company he kept. He owned a dozen shell companies that sold arms to the highest bidder. He took pleasure in delivering the merchandise to his clients on his own ships. Swanbeck also had an extremely lucrative sideline laundering money for the Russian mafia and he owned a string of brothels across the Continent."

Philip gave a low whistle. "Charming."

"Indeed. The man also had a nasty temper and took it as a personal affront if anyone dared to cross him or go to the authorities. There are a number of men who walked out their doors in the morning and have never been seen on this earth again."

"So how did you and this illustrious chap become acquainted?"

"Quite by chance. And certainly not by choice. As you know, I have always been a...connoisseur of beautiful things. And Swanbeck was known to have an extensive collection of art and—"

Philip cut him off. "Jewels. Now I get the picture. You set out to rob one of the world's most corrupt and lethal men. You must have taken leave of your senses. I never took you for a fool."

"My dear, Acheson, how many times must I tell you and Oliver that I'm one of society's most law-abiding citizens. A model of propriety, in fact. I would never dream of committing a crime—"

"Hmph," Philip snorted.

"—let alone such a brash and daring one that left no trace behind," Gregory continued as if he had not been interrupted, a slight smile playing around his lips.

"So what happened? Did Swanbeck catch you in the act of breaking into his safe? I'm surprised he didn't set the dogs on you."

"Don't be vulgar." Gregory shook his head and clucked his tongue. "Dogs, indeed. No, in conducting a...business transaction in the establishment of one of his associates, it came to my attention that Swanbeck was exchanging more than arms and dirty money with his cronies. He was peddling to the highest bidder a list of double agents working for the British in the U.K."

"I see. That's where Villiers comes into the picture, I take it?"

"Yes. Treason is so distasteful. As a loyal Englishman, I felt it was my duty to queen and country to stop such nefarious goings on. After some negotiation, I agreed to—shall we say procure?—and deliver the list into Villiers's safe hands."

"Very noble and patriotic."

"I'm glad that you agree. I'm must say that I was rather proud of myself."

Philip sighed wearily. "Longdon, I didn't miss my meeting so that I could plump up your ego. What happened with Swanbeck? And if he's dead, what does any of this have to do with Emmeline?"

Gregory pursed his lips and fell silent. His gaze drifted across the lake. For a moment, he allowed himself to be mesmerized by the graceful tresses of a willow tree dandling in the wind. It was easier than confronting the jumbled memories chasing across his mind and the nagging fear that his past would snuff out his future.

Reluctantly, he forced himself to look at Philip again. There was no point in stalling. Best to have done with it. "I killed him," he said matter-of-factly. He saw a startled expression leap into the eyes of his companion.

"I can't believe it. You may be a scoundrel, but I never would have thought—How?"

Gregory grimaced. "It wasn't cold-blooded murder. It was self-defense, I assure you. Villiers set me loose to see if I could recover the list of compromised agents and, if in the process, I could find anything else of an incriminating nature that could finally put the nail in Swanbeck's coffin. Until that point, no one could tie him to any of his crimes. To the world at large, he was simply another extremely wealthy businessman. You have to understand, I was several years younger then. The danger gave it a piquancy I couldn't resist. The whole thing seemed like a lark...until it wasn't anymore. I had insinuated myself into Swanbeck's inner circle. By that time, I had been Gregory Longdon for so long no one could trace me to the Sanborns. But Swanbeck was too clever. I was caught like a rat in a trap."

"I can't believe that Villiers would use his own so—" Philip snapped his lips together just in time, before he made a slip for which Villiers would never forgive him. He recovered quickly. "I can't believe that Villiers would send someone out into the field who was so green."

"Yes, well. As I said, I was young, and I didn't realize what

I was getting myself into. Somehow I made a careless mistake, and Swanbeck started to suspect me. He became more guarded. I felt like his eyes were always on me, watching. He was biding his time. I knew my days were numbered. I had to get that list of agents and get out. Fast. The only problem was he was waiting to pounce the night I made my move. I can still see him now in my nightmares calmly standing there in the middle of his study, his revolver aimed at my chest. For an instant, time froze. We just stood there staring at one another. Then, with a faint smile creasing his face and a flick of his thumb, he eased the safety catch off and tightened his finger round the trigger.

"I didn't think. I just lunged for him. Somehow the gun...simply...went off. And there, sprawled across the intertwined leaves and flowers of the lovely Aubusson carpet, Swanbeck lay dead at my feet. I was paralyzed with fear. I don't know how long I stood there gaping at him with the gun dangling from my hand. It couldn't have been more than a minute or two, but it felt like an eternity. Slowly, I started to gather my wits about me. I grabbed the list of agents and several computer disks and ran. I didn't stop running until I reached a safe flat near Victoria Station that Villiers had once mentioned 'in case you get into trouble.' I rang him as soon as I thought it was safe. I told him what had happened. He said that I had done well. Better than he had hoped. He told me to keep a cool head and not to leave the flat. The night seemed endless. I couldn't sleep a wink. I was a bundle of nerves. Every little noise set my teeth on edge. Villiers, his usual phlegmatic self, appeared on my doorstep as the first gray strands of dawn started to seep through the curtains. I couldn't wait to get rid of the list and the disks with what I believed were details of a number of secret arms deals. "

"I can well imagine. But obviously that's not the end of this sordid story."

Gregory leaned back against the bench and smoothed the corners of his mustache down. He huffed a weary laugh. "Sometimes I think I will never be free of the demons from my past."

Philip clapped him on the shoulder in a silent gesture of unexpected camaraderie. For some reason, this touched Gregory more than he thought possible and gave him the courage to tell him the rest of the wretched business.

"As you surmised, there's more. Much more." Gregory shook his head grimly. "To start with, the damned list was a fake."

"Oh, Lord. You mean that—"

"That the entire thing was a fiasco from beginning to end? Yes. That a string of agents were killed as a result? Yes. That I have to live with that on my conscience for the rest of my life? Yes. I—more to the point Villiers—made the mistake of underestimating Swanbeck. From the first day we crossed paths, Swanbeck knew what I was about. It must have amused him no end to watch me devour every—seemingly—careless crumb he tossed out. I was being played by a master. However, my dear Acheson, trouble seemed to dog my every step. It now came in the form of Swanbeck's son, Alastair, an attractive chap with a fierce intelligence and business acumen which verges on genius. He's a good ten years younger than I am, but he was already overseeing some of his father's vast illegal empire while he was still at university. Villiers had made certain that the murder investigation never led to any arrest. But Alastair had a good idea who had killed his dear old papa. He had made inquiries through his underworld network. He's even more ruthless than his father. Cruel and cold. Ice water runs through his veins. Men are said to quail at his very shadow.

"So you see, it was not long before my name floated to his ears. He already had his suspicions about me, of course, but by that time I had fled to the Continent. I managed to stay a step ahead of him, despite a few close calls. Then two years ago, Villiers got word that Swanbeck had died in some sort of dispute over money—what else?—with Igor Bronowski. Swanbeck was reportedly killed. His bullet-riddled body was found in an abandoned Mercedes along the Autobahn near Munich."

"Bronowski? He makes Genghis Khan look like an angel.

There is no one more revered—and feared—in the Russian mafia."

The corners of Gregory's eyes crinkled. "Ah, I see you're acquainted with the chap. Therefore, it's quite unnecessary for me to give you the highlights of his CV. Needless to say, news of Swanbeck's demise was music to my ears. I began to relax and decided to come home. And then…then I met Emmy and I was given a chance—my first chance—at happiness."

"I can't argue with you there. You're lucky to have found a woman like Emmeline."

"Yes," Gregory whispered, his fist curling into a tight ball on his thigh. "But I'm afraid that I haven't been very lucky for *her*. When I went to visit Villiers in hospital after he had been shot, he told me that Swanbeck's alive."

"What? How's that possible?"

"Apparently, Swanbeck saw the writing on the wall. He knew Bronowski would attempt a hit, so he sent one of his lackeys out in his car as a decoy. I can't say I feel too sorry for the fellow. After all, if one lies down with dogs, one must expect to wake up with fleas. He was carrying Swanbeck's identification, so naturally the German police assumed the dead man was Swanbeck. The man had the audacity to identify the body himself. It took several months to untangle the muddle. And now, Swanbeck's found me again. What's worse is that he knows about Emmy. He sent her a bouquet of coral roses— her favorites—to the office last week. He also broke into my flat and left a coral rose on my pillow. His little joke. I've also received several phone calls, where I can hear someone breathing at the other end of the line but no one speaks. It's his way of telling me that he knows where I am and can get to me *and* Emmy anytime he likes."

"It doesn't make sense. You've been back in England for two years. Why make his move now?"

"I think Swanbeck lost track of me and was stewing in frustration."

"If that's true, it's even more curious."

Gregory shook his head. "Not to me. I think the trail *had* gone completely cold…until three months ago."

"What happened in April to change the situation?"

"I'm fairly certain that a vindictive little bird whispered some sweet-nothings in his ear."

One of Philip's blond eyebrows quirked upward. "What 'little bird'?"

Gregory heaved a long sigh. "My wife."

CHAPTER 7

Philip's back stiffened and a dark crimson flush spread across the hard contours of his face. "Your wife?" he asked acidly. "Your *wife*?" He slapped his thigh with his open palm. "Damn it, Longdon, this is monstrous even for you. If you're married, why have you been stringing Emmeline along? She is under the deluded impression that the two of you are getting married in October. Why the devil did you do it? She doesn't deserve this."

"Calm down, Acheson. Do you know you have a face like thunder? You can forget pistols at dawn because I haven't been toying with Emmy's affections."

"It doesn't look that way from my perspective."

"Just listen. Emmy knows about Ronnie…Veronica. She met her."

Philip gaped at him. For a moment, no words would rise to his lips. When he had recovered his wits, he asked incredulously, "She *met* your wife? And she's still with you? I can't believe what I'm hearing. Emmeline must be losing her grip on reality. I would have throttled you long ago."

This elicited a half-smile from Gregory. "Well, thank God you're not Emmy. Mind you, it was touch-and-go there for a while. Not that I need to explain my private life to you, but I hadn't seen Ronnie in four years. I filed papers to have our marriage dissolved. There were complications. The long and the short of it is the divorce was finalized in the end. In any case, Ronnie's dead now. She was murdered back in April in Torquay. It was a rather messy business, but I'm sure you're not interested in all the boring details."

Philip's eyes became like two large saucers. "I must be the

one who is going mad. Every word that comes out of your mouth is more outrageous than the one before."

"Ah, yes, but I assure you, it's all true."

"That what makes it worse." Philip dropped his blond head between his hands and shook it as if he were trying to wipe out the last quarter of an hour. "Another murder," he groaned and lifted his head to impale Gregory with his hostile glare. "You seem to leave a trail of bodies in your wake. Don't tell me you killed your wife...ex-wife, oh, whoever the woman was... too?"

"No," Gregory replied circumspectly. "I cannot take credit for that dirty deed. But I thought about it many, *many* times. Ronnie was a viper and an opportunist of the highest order."

"And *this* is the woman you chose to marry? Why not simply down a bottle of strychnine?"

Gregory stared out across the lake again, but he was reliving the past. "In retrospect, I should have done so because I was a complete and utter fool. I allowed myself to be swayed by a pretty face. I'm not excusing myself, but sometimes loneliness distorts one's outlook. Ronnie oozed sex appeal and danger. She was exciting, but she also was damned unpredictable. I never knew what she would do from one moment to the next. She would disappear for months at a time and then return as if she hadn't been gone at all. Years passed by like that. It couldn't last, of course. A relationship like that is bound to burn out sooner rather than later."

"Why did you stay with her?"

Gregory turned back to face Philip. "Because aside from Villiers, Ronnie was the only other person who knew I had killed Walter Swanbeck. We were man and wife, as well as...business partners."

"You mean you were both thieves. Partners in crime."

Gregory clucked his tongue. "You and Oliver have one-track minds. I don't understand why the two of you persist in sullying my good name and reputation—"

"Huh. You're a reputed thief. That's what you are."

"—my good name and reputation at every opportunity. Do you want to hear the rest of the story or not?"

Philip inclined his head. "By all means, proceed," he replied facetiously. "Thus far, it's been highly enlightening. I can't wait to see how it all ends."

"I'm hoping it won't end in Emmy's death. That's why I need your help, Acheson."

Philip sobered and sat up straighter. "Sorry. I didn't mean to be flippant. Go on."

"The night I—" Gregory swallowed hard. "The night I killed Swanbeck I called Villiers as I told you, but I also rang Ronnie. I was badly shaken and I needed to see her. She came to the safe flat. I was in shock. I certainly wasn't thinking clearly. I told her everything that had happened, with the omission about Villiers's part in the whole matter. She had no idea about Swanbeck and his illegal and treasonous activities. She thought I infiltrated his circle simply to have easier access to the—"

Philip lifted an eyebrow as his mouth twisted into a faint smile. "Jewels?"

Gregory cleared his throat. "It's of no consequence what she thought. The wheels of her scheming mind were already turning furiously. I was just too blind to see it. But how I've paid for it, ever since," he muttered bitterly. "She played the dear, devoted wife role to perfection. She said it was too dangerous for me to leave the flat, therefore she would get rid of the gun. My brain was so addled, I readily handed it to her. You asked why I stayed with her. Because I was trapped from that moment. She hid the gun with my fingerprints somewhere. It amused her to know that she held my life in her hands. You can't imagine what it's been like having this threat hanging over my head for the last five years. But that was Ronnie."

"You do surround yourself with colorful characters, I must say."

"Ah, your diplomatic training stands you in good stead, Acheson."

"But how is your wife—Ronnie—tied to Swanbeck's son?"
"I think the way he traced me and Emmy is because Ronnie contacted him. She was so jealous. She wanted to destroy what

Emmy and I have. And she very nearly succeeded. I think Ronnie told Swanbeck where to find me. She may very well have sent him the gun."

"A model of true wifely devotion. You said Emmeline knows about your ex-wife, but what about Swanbeck? Does she know you killed his father?"

Gregory sighed and shook his head. "No. She knows I killed a man in self-defense, though. However, she believes it was the drunken scion of one of Spain's most prominent families who came after me with a knife in an alley in Barcelona's Gothic quarter. Ronnie's villainous part in the affair is the same, only in this version she kept the knife with my fingerprints rather than a gun."

"It's incredible how the lies tumble so effortlessly from your tongue. And to the woman you claim to love, no less. It must take tremendous skill to keep the stories straight in your mind. What was it that you said earlier about lying down with dogs?"

Gregory flapped his hand impatiently. "I suppose you think I deserve that, but frankly you can go to the devil for all I care. I don't need a lecture. Nor am I going to grovel," he said. His tone took on a sharpness that was far from his usual glib insouciance.

Philip cocked his head to one side as his eyes searched Gregory's face. He appeared to be digesting everything that he had just been told. Gregory could almost hear the unspoken question hovering on the other man's lips: *Am I supposed to believe this bizarre story?*

Philip seemed to come to a decision after some internal debate. He nodded his head once. "Right. I'll make some discreet inquiries to see what I can find out about Swanbeck and I'll have a word with Villiers to see if he can provide any insight. Then, I'll have a better idea of the best way to proceed—"

Gregory put a hand on his sleeve. "Don't be naïve. You forget that money is the great motivator. It's a weapon. The corridors of Whitehall and MI-Five are probably teeming with men who have sold themselves for thirty pieces of silver in exchange for doing Swanbeck's bidding. How do you think it's been possible for him and his father to elude justice? A greased palm here. A favor there. My dear Acheson, he knows every move you're going to make before you make it."

"I can't—I won't—accept that. Not everyone is corruptible."

"True. Not everyone. Certainly not you. That's where the danger lies. Those who have been unwilling to play Swanbeck's game have taken their scruples to the grave. Life is just another commodity for him. To be traded and sold at will. I want to make you aware of what you're up against."

A muscle in Philip's jaw pulsed. "We'll stop him."

"Not stop. Destroy. A man like Swanbeck has to be destroyed, from the inside out. And his associates. Otherwise…" He let the sentence trail off.

The hairs on the back of his neck prickled. *Tick, tock, tick, tock. Tempus fugit.* He just hoped that it wasn't already too late.

ဢ

Emmeline listened to the wind's pleasant chatter as it darted among the trees in St. James's Square, playing hide-and-seek with the light and shade. It was a very soothing sound, bringing a smile to her lips as she walked out of Royce Global Holdings' offices.

She glanced at her watch and turned right. She wended her way around the square, which was virtually empty. A gentleman in a light-gray suit passed her at one point and disappeared into one of the other buildings. Meanwhile, a gleaming black Audi slid to a stop at the curb a few yards ahead of her. Barely a minute later two men, heads bent deep in conversation, hurried out of another building and got into the car.

The stillness of the square helped her to assess her impression of Victor Royce. He was distinguished, solicitous, intelligent, and without question an astute businessman. She decided that she liked him. She nodded her head. Yes, she liked him. And yet, she was convinced that he was hiding something. She couldn't put her finger on precisely what made her think so, but she knew she was right. All her instincts told her so. Only someone who was trained to listen and observe—like a journalist or policeman—could have discerned the undercurrent of tension hovering beneath the outward appearance of cool confidence.

Let's see if I can loosen your tongue a bit on Friday, shall we? she thought. She was eagerly looking forward to the Royce summer bash. It was a stroke of luck that the invitation unexpectedly dropped into her lap. People had a way of letting their guard down at parties.

This made her quicken her pace as she turned off King Street and onto St. James's Street. Green Park was the closest Underground station. She would catch the Jubilee Line back to the *Clarion's* office in the London Bridge Quarter and start working on her story. She had already formulated the lead in her head.

But instead of cutting across the park, she walked up to Piccadilly and popped into Hatchard's to pick up a book she had ordered for Gran. The transaction took all of five minutes. Once she had the book in hand, she weaved her way in and out of the midday crowd on the pavement and hurried toward the station.

She swiped her Oyster card through the turnstile and headed for the escalator that took her into the bowels of the station. She walked down a white-tiled corridor lined with various advertisements and at last arrived on the Jubilee Line platform. The countdown clock indicated that the next train would be arriving in three minutes. Good, not long to wait.

She moved down the platform to an area that was less crowded. Her gaze was riveted on the gloomy mouth of the tunnel from where the train would soon emerge.

Out of the corner of her eye, a flicker of movement caught her attention. She shifted her gaze to find a tall man dressed in an immaculately cut light gray suit, crisp white shirt, and navy tie boldly staring at her from a few feet away. She suddenly understood what all those Gothic novels meant when they said "smoldering dark looks." If anyone could be said to smolder, this chap certainly was doing an admirable job of it.

She caught her breath as those sea green eyes seemed to hold her captive. He didn't make a move. He simply stood there staring at her. Her mouth felt dry. She took a half-step backward and bumped into a woman standing next to her. "Sorry," she mumbled.

When she turned back, the man was gone. Emmeline squeezed her eyes shut as the tension eased from her muscles. *Stupid*, she chided herself. *Get a grip on yourself. You're allowing what happened with Doyle to make you look for things that aren't there.*

The next second, the train pulled into the station with a *whoosh*. A few people got off and she quickly stepped inside and found a seat between a rather burly balding gentleman and a young woman who was engrossed in a magazine. She settled back and relaxed. It would be a short ride to the London Bridge Station.

As the bell tinkled to warn passengers that the train would be departing, the dark-haired stranger reappeared in the doorway but he didn't make a move to get in the car. He just stood there, hovering.

Emmeline stiffened and gripped her handbag tighter in her lap. This was no mistake. No coincidence. He had deliberately followed her. It was written in those mocking green eyes. But why? What did he want?

Her muscles were coiled tightly. *Shut the bloody doors already*, her brain screamed. It was another half a second before the doors obeyed her silent command. She slumped back in relief.

Just as the train started to move, the stranger gave her a wink and then his face became a blur.

∽∾∽

Philip finally arrived at his meeting at the Cabinet Office half an hour late. He was still reeling from what Longdon had told him. He should have turned around and walked in the opposite direction the minute he saw that man waiting for him. But his conscience told him that he couldn't have done that.

Really? He sighed and nodded. Yes, really. Sometimes the burdens of being one of the good guys were too much. Perhaps he should start behaving like a baddie and everyone would simply leave him alone.

"Ah, there you are, Acheson," Mark Bradford, the Minister of Defence's permanent secretary, said as he hurried across to him.

They shook hands. "I apologize for being late, Mark. I'm afraid something came up just as I was on my way out the door. I had to deal with it immediately."

Bradford, Philip's senior by twenty years, may have put on a few extra pounds since he was a strapping lad, but every inch of his bearing was a testament to his highly decorated career in the military.

"Not to worry. All of us in this room are slaves to the call of duty. We actually haven't started the meeting. As it happens, you're not the only one who is running late. We're still waiting for the last chap to arrive."

"Well, that's good. So what's this meeting all about? Raymond Haworth asked me to step in at the last minute. He mumbled something about security issues and the Russians and it being more up my alley than his."

"The PM has become increasingly worried about Putin's saber-rattling. As you know, an icy chill still hangs over Britain's diplomatic relations with the Russians since the Alexander Litvinenko affair. The PM does not, nor do any of us in the intelligence community, want a repeat of that on home soil. The Russians caught us with our trousers down. The Kremlin has a long history of silencing—forever—anyone who dares to oppose it. Putin, who was suckled on KGB doctrine rather than mother's milk, has perfected this practice in recent years. Journalist Anna Politkovskaya was gunned down outside her Moscow flat building in 2004; pro-West Ukrainian presidential candidate, Viktor Yuskenko, was poisoned in 2004; businessman Mikhail Khodorkovsky is sitting in a Russian jail; and human rights activist, Natalya Estemirova, was kidnapped outside her home just last year and found dead later the same day. The list goes on and on."

"We know all this," Philip said. "But there's not much we can do on Russian soil."

"Not in Russia, no. But *here* we can. We've intercepted a lot of chatter lately between Moscow Center and London. We think Putin and his thugs are planning assassinations here of Russian emigrés, like Boris Berezovsky. We've increased surveillance, but after Yuri Petrov's inexplicable death in March we're worried the killings haven't stopped."

Philip frowned and shook his head. "The last thing we need is to have London as the frontier in a new Cold War. Putin's arrogance is astounding. Does he really think that he can get away with it?"

Bradford clapped him on the shoulder. "Arrogance it may be, but we intend to hit back, hard. The sanctions that Britain, the United States, and Europe have imposed are not enough. That's why all of us are here today. We're the PM's new task force in this war on Putin." Bradford's outstretched arm swept over the men and handful women gathered in the room. "The members of this panel hail from the government, the security services, and the business world all of whom have dealings with the Russians. Each person is an expert in his or her own right. Our mission is to devise a strategy to make Putin think twice before sending his hooligans here again to threaten our citizens or those under Britain's protection."

"Right. So where do we start?" Philip asked eagerly, his mouth breaking into a wide grin.

Bradford returned his smile. "Enthusiasm, that's what I like to see. Ah, here he is now." His brown gaze was caught by a young man in a light gray suit, white shirt, and navy tie who had made his entrance. "Let me introduce you to the last member of the task force."

Bradford guided Philip across the room to meet the new arrival. "Philip Acheson of the Directorate of Defence and Intelligence. This is Alastair Swanbeck, managing director of the Swanbeck Corporation."

Philip had started to extend his hand toward the other man, but jerked it back as if he had been scalded.

Swanbeck pretended not to notice and instead proffered his

own hand, his green eyes twinkling with amusement. "It's a pleasure, Mr. Acheson. I've heard so much about you."

"Have you?" Philip replied warily. An uneasy flutter in the pit of his stomach told him that this man, one of the world's most ruthless criminals, knew that he had been meeting with Longdon not half an hour ago.

"Oh, yes. I believe we have a mutual friend. Two, in fact."

CHAPTER 8

Although she was back at her desk with a newsroom full of reporters right on the other side of the large picture window in her office, Emmeline was disturbed to see that she was still trembling. She tried inhaling through her nose and exhaling deeply though her mouth to steady her rapid, shallow breathing. An image of the stranger's face with the dangerous glint in his cool green eyes danced before her, teasing, taunting, goading.

"Emmeline."

She jumped up and spun around so quickly that her chair banged into the desk. "What?" Then her body relaxed, when she saw that it was Sam, the deputy features editor.

Something in her expression must have made his brow furrow "Sorry. I didn't mean to startle you. I did knock." When she didn't respond, he asked, "Are you all right?"

She swallowed and gave him a weak smile, as she lowered herself into her chair once more. "Yes, perfectly. I couldn't be better. You just caught me off guard. That's all. I have a lot on my mind, what with the wedding coming up at the end of October."

Sam gave her a quizzical look. He didn't appear convinced by her explanation, but decided to let it go and get down to business. "Right. The reason I stopped by is to go over some changes I wanted to make to the Sunday spread. I thought—"

Emmeline was only half-listening to his ideas. She nodded and made the appropriate noises in the right places. "Great. It sounds terrific. Run with it."

He rose. "Thanks. I'll get on it straightaway." Sam was at the door, with his hand on the knob, when he turned around.

"Oh, I nearly forgot. A chap has been ringing up all morning asking for you."

She blinked. Her folded hands were locked tightly together on her desk. "A chap? Who? What did he want?" She was surprised at how steady her voice sounded.

Sam shrugged and shook his head. "No idea. I don't know how he got my number. He refused to give his name or leave a message. He demanded to speak to you and no one else. He sounded a bit desperate, if you ask me. The only thing that I can tell you is that he had an accent."

"An accent? What kind of an accent?"

"I'm fairly certain it was Russian." He shrugged again. "I'll put him straight through to you the next time he calls."

"I'm not speaking to anyone who doesn't give his name. Got that?"

Sam nodded. "Right, boss."

Two strangers in one day. It was too much of a coincidence.

Emmeline reached for the phone and dialed a number she was becoming all too familiar with lately. It rang once.

"Burnell." She couldn't help but smile when she heard the superintendent's brusque greeting.

"Hello, Superintendent Burnell. It's Emmeline Kirby. I hope you had a lovely holiday."

She could hear some papers shuffling, but the change in his tone was unmistakable. "Emmeline, what a nice surprise after the morning I've had. Our new assistant commissioner is fast becoming a thorn in my side. But you didn't ring to listen to me whining on. To what do I owe this pleasure?"

Her smile grew wider. She liked the superintendent tremendously. He could be gruff, but never with her, despite his antagonism against Gregory. Burnell was solid—and it had nothing to do with the extra weight he carried on his large and sturdy frame. He was a skilled detective with an agile mind, who respected the law and had dedicated his life to seeing that the guilty were punished. She was quite certain that Burnell liked her just as much as she did him, but he would never admit it. One thing that there was no doubt about was that he respected her as a journalist and admired the job that she did every day. That was a rarity among police officers. She was happy that she had recently persuaded him to call her Emmeline rather than Miss Kirby, at least when they were among themselves.

"You know that I always enjoy chatting with you and Sergeant Finch. By the way, give him my regards. But as you've guessed, this is not a social call. I had a rather unsettling encounter on the Tube today. Perhaps I'm just being silly and there was nothing to it at all, but I'd like your professional opinion. Could I pop over to discuss it with you?"

"My door is always open for you—day or night—but I'm actually on my way out at the moment." He groaned. "A suicide. In Mayfair, no less."

"Oh, how horrid," she said, trying to keep the disappointment out of her voice. "Then I won't keep you from your duty any longer."

"Look, why don't you drop by in the morning. I promise I'll make time for you. Unless it's urgent, and I'll send Finch—"

She smiled. "Certainly not. It's nothing that won't keep until tomorrow. As I said, I've probably got the wrong end of the stick."

"I very much doubt that, Emmeline. Your instincts are usually spot on. But..." His sentence trailed off.

"But you must dash. Yes, I know. I'll see you tomorrow."

"I look forward to it."

Burnell rang off. However, Emmeline's feeling of unease lingered.

҂҂҂

Two PCs had managed to move a group of gawkers and stunned onlookers down toward the corner with North Audley Street, where they huddled *en masse* in front of the Starbucks, their necks craning and on their tiptoes as far the balls of their feet would allow.

Burnell shook his head as Sergeant Finch turned into Green

Street and pulled the car up to the curb outside an elegant, four-story red-brick Victorian mansion block. "A bunch of ghouls," he muttered. "What's the fascination in seeing the mangled body of your fellow man sprawled along the pavement?"

"Human nature, I suppose, sir. Fear about their own mortality. Perhaps, it's a matter of, 'There, but for the grace of God, go I.'" Finch shrugged at a loss himself. If people saw the kind of things they did on a daily basis, they would appreciate life a bit more.

"God help us all, if that's the case." Burnell unbuckled his seat belt and started to open the door. "Now, a little less of the philosophy and a bit more of the gritty police work."

"Right, sir."

The area had been cordoned off with yellow *DO NOT CROSS* tape. The first constables to arrive had done their best to hide the distressing scene from onlookers. The forensics team was already hard at it. Some acknowledged the two detectives with a curt nod before getting on with their gruesome task.

"Ah, there you are, Oliver," Dr. Meadows, the forensic pathologist, said as he came up behind them. "I knew you wouldn't want to miss out on all the fun."

Burnell turned toward his friend of over twenty years. "Indeed, John. It's the highlight of an otherwise dreary day," he replied grimly and thrust his hands deep into his pockets. "What can you tell us?"

Meadows lifted a white sheet to reveal a man in a charcoal suit impaled on the iron railings. The superintendent winced and Finch had to turn his head away. "Seen enough?" The two detectives nodded, and Meadows hastily covered up the body once more.

"His name is Pavel Melnikov. At a guess, I'd say he was in his late forties. Russian émigré. Lived in the three-million-pound, two-bedroom duplex penthouse. A couple of horrified residents found him like that. Apparently, he jumped from up there." Meadows jerked his thumb toward a balcony where a French door stood open.

Both Burnell and Finch shifted their gaze upward. They could see members of the forensics team wandering overhead to gather evidence.

Burnell whistled. "That must be what…at least a sixty-foot drop?"

"Give or take, yes."

The superintendent fixed Meadows with a hard stare. "You said *apparently* he flung himself off the balcony. Are you saying it wasn't suicide?"

"Well, we did find a note in his pocket." The doctor signaled to one of the constables, who brought over an evidence bag with the crumpled note. "As you can see, it's the usual 'I can't go on anymore' guff."

"But you don't buy it?" Burnell prompted.

"No, I don't. It's too neat."

"If you can call being skewered on iron railings neat, that is."

"Oliver, you know what I mean. It doesn't smell right to me. However, I'll have something more definitive once I've done the postmortem."

"I trust your instincts, but I'll wait for your official report on the cause of the death. In the meantime—" He turned to the sergeant. "Finch, you know what to do."

"Yes, sir." The sergeant took out his notebook and pen. "I'll go talk to the neighbors to see if anyone can shed light on our Mr. Melnikov. How was he behaving lately? Was there a girlfriend? Did he have regular visitors? Had any strangers been hanging about recently?"

Burnell nodded and watched him head toward the shiny black front door, where he stopped for a moment to have a word with one of the constables before disappearing inside.

The superintendent stepped into the middle of Green Street and tipped his head back. He folded one arm across his chest and stroked his beard contemplatively with the other as he studied the Queen Anne-style Dutch gabled roof. He took another half-step backward, his gaze sweeping the entire length.

"Excuse me, sir. Are you in charge?"

Burnell spun around to find two elderly women at his elbow. One was nearly as tall he was, painfully thin with a neat silver bob. The other was short and plump, with dyed ginger hair and rosy cheeks sprinkled with freckles. He could see the latter's green eyes alight with excitement.

Oh, no. This is all I need. Miss Marple and her trusty side-kick, he groaned inwardly. However, he plastered what he hoped was a polite smile on his face and aloud, he said, "Good afternoon, ladies." He showed them his warrant card. "I'm Superintendent Burnell of the Metropolitan Police. I'm afraid you cannot linger here. This is a crime scene and we must—"

"Yes, we know. It's terribly thrilling. And here we are, right in the thick of things," the short one replied with glee. "We came to assist you."

I knew it, Burnell thought. *Here we go.* "Indeed. That's aw-fully nice of you to offer, but I assure you we have things well in hand. If you'll please just move along, we can get on with our investigation."

He turned to join Meadows on the pavement, but a surpris-ingly strong blue-veined hand clamped on his sleeve and reeled him back. "But we have information that's vitally im-portant to your inquiries. You must listen."

His gaze flickered between the short one's earnest face and the thin woman, who was nodding vigorously. He sighed wea-rily. Best to get it over with. "Right. What can you tell me?"

"That man—" The short one pointed in the general direc-tion of the sheet-shrouded body. "—was not alone. We saw two other men up there with him just before he—before he—" At this point, she swallowed hard and placed a hand on her chest. "Before he fell," she whispered.

"What my friend is trying to tell you, Superintendent, is that the man was thrown from the balcony," her friend said without a trace of emotion.

Burnell's eyes widened. "That's a very serious accusation and, if it's true, it puts quite a different complexion on this case. Ladies, are you quite certain that you saw two other men on roof with the victim?"

"We know our civic duty and would swear to it in a court of law, if necessary," the tall woman replied, tossing her chin in the air and straightening her spine with solemn dignity.

"I see. Let's not get ahead of ourselves. One step at a time. Why don't we start by having you both make a statement, shall we?" He signaled to one of the WPCs. "If you'll kindly go with Constable Curtis down to the station, I would appreciate it. Try to be as accurate as possible. Tell her everything you saw, even if you think something was unimportant at the time."

"You can count on us, Superintendent," the ginger-haired lady said.

Curtis nodded and shepherded the two women toward a police car parked several hundred feet down the block.

Burnell thrust his hands in his pocket and pursed his lips. He crossed toward Melnikov's dead body and lifted the sheet. "So who helped you to shuffle off your mortal coil eh, Mr. Melnikov?"

Meadows clapped him on the shoulder. "I shouldn't think you'll get very far in your investigations if you continue to interrogate dead men."

Burnell gave him a pointed look. "Very droll. Remind me again why we're friends?"

Meadows chuckled. "Because I make you laugh, of course." Then, with all seriousness he asked, "All right for us to remove this poor devil?"

Burnell nodded. "Yes, go ahead. And, John, could you—"

Meadows put his hands up in the air to cut him off. "Put a rush on the postmortem?"

The superintendent smiled. "Are you a mind-reader now too?"

His friend's gray eyes twinkled. "I'm not just another pretty face, you know. It's about time you realized that and started taking me more seriously."

"I'll keep that in mind. Off you go," Burnell replied as he and Meadows stepped out of the way as firefighters moved in with an angle grinder to begin the gruesome task of cutting through the railings so that Melnikov's body could be taken away.

This was an unpleasant business and Burnell was glad

when the dead man was finally zipped into a black body bag and lifted into a police van.

"I'll try to have some preliminary results for you in a day or so," Meadows said as he walked toward the van.

"Thanks, John. The sooner, the better."

He frowned as the van pulled away from the curb. He pressed a hand to his stomach as his ulcer gave a cautionary rumble. "Indeed," he murmured to himself. "I can always rely on your judgment." He patted his stomach again. "There's trouble in the wind."

"Sir?" Finch called.

Burnell turned on his heel to find his sergeant and two men, who if he had to hazard a guess were from one of the security services, heading straight for him. Their appearance did not come as a surprise, but he would try to play nice to see what they wanted.

"Sir, this is—"

But the taller of the two men cut across him. "I'm Jennings. This is Drake." He jerked his head at his companion and they both flashed their identification. "MI-Six."

Burnell gave them a broad smile. "I see. How can I help you?" he asked politely.

"You're off the case. We're taking charge. As far you're concerned, you never heard the name Melnikov. Send your people home. Our chaps are on the way and will secure the crime scene. I want all notes or statements related to this case. And I do mean *everything*. Someone will come round to collect them. Well, I think that's enough to be getting on with. I'll let you know if I need anything else."

The superintendent thought his face would crack. But his smile didn't falter, not for a second, even though a vein was carrying out a full-on assault against his temple. "Oh, yes? And why is MI-Six so interested in the suicide of a Russian national?"

Jennings's mouth curved into a smile, but his brown eyes held the cold glint of finely polished steel. "That's on a need-to-know basis I'm afraid, Superintendent. I'm sure you understand."

Burnell's nails dug into his palms as he curled his fists into tight balls at his sides. "Actually, I don't understand."

Jennings laughed.

That was a mistake, thought Finch. *The guv is already on the verge of thrashing you. Don't press your luck.* He shot a sideways glance at Burnell, who appeared ready to explode.

"Really, Burnell," Jennings went on calmly, but there was a sharp edge to his voice. "Why make things difficult for yourself? It's a complete waste of energy, and I can assure you you'll end up the loser. Now, I'm certain you have other things that can occupy your time. I suggest you get on with them."

Burnell took a step toward Jennings and opened his mouth to say something. However, whatever it was died in his throat as Finch grabbed his arm. "Sir."

The superintendent's cheeks flamed as his seething blue gaze impaled Finch. An uncomfortable silence ensued for several seconds. Finally, Burnell nodded and shook himself free of the sergeant's grasp.

He cleared his throat. "Far be it from me to stand in MI-Six's way." He inclined his head at the two men. "Jennings. Drake. It's all yours." His arm swept in an arc that encompassed the street, the mansion block, and the pavement.

"Wise choice, Burnell." Jennings's gaze flickered in Finch's direction. "Your sergeant has good sense. He'll go far. Come on, Drake." He didn't hang about any longer. He simply turned his back on the two detectives. They were already forgotten.

A strangled sound emanated from Burnell as he watched them go.

"Sir, it's not worth it," Finch whispered. "He's only trying to goad you."

The superintendent squared his shoulders and swallowed hard. "He can go to the devil for all I care. There's no way we're dropping this case."

CHAPTER 9

The next morning, Emmeline arrived at *The Clarion* earlier than usual. The excuse she made to herself was that she wanted to get some work done on Victor Royce's profile before she had to go meet with Superintendent Burnell about the strange man in the Green Park Station. However, she knew perfectly well that there was not enough in her notes from her interrupted interview with Royce the day before to even draft a decent background sketch. She would have to wait until the party on Friday and her follow-up interview with him on Monday to get the real story behind the man.

So why was she here? *You know why you're here*, she said to herself. Yes, she did know. Her eyes strayed to the file that Yoav Zielinski had given her. The file about her parents. Every free moment she could spare in the last fortnight, she had spent—unsuccessfully thus far—trying to unearth anything that could lead to her parents' murderer or murderers. She needed answers. She needed the truth. But she knew that if she was not careful, it could become an obsession. And if that happened, she could lose her sanity, Gregory—*everything.* Was she willing to take such a risk for something that happened twenty-five years ago?

Yes, damn it. She needed to *know.*

"But, Emmy darling," Gran had said. "Knowing won't bring them back. Why rake all that up again?"

Because…because. Emmeline choked on the sob that caught in her throat. *Because Mummy and Daddy need to rest in peace. Because* I *need peace.* The not knowing was the cruelest part.

She sighed and impatiently wiped a stray tear trickling down her cheek with the back of her hand.

Right. She straightened up. *That's quite enough of that. It's time you did a bit more thinking and a little less wallowing in self-pity.*

She would start at the *Times*. Although she no longer worked at the paper, she was still on good terms with many of the correspondents. The only one she steadfastly refused to speak to was James Sloane—her former editor and former friend. She would never forgive him for his lack of backbone and his betrayal. *Ah, well, they say your true friends come to light in times of crisis.* Sadly, James did not rise to the occasion. No matter. She had moved on and wasn't looking back. The only concession to the past was the unresolved matter of her parents' murder.

With renewed purpose, Emmeline grabbed a pad and began making a list of the correspondents still at the *Times* who had known her mother and father well.

She spoke to one or two. Although they were happy to talk to her about her parents, not one could provide any information. Emmeline was determined not to let this upset her. She was a journalist after all. Digging for a story was in her blood. She would have the truth, one way or the other.

ᥱᓭᥱᓭ

"Ah, there you are, Burnell," Assistant Commissioner Cruickshank said as he waylaid the superintendent in the corridor.

Terrific. If it isn't the Met's very own little ray of sunshine, Burnell thought. *And to think, I could have missed him entirely if the Tube had been delayed. Reliable service leaves a lot to be desired.* Aloud, he replied with an obsequious smile, "Good morning, sir. I trust all is well."

"It most certainly is not."

"Isn't it? I'm sorry to hear that, sir. Perhaps your day will get better. Now, I must dash. I'm—"

"Burnell." Cruickshank raised his voice slightly. His tone was stern. Well, as stern as the Boy Wonder could muster, the superintendent supposed.

"I would like a word." Cruickshank jerked his head toward a quiet spot, where they would not be overheard.

Burnell sighed and reluctantly followed. "Yes, sir."

"I had a rather unpleasant call last night from MI-Six."

"Did you? It's shocking the lack of common courtesy in the world today. Never mind. I wouldn't dwell on it if I were you."

"I am not amused, Burnell. This is a serious matter. MI-Six complained that you were extremely uncooperative yesterday at the scene of the suicide of that Russian fellow."

"Alleged."

"What? What are you driveling on about?"

"Alleged suicide, sir. There are strong indications that Melnikov was pushed off the balcony."

"That's entirely beside the point. I was informed that you made a nuisance of yourself with Agents Jennings and Drake."

"I think you'll find that they were the ones who were rather heavy-handed—"

Cruickshank cut him off. "Enough. The case is no longer your concern. And in future, you will give MI-Six all the assistance it needs. Do I make myself clear?"

Burnell bit his tongue and silently counted to ten. "Perfectly, sir."

"Superintendent Burnell," a familiar voice called.

Involuntarily, a smile spread across his face before he realized he was still facing his new boss. He quickly pursed his lips and spun around to be greeted by the sight of Emmeline walking toward him.

Her lips curved into a smile and she extended a hand when she reached his side. "Good morning, Superintendent Burnell."

He accepted the small hand she proffered and inclined his head slightly.

Before he had a chance to say anything, Cruickshank piped up, "Burnell, you must introduce me." He flashed what the superintendent assumed was intended to be a dazzling smile at Emmeline, but which, in reality, made the assistant commissioner look rather silly.

Burnell rolled his eyes. *Good God, the man is actually preening like a peacock. Can't he see what a fool he's making of himself? It's going to be a pleasure bursting his bubble.*

Burnell rubbed his hands together with glee. "Certainly, sir. Assistant Commissioner Cruickshank, this is Emmeline Kirby. Miss Kirby, Assistant Commissioner Cruickshank."

Cruickshank extended his hand. "A pleasure, Miss Kirby."

She smiled and shot a questioning look at Burnell, whose features were schooled to be deliberately bland.

"Kirby?" Cruickshank murmured. "Why does that name ring a bell?"

Burnell cleared his throat. "Perhaps, I can help on that score, sir. I believe it's because Miss Kirby has been instrumental in helping the Met—me, in particular—in cracking several recent cases."

"Has she? You're to be commended, Miss Kirby. We need more civic-minded people like you," Cruickshank said, giving her an appreciative nod.

A slight flush tinged Emmeline's cheeks. "Oh, Superintendent Burnell, you give me too much credit. You mustn't forget Gregory. His contributions were invaluable," she replied modestly.

"How could *anyone* forget Longdon," Burnell muttered, his voice laced with sarcasm. Then, to Cruickshank he said, "In any event, Miss Kirby might be known to you because she works in that profession you regard in such high esteem."

"Oh, yes?" The assistant commissioner's glance settled once more on her attractive face. "And what do you do, Miss Kirby?"

"She's a member of the Fourth Estate," Burnell answered matter-of-factly. He let this information sink in, before he added, "Miss Kirby is the well-respected editorial director of *The Clarion*."

Emmeline beamed with pride at this description, but Cruickshank's brown eyes widened in disbelief. Burnell could almost hear the man's illusions shattering.

The assistant commissioner swallowed hard as he took a half-step backward. "The *press*? Of course." He wagged an accusatory finger at Emmeline. "You're the one who—"

"Writes such balanced and insightful articles? Indeed, she is, sir," Burnell said, as he heaped more salt on the wound.

"You're the one who nearly destroyed the Metropolitan Police with that scurrilous report on Fenton. And to make matters worse, you're engaged to that thief Longdon."

Burnell saw Emmeline's back stiffen and her dark eyes narrow.

Uh, oh, now you've gone and done it, old chap, he thought. *I would run while I still had the chance, if I were you. She may be all of five-foot-two, but her temper is that of a lioness protecting her cubs.*

"For the record, Assistant Commissioner Cruickshank." Her tone was clipped and her bearing rigid. "Everything—and I do mean *everything*—was corroborated by several sources. As my stories always are. I do not appreciate my professionalism being brought into question simply because the truth is inconvenient."

Take that, Burnell silently cheered.

"And another thing, my private life is no one else's business. You have no right whatsoever to cast aspersions on Gregory's character. Symington's would not have hired him as its chief investigator if there were any doubts about his soundness."

Character? I'll have to disagree with you on that score, Emmeline, Burnell thought. *Longdon is a thief and always will be. Playing at insurance investigator will soon begin to chafe.*

Cruickshank opened his mouth to say something, but quickly snapped it shut.

Wise move, Burnell quietly applauded. *I suggest a tactical retreat.*

Cruickshank straightened his shoulders and drew himself up to his full height of six-foot-three.

In Burnell's eyes, though, Emmeline still dwarfed the man in stature even as she stood there seething with indignation.

The assistant commissioner held out his hand again. "Miss Kirby, I'm afraid I must go. A pleasure to have met you." Burnell noted that the latter was uttered with quite a bit less enthusiasm than it had been only moments ago. "I have…a meeting."

Emmeline gave his hand a perfunctory squeeze. "Of course, Assistant Commissioner Cruickshank."

"Before I go, though, I would like to make it perfectly clear that Scotland Yard is willing to cooperate with the press. To a point. However, I must ask you not to harass my officers." He cast a sharp glance at Burnell. "They have more important things to do than to spend all day answering inane questions."

He gave a curt nod and turned on his heel before she could respond.

She started to go after him, but Burnell grabbed her arm. "He's not worth it, Emmeline." He used her given name, now that they were left alone.

Her dark eyes scoured his face. "The pompous bastard."

Burnell chuckled. She didn't normally swear. "Welcome to my world."

A throaty laugh burst forth from her lips. "You have my sympathies. I'd throttle him if I worked with him day in and day out."

"I just do my best to ignore him. Now, how can I help you?"

Her face sobered and her body seemed to tense. "It may be nothing."

"Despite what Cruickshank might think, I *know* you wouldn't ring me up if it were nothing. Let's go to my office. Then we can sort out your problem, all right?" He patted her arm reassuringly.

She gave him a wan smile and nodded.

"Finch," he yelled as the sergeant stepped out of the lift. "My office."

"Right, sir." He smiled and inclined his head when he noticed Emmeline by the superintendent's side.

Once Burnell was ensconced behind his desk and Finch was settled in the seat beside her, Emmeline took a deep breath and told the two detectives about the incident in the Tube yesterday. "I must admit," she concluded. "It sounds rather silly now. I think I allowed my imagination to make more of it than it really was. After all, he didn't approach me or say anything. And yet…" Her voice trailed off.

Burnell and Finch exchanged a look.

"Yes, Emmeline? And yet what?" the superintendent prompted.

Her dark gaze flitted between the two detectives. "And yet, I can't help feeling that he followed me deliberately. He wanted to frighten me." She paused and shivered involuntarily. "And he did. Why?" she whispered.

Burnell's hands curled into tight fists. "I don't know, Emmeline. But I promise you, we're going to find this bloke and then we're going to have a nice long chat with him. It's ungentlemanly to go around frightening young ladies."

Emmeline sat back and relaxed. "I was worried that you would think that I had made too much out of the incident. But the look in his eyes was so cold and calculating."

"Leave it to us. Since the encounter, you haven't seen him again have you? Or any other strangers hanging about?"

She shook her head.

"Good." He turned to Finch. "Start checking into this matter, will you?"

"Yes, sir."

"Thank you both. You've eased my mind."

Burnell bestowed a rare smile. "We're merely doing our duty. Please don't worry. But ring us immediately if you see the chap again."

Emmeline rose to go. "I will. Thank you." She shook hands with both of them. Then her face froze. "I must ask you one thing."

"Of course, anything. What is it?"

"Please don't tell Gregory."

"Don't tell Gregory what?"

They all turned to find Gregory leaning against the doorframe with his arms crossed over his chest.

CHAPTER 10

D on't tell Gregory what?" he repeated as he pushed away from the door and strode across to the desk.

He took Emmeline by the elbow and leaned down to brush her cheek with a kiss. "Hello, darling. This is an unexpected surprise. You didn't mention that you would be popping over to have a secret natter with old Oliver today."

"No, I—Well, you see—" Emmeline stammered, as a dusky pink flush slowly crept up her cheeks.

Burnell cleared his throat noisily at the utterance of his given name. Gregory merely smiled. He so enjoyed needling the detective. At every opportunity, he would "forget" to address Burnell by his title.

"What was that, *Oliver*? I didn't quite catch what you said." Another smile was rewarded with a scowl from the superintendent. "Never mind." Gregory sidled closer to Emmeline and put an arm around her shoulders. "Now, do tell me what this secret is that I'm not supposed to know about." Although his tone was soft, there was an undercurrent of concern behind the words.

Her gaze met his and she pressed a hand to his chest. "It's hardly a secret," she murmured.

"No? Good. Then, as I'm your fiancé, you can tell me what this little *tête-à-tête* is all about."

Emmeline cast a sideways glance at Burnell and then dragged her gaze back to Gregory. She sighed. "I didn't want to worry you. It may be nothing."

His body tensed, all his muscles suddenly alert. "What's happened?"

Reluctantly, Emmeline proceeded to tell him about her encounter with the stranger in the Green Park Station.

With each word, Gregory could feel the color draining from his cheeks. His mouth went dry. Emmeline's description of the man left him in no doubt as to his identity.

Swanbeck.

Blood raced through his veins. Wave upon thunderous wave crashed with ferocious intensity against the walls of his heart.

He grabbed Emmeline roughly by the arms and shook her. "From now on, you are not to go anywhere alone. Not even for five minutes. Do you understand?"

"Ow, Gregory, you're hurting me." She tried to loosen his grip, but his fingers were clamped around her upper arms like a vise.

Burnell jumped to his feet and pounded his open palm on his desk. "Longdon." His tone held a note of severe warning. He had never known the man to resort to violence, certainly not against women. Longdon was a charmer by nature, not a hardened murderer.

Finch was hovering near Longdon, ready to step in if the situation escalated.

Gregory saw fear and confusion reflected in the dark depths of Emmeline's eyes. He abruptly let her go and drew her into his embrace. He rested his chin on the crown of her head. "Sorry, darling." He pressed a distracted kiss against her soft curls. "Sorry," he mumbled again.

She pulled away and tilted her head back to look up at him. "This is why I didn't want to tell you. After everything that happened with Doyle, I didn't want to worry you unnecessarily. I freely admit that I was frightened yesterday, but nothing actually *happened*."

Gregory kissed the tip of her nose. "You're right, darling. I didn't mean to overreact."

Emmeline smiled up at him and traced a finger along his jaw. "You know I love you, but I don't need to be coddled. You can't protect me all the time. I'm a journalist. I have a job to do. I can't stay locked up in my office. And I *don't* need a bodyguard. What happened yesterday—" She paused and took a breath. "—was probably nothing." She turned to Burnell seeking support on this point. He nodded. "And if it wasn't…well, then it's in the capable hands of Superintendent Burnell and Sergeant Finch. I have every confidence in them and so should you."

Gregory tossed a grudging smile at Burnell and sketched a little salute. "Oliver is well aware that the depth of my admiration for him knows no bounds."

The superintendent snorted and waved his hands in the air in a dismissive gesture.

"No, truly, Oliver, old boy. I sleep soundly each night knowing that you—and Finch—" He inclined his head toward the sergeant. "—are at the helm of Scotland Yard. Protecting the city and its humble citizens from those with evil intentions."

Burnell grunted. "Pull the other one, Longdon. If you had any respect for the law, you wouldn't make a career out of stealing other people's jewels."

Gregory let Emmeline go. "Oliver, you don't know the pain it gives me right here—" He pressed a fist to his heart. "—to hear such hurtful—not to mention slanderous— accusations spilling from your lips. Clearly, someone is trying to poison your mind against me. I would have thought that the bonds of our friendship were strong enough to withstand anything." He shook his head sadly and clucked his tongue.

"Longdon, not in this lifetime nor in the next world will we ever be friends. I don't consort with criminals."

"Criminal? Oh, Oliver. Rubbing salt into the wound. I never thought you could be so cruel."

Burnell groaned in apparent exasperation.

Finch rolled his eyes. "Sir, would you like me to escort Mr. Longdon off the premises?"

"You too, Finch?" Gregory sniffed. "I must say that my opinion of you has sunk very low."

"I'm crying," the sergeant retorted sardonically. "The day I'm concerned what the likes of you thinks about me will be the day it's time for me to quit the force. Until then, I'll be waiting. You've had a good innings, but it can't last forever.

You're going to slip up one of these days because you're too cock-sure of yourself."

Gregory stepped away from Emmeline and clapped Finch on the shoulder. The grin he flashed was intended to infuriate, and he could see it succeeded in its mission. "Such hostility is unseemly, Finch. An officer of the law should show a little decorum. Perhaps a psychiatrist can get to the root of your problem."

Finch opened his mouth to say something and then appeared to change his mind. He pressed his lips together and shrugged his shoulders in resignation. After all, he would only lose the argument.

"Gregory." Emmeline nudged him in the ribs with her elbow and shook her head in disapproval.

"Yes, darling? I was only trying to help Sergeant Finch."

"What you've done—as you usually set out to do—is to put everyone in a thoroughly foul mood," Burnell said through gritted teeth.

"Me?" Gregory replied, his tone infused with innocence. "I'm the most agreeable of chaps. That's not possible."

Burnell muttered something unintelligible under his breath.

"Gregory, I think we should go. Superintendent Burnell and Sergeant Finch have work to do." Emmeline tugged at his sleeve. "We've taken up quite enough of their time." She offered both detectives an apologetic smile.

Burnell unbent slightly and extended his hand. "I always have time for *you*, Emmeline. You're never a bother."

She blushed as she shook his hand.

"And me, Oliver?" Gregory fluttered his eyelashes coquettishly at the superintendent. "Will you be there for me day or night?"

The smile disappeared from Burnell's face as he shifted his gaze. His voice was as hard as broken glass. "One of these days you're going to push your luck too far, Longdon. Now, get out." He jerked his head toward the door.

Gregory patted Emmeline's small hand. "Emmy, I have business with these illustrious gentlemen. If you'll wait, I'll see that you—"

She cut across him. "Weren't you listening to me a few moments ago? I'm perfectly capable of taking care of myself. I don't need you lurking in the shadows. We both have work to do. Please let me get on with mine."

Her jaw was set with determination as she tossed her chin in the air, as if daring him to contradict her.

After a moment's silence, he lifted her hand to his lips and brushed her fingertips with a kiss. "Go." And then, he stood aside and watched her quietly slip out of the office.

Once Emmeline had left, Gregory whirled round, all tenderness gone from his demeanor. "Oliver, I want Emmy watched night and day. You are not to let her out of your sight."

Burnell arched one eyebrow upward. "Since when do you think you can stroll into my office and order me about? Scotland Yard is not at your beck and call."

Gregory placed both hands on the desk and leaned forward so that his face was only inches from the superintendent. "Damn it, man," he hissed. "This is no joke. Emmy is making a target of herself. A very easy target."

Burnell straightened up. His gaze raked Gregory's handsome features. There was a haunted look in in the other man's eyes. And there was something he had never heard before in Gregory's voice. It was a desperate urgency—and fear.

"Oliver, you don't understand."

The superintendent waved toward a chair and dropped into his own. He propped his elbows on the desk and rested his chin on his hands. In a gentler tone, he said, "No, you're right there. I'm completely in the dark. So why don't you enlighten us."

Gregory hesitated for a fraction of a second and then sat down in the chair Emmeline had occupied only a few moments ago. Finch resumed his own seat.

"Good. Now, talk."

CHAPTER 11

Emmeline exited the New Scotland Yard building on the Dacre Street side since it was directly opposite the St. James's Park Tube station. She intended to catch the Circle or District Line and switch at Monument to go back to the office. But just as she was about to swipe her Oyster card through the turnstile, another idea struck her and she hurried back out into the brilliant sunshine.

She pulled out her mobile and punched in a number. She crossed her fingers and mumbled, "Please be there."

It was answered on the second ring. "Acheson."

She smiled. "Hello, Philip. It's Emmeline."

"Hello there." He sounded pleased to hear from her, but there was a hint of wariness in his voice that she couldn't fathom.

"Philip, are you all right?"

"Yes, of course. I'm perfectly fine. Why do you ask?"

"You just don't sound like yourself." A knot suddenly lodged in the pit of her stomach. "Is something wrong? Are Maggie and the boys all right?"

"Everyone's fine. Maggie has thrown herself into her work again and the twins are as infuriating as two five-year-olds can be."

Emmeline let out her breath, which she hadn't realized she had been holding.

"Tell me why London's most intrepid journalist has rung me up."

"I'm in the neighborhood and I was wondering if I could bribe you with a coffee. I'd like to discuss something."

"I've got a lot on this morning. What's all this about?" The caginess was back in his tone. *Why*?

"I realize that you're busy. I know it's a bit of a cheek turning up on your doorstep without warning, but it's important. I promise it won't take long."

"Well—"

She heard papers rustling in the background.

"Please, Philip. I need help. It's something personal. It's about…It's about my parents."

"What?" Was that relief mingled with confusion that she detected in his tone? "Your *parents*?"

"Yes, my parents," she replied quietly. "What did you think I wanted?"

"Nothing."

Emmeline pulled the mobile away from her ear and gave it a quizzical look. *What are you hiding?* she silently asked Philip. She would get to the bottom of things. Then, she resumed the conversation. "I could meet you at the Caffè Nero in Trafalgar Square in say half an hour, if that's all right?"

There was a prolonged pause. Then she heard him sigh. "Fine. But I can't stay long."

"Thanks, Philip. I'll be brevity itself."

He said goodbye and severed the connection.

Emmeline beamed as she started to wend her way toward Birdcage Walk.

By the time she reached the pavement on the outer edge of St. James's Park, hope started to bubble within her. Surely with Philip's help—if he was willing to give it and why wouldn't he once he heard her story?—she would be able to find her parents' murderer. He *must* be able to provide some kernel of information or know someone who could lead her to the truth.

There was a bounce in her step as she turned onto Horse Guards Road.

When she was opposite the Cabinet War Rooms, her mobile started to scream and she rummaged in her handbag to dig it out.

"Oh no, you don't," she said as she flipped it open. "Philip, you're not going to stand me up. A promise is a promise."

"Miss Kirby. Is that Emmeline Kirby?" She stopped short

at the sound of the strange male voice with a Russian accent at the other end of the line.

"Who is this?"

"My name is Yevgeny Sabitov. I've been calling your office, but they wouldn't let me speak to you."

The hairs on the back of her neck stood on end. "This is my private number. How did you get it?"

"That's not important. I must see you. They killed Pavel and now I'm next."

She gripped the mobile more tightly between her fingers. "Mr. Sabitov, I don't know why you're calling me. If you're in some sort of trouble, I suggest you go to the police—"

He snarled in her ear. "Bah. The police are useless. Swanbeck has spies everywhere. Can't you understand? I need *your* help."

"No, I don't understand anything. What can I do? Why come to me?"

"Because Charles Latimer was my friend and he trusted you. I'm a dead man, unless you help me. Please."

At the sound of Charles's name, she sucked in her breath. "Charles? Charles is dead." Her voice was low and hoarse.

"Yes, I know. We both know that he was a very good man and a superb journalist. He spoke of you often. I have nowhere else to turn. Will you meet me?"

Poor, dear Charles. A lump formed in her throat. She missed him terribly.

She squared her shoulders and made a split-second decision. "Where do you want to meet?"

"Somewhere so public they won't dare to try anything." He paused for a moment. "How about tea at the Dorchester Hotel this afternoon?"

They? What was she getting herself into? "I can't today. What about tomorrow?"

The silence was so long that she thought he had rung off. "All right. Tomorrow. The Dorchester. Four-thirty."

Then his voice was gone and she was left listening to dead air. What would tomorrow bring?

ळ৩৩

The Caffè Nero wasn't crowded. The aroma of ground espresso beans filled her nostrils as soon as Emmeline pushed open the door. The floorboards creaked slightly as she climbed the three wide, flat wooden steps and made her way past the counter to the back of the café. She sank into a cracked leather armchair that had seen better days, but was still comfortable. As she waited for Philip, she glanced out the window that overlooked Admiralty Arch. Cars, taxis and other vehicles ducked in and out of the monument's shadows as they made their way along the Mall.

Her mind replayed the odd conversation she had just had with Yevgeny Sabitov. The name was familiar. "Sabitov, Sabitov," she mumbled under her breath.

Of course. How could she be so stupid? He was the outspoken Russian opposition journalist. She admired his work—that is, what little had leaked out to the West. It took tremendous courage to investigate corruption in the Kremlin. The last she heard, Sabitov was doing a series on the criminal activities of officers in the FSB, the KGB's successor.

Now that she confirmed his *bona fides* in her mind, she was itching to hear what Sabitov had to say. How could she possibly help him? What were those names he mentioned?

Pavel and Swanbeck. She shrugged. They meant nothing to her.

"Careful, if you frown anymore those lines marring your lovely forehead will become permanent."

"What?" The pleasant timbre of Philip's voice dragged her thoughts away from speculation about the intrepid Mr. Sabitov. "Hello, Philip."

She made to rise, but Philip waved her back. "Sit, sit." He bent down and brushed her cheek with a kiss. He dropped down into the armchair opposite her. "You're looking well. I'm glad to see that there are no ill effects from crossing swords with Doyle." He raised a blond eyebrow in askance.

She looked down at her hands in her lap and replied quietly, "No, I'm all right in general. Just a bit nervy these days, but I suppose that will pass soon. Work is a great help. And of course, I have Gregory."

"Yes, of course, Gregory," he murmured.

She saw a shadow cross his face. "Look, Philip, I'm well aware that you don't like Gregory but you'll have to get use his being around sooner or later." Her tone sounded sharp to her own ears. "We're getting married in October, so unless you and Maggie banish us from your home, you'll be seeing a lot of Gregory from now on."

His blue eyes widened and then crinkled at the corners in amusement. "What? Banish you from the house? The way Maggie has been working to push you two together? And the way the boys adore Auntie Emmeline? Heaven forbid. I'd never live to see another day, if I even suggested such a thing—which I hope you know I wouldn't. Longdon and I are big boys. I think we've proven that we can be civil to one another for the sake of the women we love."

He reached out and squeezed her hand. Her cheeks suffused with heat as she returned the pressure.

"Thanks. I know Gregory and I have had our problems, but we've dealt with them...well, most of them." She jutted her chin in the air. "I'm determined to make things work."

Philip laughed and got to his feet. "I have no doubts on that score. Now, how about some coffee and then you can tell me why you wanted to see me?"

She felt her smile falter just a teeny bit, when she remembered why she needed to talk to him. "Right. I need a bit of Dutch courage today. I'll be naughty and have a Hot Chocolate Milano."

One blond brow arched upward but Philip replied, "One Hot Chocolate Milano, it is."

She watched as he strode to the counter to order their drinks. Then she fumbled in her handbag and pulled out the photo of her parents that she always carried with her. It was taken that last summer before they died. Their family holiday together in Cornwall. She traced her finger over their well-loved faces.

"I will find out who took you away from me. I promise," she whispered.

A tear pricked her eyelid and she tucked the photo carefully back into her wallet. Her emotions seemed to be very fragile of late. She supposed almost dying had something to do with that.

She turned her head toward the window to get herself under control before Philip returned. She had to present the facts—what little she knew of them—in a cool, detached, and objective manner. She had to approach this as she would any other story she was investigating. It was the only way. She couldn't allow her emotions to cloud her judgment. Then where would she be?

"A hot chocolate to tempt the lady," Philip said as he carefully placed her drink in front of her.

She swiveled around as he settled into his chair. She watched over the rim of her tall glass cup as he put sugar into his double espresso and gave it a quick stir it with his spoon. He took a sip and, seemingly satisfied, leaned back.

They fell silent for a few minutes as they sipped their drinks. He swirled the cup around between his hands and lifted his gaze to her face. "As much as I enjoy your company, don't you think it's time you told me what all this in aid of? You mentioned something about your parents."

She took one last gulp of her chocolate and set the glass carefully on the saucer. "Yes, you see—" She moistened her lips with her tongue and started again. "I recently found out—that is, I recently received information from Yoav Zielinski—that my parents didn't die while on assignment in Beirut. They were—" The words caught in her throat, sending a tremor through her voice. "They were murdered."

Philip sat bolt upright. His cup made a jarring chink against the saucer as he banged it down on the table between them. He glanced around, before he hissed, "Murdered?"

She nodded. "Yes, the file that Mr. Zielinski sent me reveals that my parents were not killed in the crossfire between guerrillas and Israeli troops trying to rescue two captured soldiers. That's what my grandmother had been told. The file said—" Her voice quavered again. She gripped her hands tightly together in her lap to stop them from shaking. "The file said that there was no fighting that day. And that—That my parents were found in their hotel room, each with a single bullet hole in the chest. Professional, neat."

Philip reached out and touched her arm lightly. "Oh, Emmeline, I'm so terribly sorry. I had no idea."

She pounded one fist against her thigh and straightened her spine. "I want to find out who killed them. I need help—official help. That's why I came to you. Please, Philip. My parents deserve justice."

The pained expression in his eyes made her flinch. "I'll try to find out anything I can. But, Emmeline, you must realize that after twenty-five years it will be extremely difficult, if not impossible, to pick up the trail."

She shook off his hand. "Don't spout bureaucratic mumbo-jumbo at me." She lowered her voice. "You're MI-Five, for God's sake. You *know* everything."

His tone matched her own. "You are correct to a point. But this wouldn't fall under MI-Five's purview. It's more in MI-Six's line."

She snatched up her handbag and scooted to the edge of her seat preparing to jump to her feet. "Fine. If you won't help me, tell me who I need to speak to at MI-Six."

He put a restraining hand on her arm and firmly pushed her back in her chair. "Emmeline, please calm down."

Ooh, how she hated when someone said that to her. "Don't tell me to calm down," she replied through gritted teeth. "I'm perfectly calm."

"Not from this vantage point. I can feel the daggers from those dark eyes of yours piercing parts of my anatomy."

At that, her body relaxed slightly. "Philip, I haven't been able to sleep since I found out. It's not something that I can turn my back on. I need to know the truth."

"I didn't say I wouldn't help you. Just that things could be a bit tricky."

She gave him a half-smile. "I'm sorry."

He waved a hand dismissively in the air. "Nothing to be sorry about. I have a thick skin. In my world, you have to. I'll start by having a quiet word with Yoav. Obviously, he tried to find out all he could without attracting attention on the Israeli end. He must suspect that the key to this puzzle is to be found here in the UK. Why?"

She shook her head and leaned in closer. "You tell me."

"It's no use speculating at this stage." He patted her arm reassuringly. "Leave it to me. I'll get back to you in a few days."

"Thanks, Philip. I'll be in your debt forever."

"I'll remind you of that the next time Janet is ill and we need someone to watch the twins."

A laugh burst from her lips. "Consider it done. Anyway, you know how much I love spending time with Henry and Andrew."

Philip grinned. "The little monsters have got you wrapped around their fingers, you do realize that?"

"Nonsense."

Philip glanced at his watch and rose. "Emmeline, I'm afraid I must dash. So if there's nothing else, I'll—"

"Actually, there is one more thing I wanted to ask you about before you go."

"Yes?"

"Have you ever heard of a Russian named Pavel—I don't know whether that's his given name or his surname—or another chap called Swanbeck?"

Philip licked his lips. This was one of those times when he would have to draw on his well-honed diplomatic skills to give her an answer without really answering her question.

He hated being evasive, but what choice did he have? It was better than telling her that a ruthless businessman with ties to the Russian underworld, as well as the Kremlin, had a vendetta against Longdon and those closest to him.

That was completely unacceptable. So, his only option was to—massage the truth.

CHAPTER 12

S wanbeck. Alastair Swanbeck," Superintendent Burnell mumbled aloud as he flipped through the file Finch had pulled together for him.

There was nothing—not even the tiniest morsel of information—to seize upon that would give him an excuse to pay Mr. Swanbeck an official visit. He slammed the file down on the desk. "Damn and blast."

"Swanbeck?" Finch asked from the doorway.

The chair groaned as Burnell turned to face him. "Yes. There must be something. Somewhere," he said as Finch plunked down into the seat opposite him.

"Sir, I've checked and double checked. There are a lot of whispers, which could merely be corporate jealousy, but no evidence to tie Swanbeck to anything illegal. In the eyes of the law, he's a model citizen."

The superintendent snorted. "In my experience, there's no such thing. We have to find the chink in his armor. He's as cool as a cucumber, but there has to be a loose end somewhere. A disgruntled employee. A bitter rival. Something."

"If Longdon is to be believed, Swanbeck likes things neat and tidy. Anyone who gets in his way conveniently seems to disappear."

"Precisely." Burnell sat back and stroked his beard. "I don't want the bodies to start piling up around London."

"Speaking of bodies, sir. Dr. Meadows slipped me Melnikov's autopsy report on the sly." Finch waved a manila folder back and forth in the air. "He said that you owe him a large pint on Friday. He also stressed that he can only stall Assistant Commissioner Cruickshank for a couple of hours so you had better make good use of your time."

The superintendent sat up and rubbed his hands together. "Good old John. A truer friend there never was." He waggled his fingers impatiently at Finch. "Come on. Give it to me."

Burnell snatched the folder and laid it open on his desk. His practiced eye quickly perused the contents. "So, it's as we suspected. It wasn't suicide. Melnikov was helped off the balcony."

He leaned back in his chair and steepled his fingers over his ample stomach. "What was it that made this Russian such a threat that he had to be silenced? Did you find anything in his flat?"

"Not much. Melnikov was certainly not short of a bob or two. Robbery was certainly not the motive. There was a safe with ten thousand pounds in cash untouched. And he was still wearing his solid gold Rolex when he died."

"What's so special about him? Why did MI-Six muscle their way into this case? I want to know."

"Right, sir." Finch scooped up the report and stood to go. "I'll do a bit more digging."

"But on the quiet. We wouldn't want ruffle MI-Six's feathers a second time."

Finch nodded. At the door, he paused and turned back. "Sir, did you ever consider the fact that Longdon concocted this story about Swanbeck to distract us from something that he's up to?"

The image of Gregory's haggard face when he was telling them about Swanbeck flashed before Burnell's eyes. He shook his head. "No, Finch. I think for once Longdon is telling the truth." He winced as he rubbed his stomach. "My ulcer is starting to do somersaults. I have a nagging feeling—and mind you, my instincts have never failed me before—that we're starting two steps behind Swanbeck."

☙❧☙

"It's out of the question, Emmy," Gregory hissed as he dabbed at the corners of his mouth with his napkin. What had been a lovely dinner at their favorite Italian restaurant had taken an unexpected turn when the coffee and dessert arrived. The mood had become distinctly frosty.

"This Sabitov chap sounds a bit dodgy. You are not going to keep that meeting with him tomorrow. I will not allow it. That's an end to it." He dropped the napkin down on the table and leaned back in his chair.

Emmeline skewered him with her dark gaze over the rim of her cup. "I beg your pardon. You will not *allow* it. Allow it? Since when do you issue orders? I'm your fiancée, not your lackey." She set her cup down on the saucer with great care. "But if you go on like a Neanderthal—" Her voice was dangerously low. "—then you had better find yourself another fiancée because it won't be me."

"Darling—"

She propped her elbows on the table and rested her chin on her hands. "Don't darling me. If you do not respect my work, we have nothing to talk about."

Gregory groaned and tilted his head to stare at the ceiling. "Bloody stubborn woman. Give me strength, Lord," he muttered.

"Let's leave God out of this, shall we?" she said. "Divine intervention will not help you."

He met her gaze and began to chuckle. "Oh, Emmy."

"Nor is this a laughing matter." Her fingers rapped an angry tattoo on the table.

He reached out and covered her small hand with his larger one, arresting her fingers in mid-tap. "Darling, be reasonable."

She snatched her hand free and leaned across the table.

Clearly that was the wrong thing to say.

"Reasonable?" Her tone was clipped. "You do realize that with every word that comes out of your mouth, you're digging a deeper grave for yourself."

What I'm trying *to do, Emmy—and you're making it very difficult, as usual—is to keep you safe—and alive*, he thought.

He raised his hands in the air. "I surrender. Truce?"

She settled back in her chair, her chin thrusting up at angle. She sniffed, slightly mollified. "Truce."

He took the hand that still rested on the table and rubbed

his thumb along the soft web of skin between her forefinger and thumb.

Neither of them uttered a word for a few minutes.

He flashed one of his most brilliant smiles. "How about a compromise?"

She was instantly alert. Her eyes narrowed suspiciously as they raked his face. "What kind of compromise?"

"How about if I come with you tomorrow when you meet Sabitov?"

"No. He sounded very skittish on the phone. You may scare him off."

He raised her hand to his lips and kissed her fingertips. "I promise I'll employ my considerable charms—of which you can attest that I have many—" She rolled her eyes and his smile only grew wider. "—to put Mr. Sabitov at his ease."

"No. I don't need a chaperone to do my job. This is a routine—" One of his eyebrows arched upward at this. "Yes, routine." She gave a defiant nod of her head. "A routine meeting with a colleague."

"Ha," he retorted derisively.

"I thought we had a truce."

"Emmy, either I join you for tea at the Dorchester tomorrow or I ask Oliver to find some pretext to hold you at the station for the entire afternoon. The choice is yours."

"You wouldn't dare. Besides, Superintendent Burnell would never do such a thing."

He lowered his voice and grinned. "Are you willing to take the chance, darling? I can be extremely persuasive when I want to be." He waggled his eyebrows up and down at her.

She folded her arms across her chest and replied with a good deal of asperity, "I never dreamed you would stoop to blackmail."

"When a man has to contend with a stubborn woman—" Her eyes kindled and her mouth pressed into a grim line, but he went on, "—stubborn in the extreme, if the sad truth be known, then any means necessary must be employed."

"You—you," she sputtered.

"Am joining you tomorrow at the Dorchester for tea with

Mr. Sabitov. I'm so glad that we settled that little matter. More coffee?"

"Only if I can pour it over your head."

He clucked his tongue. "Really, darling. That would be very unladylike." He lifted his cup to his lips and took a sip. "Not to mention a waste of a perfectly lovely cup of coffee."

CHAPTER 13

Emmeline checked her watch as she exited the Hyde Park Corner Tube station the next afternoon. Five past four. She had plenty of time. It was only a short walk up Park Lane to get to the Dorchester. Gregory said he would meet her at the hotel at a quarter past and they would go in together to meet Sabitov.

Why did I agree? she grumbled as the light changed and she crossed the road. *It's absolutely ludicrous. It's the Dorchester for goodness sake, one of London's luxury hotels, not some back alley. What can possibly happen? If Gregory thinks that he can be so heavy-handed after we're married, he had better think again.*

By this time, she had reached the little garden in front of the Dorchester, whose cream-colored stone reflected the afternoon sun. Solid and staid, it rose with distinction to scrape the wisps of cloud drifting across the July sky. The fountain in the center of the garden chattered merrily as its waters sprayed into the pool surrounding it, which was bordered by a profusion of the red and white impatiens. She found a shady spot and carefully sat down on the stone border to wait for Gregory.

She watched taxis and cars roll up and depart at intervals along the semi-circular drive in front of the hotel. A doorman, dressed in a long, black coat trimmed with gold braiding that reached his mid-calves, held car doors open and touched the brim of his hat as he wished guests a good stay or alternately bid them goodbye.

She sighed as the minutes ticked by. Four-fifteen. Four-twenty. Four-twenty-five. Right. Gregory was ten minutes late.

Not blessed with natural patience, Emmeline decided she had waited for him long enough. He only had himself to blame.

The doorman smiled at her as she crossed the drive and held the door open for her. "Good afternoon, miss," he said quietly.

She returned his smile and inclined her head slightly. She hoped her annoyance with Gregory was not reflected in her face. "Good afternoon."

She stepped into the lobby, whose floor of white marble scattered with a pattern of black diamonds had been polished until it gleamed like a mirror. The reception desk was directly opposite the doors. Emmeline saw a male guest in a sports jacket speaking to the middle-aged gentleman on duty behind the desk. He appeared to be giving the guest directions. Next to him, the concierge was speaking on the telephone and jotting down a note.

Her heels echoed against the marble as she traversed the lobby and headed to the right of the reception desk down a set of wide, shallow steps shaped like a gray-and-white-striped fan. This led to the Promenade, the heart of the hotel where afternoon tea was served. Emmeline stopped for a moment to soak in the ambiance. It was no wonder that the Promenade was often referred to as "the drawing room of Mayfair." It was elegant and cozy all at once. The perfect place for a chat with an old friend or, if one was the naughty type, a rendezvous with a lover. There were high-backed divans and large urns overflowing with huge bouquets of flowers, plush loveseats and armchairs upholstered in moss green velvet, and potted palms and drapes to muffle whispered conversations in discreet corners. At the far end of the room, there was a leather oval bar with a backdrop of deep crimson glass.

Emmeline hesitated, her eyes scanning the faces around her. She suddenly realized that she had no idea what Yevgeny Sabitov looked like. She stood there for a few seconds shifting from foot to foot. Then above the snatches of conversations that rose to her ears, she heard an insistent voice that was slightly louder than a whisper.

"Miss Kirby, over here."

A burly man with thinning gray hair and a round face was half-standing at a table for two on the left-hand side about midway down the Promenade. He almost melted into the red marble column and potted palm behind him. He flicked his wrist once to wave a white cloth napkin in the air and then sat down again. She saw him cast a furtive glance to his right and left as she hurried toward him.

"Mr. Sabitov?" she asked when she came level with the table.

He gave a curt nod and motioned with his pale blue eyes at the chair opposite him.

"I took the liberty of ordering tea. It should arrive shortly."

As she had noted on the telephone yesterday, though his Russian accent was heavy his English was flawless.

She lowered herself into the chair. "It sounds lovely. Why did you want to see—"

He put up a hand to cut her off.

A waiter in a dark morning coat, white shirt, navy tie, dark waistcoat, and gray trousers had materialized at her elbow with a trolley. They were silent as he placed a steaming pot of tea in the center of the crisp, white tablecloth. Next appeared a two-tiered silver tray with a selection of finger sandwiches, plump scones, clotted cream, strawberry jam, and pastries.

"I'll be mother, as you English say, shall I?" Sabitov asked as he lifted the pot and extended a hand for her cup.

She nodded her thanks and selected a scone. She placed a dollop each of clotted cream and jam on her plate, while he chose the smoked salmon and chicken sandwiches.

She broke off a piece of scone and spread cream on it before topping it with a dab of jam. She studied him as she nibbled. He had a broad face with a fair, almost bloodless complexion. His most arresting feature, though, was his eyes. They were not blue as she had first thought, but rather a clear gray with the merest hint of blue. She suspected that his overall colorless appearance masked a fiery intelligence.

He gobbled up his smoked salmon in a single bite and washed it down with a lusty gulp of tea. "I've always appreciated your tradition of afternoon tea. It's all very civilized, is it not?" His hand swept in wide arc that encompassed their little nook, the Promenade, and the other patrons. A shadow fell over his face. "A civilized setting to discuss something that is not very civilized at all."

Emmeline took a swallow of the strong tea, which was the Dorchester's own blend of Sri Lankan Ceylon and Assam. It was just the thing to steady her nerves and help her mind to focus.

"On the phone, you mentioned Charles Latimer. How—how did you know him?"

His mouth twisted into a half-smile and he seemed to relax a little. "Ah, Charles. We became friends when he was the BBC's Moscow bureau chief. It was not easy because we were watched all the time. Putin and his coterie in the Kremlin and FSB view the press as an enemy of the people. Charles pushed his luck once too often, and they killed him."

Yes, Emmeline said to herself, *poor Charles, one of Daddy's closest friends, was murdered because he posed a threat to someone. Just like Mummy and Daddy.*

She shook her head to clear her mind of this train of thought. This was not the time.

Sabitov was still speaking. "Charles talked about you many, many times. He was very proud of you. In his mind, you were like a niece."

Emmeline smiled. "When I was little, I used to call him Uncle Charles. He and my father had been friends since university."

"That's why I came to you, Miss Kirby. I need someone I can trust. I'm running out of time. At any moment, I can be killed just like that." He snapped his fingers. "Putin's reach is long. No one escapes it."

She shivered involuntarily but squared her shoulders. "Please call me Emmeline. I will help you in any way I can for Charles's sake and for the truth."

His lips tightened into a grim line. "Hmph." He tossed his head back and scoffed, "The truth. That is something that Putin is quite unfamiliar with. His obsessions are power and money. He never has enough of either one. He doesn't care what he has to do or who he has to crush to get more. He has no respect for the law. From the upper echelons to the lowliest clerk, the Kremlin is riddled with corruption. And if anyone dares to say anything—" He spread his hands wide and shrugged. "—he will never be seen in this world again. Pavel thought he could outsmart Putin and Swanbeck, but his gamble didn't pay off."

"Who is this Pavel? Was he a friend of yours?"

Sabitov lifted his cup to his lips and cast a sideways glance to his left, before he answered. Emmeline casually allowed her eyes to roam around too, but no one seemed to be eavesdropping. The middle-aged couple at the table in the center aisle several feet from them was holding hands and appeared engrossed in their conversation. A waiter passed by and seated a young woman at the table behind Sabitov. She was wearing a white silk sheath dress and a dainty fascinator hat set at a jaunty angle. The minute she sat down she pulled out her mobile, oblivious to everything around her.

"No one's listening," Emmeline whispered.

Sabitov hesitated for a second and then plunged ahead. "Pavel Melnikov was what's known nowadays as a whistleblower. He was—murdered yesterday. Right here in London." He paused to let this sink in. "Putin's friends—more likely Russian gangsters tied to Swanbeck—pushed Pavel off the balcony of his flat in the posh environs of Mayfair."

Emmeline slumped back in her chair, stunned. "You can't be serious."

"Oh, but I am. These are ruthless men."

She leaned forward and picked up her cup. "But it's not possible," she hissed over the rim. "They can't go about London killing people."

"Putin and Swanbeck can. They're two of a kind. An alliance made in hell. Besides, the killings outside Russia were given a legal blessing by the Kremlin. So you see, the government is granted free rein to use the FSB to liquidate its enemies. Business leaders, lawyers, rights advocates, anyone who goes against Putin is considered a traitor." His tone was a mixture of bitterness and disgust—and fear.

"What did Pavel find out that they had to silence him? Is this Swanbeck chap a FSB officer?"

"Let's start with Pavel. He came to me to expose a major money-laundering scheme involving FSB officers, the Russian mafia, and the Kremlin. A one-hundred-fifty-million-pound fraud. Can you imagine? He gave me names, dates, files—everything. I had enough information to do a series of articles. However, the day the first article appeared Putin had every last copy of the paper pulled from the streets, and he even had the printing plates destroyed. From that day, I have been a marked man. Pavel fled to London six months ago and had been talking with MI-Six. He was living on borrowed time."

Emmeline poured herself another cup of tea. She wrapped her fingers around the delicate porcelain, hoping to warm her hands and ward off the chill that had settled into her bones. "If MI-Six knew he was in so much danger, why didn't they place him in a witness protection program and hide him in some remote village in the country?"

"Pavel was a fool and refused. He thought Putin and the mafia wouldn't dare touch him if they knew he was talking to MI-Six."

"Who is this Swanbeck chap?"

"Alastair Swanbeck. Son of the late Walter Swanbeck. Ever heard of him?"

Emmeline shook her head.

"He was a billionaire. An oil and shipping magnate, who counted the Russian mafia and members of the Kremlin elite among his closest associates. Swanbeck the father was involved in everything from gun-running to brothels all across Europe. The dirtier it was, the better he liked it. As far as the law was concerned, no one could touch him. He was very clever, but not clever enough. Walter was killed several years ago. No one really knows the exact circumstances. However, his empire didn't suffer. He had been grooming his son Alastair to take over the business since he was in knee pants. The day after the funeral, Alastair stepped into his father shoes without any hesitation, and he has never looked back. They say he's a thousand times more cunning than his father. If the rumors are to be believed, Putin is a silent partner in the business."

"My God. They have to be stopped."

"Yes. Pavel tried. But now Pavel is dead, and I'm next. So is Rutkovsky."

"Rutkovsky? Who's he?" Her mind was already reeling. "Another whistleblower?"

"In a way you could say that. Rutkovsky is...special. So special, in fact, that no one even suspects that he is helping the British to cut the snake's head off. He's above suspicion. He's not an agent, but he has high connections and he can move around more easily because of his business dealings. However, I've said too much. If Rutkovsky's cover is blown, then it's truly the end. None of us are safe. Putin and Swanbeck don't like loose ends. We're all living on borrowed time." His sad, gray eyes found hers. "I needed someone else to know. It's important that the story is told. Promise me you'll do it, if anything happens to me."

"This is madness. You have to go the police. Superintendent Burnell can help—"

He reached out and grabbed her wrist in a vise-like grip. "No," he snapped. He darted a worried glance to his left and then lowered his voice, when he saw several heads turn in their direction. "No police. Swanbeck has his spies everywhere."

Emmeline leaned forward and hissed, "You're hurting me." She managed to wrench her hand free. "Let's get one thing straight, Mr. Sabitov," she said as she rubbed her wrist, "I'm not going to be bullied. Your friend Pavel is dead. Your only choice is to go to the police."

"I said no." His voice was rising, once again attracting unwanted attention. "You call yourself a journalist. Bah." He made a disgusted gesture with his hands.

Emmeline threw her napkin down on the table. "Do you want to die? Because you certainly will if you continue to be so stubborn. Then all your hard work will have been for nothing, and Putin and Swanbeck will have won. Is that what you want? I'll help you. I agree this story has to be told, but we can't fight them on our own. You *must* go to the police. Don't you see—"

A waiter cut off whatever she had been about to say. "Excuse me, Miss Emmeline Kirby?"

They both looked up, startled. "What? Yes," she stammered and then cleared her throat. "I'm Emmeline Kirby."

"Would you come with me to reception, madame?"

She frowned. "Why? Is there a problem?"

"Please, Miss Kirby. I think it would be best if you would just come with me."

She exchanged a look with Sabitov, who shrugged and shook his head.

Emmeline rose and pushed her chair back. "All right. But I don't understand what this is all about." Then to Sabitov, she said, "Please excuse me. I'll be back as quick as I can."

She started to follow the waiter. But over her shoulder to Sabitov, she whispered in parting, "Think about what I said."

He scowled in response, his jaw clenching into a tight, hard line. "*Nyet*," he defiantly tossed back at her.

Hmph. Why are men always so pig-headed, she thought as she wended her way out to the lobby.

Sabitov savagely crumbled a scone between his fingers. He watched Emmeline's retreating back until she disappeared up the steps into the lobby. He was beginning to regret ever contacting her. *Why did Charles think she was so brilliant?* He didn't see anything to warrant such admiration.

He glanced at his watch and took a gulp of tea. If she didn't return in the next five minutes, he decided he was going to leave. He had wasted too much time already. And he had exposed himself too much. This unsettling thought prompted him to sweep his nervous gaze over the surrounding tables. His eyes lingered on the faces of the other patrons. But no one seemed to be taking an unhealthy interest in him. He sagged in his chair and closed his eyes. Some of the tension uncoiled from his muscles. He was becoming paranoid.

"What do you mean you're not coming, Ralph?" The grating tone of the woman seated behind him made him open his eyes. She was on her mobile. "I've been waiting here for the last quarter of an hour. This is the third time in the last week that you've stood me up. You had better have a *very* good explanation."

Sabitov sighed. She sounded extremely spoiled. He pitied poor Ralph. However, he was intrigued and leaned his head back just a touch so that he could hear a little better.

"*Your wife?*" The woman's voice was laced with fury. "You stood me up so that you could accompany your wife to some bloody charity event."

Sabitov smiled and shook his head. What did she expect? The woman had paused in her tirade, apparently because Ralph was trying to justify himself.

"Stuff your feeble excuse. This is the last straw, Ralph. Don't bother coming round anymore. I'll set the dog on you if you do."

Sabitov leaned forward when he heard her chair scrape back. She was muttering under her breath. Out of the corner of his eye, he saw her stop just over his left shoulder to take out a small mirror and freshen up her lipstick. He clucked his tongue silently. *Very poor manners*, he thought. *Ralph, I think you've had a lucky escape.*

When she was done, she zipped her clutch with such violence that it became stuck. "Oh, for goodness sake. Is everything going to go wrong today?" she mumbled as she continued to tug at the zipper with increasing impatience.

In the process, her hat slipped from her hand and landed beside Sabitov's left foot. He bent down to retrieve it for her.

She snatched it out of his grasp. "Do you mind? What do you think you're playing at?"

He cleared his throat and replied apologetically, "Nothing, madame, I assure you. I was just trying—"

"Keep your grubby hands to yourself." She set the hat on her head at an angle before storming off, her hips swaying and her heels clicking.

He shrugged and exchanged a conspiratorial look with the couple across from him. At least the insufferable woman had gone.

He reached out to pour himself another cup of tea and was

surprised to see that his thumb was bleeding. He pressed it to his lips. Oh, yes, he remembered now. A hat pin cut him when the woman grabbed her hat out of his hand. He sucked on his thumb for a few of seconds. *Stupid woman.*

Speaking of women, where was Emmeline Kirby? He coughed. His mouth suddenly felt parched. He fingered his collar. He hadn't realized until that moment that it was very warm in the hotel.

He managed to get some tea into his cup, after sloshing a good bit of it onto the saucer. He took a greedy gulp and filled his cup again to try to quench his overwhelming thirst. He raised the cup to his lips, but immediately banged it back down, rattling the saucer. He was having trouble drawing air into his lungs. What was happening to him? His pulse was racing. He hoped he wasn't having a heart attack. He gripped the arms of his chair and blinked rapidly. The bright lights were causing his vision to blur. He wished it all would just stop.

He sat up abruptly, his curled fists sending plates and saucers tumbling to the floor with a crash. He was desperate for air. He couldn't breathe. He looked about frantically. Why were people staring at him?

In that instant between heartbeats, the terrifying truth dawned upon him.

He was dead. They had killed him.

CHAPTER 14

I f I get my hands on the practical joker, I'll throttle him with my bare hands," Emmeline muttered under her breath as she hurried back to the table. She had spent the last ten minutes trying to explain to the concierge that she had not ordered five dozen roses. She liked roses. But five dozen? What would she *do* with five dozen roses? At last, the dim-witted man saw reason. She left him to deal with the florist.

"Oof. Open your eyes and look where you're going," the woman in white said as she jostled past Emmeline.

"You're the one who bumped into me," Emmeline spat back, her voice edged with irritation. She was in no mood for rudeness this afternoon.

The woman looked down her nose at her, a ghost of a smile playing around the corners of her mouth. Without another word, she turned on her heel and continued on her way toward the lobby.

Emmeline wrinkled her nose behind the woman's back and mumbled, "Hoity-toity. It's beginning to rain. I hope your spotless dress gets splashed by a taxi and is ruined beyond repair." It was spiteful, but in the circumstances she felt it would do.

Now, back to more important things. Sabitov.

Emmeline had only taken a few steps, when the jarring sound of plates smashing against the floor floated to her ears. Her eyes were immediately drawn to their table. Sabitov looked as though he was having a fit of some kind. People at nearby tables were beginning to take notice. A nervous murmur of voices rose upon the air.

Emmeline ran the last few feet to the table. Sabitov's face

was scarlet, as if he had fallen asleep in the sun and woken with a bad burn. His skin was slick with perspiration. He was thrashing about. There was a glazed look in his eyes.

"Mr. Sabitov, tell me what's wrong so that I can get you some help?"

At the sound of her voice, his head snapped up and he tried to focus. "You." He tried to stand, but plopped back down onto his chair.

He grabbed her wrist and snarled, "There is no help for me. Can't you...see...I'm dead?"

His fingers bit into her skin, branding her with his fear. He wouldn't let go.

"What's going on?" a man behind her asked.

Sabitov's confused gaze drifted to some point over her shoulder. "She...killed me." It was a hoarse whisper. "She—" But that was the last word he would ever utter.

A frisson slithered down Emmeline's spine. There were several audible gasps from the semicircle of people now hovering around the table. She heard "Did he say murder?"

"I heard him say, 'She killed me.'"

"Oh, my God. He's dead."

Emmeline craned her neck around to find herself in the crosshairs of several horrified stares. She caught a whisper of movement out of the corner of her eye. She turned and saw the woman in white crossing the lobby. She broke her stride for only a second, long enough to cast a quick glance over her shoulder. Instinct told Emmeline that the woman had to be stopped.

With little grace, she prized her hand from the dead man's hold. If she could just prevent the woman from leaving the hotel.

She found her way blocked by several patrons. "Where do you think you're going?"

Emmeline's back stiffened. "Would you please get out of my way? I have to stop that woman. It's very important."

A portly gentleman with a smug, craggy face clamped his sausage-like fingers around her upper arm. "So that you can scarper to Argentina or wherever it is criminals go these days?

I don't think so. I was not born yesterday, you know. You're staying right here until the police arrive."

She struggled against his grasp. "Criminal? You don't understand."

"Emmy, what the devil is going on?"

Her head whirled round when she heard Gregory's voice. The voice of sanity. At last.

"Gregory, Sabitov's dead." She jerked her chin in the direction of the table. "He's been murdered." This last word was barely audible.

His cinnamon eyes widened in disbelief and then became narrow slits as he turned back to her. "I thought I told you to wait for me," he hissed through clenched teeth.

"You can lecture me later. Right now, we have to stop that woman in the white dress." She pointed toward the lobby. "I think she's the one who killed him, but this oaf won't let me go." She lifted her arm, indicating the beefy hand attached to it.

Before the man had a chance to react, the pointy part of Gregory's elbow jabbed him in the ribcage. "Oof," he grunted as he staggered back several steps, landing with a heavy plop in an empty chair nearby.

Gregory shot his cuff and took the man to task. "It's awfully bad manners to treat a lady with such a lack of respect."

The man opened his mouth, but he was apparently too stunned by Gregory's impudence to offer a response.

Without another word, Gregory grabbed Emmeline's hand and they broke into a run.

"Stop that woman," she called out. "Don't let her leave the hotel."

Heads were turning around to see what the commotion was about. People were scattering to get out of their way. Emmeline didn't bother to glance back, but she could hear several waiters and others close on their heels. Bloody stupid fools. Did she and Gregory really look like criminals? Well, Gregory was a jewel thief—*was* being the operative word as in no longer is, she hoped. But this was no time for second guessing him.

As they skidded across the marble floor of the lobby, some plainclothes hotel security officers came running toward them. Emmeline saw the woman in white squeeze through the revolving door. If she got into a taxi, they'd never find her again.

Gregory dropped Emmeline's hand and muscled his way past two of the security men. With his longer stride, he was through the door and outside on the pavement before her. She momentarily got tangled up with the security men and had to struggle to shrug off their hold on her arms.

Three taxis and a silver BMW pulled up to the curb. The first taxi had already disgorged its passengers and was preparing to depart with its next fare.

Gregory yanked the door open. "My word. What do you think you're doing?" an outraged older gentleman asked.

Gregory dipped his head in chagrin. "Sorry. Wrong taxi."

"I should say so. Now, please close the door. I'm in rather a hurry."

Frustration made him slam the door harder than was necessary.

"Gregory, the last one," Emmeline said. She had finally caught up to him. She had no regrets about giving security men a swift kick in the shins. "I saw her get into the last one."

The BMW screeched past just as Gregory put out his hand and wrenched the taxi door open. He heard a startled cry from the interior and then a sharp gasp from Emmeline at his side.

He spun his head round. "Emmy, what is it?"

She clutched at his sleeve as her dark eyes found his. "She's dead."

CHAPTER 15

Gregory blinked for a second and then ducked his head into the taxi.

There was Sabitov's murderer, slumped in the corner, chin on her chest and a trickle of blood seeping from a bullet hole in her left temple.

"Bloody hell. Why did she have to go and get herself knocked off in my cab?" the driver asked philosophically. "I've got a wife and kids to feed. Do you know what this going to do for business?"

"I rather doubt her intention was to sabotage your business. I think you'll find this was as much of a surprise to her as it was for you," Gregory replied imperturbably as he stepped back and shut the door.

The driver shook his head in disgust. "Women. No consideration whatsoever."

"There they are, Constable. Hurry before they get away," a clipped voice said.

Gregory and Emmeline turned their heads in unison to find a tall, thin woman with a haughty expression on her pinched face bearing down on them. She was virtually dragging the weary-looking constable at her side.

The two came to a halt in front of them. The woman raised her arm in a dramatic fashion and ordered, "Here are your culprits, caught red-handed. Arrest them, Constable."

The constable, who had to be in his early fifties, flicked a glance between Emmeline and Gregory as he pulled out his radio to report the incident to his superiors. Emmeline could tell from the skeptical expression reflected in the depths of his pale blue eyes and the tone of his voice that he had a hard time believing that she and Gregory were a modern-day Bonnie and Clyde.

"Well," the woman demanded. "Why don't you do your duty and arrest them?"

He put a hand in the air. "Madame, please." He was not to be hurried. With deliberate care, he drew out his notebook and a pencil from an inside pocket of his tunic. "There are procedures that must be followed. If you'll excuse me, I must speak with hotel security."

He gently sidestepped her and leaned an elbow down on the taxi window. He told the driver, "Sir, I will have to ask you to step outside and lock your vehicle. We'll want as little contamination as possible."

"Of course, Constable," the driver said.

The constable turned away for a moment to have a murmured word with the security officers. Then he raised his voice so that he could be heard above the din of nervous chatter of those gathered on the pavement. "Ladies and gentlemen, I must ask all of you to go back inside the hotel. We will need statements from you."

A collective groan rose up as the security officers began herding everyone indoors. Bang went a series of plans for the day.

As one, they moved like sheep toward the revolving doors, all except the woman at his side.

"Madame, I'm afraid that includes you," the constable said with polite forcefulness to the pushy woman, who had wanted him to make an arrest.

She shot him a withering look. "*This* is what we pay taxes for." Her tone was laced with scorn. "Honestly. Your superiors will hear about this." She sniffed and pivoted on her heel.

"I'm sure they will," he mumbled *sotto voce*. Aloud, he said, "Yes, madame."

Emmeline bit back a smile and then her mood quickly sobered. How could she smile when two people had been murdered that afternoon in the rarefied confines of the Dorchester?

လွၤသ

By the time Superintendent Burnell and Sergeant Finch arrived on the scene, a sort of calm had settled over the hotel staff and patrons. A number of statements had been taken and many people—to their immense relief—had been allowed to leave.

The hotel had graciously made a private room available so that they could conduct their interviews, while the forensics team got on with its grim task of photographing and collecting evidence from the taxi and the Promenade. And, of course, when given permission by Burnell, Dr. Meadows and the team would remove the bodies for further examination.

Burnell hitched a hip on a corner of a table as Finch sat with pen poised over his open notebook. Emmeline and Gregory sat in two armchairs opposite the detectives.

Emmeline felt the full force of Burnell's deep blue gaze on her face. "Tell me what happened?"

"Oliver, you can't seriously think Emmy had anything to do with these murders."

The superintendent flicked a glance at Gregory. "*Superintendent Burnell.*"

Gregory pressed a hand to his chest and bowed his head in mock apology. "If you insist on formalities, Superintendent Burnell."

Burnell nodded. "That's better. Now, I wasn't talking to you. Yet. I'll get to your part in this later."

Gregory crossed one elegantly tailored leg over the other and flashed a cheeky grin at him. "I can hardly wait."

Burnell rolled his eyes. He cleared his throat and shifted his attention back to Emmeline. "I'd appreciate it if you would please go over it all again."

She gave a resigned shrug of her shoulders. "All right." She took a deep breath and told them everything from the moment she received Sabitov's call asking to meet with her to their discussion about Swanbeck and Putin, and Sabitov's allegations that Pavel Melnikov had been murdered because he posed a threat to their nefarious business dealings.

Emmeline shivered involuntarily. "Sabitov was certain he would be the next one to die." She lowered her voice. "And he was right. He also said that Rutkovsky was in danger."

"Did he mention who this Rutkovsky chap is?"

She shook her head. "All he said was that Rutkovsky was 'special,' but he stressed that he was not an agent. Apparently, no one suspects that Rutkovsky is helping the British government to bring down Swanbeck and Putin."

Unfortunately, Emmeline caught the look Burnell traded with Finch and Gregory at the mention of Swanbeck's and Putin's names.

"Why do I get the distinct impression that the three of you are keeping something from me?" Her dark gaze accused each of them in turn.

Gregory reached over and took one of her hands. "Darling, would we really do such a thing?"

She yanked her hand free. "Yes. You've done it in the past. I've told you—all of you—" Her eyes raked over the three men. "—that I don't need to be coddled. It's clear by the furtive expressions on your faces, *and* the cowardly way you refuse to look me in the eye, that you're hiding something."

Gregory shot a glance at Burnell. "Cowardly? I don't know about you, Oliver, but I for one am deeply wounded that my own fiancée would doubt my word."

Emmeline crossed her arms over her chest. Her eyes narrowed and two vertical lines formed between her brows. "Hmph." She was having none of it.

Ah, well, Gregory sighed inwardly, *it had been worth a try. Nothing ventured, nothing gained.*

"The game's up, Longdon," Burnell said. "I think we have to come clean about what we know at this stage, which is precious little."

A triumphant look flitted across Emmeline's face. "I'm very glad to see that *someone* around here is being sensible." She favored Burnell with a sweet smile and then gave Gregory a quelling look.

"Emmy, it's no good giving me the evil eye."

"Stop stalling. I can tell from the way Superintendent Burnell and Sergeant Finch are holding their tongues that you're the one with all the answers. Why am I not surprised?"

Gregory gave her a smile that was intended to melt her heart. "It's quite flattering that you consider me a fount of knowledge."

"Charm will not work." Obviously, the smile failed.

More's the pity, Gregory lamented silently. *Darling, why do you always have to be so...so headstrong?*

He smoothed the corners of his mustache down and lifted his eyes to meet hers. Then he told her, without embellishments, about how his life got entangled with Walter Swanbeck and his son, Alastair. And the consequences that they must deal with now because of that twist of Fate.

Emmeline listened without interrupting, but the blood slowly began to seep from her cheeks. By the time he had finished his unpleasant tale, her complexion had taken on a grayish hue.

A heavy, tense silence loomed in the space between them for several seconds. She could feel three pairs of eyes concentrated on her, waiting for a reaction.

Right. She swallowed down the fear that had risen in her throat. Thrusting her chin in the air, she said, "Well, now I know. Knowledge is power. Our only option is to go after Swanbeck. I'll pick up the story where Sabitov left off—"

Gregory shot to his feet, cutting her off. "You most certainly will not."

She frowned up at him. "I beg your pardon. I hope you are not *forbidding* me to do my job."

"Lord knows I can't stop you doing anything you set your mind on, but darling, see sense. This is not a game." He crouched down before her and took her hand in his larger one. He softened his tone. "I've just told you how ruthless Swanbeck is. His connection to the Russians only makes the situation that much more dangerous. He's already made it very clear that he can get to you any time he wants. Look at what happened in the Underground."

Her eyes widened and her grasp tightened on his hand. "Do you think...Do you think that was him?"

Gregory gave a weary nod of his head. "From your description, I'm afraid it sounds like Alastair. But that's not all, Emmy. Those roses that were sent to your office—they weren't from me." He let this sink in before he continued. "He broke into my flat and left a rose on my pillow to make sure I knew that it was him."

A shadow of concern dimmed the brilliance of his cinnamon eyes.

"I see," she murmured. Her gaze strayed to Burnell and Finch, who had kept quiet throughout their verbal tussle. "What's your professional opinion?"

The two detectives exchanged a cynical look. As if by tacit agreement, Burnell was the one to speak. He responded carefully, measuring his words. "I think that there is a compelling case against Swanbeck. In my professional opinion, he poses a grave threat to you and society at large." He paused and sucked in his breath. "However, the devil of it is we can't prove a damn thing against him. He's wiped his tracks clean."

"But can't you use what Sabitov told me to at least go after him for Melnikov's murder? After all, you yourself raised doubts from the outset that it was suicide. Now, you have probable cause."

The corners of Burnell's mouth curved into a lopsided smile. "No. Unfortunately, whatever Sabitov told you is hearsay. No magistrate in his right mind would issue a warrant if I went to him with that kind of evidence. Besides, MI-Six has taken over the Melnikov case. As far as Scotland Yard is concerned, he never existed. Our hands are tied."

"Hmm. Yes, of course. You're in an untenable position. Right, you've given me a lot of food for thought." She stood up and hitched her handbag over her shoulder.

Gregory straightened up to his full height and stared down at her, relief creasing his handsome features.

"Everything is perfectly clear. The only way to get Swanbeck is if I pursue the story. So I had better get cracking." She reached up and gave Gregory a peck on the cheek. "Bye, darling, I'll ring you later."

She scurried from the room before the three men could gather their wits long enough to stop her.

CHAPTER 16

Philip tapped his pen absent-mindedly on his desk as he stared at some spot on the opposite wall. He had been unable to concentrate on the job at hand ever since he came face-to-face with Alastair Swanbeck the other day. On the surface, the man was suave and pleasant with an extraordinarily sharp intellect. He could speak with great insight on a range of issues. But in unguarded moments, Philip caught a glimpse of the real man through the cracks in his well-constructed façade. No matter what Swanbeck did, he could not hide the expression of callous arrogance reflected in his sea green eyes. Philip could well imagine the man ordering his enemy's death without batting an eye.

Or was he losing professional objectivity? Had he allowed himself to be influenced by Longdon's story and his friendship with Emmeline? His mind wrestled with these questions. After several seconds, he shook his head and sat up straighter in his chair. No. Swanbeck was every inch a menace. Philip may not like Longdon, but in this instance he concurred with him one hundred percent.

There had to be a way to bring down Swanbeck. But how? From what Longdon said, Swanbeck's criminal empire was like an octopus whose tentacles extended across the globe. And now, Swanbeck had insinuated himself onto the task force.

Whose brilliant idea was that? Philip wondered. In one sense, he could keep an eye on Swanbeck over the next few months while the task force drafted its report. But how often would the panel meet? Once, perhaps twice a month? Why was the bloody man even on the task force at all? Surely they could have found someone else? There was an endless supply of industry leaders in the UK who could provide insight on Russia and Putin's inner circle.

Philip's eyes narrowed and his back stiffened. No, there was something else going on here. Something calculated, methodical. He could almost see the shadows twitching as the pawns were being moved across the chessboard.

He snatched up his phone and dialed Mark Bradford's number. His secretary answered, but she put him through straight away.

"Philip, old chap. How are you?"

"I'm fine. Thank you. Mark, I won't mince words. I need to have a chat with you about the task force."

The other man's voice was tinged with caution. "Really? Your enthusiasm does you credit, but can't it wait until the next—"

Philip cut him off. "No, it can't. We need to meet as soon as possible. I think you know why."

"Actually, I have no idea at all. These days I don't have a minute to spare. As I'm sure you know from the briefings, the Minister of Defence is in the midst of delicate negotiations with—"

Philip pounded his palm on his desk. "Stuff the minister. I want to know about Swanbeck."

After a long pause, Bradford cleared his throat. "I'm afraid that's on a need-to-know-basis. I'm sure you understand."

"Don't give me the party line, Mark. You just confirmed my suspicions. Tomorrow. Lunch at Rules. I must warn you that if you don't show up, you'll find me on your doorstep. Or better yet, I could drop a word to the press—anonymously, of course."

"You wouldn't dare." Bradford's voice trembled with outrage. "It's more than your career is worth Acheson."

So it was Acheson now, no longer Philip. Had he struck a nerve?

"It's your choice, Mark."

The silence was longer this time. Finally, Bradford replied in a clipped manner, "Rules. Tomorrow. But if I find out that you've opened your mouth to say more than hello to Emmeline Kirby, I will bury you personally."

"Right. At least we know where we both stand. Until tomorrow." Philip rang off without saying goodbye.

Emmeline. He didn't like it one bit that her name got introduced into a conversation about Swanbeck.

e⁄ɔe⁄ɔ

Emmeline launched her campaign—for it was executed with military precision—to draw out Swanbeck by featuring as the leader on *The Clarion*'s front page the story about the double murder that took place the day before at the Dorchester. After all, the deaths of activist journalist Yevgeny Sabitov, a critic of the Kremlin and the FSB, and the woman in white were news. Gruesome, shocking and deeply unsettling, but news nonetheless. What would be trickier would be Melnikov's "suicide." Thus far, MI6 had been extremely tight-lipped, not even a tiny ripple on the pond escaped. It was—like Superintendent Burnell had said—as if Melnikov had never existed. But you couldn't sweep a dead body under the carpet, especially one that was flung off a balcony in the middle of London. She simply had to find a way to get someone to talk. Then she could raise further questions and bring to light his link to Sabitov and, ultimately, to Swanbeck.

Yes, that was extremely important. They had to nail Swanbeck for his crimes. The trail of bodies that led to his door had to come to an end. He could no longer be allowed to strut about, smug in the knowledge that no one was going to touch him.

Oh, no. His house of cards had to come tumbling down. But how was she going to find the evidence against him without becoming one of his victims?

"He's already made it very clear that he can get to you any time he wants. Look at what happened in the Underground."

Gregory's words reverberated in her ears as an icy tendril of fear curled itself around her heart.

Yes, well. She pushed herself to her feet and tossed her

chin in the air. She walked around her desk to the window overlooking the Thames. She would simply have to be on her guard and more aware of her surroundings. She would *not* cower behind closed doors. Then Swanbeck would have won.

"No, that is quite out of the question," she said aloud to her empty office as she pivoted on her heel and installed herself once again at her computer.

She would not allow fear to rule her life. She would find the chink in Swanbeck's armor. There had to be one. A thought struck her. If she could find Rutkovsky, perhaps she could persuade him to talk. It was a long shot, but it was the only tangible thing she had to go on.

The problem was who *was* Rutkovsky and where should she begin her search for him?

Perhaps, she should try Philip again. He became very taciturn, positively evasive, when she had brought up Melnikov and Swanbeck.

Yes, Philip had some explaining to do. She reached for her phone. This time she would not be brushed off.

e∕ɔe∕ɔ

Superintendent Burnell wished that he had heeded his impulse to turn over and pull the bedclothes over his head this morning. There was something to be said for gut instinct. Or was that his ulcer stirring with displeasure?

Thus far, it had been a thoroughly rotten day and there were still many hours left before it came to a close and he could slink off to his favorite pub for a nice, restorative pint. He sighed wearily. It was on days like this that he contemplated what it would have been like if he had acquiesced to his parents' desire for him to become a barrister.

Ah well, there was nothing he could do about that now. Fate had made his choice for him. He would just have to get on with job at hand. Two more murders. He shook his head and sighed again. It would be so much easier if he didn't have to deal with the Boy Wonder. Cruickshank made his skin crawl. He was so eager to impress and make a name for himself that he had forgotten what was important. Seeing that the baddies were put in jail where they couldn't harm anyone ever again. A safe society. That's all Burnell wanted. Was it too much to ask for? He didn't think so and that's what made him get up every morning.

So Cruickshank be damned, he and Finch were going to investigate the murders of Sabitov and the "woman in white," whom they still hadn't been able to identify. If their inquiries circled back to Melnikov and they could make a direct connection, they would pursue the case to the bitter end. He didn't care if he stepped on MI6's toes. Maybe the next time they would extend some professional courtesy and share their information. After all, they were *supposed* to be on the same side.

"Oliver, scowling like that is doing the most unattractive things to your features. You look positively menacing."

Burnell snatched off his glasses and his head shot up to find Gregory's tall, trim form leaning against the doorframe. An impish smile was playing about his lips.

Damn and blast. How the devil did the man always manage to exude an aura of unflappable, crisp elegance? He was a walking advert for Savile Row. He virtually crackled with masculine grace and sex appeal. It was no wonder women were always fawning over him.

Longdon was well aware of the power of his charm and how to wield it. However, Burnell had to admit that his nemesis was not a conceited man and the only woman he had eyes for was Emmeline. A point in his favor. The only point in his favor.

"What do you want, Longdon? I've quite had my fill of headaches today. If you've come here simply to be a nuisance, you can turn around right now."

Gregory ignored this and entered the office. He lowered himself into the chair opposite Burnell, opened a button on his suit jacket, leaned back, and crossed one long leg over the other. His mouth curved into another infuriating smile.

"You know, Oliver—"

Burnell grunted.

"Oh, sorry, I meant Superintendent Burnell. I forgot that I was on the hallowed ground of Scotland Yard. I assure you that it was a mere slip of the tongue."

"Hmph. I'll bet," Burnell muttered under his breath.

"Pardon, I didn't quite catch that."

"Never mind. Why are you cluttering up my office yet again? I was under the impression you had a job these days. Although I must say, I see very little evidence that you actually *do* anything. Except perhaps plotting your next heist."

Gregory put a hand to his chest. "That hurts, *Oliver*. It really does. I never thought I would hear such cruel words from a *dear* friend."

"Ha," Burnell snorted. "First of all, your skin is as thick as an alligator's back. Words just bounce right off you. Second, and most importantly, I'd rather live as a hermit in some remote corner of the Antarctic than have you as a friend."

One of Gregory's eyebrows arched upward. But damn the man, there was a mischievous gleam in his eyes. Burnell wished he could wipe the bemused smirk off his face.

"Wouldn't it get a bit nippy, Oliver? And only penguins and the occasional polar bear for company? Oh, no. It's definitely not the life for you. Besides, you'd miss me terribly."

The superintendent tossed his chin in the air. "You must be joking." His voice was infused with disgust.

"Admit it. You'd miss our stimulating conversations, our camaraderie and, above all—" Gregory leaned forward propped his elbows on the desk and rested his chin on his hand. "—our close working relationship."

Something rumbled forth from deep within Burnell's chest and exploded as a harsh bark of a laugh. "You've flipped your lid and are living in the realm of fantasy. Stop wasting my time and tell me what you came to see me about."

Gregory sat up straight in his chair. His flippant manner disappeared. "I'm sure you read Emmy's article about what happened at the Dorchester."

Burnell exhaled a long, slow breath. "Yes. And the ones in all the other papers. My phone was ringing all morning." He curled his lip at the detested instrument. "I was seriously considering ripping it out of the wall and hurling it out the window."

Gregory gave a half-hearted chuckle. "I don't think it would have solved anything. The press is very persistent, especially on a story like this one." He paused, his eyes locking on Burnell's face. "Oliver, you and I both know that a man like Swanbeck needs very little encouragement. Emmy is waving a red flag in front of a bull. And the devil of it is, I can't do anything to stop her. You know how she is."

"Yes," Burnell replied grimly. "She's admirable and courageous, and a bloody menace to my ulcer." He gave his stomach sympathetic rub.

Gregory's mouth quirked into a crooked smile. "For some strange reason, she likes you too, Oliver."

Burnell stroked his beard. He felt certain that the heat warming his cheeks was a blush. He hoped Longdon didn't notice. "Yes, well. Emmeline is a very discerning judge of character. Except where you're concerned."

"Ah, ah. There's no need to be jealous."

The awkward moment had passed. They were back on familiar ground. "Save it, Longdon. As for Emmeline, don't worry. We'll get Swanbeck. He'll make a mistake. They always do. Please go away and let me do my job."

Gregory pushed himself to his feet. "Right. You'll let me know if you discover anything new about Sabitov or Melnikov?" Burnell nodded. "Good," Gregory said. "In the meantime, I wanted to let you know that I have an idea."

"Oh, yes?" Burnell didn't like the spark of mischief kindling in Gregory's eyes. "Anything you'd care to tell me about?"

Gregory's mouth broke into a roguish grin. "You know what they said about curiosity and the cat. I wouldn't want that to happen to you, Oliver. After all, you have an ulcer to consider."

Burnell grunted and wagged his forefinger at him. "I should have thrown you out the minute you trespassed into my office."

"Trespassed? Really, Oliver. I thought the door to your inner sanctum was always open."

"You're wrong. It is the door to the jail that's always open to you, Longdon. There's a cell reserved for you any time you like."

"How frightfully kind. But I'm afraid I can't accept such generous hospitality."

"No? Pity. I think it would be just the thing."

"If—"

Whatever Gregory had been about to say was cut off when Finch burst into the office.

"Sir," he paused, nodded at Gregory, and turned back to his boss. "Sir, I wanted to warn you that Cruickshank is on walkabout and he's headed this way."

Burnell groaned and slammed his open palm on his desk. "What the devil does he want? I gave him an update this morning."

Finch shrugged. "No idea, sir."

"Cruickshank?" Gregory piped up. "Is this your illustrious new leader?"

Burnell nodded.

"Emmy told me about him. Bit of a prat, is he?"

Burnell touched the side of his nose with his forefinger. "Got it in one."

"I must stay to meet him. It would be bad manners to rush off."

Burnell's ulcer gave a violent lurch. This day was never going to end.

CHAPTER 17

The next day was Friday. Emmeline could hardly believe the week had come to an end. So much had happened—and her questions kept multiplying. About Sabitov. About Melnikov. About the shadowy Rutkovsky. The fact that she had no answers didn't sit well with her. To add to her frustrations, Philip appeared to be avoiding her calls. She had left three messages and he had yet to ring her back. This only confirmed her suspicions that he knew something. Two could play at that game.

Maggie had invited her and Gregory round to the house on Sunday for lunch so that they could discuss ideas—Maggie's ideas—for the wedding. Gregory had cried off, giving some vague excuse. *Coward,* Emmeline thought. Oh, well. That left Philip defenseless. He stood absolutely no chance, especially if she enlisted Maggie's help to buttonhole him. He was going to talk to her whether he liked it or not.

Emmeline glanced at her watch and pushed herself to her feet. However, all of that would have to wait until Sunday. She flicked off her computer and gathered up her handbag. Right now, she had to rush home to shower and change for the party at the Royce mansion in Cheyne Walk. Gregory would be coming to collect her at seven-thirty and she didn't want to be late. She was hoping that the less formal setting of the party would help to loosen Royce's tongue. They had struck up a rapport the other day and he had started opening up to her about himself when his arrogant son had rudely interrupted their interview. She was a good judge of character. She was certain that she had gained Royce's confidence. She would build on that tonight. More than anyone else she had profiled,

Victor Royce intrigued her. She wanted—no, needed—to know more of his story. When his guard slipped for a fraction of a second, she had caught a glimpse of *something* in the depths of those shrewd dark eyes. She couldn't quite put her finger on what it was, but she was going to try to peel away the layers to get a better picture of the real man.

೭ഐ೨

Gregory unlatched the beautiful wrought-iron gate and stepped aside, allowing Emmeline to enter the short walk leading up to the Royce mansion. The gate clanged with gravitas as he closed it behind him.

He cast an appreciative eye over the sleeveless crimson lace dress that delicately hugged the curves of her body and dipped in a deep U-shape in the back, exposing the nape of her neck and the expanse of skin between the top of her shoulder blades. "You look particularly ravishing tonight, love," he said as he looped her arm though his and patted her hand. He smiled as he felt her pink sapphire engagement ring graze his palm. In less than three months she would be his wife. If Swanbeck didn't kill them first.

This sobering thought sent a slight shudder through his body. He hoped Emmy hadn't noticed.

Apparently, she hadn't because she stopped and reached up to give him a soft kiss on the cheek. "Thank you. Of course, you already know that you always cut a dashing figure in a tuxedo."

He shot his cuffs as she straightened his tie, which had become slightly askew. "Naturally, that goes without saying."

Emmeline rolled her eyes, but a chuckle escaped her lips. "You are incorrigible."

He leaned down and gave her a cheeky wink. "But you must admit that I'm completely irresistible."

She laughed again. "And swell your ego, even more? I think not."

She took a half a step toward the door, but he put a hand on her arm and drew her back.

"Really, darling. You do know how to wound a chap. We lowly, inferior men are sensitive creatures at heart." He gave a dramatic sigh to emphasize his point.

"Hmph," she snorted. "Spare me."

"I must say you've opened my eyes to a side of your personality that is quite... unsettling."

"Indeed? Good." She beamed up at him. "Then, maybe it will keep you on your toes. At the moment, we have a party to attend and I, for one, do not intend to spend all evening out here on the flagstones."

He tucked her arm through the crook of his elbow once again. "If you put it that way, as a gentleman I cannot allow such an enchanting creature to go alone. Shall we?" He waved a hand toward the door.

She inclined her head and he guided them up the handful of wide steps. He pressed the doorbell. As they waited side by side for someone to answer, he bent down gave her another kiss.

"I do love you," she whispered.

He was about to respond when the door was flung open.

Emmeline's eyes widened when she saw that it wasn't the butler, but the master of the house himself standing on the threshold.

"Emmeline, good of you to come," Victor Royce said. "Come in." He made an impatient gesture with his hand and opened the door wider, stepping aside in the process. If she didn't know any better, it was almost as if he had been watching from the window for their arrival. But that would be ridiculous.

Once they were inside the grand front hall and the door was bolted behind them, Emmeline introduced the two men. "Mr. Royce, this is my fiancé, Gregory Longdon." She turned slightly toward Gregory. "Darling, this is Victor Royce."

Gregory extended a hand to the older man. "A pleasure, sir. Thank you for inviting us this evening."

Royce's grip was strong and firm. "You're very welcome. The more the merrier I always say. Besides, I had to make amends for the shabby way your charming fiancée—" He took

Emmeline's hand between both of his. "—was treated the other day when she came round to my office for the interview.
Again, my dear, I must apologize. I promise there will be no
interruptions whatsoever on Monday. I've given Delia strict
orders that we are not to be disturbed. You will have my complete attention."

Gregory saw a very becoming rose flush creep up Emmeline's cheeks. His glance shifted to Royce. Surely it was
time for the man to release her hand. But no, he continued to
hold onto it.

Emmeline murmured something in response, but he didn't
quite catch what it was. His attention was concentrated on
Royce, whose dark brown eyes seemed to be memorizing every contour of Emmy's face. There was a hunger in that look. A
desire to know more. To know her better.

Gregory frowned. Royce must have sensed his intense
scrutiny because a veil came down and a neutral expression
entered his eyes. He abruptly dropped Emmy's hand. "Yes,
well. My wife always says that I'm a very poor host. Please
follow me. I must get you some champagne. We have cock-
tails and canapés upstairs in the drawing room and there's a
buffet set up in the dining room." He waved at a double door
across the hall. "Or I could give you a tour of the house, if you
like. We bought it twenty years ago. It dates back to 1718."

"Really? How fascinating. I wish that it could talk. I bet it
has some interesting stories to tell about its past owners and
the times they lived in," Emmeline said, an excited gleam in
her dark eyes.

Encouraged by her remark, Royce continued to chatter on
as he led them up the magnificent sweep of the staircase that
was surrounded by lushly painted walls. Emmeline tipped her
head back to drink in the rich colors of the Baroque mural on
the ceiling depicting Venus in all her seductive glory. Gregory
held onto her elbow and murmured appropriate responses, his
gaze fixed firmly on the back of their host's head. Emmeline
stopped briefly to cast a glance out the window on the half-
landing that provided a view of Cheyne Walk. She hurried up
the last few steps to the first floor, eager to see more.

Her eyes roamed over all the antiques. "Mr. Royce, your home is beautiful."

"Thank you." Royce preened. "I fell in love with it the minute I clapped eyes on it. It always pleases me to see others appreciate the house as much as I do."

He gave her another warm smile.

"Yes, Mr. Royce, I must compliment you on your exquisite taste," Gregory chimed in.

Despite the polite smile Gregory plastered on his lips, he could not keep the edge of irritation from his voice.

Royce cleared his throat and hastily dragged his gaze from Emmeline. Again. An awkward silence filled the air between them as he appeared to be sizing Gregory up.

The low hum of voices mingled with the strains of Mozart drifted to their ears from behind the doors of a large room to their left. Emmeline assumed it must be the drawing room.

"We can't have you two hanging about in the corridor all night." Royce crossed to the door and with his hand on the knob turned back to them, "Time for a little champagne."

The door opened onto a bright, rectangular-shaped room filled with more antiques and two fireplaces directly opposite one another. The room was intimate and elegant at the same time. It was the perfect space for the two dozen or so guests to chat and mill about, while a footman and a maid circled the room with silver trays offering all sorts of tempting *hors d'oeuvres*. Another footman carried a tray of champagne flutes.

Royce caught the latter's eye. "Paul, over here. Miss Kirby and Mr. Longdon need some champagne."

The three of them accepted a glass from Paul, who gave a deferential nod and quietly slipped away again.

Royce lifted his glass. "A toast, I think."

"What shall we toast to?" Emmeline asked.

"How about to delightful new acquaintances?"

She smiled up at Gregory. "And to love."

He squeezed her fingers with his free hand and lifted his glass. "To love."

"Yes, of course. To love," Royce mumbled. He stole a glance at them over the rim of his glass.

Gregory flashed a smile in his direction and was pleased to see the man's back stiffen slightly.

Royce took another sip of his champagne and started looking about him. "I must introduce you to Lily, my wife. I don't seem to see her. Where can she have got to?" He signaled to the maid, who hurried over to them.

"Yes, Mr. Royce."

"Where's Mrs. Royce?" he asked, clearly annoyed.

"I believe she went down to speak to Mrs. Mellet about the buffet. Shall I go and fetch her, sir?"

He gave a dismissive wave of his hand. "No, that won't be necessary."

"Very good, sir. I'll be getting on then." She moved off without another word.

"Ah, well. You'll have to meet Lily later. Now—" He rubbed his hands together. "Emmeline, how about that tour of the house and garden?"

She nodded her head enthusiastically. "Oh, yes, please."

Gregory raised an eyebrow.

"And you, too, of course, Longdon. If you feel your fiancée needs a chaperone with a harmless old man."

"Harmless? I hardly think so." Gregory muttered *sotto voce*. Aloud to Emmeline, he said, "Go by all means, darling. I can see that you're keen to explore every nook and cranny." He leaned down and gave her a peck on the cheek. To Royce, he replied, "I expect you to return her to me before the carriage turns into a pumpkin."

Royce gave a hearty chuckle and clapped him on the shoulder. "Of course. You needn't have any fears. I'll keep a very close eye on her I assure you."

Gregory inclined his head politely, but said nothing.

"By the way, Longdon, before you leave this evening I'd like your advice on insuring some pieces in my collection. I understand you work for Symington's."

Gregory held the other man's gaze. "And how would you know that?"

Royce shrugged his shoulders. "I suppose Emmeline must have told me."

Gregory smiled. "Yes. That must be it." He saw her brow furrow as if trying to recall when she had mentioned his occupation to Royce. "How else would you have known?"

"Precisely, old chap. Shall we, Emmeline?"

Royce proffered his arm, which she accepted as she waggled her fingers at Gregory.

"See you later, Longdon."

Gregory took a sip of his champagne and watched them slip from the room. Royce bent his head close to say something to Emmeline. He saw her nod and then the door shut behind them.

"I can hardly wait, old chap. I'd like to know what the devil you're playing at."

CHAPTER 18

Emmeline gently disentangled her arm from Royce's once they were in the corridor. Although this was a party, she could not afford to compromise her professional integrity. It was very kind of Royce to invite them, but she had to maintain that line between the personal and the professional. Besides, one would have to be blind not to have seen the way Gregory and Royce had eyed one another. She had no wish to inflame situation further—no matter how silly she thought the two men were.

They reached the bottom of the stairs. Royce's arm swept in a wide arc around the front hall. "As I said earlier, that's the dining room over there and that's the sitting room. And there is my refuge. The library. I use it as my study. Why don't we start with the library? It looks out over the garden. I'm an avid gardener."

Emmeline shot a surprised look at him. "I can't picture Victor Royce, industrialist, philanthropist, and art collector, on his knees rooting out weeds in the garden."

He threw his head back and laughed. "Believe it. I like nothing more than feeling the earth between my fingers and watching the seeds I've planted grow into the most magnificent flowers. I'm particularly proud of my roses. I've created my own hybrid, which has the most intoxicating scent. I call it Heart's Desire."

Emmeline giggled. It was amusing to see Royce gushing over his garden. "It sounds lovely. Gardening is something that we have in common."

Royce stopped in the middle of the hall. "Is it?"

"Yes. You remember I mentioned that I was raised by my

grandmother after my parents—" She swallowed hard. "—after my parents died."

A shadow crossed his face, but he nodded.

"Well, she is Mother Earth herself." Royce laughed. "It's quite true," Emmeline assured him. "I'm not exaggerating. She taught me everything there is to know about flora and fauna." She grinned. "We've spent many happy hours together digging around in the garden, so I quite understand your enthusiasm."

"Marvelous. It will be nice to talk to a fellow gardener for once. Perhaps you can give me some ideas. My wife unfortunately does not share my passion for gardening."

"That's a shame. However, I'm certain you share other interests."

His brow furrowed. "Yes," Royce replied noncommittally.

He put a hand in the middle of her back and ushered her forward. "First stop, the library."

Emmeline stiffened when his fingers brushed for an instant against her bare skin where her dress dipped in the back.

She slid a sideways glance at him, but he didn't seem to have noticed. Her body relaxed. So it was just an accident. Nothing untoward.

☙❧☙

Lily Royce noticed, though. She walked out of the dining room at the precise moment that her husband had placed his hand on Emmeline's back. Her eyes narrowed as she watched them disappear into the library.

"There you are, Mum" a male voice called.

Lily reluctantly tore her eyes away from her husband and the unknown young woman. She looked up to find her son, Adam, making his way down the stairs.

She managed a weak smile and proffered her cheek for her son to kiss. "How are you, darling?" she asked distractedly, her mind still on Victor and the woman, whom she had every intention of identifying before the evening was over.

She reached up and straightened her son's tie. "You look very handsome tonight."

"Thanks, Mum. Needless to say, you're the height of chic. You put the younger women here tonight to shame."

Lily's silvery laughter hung upon the air for an instant. "Thank you for being kind to your old mother."

"Come off, it," Adam snorted. "You *know* you're very far from old."

She merely smiled at him as she caught a glimpse of herself in the gilt-edged mirror hanging on the opposite wall. Her red-gold hair came out of a bottle these days and there were a few more fine lines around her eyes and her mouth, but she had to admit that she was still an extremely attractive woman at sixty-three. She had kept her trim figure and her clothes were only of the finest quality. But it was her eyes—an envious shade of turquoise smoldering with fiery intelligence—that drew one to her. She patted a stray strand of hair that had come loose from her upswept coiffure and smiled at her reflection. *Yes*, she thought, *I can still turn heads*. This delighted her no end.

"What was that, darling?" she asked, focusing her attention on her son again.

"I said that everyone is having a smashing time. I was on my way to the dining room. Can I make a plate for you?"

Lily touched his arm lightly. "No, thank you. I'll get something to eat later. Just now, I have things to do." She cast a glance at the closed library door and frowned. "A hostess's work is never done."

"All right, I'll see you later." Adam bent down and kissed her cheek, leaving her standing there in the middle of the hall.

઒৩઒৩

Emmeline fell in love with library the instant she stepped over the threshold. The evening light cascaded in from two tall windows and danced upon the parquet floor. It reflected off the cream-colored paneling and moldings enhancing the airy feel of the room. Her eye was immediately drawn to the Venetian glass chandelier whose sinuous pale blue branches ended in clusters of red-pink roses. It dangled from the ceiling in the center of the room above a desk with intricately carved scrolls of leaves and flowers that were inlaid with mother of pearl, lapis lazuli, and other semi-precious stones.

She crossed the room and slowly circled the desk. Her fingers grazed over the carvings. She looked up at Royce, who had a bemused expression on his face. "It's lovely. I've only seen desks like this in Italy."

He clapped his hands. "Very good. The lady has a keen eye. I purchased the desk in Italy several years ago. In Florence, in fact."

"Yes, I thought as much," she murmured as she cast another reverent look at the desk. She tilted her head back. "And the chandelier of course is from Venice, specifically Murano."

"Right, again. I see I was right about you, Emmeline. A beautiful lady with an eye for the beautiful."

She lowered her gaze to meet his across the room and felt her cheeks suffuse with heat. "Thank you," she mumbled, her voice slightly hoarse from embarrassment.

What was it about this man that unsettled her so?

In a bid to regain her composure, she walked toward the corner where the bookcase was flanked by two creamy Greco-Roman columns. She allowed her eyes to roam over the shelves, where books shared space with Sèvres vases and a handful of family photographs. There were a number of black-and-white photos of a handsome couple with a baby and then a little boy. She guessed that these must be his parents and Royce as a child. These jostled with color photos of three children, two boys and a girl, with a stunning woman who had the most extraordinary eyes. Obviously, these were Royce's wife and children.

Out of the corner of her eye, she could see Royce leaning against the marble mantelpiece. He didn't say a word. He simply watched her, affording her senses an opportunity to drink in the beauty of the room.

She moved to the window closest to the bookcase and saw that it looked out over the garden. From this vantage point, it appeared to be everything that Royce had boasted.

She swung round to face him, her back pressed against one

of the sashed drapes. "It's the most magnificent room I've ever seen. I can well understand why you would want to escape here every moment possible." She cast another glance about her. "It's so peaceful and soothing."

He pushed away from the fireplace and walked to the middle of the room. "Somehow I knew you would appreciate it. That's why I wanted to show you this room in particular."

She felt the blush warming her cheeks again. "Thank you. I feel honored." Her gaze strayed to the window. "I'd love to see the garden."

"The garden it is then." Royce extended an arm, a gleam in his dark brown eyes. "Prepare to be dazzled."

Emmeline couldn't help but laugh as she cast one last glance around the library and then followed him out.

After Royce had given her the tour of his prized roses, which were as lush and fragrant as he had promised, and asked her opinion about what he should plant in a newly dug nook, they sat down for a few moments at the wrought-iron table on the terrace.

"What would your grandmother say?" Royce asked playfully.

Emmeline smiled. "Gran would be in heaven. It's truly amazing. And such a large private garden in the middle of London is unusual."

Royce threw his head back and let out a throaty laugh. "I'm glad to hear that my garden would pass muster with your grandmother. She sounds like a fascinating woman."

"Indeed, she is. And I'm being completely unbiased when I say that."

He nodded indulgently. "Of course, you are."

They lapsed into a companionable silence as they stared out over the delicate blooms and shrubs, and listened to the breeze rustling through the trees. At one point, Royce glanced over at her and smiled. But she was taken off guard by the sadness that shadowed his eyes. This was a man who had experienced unhappiness, and loss. She had to look away. It felt like she was intruding upon his secret pain. It also brought to the fore everything that she had lost. Her parents. *The baby.*

The baby. She drew in a ragged breath. How she missed the baby. The ache and emptiness never went away. The pain wasn't as raw as it had once been, but it was always there. Always.

Her mind was jarred from these agonizing thoughts by the sound of Royce's voice. She wasn't sure how long he had been talking. She discreetly wiped away a tear from the corner of her eye and tried to concentrate on what he was saying.

"You see, I think the problem was that we were never really suited to begin with. Lily was the most beautiful creature I had ever seen. She was a student of my father's. That's how we met. She was top in his class. She excelled at everything that she did. I was instantly bowled over and she was too. I had never felt such a strong attraction to any woman." He leaned back in his chair and mused, "Hmph. I thought I was in love. We both did." He shook his head and sighed. "But we were too young to see the problems."

Emmeline wondered why he was telling her all this about his troubled marriage. But perhaps it was an instance of it being easier to talk to a stranger than a close friend. She quietly prompted, "When you're in love, you don't think anything can stand it in your way."

He shifted his head slightly and she saw his mouth curve into a half-smile. "That's just it. Now, I can see clearly that we were never in love. It was merely blind infatuation with a heavy dose of physical attraction tossed in. My parents saw it, especially my mother. She pegged Lily's character from the outset. I was simply too pigheaded to admit that they were right. I should have seen it. My parents and Lily got on like chalk and cheese when I brought her home that first time. But I blamed them for being unreasonable snobs. Of course, it didn't help matters that Lily wasn't Jewish. I didn't care, though. I married her anyway. A bit earlier than I had intended, if you understand my meaning."

Emmeline nodded, but didn't interrupt his narrative. She recognized his need to get things off his chest.

He sighed. "Unfortunately, Lily lost the baby." She sucked in her breath, but he didn't seem to hear. "I've always wondered if our life would have been different if she hadn't."

She watched him as dusk crept in on silent feet to wrap them in its soft embrace.

"When Lily became pregnant with Jason the next year, I thought, 'Here's our chance to start fresh.' But no. She had a very difficult pregnancy and delivering him drained her physically. She blamed me. The gulf that had already formed between us only seemed to grow wider. She showered all her attention on Jason, and I threw all my energy into building up the company. I worked all hours, even some that even God himself didn't know existed. That's why it came as a shock to both of us when Lily became pregnant with the twins, Adam and Sabrina.

"I was surprised, but delighted. Again, I snatched at the hope that we could put all the unhappiness behind us and at last become a close-knit family like I had growing up." He shook his head sadly and exhaled a pained breath. "It was a dream. Lily had an even rougher time with the twins. The doctor ordered complete bed rest for the last two months, but she had a terrible time in labor. It took her a month to recover. She didn't want to look at the twins. Instead, she concentrated on Jason, and Jason alone, from that moment on. She kept the twins at arms-length and as for me...well, you can imagine. We were married in name only. We lived separate lives. It was awful. Once I broached the subject of divorce, but Lily wouldn't hear of it. She considered it distasteful, an attack on her good name.

"So we lived in a state of tense truce, merely keeping up appearances for the children's sake. Year in and year out it was like that. It was mentally exhausting...and lonely, very lonely. Until one day, when the sun entered my life again. I met a woman. She was quite a bit younger than I was, but she was warm and witty, intelligent and full of life. She was a breath of fresh air. We fell in love and began an intense affair. I couldn't imagine another day without her. I was about to ask Lily for a divorce. I didn't care how long it took. I wanted to marry this woman. And then—" His fist clenched and he choked on a sob. "Then she sent me a letter ending it. Just like that, it was over. I never understood why. She simply went away and I never saw her again. And there's been no one else ever since."

Emmeline's chest constricted. "How terribly sad. I'm truly sorry, Mr. Royce." Her voice was low and thick with emotion.

He fixed her with a strange look and reached out to take her hand in his. He lifted it to his lips. "You're a sweet young woman. I hope I haven't shocked you."

She shook her head.

He continued to hold her hand, but turned it back and forth in the air to admire her pink sapphire engagement ring. "That's an exquisite ring. Longdon obviously has good taste and an eye for beauty. I hope he appreciates and loves you as you deserve."

Royce's dark eyes searched her face for confirmation. She could see he was concerned on this point.

"Yes, he does. We've had our problems—quite a lot of them, in fact. And we've gotten a bit battered along the way, but we're still standing. I think—no, I know, we've put all of that behind us."

He squeezed her hand. "Good. I'm glad to hear it. But Longdon is not Jewish."

"No," she replied quietly.

"It could become a problem, when you have children that is. I know it caused a major row with Lily. She insisted that children were not going to be Jewish. In the end, I gave in, hoping it might ease things between us. As you see, it didn't work. I don't want the same thing to happen to you."

Emmeline smiled. "Please don't worry. Our situation is quite different. We haven't discussed the subject, but I know Gregory respects me, and we will come to a mutual decision. As we will with all matters. We will be open and honest about everything in our marriage."

"Yes, that's as it should be." He let her hand drop and rose to his feet. "I think if I don't return you to your fiancé, it will be pistols at dawn. Not that I really blame him."

She chuckled as he tucked her arm through his and led her across the terrace. "You flatter me, Mr. Royce. I'm hardly in the same league as Helen—not my grandmother, although she is by far the better woman—but the one from ancient Greece who launched all those ships."

He stopped and turned to her before they reached the French door into the dining room. "Emmeline, you sell yourself far too short. Longdon is an extremely lucky man. I hope he knows it."

Without another word, he turned the handle and they were immediately swallowed up by the buzz of conversation as guests wandered about the table filling their plates.

CHAPTER 19

Royce and Emmeline's appearance caught Lily's eye and she interrupted her son in mid-sentence. She nodded with her chin. "Jason, who is that woman with your father?"

"What woman?" Jason's green-gray gaze scanned the room until he saw them. He smirked and rolled his eyes. "Oh, her. She's the journalist I told you about. Emmeline Kirby. You know, the one who wants to do that big profile on Dad for *The Clarion*. I can't believe he invited her."

Lily's eyes narrowed as she watched them. "Emmeline Kirby." The name lingered on her tongue. "A journalist. He didn't say a word to me about her."

"She probably twisted his arm," Jason ventured as he munched on a large prawn. "You know how pushy these journalists can be. Always looking to insinuate themselves where they don't belong."

"Yes, very disruptive and intrusive," his mother murmured.

"Would you like me to have her thrown out?"

"What? No. We can't possibly do that. It will cause an unpleasant scene. We just have to hope she knows how to behave."

"I think you give the woman too much credit, but it is your house."

"Exactly, darling." She tapped his arm. "Finish up eating. I want you to introduce me to this paragon of the Fourth Estate."

"Why, Mum?"

"Don't be argumentative. I must make sure that all my guests are happy."

He guffawed, but did as his mother bid. He popped the re-mainder of the shrimp in his mouth, wiped his fingers on a napkin, and put his plate down on the mantelpiece.

He took her elbow and guided her across the room. He cleared his throat. "Dad."

Royce turned around, but the smile that had been on his lips quickly faded when he saw his son and his wife.

"Yes, Jason. What is it?" There was a sharp edge to his father's tone.

"I came to introduce Mum to *Miss* Kirby." He shot a smarmy smile in Emmeline's direction as he stressed her title. He was gratified to see her stiffen.

He waved a hand toward Emmeline. "Mum, this is Em-meline Kirby, the editorial director of *The Clarion*. *Miss* Kir-by, this is my mother, Lily Royce."

Emmeline extended a hand toward Lily and smiled. "Mrs. Royce, it's a pleasure to meet you."

Lily looked down at her proffered hand for a moment be-fore reluctantly clasping it with her own manicured one.

Cool, curt, and perfunctory, Emmeline thought. Mrs. Royce was still a striking woman, but the air of frosty reserve that clung to her was unnerving. It was no wonder that her husband had sought solace in someone else's arms. She pitied him anew. How could people ruin their lives like that?

Emmeline attempted to fill the uncomfortable silence, as Mrs. Royce looked her over from head to toe. "Thank you for inviting me and my fiancé this evening, Mrs. Royce. You have a lovely home. Your husband kindly gave me a tour."

"I didn't invite you. My husband did. You have him to thank. I was not consulted." She threw Royce a withering look.

"Lily, I—"

She cut him off and directed herself to Emmeline. "Miss Kirby, is it true what I hear? The police questioned you about that sordid business yesterday at the Dorchester?"

Emmeline swallowed hard but replied calmly, "Yes, the police did question me, but they let me go. I was…a witness."

"Well, see to it that whatever squalid mess that you're involved in does not disrupt my party or touch my family. This is a respectable home."

Emmeline tossed her chin in the air and cleared her throat. She opened her mouth to respond, but Royce intervened. "Lily, Emmeline is our guest. I think we must show a little hospitality and decorum."

"*Your* guest," his wife snapped. "Not mine. As far as I'm concerned, she's a party-crasher."

Jason stood beside his mother with a bemused smirk on his odious face.

Emmeline felt the vein in her temple begin to throb as blood raced through her veins. She narrowed her eyes and wished that all the plagues in Pandora's Box would be let loose on Mrs. Royce's head.

"There you are, darling." Gregory's voice floated to her ears.

The next second she felt his strong hand on her elbow. She looked up and gave him a grateful smile. A minute longer and she might have done bodily injury to Mrs. Royce if she had continued to go on in the same malicious vein.

Mrs. Royce turned on him. "And you are?"

"Do forgive me, Mrs. Royce. I'm Gregory Longdon, the man lucky enough to be Emmeline's fiancé."

"I see. I suppose you're another journalist and you've both come into my home to do a sleazy exposé on my family."

Gregory pressed his fingers into the fleshy inside part of her upper arm. He probably sensed that she wanted to give Mrs. Royce a good, hard cosh on the head.

"Ah, there you are mistaken on two counts, Mrs. Royce. First, Emmy is a highly-respected journalist." He ignored the woman's snort of disbelief. "And second, I'm the chief investigator at Symington's."

It amazed Emmeline that he could remain calm, even going so far as to flash one of his charming smiles. Alas, this failed to melt even a corner of Mrs. Royce's arctic heart—if she had one.

Mrs. Royce's turquoise gaze shifted from Gregory to her husband and finally came to rest on Emmeline's face. "Good

night. Please see to it that you don't harass my other guests."
Then to her son, she said, "Jason, I suddenly need some air. I
feel a headache coming on. Will you come with me out into
the garden?"

"Of course, Mum."

Royce put out an arm to restrain his wife. "Lily, your behavior is quite intolerable," he hissed through clenched teeth.

Mrs. Royce's lips pressed into a thin line. She looked down
at her husband's offending hand and removed it with disdain.
"Victor, I think you've caused quite enough embarrassment
for one night."

She turned her back on him and allowed her son to lead her
toward the French door.

Two ugly crimson stains appeared on Royce's cheeks and
his nostrils flared as he watched them go. His hands were
curled into fists at his sides.

"They say home is where the heart is," Gregory muttered
under his breath.

Emmeline heard him and swatted his arm.

"What was that for, my love?"

She gave a disapproving shake of her head. "You know
why."

Royce had managed to get himself under control. He
cleared his throat. "I must apologize for my wife's inexcusable
behavior. Obviously, she's unwell tonight."

"Yes, of course. I'm sure on a good day she's the life of the
party. Full of verve and scintillating conversation," Gregory
retorted glibly.

Emmeline threw a reproving look at him, but it didn't make
any impression because he gave her a cheeky wink in reply.

Completely and utterly incorrigible. Why was she marrying
this man?

Royce waved a hand at the buffet. "Emmeline, you must be
starving. Please have something to eat. If you don't mind, I'd
like to steal Longdon for a few moments to discuss those insurance matters I mentioned earlier. I promise I won't keep
him long."

She saw Gregory's brow furrow.

"It's up to Gregory. I'll be fine if the two of you would like to talk."

"Longdon, will you come with me to the library? It'll be quiet in there."

"Right. Lead the way."

e/>e/>

"Step into my parlor," said the spider to the fly. This line from the old nursery rhyme flew into Gregory's head as Royce closed the library door behind him.

If this was some sort of a trap, Gregory mused, not much could happen with dozens of guests scattered about all over the house. Royce was far from a stupid man. But as much as Gregory despised Lily Royce, he didn't trust her husband one iota. He certainly didn't like the way Royce looked at Emmy. It was too familiar. Almost possessive.

Royce gestured to two high-backed claret-colored leather armchairs positioned in front of the fireplace. "Please have a seat, Longdon."

Gregory settled his long limbs into one of the chairs as Royce crossed to a console table in the corner by one of the windows. He lifted a decanter. "Join me in a Scotch?"

Gregory inclined his head. "Thank you. I will."

"Good. I'll make it a large one. I pegged you as a Scotch man. I'm the only one in the family who has acquired a taste for the stuff."

"Their loss. There's nothing better than a good Scotch."

A ghost of smile touched Royce's lips. "A purist after my own heart. Single malt is meant to be savored without distractions, don't you find?"

He walked over and handed a crystal tumbler to Gregory. They clinked glasses.

"Cheers," Royce said as he took the chair opposite Gregory.

They both were silent as they sipped the amber liquid. Gregory rolled it around his tongue and then allowed it to glide down his throat. Perfect. It was smooth without that smoky taste one often encounters. He eased back into his chair and propped his elbows on the armrests. He studied Royce over the rim of his glass as he took another swig of his drink.

Victor Royce was definitely not what he appeared to be. As one who had his own share of secrets, Gregory was struck by the subtle furtiveness he detected in the other man.

What could Royce want? He certainly hadn't dragged him in here to discuss insurance. However, his natural patience supplanted his curiosity. So he held his tongue and waited until Royce was ready.

As if sensing this scrutiny, Royce downed the rest of his Scotch in one gulp and rose to his feet. He set the tumbler down on the mantelpiece and turned to face Gregory. "I suppose you're wondering why I wanted to speak to you privately."

Gregory smiled up at him. "Advice on insurance, wasn't it?"

Royce thrust his hands into his pockets. "We both know that was not the reason." There was a hint of irritation in his voice.

Gregory tilted his head to one side and asked in mock innocence, "No? Then you have me at a disadvantage, Mr. Royce. Perhaps you'd care to enlighten me."

If Royce thought his hard stare would unfaze him, he was mistaken.

"Longdon, you're everything I despise. You're arrogant, indolent, and above all, a thief."

Gregory raised an eyebrow. "When one listens to idle gossip, one is certain to get burned."

"Oh, come off it," Royce snapped. "We both know the truth."

"And what truth would that be?" Gregory asked casually, as he brushed an imaginary piece of lint from his trouser leg.

"That the only reason you're parading around as Symington's chief investigator is because Laurence Villiers placed you in that position. God knows why the man has chosen to put his trust in you. Nothing about you is real. Even your name is an alias. What was wrong with Toby Crenshaw?" He paused, but Gregory remained silent. "One thing I must compliment you on is your talent for obfuscation. Your past is buried under so many layers of secrets, it's like getting lost in a byzantine maze. On the other hand, I suppose Villiers feels having a thief as a part-time protégé has its advantages."

Gregory took a slow swallow of Scotch before he responded. "What I'm curious about is why a complete stranger found it necessary to do a background check on me?"

"Do you think I would allow just anyone into my house?"

Gregory smoothed down the corners of his mustache as his lips curled into a broad grin. "To use your own colorful expression, Mr. Royce, come off it. I don't think it was merely a question of the security of your home. How do you know Villiers?"

"Suffice it to say we're acquaintances. I know he's the deputy director of MI-Five and that you've worked for him from time to time. That's the only reason you're here tonight. And the fact that you're Emmeline's fiancé."

Emmy? He frowned. Why mention her? As far as she was concerned, Royce had never heard of her until a few days ago.

"Look, Longdon, one thing we both can agree on is that we don't like each other. Frankly, I could care less what you think of me. But I need you to get a message to Villiers. I've been trying for days but haven't been able to get in touch with him."

That was not surprising. After Villiers had been shot, MI5 had swept in and brushed the entire incident under the carpet. Only a very small group, which included Gregory, Emmeline, Philip, Burnell, and Finch, knew how gravely wounded Villiers had been. The man had taken a bullet that had been intended for Gregory.

While it had been touch-and-go, the sixty-eight-year-old Villiers had survived the surgery but his recovery was expected to take a long time.

"Let's just say Villiers is on extended leave."

Royce pounded his fist on the mantelpiece causing a Sèvres vase to jump precariously close to the edge. "Damn the man. He picked a fine time to go on holiday." Royce gave an annoyed shake of his head. He paced back and forth in front of the fireplace for several seconds and then came to an abrupt halt.

"I see I'm left with very little choice but to trust you." The chilly look of disdain in his eyes told Gregory that he was not best pleased by this prospect.

"I can't tell you how gratified I am to hear that."

"Put a cork in it and listen. It's important that this information gets to the right ears. It has to do with a very nasty chap called Alastair Swanbeck."

Gregory felt the blood drain from his face.

ʊ˧ʊ˧

Never did Royce think he would set eyes on Swanbeck again after he pulled out of that ill-conceived partnership he had been contemplating on a project six years ago. He had extricated the company, albeit at a huge loss, just in time. He didn't regret it. Ups and downs were expected in business. What he did regret was ever crossing paths with Swanbeck. He hadn't realized how vindictive the man was. He took it as a personal affront when Royce Global Holdings won the North Sea oil drilling lease. Then he mounted a hostile takeover, which failed. The final straw was when Royce outbid him for the Empress Diamond at the Christie's auction. Royce dismissed his talk of revenge as simply idle bluster. He was wrong. Swanbeck deliberately sabotaged three subsequent deals that Royce and Jason had painstakingly negotiated. Millions in contracts were lost. Then word came that Swanbeck had died and the business started to recover.

But Swanbeck isn't dead, Royce thought as he stared out at his garden, so quiet and peaceful as dusk caressed his roses. *It had only been a bloody rumor. And now he's back to settle old scores.*

He let the drape fall back into place and poured himself another large Scotch. He definitely needed it. Tonight his past had come back to haunt him. He tossed back his drink. He didn't taste it, but the alcohol burned as it slithered down his throat. He slammed the tumbler down on the table.

He pressed the heels of his hands to his eyes. There were a lot of things he couldn't control, but there was something he could do to make amends for his past mistakes.

He crossed to his desk and picked up the manila envelope that the messenger had delivered that afternoon. He emptied its contents and carefully read through every page again.

Yes, everything was in order. He glanced at his watch. It was only nine o'clock. It wasn't too late. He knew Stan would probably be locked up in his study still hard at work, even on a Friday night. He reached for the receiver and dialed his friend's home number.

His call was answered on the second ring. "Hello, Stan. It's Victor."

"Hello, Vic." Royce could hear the genuine pleasure in his old friend's voice. "Everything all right?"

"Fine. Thanks for making all the changes I requested. I'll pop round your office on Monday afternoon to sign both copies. I'd rather do it there, away from prying eyes. No need for anyone to know until the time comes."

"It's your decision, but are you quite sure about all of this? It's bound to be a—"

"A shock. Yes, I've no doubt about that."

But it was right thing to do, even after so many years.

CHAPTER 20

Everywhere he turned there was Swanbeck. He couldn't escape the bastard, even here in the rarefied environs of Cheyne Walk.

Gregory stared at the closed library door and mulled over his conversation with Royce. He smiled. Granted, it was a risk. Anything could happen, but what did they have to lose. It could very well work. It bloody well *had* to work. Swanbeck had to be brought down to his knees and his entire crooked empire had to be dismantled. The only way to do that was to play on the man's ego and his greed. Those were his Achilles heel.

His smile grew wider. Yes, the more he thought it about it, the more he warmed to the plot that he and Royce had hatched up. It merely needed some refinement, but that was where his former *métier* could prove an enormous asset. He couldn't wait to see Acheson's reaction when he presented the plan to him. He was quite sure that old Oliver would be left speechless as well. The image of Superintendent Burnell's face flush with incredulity floated before his eyes and for the first time that evening he chuckled. Oh, they were going to have a jolly old time.

Then, he sobered. *What if something went wrong?* He shook his head. No, that was not an option. It had to be foolproof. Emmy's life depended on it.

❦❦❦

Emmeline had spooned a little rice onto her plate and was just reaching for the tarragon chicken, when a voice hissed in her ear, "You can't take a hint, can you? You're not wanted here."

She swung round so swiftly she nearly dropped her plate.

Jason was looming over her, his expression full of disdain. "Why don't you leave?'

Emmeline pursed her lips. She was not going to be intimidated. She shot back, "Were you born rude or is it a talent you cultivated over the years?"

"Spare me. You should talk. 'Journalists' in inverted commas are nothing more than gossipmongers out to make a name for themselves without any regard for the truth."

She squared her shoulders and straightened her spine. This was not the first time that she had encountered such an attitude. "We live in an open and free society. The press plays a vital role in maintaining the delicate balance. The public has a right to know the truth."

Jason snorted. "And what truth would that be? From what I read every day, the press has only a passing acquaintance with the truth. You people make it up as you go along. The more outrageous, the better, right? The only thing you're interested in is selling more papers. You could care less about the plight of the poor sod struggling to put food on his family's table."

She cast her eye about the elegant dining room and caught a glimpse of Mrs. Royce glaring at her. "And you do, Mr. Royce? From what I see, you have very little in common with the 'poor sod' for whom you purport such concern. You probably walk quickly past him on the pavement. In fact, your ego is so inflated that you think that you're better than everyone else."

"Why you little—"

"Jason, that's enough." His mother's voice cut across him. She stepped between them and although her comments were directed at him, they were clearly intended for Emmeline. "Don't make a bad situation worse. She's here and we'll simply have to lump it for the evening. Let's go upstairs."

Emmeline knew she shouldn't have but she couldn't resist. "Yes, do follow Mummy."

Jason opened his mouth, but his mother put a restraining

hand on his arm. "Don't sink to her level." Then to Emmeline, in a lower voice she said, "The only reason you haven't been tossed out on your ear tonight is that I don't want a scene. But if you ever dare to darken my doorstep again, I will have you arrested for trespassing."

"You can't do that."

Mrs. Royce's turquoise eyes gleamed with malice. "Try me."

Jason allowed himself a smug smile, took his mother by the elbow, and turned his back on Emmeline.

Emmeline gripped her plate hard to stop her hands from trembling. She took a couple of deep breaths to slow her racing pulse.

"Evil witch," she muttered. "As for you, Jason, I hope you get run over by a lorry."

"He is a spiteful bugger, isn't he?" a male voice mused beside her.

"What?" Emmeline was taken off guard. She craned her neck to find herself looking up into a pair of laughing dark eyes.

The man must be in his late thirties. He was attractive—not as handsome as Gregory, but then no one was—and he had an open, honest face that hinted at an easy-going disposition. He looked vaguely familiar, but she couldn't place him.

"I didn't think anyone had heard me."

He smiled down at her. "Don't worry. I was the only one close enough. I've often wanted to throttle Jason. He brings out the worst in people."

Emmeline returned his smile. She liked this fellow. "He's just so…so hateful."

The stranger tossed his head back and laughed. "You're being too polite. I could think of a lot worse to say about him."

"I gather you've known him a long time."

"You could say that. He's my brother." He smiled and extended his hand. "I'm Adam Royce."

Emmeline's mouth went dry. She felt the heat rising to her cheeks.

"You know you're turning the most becoming shade of pink." This only made her blush more.

"I—I—" It came out as a strangled croak. She cleared her throat and tried again. "I seem to have inserted my foot in my mouth. I'm terribly sorry. Please forgive my rudeness."

"Not a bit of it. You were spot on about Jason. He's always been absolutely insufferable. Be thankful you didn't have to live with him."

His laughter was infectious. The awkwardness quickly dissipated.

"Now, you have me at a disadvantage. You know my name, but I don't know yours."

She proffered her hand. "I'm Emmeline Kirby. Your father invited me and my fiancé."

The corners of Adam's mouth drooped. "Ah, fiancé. Then I'm out of luck. Naturally such a lovely woman would have a fiancé."

"You're very kind."

"There's that blush again." He winked at her. "No, don't be embarrassed. You truly are lovely. How do you know Dad?"

"I'm the editorial director of *The Clarion*. I'm doing a profile on your father for the paper."

"Oh, yes. Dad did mention it. Frankly, I was surprised that he agreed. He usually doesn't do interviews. You must have been very persuasive. I suppose Mum and Jason are not too keen on the idea. Mum can be a bit tetchy. Is that what all that unpleasantness was about?"

She sighed. "I'm afraid so."

"Never mind. You have one Royce in your corner." He flashed another smile at her. "I'll have a quiet word with Jason. I'm not promising anything, but he won't be quite so disagreeable."

"Thanks. I don't have any underhand agenda. I simply thought our readers would like to know more about your father. He's a fascinating man and his business acumen is well-regarded in the industry."

Adam chuckled. "Dad will be tickled to see that he has gained another admirer. Mum and Jason have nothing to fear.

I'm certain your interview will be very flattering."

"It's not a question of flattering. I strive to present an objective portrait so that readers can garner a better understanding of the person."

"Yes, in the few minutes I've spent talking to you, I can see that you take your job seriously and are determined to be fair."

"Why, thank you, Mr. Royce."

"Adam please. And I will call you Emmeline. Friends don't stand on ceremony."

Emmeline threw him a questioning look. "Are we friends? We've only just met."

"Of course we are. Friendship, like love, is a matter of instinct and can happen in an instant." He snapped his fingers to emphasize his point.

"I never thought of it that way. But I suppose you're right."

They grinned at one another.

"New girlfriend, Adam? Where have you been hiding her?" A woman with inquisitive green eyes and dark hair that fell in thick waves about her shoulders, asked as she looped her arm through Adam's.

He slipped his arm around her waist and gave her an affectionate peck on the cheek. "Sabrina, you monkey. I've left you three messages in the last two days and you haven't returned my calls."

Sabrina gave a casual wave of her hand. "I've been around. I meant to ring you back, but something always seemed to get in the way."

"Uh. Huh. We'll discuss it later. Let me introduce you to Emmeline Kirby, the editorial director of *The Clarion*. Emmeline, my twin sister, Sabrina."

Emmeline inclined her head and clasped the other woman's outstretched hand. "How do you do?"

She studied the brother and sister. Adam resembled his father, only his looks were darker. Sabrina, on the other hand, while she shared her brother's dark hair there the resemblance ended. Her finely drawn features, with the long delicate nose and wide eyes, could be mistaken for no one other than their mother.

In Sabrina, Emmeline got a glimpse of what Lily Royce must have looked like as a young woman. Breathtaking was the only way to describe her. A woman who could have any man she set her cap at.

Sabrina's handshake was brisk and firm. A slight smile played around her lips. "So you're the one doing that interview on Dad? No wonder Mum had a face like thunder when I saw her in the hall. Mum likes her privacy."

"I assure you, Miss Royce, I have no intention of being intrusive."

"It's Sabrina. And aren't you? Intrusive, I mean. That's a journalist's stock in trade, isn't it? Sticking their noses in where they jolly well don't belong."

Emmeline gritted her teeth. It was obvious which brother she took after.

"Ooh, the evening is starting to look up. Isn't he dishy? I wonder who he is."

Emmeline followed Sabrina's gaze. It was locked on Gregory, who was threading his way toward them.

With a touch of asperity in her tone, she replied, "That is *my* fiancé."

Sabrina's cool gaze snaked toward Emmeline for a second and then settled on Gregory again. "Is he? Hmm. You are a lucky girl."

"I would say that we were both lucky."

"Is that what he says? Or what you *hope* he says? I find men don't like the clingy type. If you're not careful, someone could snatch him out from under your nose."

Emmeline clenched her fists at her sides. The bloody nerve of the woman. "I suggest you look elsewhere. He's taken," she hissed.

Sabrina's mouth curved into a feline smile. "Feeling a little insecure are we, dear?"

"Right, Sabrina. That's quite enough. Pull the claws back in," Adam scolded.

Sabrina ignored him and directed her comments to Emmeline. "Like all men, my twin can't stomach even the merest whiff of controversy. But we women are not afraid to fight for what we want, are we? No matter how dirty it gets."

Emmeline thrust her chin in the air and returned her smile. "You don't stand a chance."

Sabrina's silvery laughter floated upon the air. "We'll see."

Gregory's arrival forestalled the acerbic retort that danced on the tip of Emmeline's tongue.

He slipped his arm her around waist and drew her into his side. "There you are, Emmy. I'm sorry to have left to your own devices for so long."

He pressed a kiss to her temple and she beamed at Sabrina.

Sabrina broke free of her brother's embrace and boldly stepped toward Gregory, her hand extended. "I'm Sabrina Royce." Her tone held a husky promise.

She made certain that she moved in such a way that her dress shifted just enough that he got a glimpse of her cleavage.

Emmeline took a half step forward, her body trembling as a hot flash of fury surged through her. Her fingers were itching to claw out the other woman's eyes. For a start.

Gregory, on the other hand, flashed one of his most engaging smiles and tightened his grip on Emmeline, drawing her closer to him and preventing her acting upon her murderous intentions. He accepted Sabrina's hand, shaking it briskly.

"A pleasure to meet you, Miss Royce. I'm Gregory Longdon."

"Call me Sabrina. I have a feeling we're going to become *very* good friends, don't you?"

His smile only grew wider.

Traitor. How can you be taken in by this...this oversexed viper? Emmeline's brain screamed. She wanted to stomp on his foot with the heel of her elegant black pumps.

"You flatter me, Sabrina."

I'll flatten you with a punch on the nose, Emmeline thought silently. *With every word that comes out of your mouth, you're digging yourself a deeper grave.*

As her rage stewed, he went on chatting amiably. "But I'm afraid my inner circle of friends is already so large that I couldn't possibly contemplate adding another to the mix. Besides with our wedding fast approaching on the twenty-ninth of October, you can well imagine that Emmy and I are quite busy with preparations."

Emmeline relaxed her body against his. She tipped her head back and smiled at his profile. *I adore you. Forgive me for being a jealous fool*, her head murmured.

He seemed to sense the internal battle that had been raging within her for the past few minutes because he looked down at her and winked.

The only one who was not smiling was Sabrina. To Emmeline's delight, her eyes kindled with a mixture of anger and embarrassment.

Sabrina sniffed. "I can't spend all night hanging about here with such deadly dull people." With that, she swept off in a huff.

"Dull, darling? *Us*? I would have said that we're quite the opposite, wouldn't you?" Gregory asked facetiously.

Adam shook his head. "I must apologize for Sabrina. She never learns. It comes from being spoiled all her life. She thinks the world dances attendance on her."

Gregory clapped him on the back and put out his hand. "Don't worry, old chap. Nothing to do with you. You're not her keeper. Gregory Longdon, by the way."

Adam clasped his hand briefly and favored him with a lopsided smile. "Yes, forgive me for being rude. It's often difficult to get a word in edgeways when Sabrina's around. I'm Adam Royce, her long-suffering twin. I assure you I am quite different in character and temperament from both my sister and my brother. Odd man out I'm afraid. My father tells me I take after my grandfather, his father."

"From what I've seen, that's a good thing," Emmeline mumbled under breath.

The corner of Adam's mouth quirked upward. "Yes, unfortunately, Jason and Sabrina take after Mum. Don't get me wrong. I love Mum, but she's a prickly sort of person. You can never relax around her." He shrugged. "I've always been closer to Dad. We seem to view things the same way."

Emmeline nodded. From the time she had spent with father

and son this evening, she recognized the similarity in their characters. Both were intelligent, charming, and had a sense of humor. The difference between the two men was that Victor Royce's life was scarred by unhappiness and he harbored secrets in his soul.

She shivered involuntarily and clutched at Gregory's sleeve.

Secrets. How she hated them. Why did people have to keep secrets? Secrets always had a way of leaching out. They simmered, they percolated in the dark, but they never remained hidden. Never. All they did was to wreak havoc and ruin lives.

CHAPTER 21

Despite his surprise, Sergeant Finch had known better than to question the guv when Superintendent Burnell unexpectedly announced an hour ago in his office, "Finch, we need a spot of culture. Our souls are in danger of moldering away. We need to remedy the situation immediately. Let's go to the National Gallery."

Culture? The National Gallery? "Yes, sir," was the only response he could give.

And now, here he was passing through the portico of the imposing building that looked down upon Trafalgar Square. Without speaking, they climbed the marble staircase in the Central Hall to Level 2. Burnell had picked up a map of the museum along the way, but it was just for show. He didn't even glance at it. He merely twisted it into a tight scroll between his hands.

Finch followed Burnell to Room 38. It wasn't crowded today. Their footsteps echoed as they crossed the highly polished parquet floor and lowered themselves onto a black leather-covered bench in the center of the room. The red damask walls featured paintings by Canaletto and Guardi, as well as Bernardo Belloto and Giovanni Panini. Burnell folded one arm over his chest and stroked his beard meditatively as he studied Canaletto's *View of the Doge's Palace and the Riva degli Schiavoni*. The warm crimson of the wall only seemed to bring out the painting's bold brushstrokes and exquisite details into sharper focus.

Finch stared at his profile incredulously. "Sir—"

Burnell cut him off with a whispered, "Shh. This is my favorite painting."

Finch shifted his gaze to the painting. It was breathtaking. It teemed with life, activity, and color. And yet, they had leads to follow up on in the Sabitov case, not to mention the threat posed by the unpredictable Swanbeck.

He cleared his throat and ventured again, "Sir, far be it from me to question a superior officer. But do you think that visiting the National Gallery is the wisest use of police time when we could be working on the Sabitov case?"

Burnell sighed. "We are working on the Sabitov and Melnikov cases." He turned to face him. "Never second guess your elders."

"Yes, sir. Sorry I said anything. However, I'd like to point out that if Cruickshank hears of this little excursion, he's going to make life uncomfortable."

The superintendent rolled eyes. "Cruickshank. Bah." He made a disgusted gesture with his hand. "Don't mention that fool's name. When he was born, he probably made the doctor uncomfortable. It's in his nature to be irritating."

"Burnell, Finch."

Both detectives turned around to find Philip looming over them.

The superintendent smiled at Finch as Philip eased himself onto the bench. "Feel better, Finch?"

Philip's blond brows knit together as he searched the sergeant's face. "Have you been ill?"

"No, Mr. Acheson, I—"

Burnell cut him off. "No, his conscience was offended because he thought we were neglecting our work."

Philip's face broke into a smile. "We all know that there's only one person who is nonchalant about his work, and—"

"You know it's not polite to talk about a person behind his back, Acheson. I was wondering why my ears were burning."

Their heads snapped up in unison. They found themselves looking up into Gregory's laughing eyes.

"Room for one more or is this a private party?" he said as he proceeded to squeeze himself between Philip and Burnell.

"Longdon," Burnell grumbled. "What are you doing here?"

Philip sighed. "Mea culpa, I'm afraid. Like it or not, we

have to work together. There seems to be an awful lot of people—all with their own agenda—who want to hush up the connection between Swanbeck and the murders of Melnikov and Sabitov."

Gregory beamed and elbowed the superintendent in the ribs. "Oliver, deep down, you're positively thrilled that we'll be spending even *more* time together."

"The only reason I tolerate you—and that's just barely—is because of Emmeline."

"For the life of me, I can't understand what she sees in you, Longdon," Finch chimed in.

"While you lack imagination, Sergeant, Emmy is very discerning. She has taken the time to scratch beneath the surface to discover the inner man. A handsome devil, I modestly admit, whose intelligence, wit, and charm are completely irresistible."

Finch shook his head. "You are the most conceited man I have ever met. I'm surprised the ladies fall at your feet."

"All right. That's enough," Philip said. He had to nip this conversation in the bud. "Let's not get distracted by personalities. Let me bring you up to date with what I found out about Swanbeck."

He proceeded to relay the information he had extracted from a reluctant Mark Bradford over lunch the other day. Bradford said that the Ministry of Defence and the Foreign Office had long been suspicious about Swanbeck's business dealings and his cozy relationship with the Russians. MI6 had managed to "persuade"—by way of blackmail—someone with intimate knowledge of his company to become an informer. What he provided was good, but the flow was choked off when the informer was found dead in alley in Edinburgh with a bullet hole between his eyes. Then Melnikov fell into MI6's lap and he was pure gold. Until he was shoved off a balcony.

Outwardly, Gregory was cool reserve, but his stomach was a churning ocean. The informer's story perilously mirrored his own experience when Villiers inserted him in Walter Swanbeck's inner circle. *There, but for the grace of God, go I*, he thought. He could still suffer the same fate. Only now Emmy was involved, and it was entirely his fault.

"Not only was Melnikov about to betray a ring of Russian agents operating undercover here in the UK," Philip went on, "He told MI-Six that Swanbeck is trading guns for diamonds. That's why the Ministry of Defence and MI-Six cooked up this task force in the hopes of somehow flushing him out. A bloody great waste, if you ask me. It's putting the cat among the pigeons and could do more damage in the end. The man is too wily to let anything slip about his dealings with the Russians." He paused and cleared his throat. "Longdon, I don't want to alarm you, but Swanbeck as good as told me that he's coming after you and Emmeline. Her article on Sabitov's murder is only going to lead to more problems, especially her determination to pick up where he left off. If she starts digging into Melnikov and this mysterious Rutkovsky she was pestering me about when she came to the house yesterday, well..." He let the sentence trail off.

"Yes," Gregory replied quietly. "I know. I'm marrying a mad woman with a will of iron and a stubborn streak to match."

This elicited a half-hearted laugh from the other three men. A gloomy silence quickly ensued as they stared at Canaletto's painting without really seeing it. Each was lost in his own troubled thoughts.

"Right," Gregory said suddenly as he slapped his thigh. "The only way to get Swanbeck is to beat him at his own game."

"Very profound, Longdon. Tell us something we don't know," Burnell retorted somewhat huffily.

"I'll do one better, Oliver." This provoked a frown from the detective. "Oh, I forgot, Superintendent Burnell. My memory is not what it used to be these days."

Burnell folded his arms over his broad chest and fixed his far-from-amused gaze on Gregory. "Do you have something constructive to contribute or are you just going to spew your usual rubbish all afternoon?"

"Really, *Oliver*, your temper seems to be getting the better of you lately. Perhaps if you take up meditation, you'll curb your impatience. I also hear that yoga is a great stress reliever." He gave Burnell a cheeky grin.

Finch couldn't help himself. A laugh burst forth at the image of the superintendent taking up yoga.

Burnell rounded on him. "Something you wanted to say, Finch?"

"No, sir." He shook his head. "Nothing at all. Just a tickle in my throat."

"Keep it that way." Then to Gregory, he said, "Get on with it and stop wasting time."

"Right." Gregory rubbed his hands together. "Gentlemen, I have a plan. A deliciously wicked plan, where I can apply skills I've honed over the years."

"Already I hate it," Burnell muttered.

"Let's hear Longdon out," Philip urged, although a wary skepticism was etched in the lines of his face.

They all leaned in closer. Gregory lowered his voice and first told them about what Victor Royce had revealed about how his ill-fated business ventures had garnered Swanbeck's ire and enmity for perpetuity. Royce had confirmed that he had heard the rumors about Swanbeck's trading arms for diamonds.

"That's what put the idea into our heads."

"Our heads?" Philip prompted. "You and Royce concocted this plan?"

"Yes, I don't totally trust the chap, but he has a brilliant business mind. Apparently, he's passed on information to Villiers in the past."

Philip held his tongue at the mention of Villiers.

"Royce actually had been trying to get into contact with Villiers, but couldn't. We all know why. So instead, he sought me out. How my name came to his ears I don't know, but that's neither here nor there at the moment. What's important is that Royce gave me the details of Swanbeck's next major buy. He provided names and the date. It's all here." He unobtrusively slipped a handful of papers from the inside pocket of his suit jacket and handed them to Philip.

Philip flipped through the papers as the others looked on. He lifted his bright blue eyes to Gregory's face. "How did Royce get a hold of this?"

Gregory tapped a finger to his lips. "Acheson, you're in the spy business. Haven't you learned that in some situations it's better not to ask? Good stuff, is it?"

"Good stuff? This is the break we've been after. However, it says that Swanbeck is demanding the—" He looked down at the papers again. "—the Blue Angel. I suppose that's some sort of code."

Gregory grinned and shook his head. "Your ignorance is astounding. And here I thought you were a cultured chap. My dear Acheson, the Blue Angel is the most beautiful, seductive creature on this earth—Emmy excepted. I saw her only once. She took my breath away. The Blue Angel is a flawless twelve-carat blue diamond. It is up for auction at Sotheby's on Thursday. The estimate is thirty-five million to fifty-five million pounds. There are only a handful of people in the world with the means and desire to acquire such a jewel."

Burnell emitted a low whistle. "I should say so."

"But the Russian mafia is floating in more money than it knows what to do with," Gregory went on. "In this case, Igor Bronowski appears to be willing to overlook past disagreements to do business with Swanbeck again. Bronowski launders his dirty money by buying the Blue Angel. He gets his guns and Swanbeck gets the diamond. All neat and tidy."

"The cunning bastard," Finch murmured. "But how can he be certain that he'll have the winning bid."

Gregory slid a sideways glance at the sergeant. "I'm sure more than a few palms have already been greased. I also wouldn't put it past him to have obtained a secret list of his rival bidders. Bronowski has probably sent his thugs on a little visit to each one. Fear and the desire to live are powerful motivators. However, Royce, who is a well-known collector, is willing to bid for the Blue Angel to do his bit for queen and country, but especially to take down Swanbeck."

Philip shook his head. "That's out of the question."

"Why? It's our only chance to catch Swanbeck off guard. He'd never suspect Royce is helping us."

Philip stared at Gregory for a long moment. Gregory could see him mentally weighing the pros and cons of the scheme. Then his gaze strayed to Burnell.

"No," Burnell responded adamantly to the unspoken question in the other man's eyes. "It's madness. The auction is in three days. There are too many things that could wrong."

Philip nodded. "I won't argue with you on that score. But think about what we'd gain if Royce manages to buy the diamond from under Bronowski's nose. Swanbeck would be furious. Furious enough to come after Royce, and we'd be there waiting for him. I'll get on to my superiors at MI-Five so that we can coordinate with MI-Six on surveillance of Swanbeck and Bronowski. We'll have to put a team of agents undercover at the auction."

Gregory smiled. "That's a good start, Acheson. Royce has agreed to keep increasing his bid to bump up the price. But if either Bronowski or Swanbeck smell trouble, they'll go so far underground you'll never catch them."

"What do you propose?" Philip asked warily.

"We have to play one against the other. While Royce's overall idea is sound, I felt it needed some improvement, a bit of panache. Therefore, I came up with my own twist."

"Yes, about this plan of yours. You haven't actually told us what it is."

"Haven't I? And you're dying of curiosity. I won't keep you in suspense any longer. We're going to allow Bronowski to have the winning bid. Then we'll steal the Blue Angel."

Philip's jaw dropped. "*We?*" He exchanged an uneasy look with the two detectives.

"I always knew the man was unhinged," Burnell mumbled.

Gregory grinned as he rose to his feet. "No need to feel embarrassed or to shower me with praise, gentlemen. I told you it was a brilliant plan. Of course, I have to work out the finer points to ensure that it goes off without a hitch. That's why I must leave you."

He gave a little wave of his hand, which was almost regal

in its execution, and pivoted on his heel. They heard him chuckling all the way to the exit.

CHAPTER 22

Royce was as good as his word. He had set aside two hours that morning and had patiently answered all of Emmeline's questions during the interview. She felt she had more than enough material to give her readers better insight into a man whose face they occasionally saw staring up at them from the papers when Royce Global Holdings made an acquisition or embarked on a new project.

Royce had graciously agreed to allow Tom, *The Clarion*'s best photographer, to follow him around to take a few candid shots to complement the article. In the interim, she had returned to the paper to write up the profile. She made a few minor edits to polish it and now all that was left was for Tom to get back so that she could select a few photos. The profile would be the leader in tomorrow's Business section.

As proud as she was for having landed the exclusive Royce interview, she was itching to sink her teeth into the Melnikov story. She had to play up the connection to Sabitov's murder. In the confusion at the Dorchester, no one had seen her slip Sabitov's notebook into her handbag. However, her triumph had quickly turned to disgust when she flipped through it. It was utterly useless because all his notes were in Russian. There was only one word that stood out in block letters: *RUTKOVSKY?*, underlined twice in heavy pencil followed by a question mark as if Sabitov was angry or *frightened*. A ghost at the center of this deadly puzzle. She had to draw Rutkovsky out of the shadows otherwise he would wind up dead like his compatriots.

She had to keep Sabitov in the headlines, highlighting the fact that his murder came in the midst of an exposé he had been working on corruption in the Kremlin. *A mere coincidence*, she would posit, *or was something more sinister at work*? She also would note that Sabitov's death came one day after Pavel Melnikov, a Russian defector, who had allegedly committed suicide by hurling himself off the balcony of his Mayfair penthouse.

Yes, I think that will attract attention, she thought.

She picked up the phone and dialed Superintendent Burnell's number. She drummed her fingers on her desk as she waited for the call to go through.

"Burnell," the detective barked in her ear.

"Hello, Superintendent Burnell. It's Emmeline. I hope I haven't caught you at a bad time."

"Oh, hello." His tone softened a bit, but the irritation remained. "Suffice it to say that I wish I had never returned from holiday," he grumbled. "I have Cruickshank looking over my shoulder and making a nuisance of himself every five minutes. Swanbeck is roaming about bold as brass thumbing his nose at the law. Russians are going about London killing one another. And to top it all off, there's *your* fiancé plotting to commit a crime."

Her ears perked up at the mention of Gregory's name. She sat up straighter in her chair. Her pulse began to thrum with anxiety. "Gregory? What do you mean? What has he done?"

After a long pause, Burnell replied, "Nothing. Longdon hasn't done anything."

His voice trailed off, but she thought his last word was "Yet."

"Superintendent Burnell, please don't shield me. Tell me if Gregory's in any trouble. I must know."

She held her breath as he let out a long sigh.

"No, Longdon is not in any trouble. Never mind me. I'm a bit out of sorts today."

She wasn't convinced, but she chose not to pursue the matter for the moment. "I'm terribly sorry. I'm only going to add to your aggravation. I'm afraid this isn't a social call, much as I enjoy chatting with you." She hoped this would improve his mood. It was true, though. She did like him. "I was wondering whether Dr. Meadows has completed the postmortem on Sabitov." She hesitated before adding quickly, "Are you willing to make a statement to the press?"

There was a brief silence followed by a grunt. She heard papers rustling, as if he were riffling through a file.

He cleared his throat. "The toxicology report has come back."

"Yes." She tried to keep the eagerness out of her voice. She snatched a pad and pen. "Can you tell me anything on the record?"

"According to the report, Mr. Yevgeny Sabitov, the crusading Russian journalist, did not die of natural causes. He was poisoned."

"We suspected as much. Was Dr. Meadows able to identify the poison?"

"Yes, it was atropine. It took a devil of a time to find it because the symptoms can be mistaken for alcohol intoxication. Meadows said that it takes between five and twenty minutes for atropine to kill. It can be injected, breathed, or absorbed through the skin."

Emmeline was writing furiously. She heard more paper shuffling.

"Let's see. Among the symptoms are blurred or double vision, dry mouth or extreme thirst, difficulty breathing, turning red/flushing, rapid pulse, gasping, aggression, delirium, and convulsions or seizures. All of which were confirmed by you and the other witnesses we questioned."

"Did Dr. Meadows determine how the atropine was introduced into Sabitov's system?"

"He did. He found a tiny pinprick on his thumb."

"A pin?" She stopped writing, baffled. Her mind flew back to the afternoon at the Dorchester. "We know it had to be the woman in white. But how did she do it?"

"We're not sure. That's all I can tell you for the moment, Emmeline."

"It's quite enough to be getting on with. I appreciate it, Superintendent Burnell. Can I quote you or shall I attribute it to *a source close to the investigation*?"

"Go ahead and quote me."

She smiled. "Thanks. I don't want to push my luck or impose on your good nature, but have you found out anything new about Melnikov and Swanbeck? Something I can include in the article?" She made her voice soft and cajoling.

Burnell was silent so long she thought that they had been disconnected. "Superintendent, are you still there?"

"I'm here," he said at last. "The answer is no. Nothing new on Melnikov or Swanbeck."

"I see. Well, you've been very helpful. I won't keep from your work any longer."

"Emmeline, humor a crotchety old policeman and be careful. These men won't even bat an eye if they kill you."

"I'm touched by your concern, Superintendent. Please don't worry, though. I'm always careful."

He sighed wearily again. "Right. I knew you wouldn't listen, but it was worth a try. I'll keep you informed." With that, he rang off.

Will you? she asked herself as she replaced the receiver. *What have you found out that you're* not *telling me? And what the devil is Gregory up to?*

Why did these men always feel it necessary to keep her out of the loop? It only made her more suspicious. Didn't they know by now that she always found out whatever *it* was in the end?

છૐછ

Victor Royce skimmed through the document one final time before picking up the pen and signing it in his neat angular hand at the bottom of both copies. One of Stan's colleagues served as a witness and put his signature on the line below.

"That's everything, Vic," Stan said. "Here's your copy." He hesitated before handing over a manila envelope to this friend. "The other one will remain here in your file. But are you sure? There's no possibility of a mistake? "

Royce stood and tucked the envelope under his arm. He clasped his solicitor's hand. "No doubt at all. I had a test done."

Stan, a tall, slim man of sixty with a round face and clear gray eyes, which always held an amused gleam, assumed a serious expression as he clapped Royce on the back and walked him to the door. He pursued his lips. "I see. Does she know?"

Royce shook his head. "I'd appreciate your discretion."

"Naturally, that goes without saying. However, I still think you should say something. At the very least to Lily. After all—"

Royce stopped and shook his head. "No," he replied in a clipped tone. "Lily is an extremely self-centered woman. She would never understand about justice."

"Yes, yes. Very commendable. But, Vic, think of the scandal. This is your family."

Royce threw his head back and laughed. "The only sensible one of the lot is Adam and he has a strong head on his shoulders. He'll be all right. As for the others, well—" He spread his hands wide and shrugged his shoulders. "—perhaps they deserve a bit of a jolt. It's just too bad that I'll already be dead and won't get a chance to see the fireworks."

CHAPTER 23

There had been talk of nothing else the past few days. It had even eclipsed the news about Sabitov and Melnikov. As Emmeline glanced down at the glossy color photo of the Blue Angel in the catalogue, she could well understand why this famous diamond was the star of today's auction. Lot 23.

The room was nearly filled. The low buzz of excited conversation rippled across the neatly lined rows of chairs. She found an aisle seat toward the back and took out her notebook. At the last minute, she had stepped in to cover the auction because the reporter she had assigned to the story had a death in the family.

She craned her neck this way and that as she studied her fellow audience members. All the ladies and gentlemen were well-heeled and oozing self-assurance. There was no doubt about the health of their bank accounts. Were they all here to bid on a particular item? Or were some merely observers like herself? she mused.

The auction should be starting in a quarter of an hour. She leafed through the catalogue and lingered over the Blue Angel's history. She looked up when two men did a sound check of the microphone at the lectern in the center of the stage.

With five minutes to go, she saw that there wasn't a single chair free. The few late-comers who had straggled in had to stand either at the back or along the walls. Her eyes widened in surprise when she saw Sergeant Finch and Superintendent Burnell, heads bent together deep in conversation, against the wall on the right side of the room. A Sotheby's auction seemed a little outside of the detectives' jurisdiction.

Just as this thought struck her, she caught a glimpse of a familiar blond head several rows ahead of her. Philip too? What was going on? Why had the Foreign Office and Scotland Yard taken an interest in what was ostensibly a typical auction?

Philip's attention appeared to be riveted on his catalogue, but he did cast several sidelong glances to his right at a man with closely cropped salt-and-pepper hair in the row in front of him. The man was flanked by two younger chaps, whose eyes never stopped scanning the audience. Their posture and concentration marked them as bodyguards. She wondered who the man was they were protecting. She wished he would turn around. She scooted to the edge of her chair and leaned forward to try to get a better look at him.

A movement to her left across the aisle caught her eye. She tilted her head slightly and froze.

The man from the Underground, the man who could only be Swanbeck, raised his catalogue and gave her a little salute. His mouth curved into a lupine smile of malicious satisfaction at her discomfiture.

Emmeline's heart began to hammer in her chest. She was surprised that the woman sitting next to her couldn't hear it.

Her eyes strayed to the spot where Burnell and Finch had been standing only moments before, but they were gone. She shot a look at Philip's row, but his seat was now empty. Where were they? She desperately searched the room, hoping to alert one of them to Swanbeck's presence.

She drew in a ragged breath as her blood raced. It had become very warm in the room. Her head began to swim. She thought she was going to faint. Instead of finding the two detectives, her gaze locked on someone she wished with all heart was a thousand miles away. Gregory. He was standing next to the phone bank to the right of the stage talking to one of the Sotheby's employees.

She licked her lips and casually ventured another glance in Swanbeck's direction. He inclined his head and beamed at her. That's what she had feared. He had seen Gregory too.

The world had suddenly shrunk, and she was trapped.

The auctioneer took up his position at the lectern. The last whispers petered out and silence reigned. Everyone's attention was riveted on the screen behind the auctioneer, where the image of a platinum necklace with a cascade of 191 carats of emeralds set between sixteen carats of diamonds was projected. Emmeline held her breath. It was stunning. The auctioneer provided some background on the piece as a Sotheby's employee modeled it live. Hands shot into air almost as soon as the auctioneer had asked for bids. The day's sale was off to a furious start. The necklace sold for a cool £3 million.

The necklace was followed by a succession of rings, bracelets, earrings, and polished jewels as large as goose eggs. Each lot was more dazzling than the previous one. The bidding was brisk and the sale prices were mind-boggling. The audience's appetite appeared insatiable.

It was difficult not to get swept up in the excitement. Emmeline soon forgot about Swanbeck.

Finally, it was Lot 23's turn. A reverent hush descended when the Blue Angel flashed up on the screen.

"Ladies and gentlemen," the auctioneer said, "shall we open the bidding for this exquisite diamond at thirty-five million pounds?"

A paddle toward the front was the first to wave at the auctioneer.

"Do I hear forty million?"

Several people at the phone bank signaled their interest, as did the man with the salt-and-pepper hair who had captured Philip's attention.

The frenzied bidding quickly escalated £50 million, £60 million, £65 million, £70 million, £75 million. When it reached £80 million, even the auctioneer appeared impressed. Clearly, the bidding had exceeded expectations and it was not over yet—*£95 million, £100 million, £110 million.*

The bidding was spiraling to dizzying heights. The faint of heart dropped out. These fabulous amounts were only for intrepid souls, or the insanely obsessed.

It was now a war between the paddle in the front and the man with the salt-and-pepper hair. From this angle, Emmeline couldn't see the bidder in the front but if she leaned forward just a tiny bit she got a good view of the latter. His profile was set with grim determination. At one point, he swiveled his head around and she got a good look at his face. Her grip tightened on her notebook and she sucked in her breath. It was Igor Bronowski, the Russian mobster. He was looking directly at Swanbeck. Some sort of silent question passed between the two men. Swanbeck gave an almost imperceptible jerk of his chin. Her gaze was drawn back to Bronowski, whose face was creased with fury. As he raised his paddle to make another bid, he glared at his rival in the front. She wished she could see who would be insane enough to challenge Bronowski. She craned her neck as far as possible but it was no use.

And it went on—*£115 million, £120 million, £125 million*

"Do I hear one hundred thirty million?"

The audience held its breath. The waiting was agonizing torture.

The auctioneer looked toward the bidder in the front. "Sir, it's up to you."

The man must have given up.

"I have £125 million. Going once, twice." The auctioneer banged his gavel down. "Sold to the gentleman on my left."

He pointed the gavel in Bronowski's direction. The audience burst into applause. Bronowski, on the other hand, appeared far from pleased by his victory. He jumped to his feet and made his way down the row, stepping on several toes as he made his brusque exit. His nostrils flared and his cheeks were flushed. His bodyguards were close on his heels. She saw Bronowski scowl at a young Sotheby's employee, who stopped him in the aisle. However, he listened closely as she explained something. Emmeline saw the woman gesture with her arm toward a door on the far side of the room. Bronowski sighed and nodded reluctantly as he followed her.

There were only a few lots left and people started to leave. To her surprise, she saw Victor Royce rise to his feet. *He* was the mystery bidder against Bronowski. It had to be more than a coincidence that Royce, Gregory, Philip, Burnell, and Finch were all here today. What scheme did they have up their sleeves? Her eyes narrowed. Whatever it was, they had kept her in the dark. Just wait until she cornered Gregory.

Her wayward fiancé must have sensed her intense scrutiny because he turned around at that precise moment. He froze and his complexion took on an ashen hue when he saw her.

Oh, yes, my darling, she thought, *you are in trouble. It's not nice to go behind my back.*

Gregory threw a worried glance at Swanbeck and then shot her a pointed look.

She nodded and gave a helpless shrug of her shoulders. Her anger was forgotten. The fear returned.

Swanbeck was too smart to try anything in the auction house. Certainly, he wouldn't dare to approach her or Gregory himself. It was too public. Too messy. As far as the world at large was concerned, there could be no connection between them.

The hairs on the back of her neck prickled. *But what if his associates are waiting for us outside?*

Her blood started to thrum through her veins. The woman next to her gathered up her handbag and the catalogue and stood up. Emmeline did as well. She would use the woman for cover until she got outside. She'd like to follow her to the ends of the earth, but that was not possible. Once she was on the pavement, she knew she was on her own but she would figure out her next move. She cast a glance over her shoulder to try to signal Gregory. He was still by the phone bank, but he was distracted by a Sotheby's employee who was whispering in his ear. Damn. She was hoping they could leave together, but she knew he would be all right.

Emmeline stiffened when Swanbeck entered her line of vision. Only two men separated them. She faced forward again and quickened her pace.

Only a few more feet and she would be out the door. Once in the corridor, she would bolt and hail the first taxi that rolled up to the curb. Why the devil didn't these people move faster? They were like a sleepy flock of sheep shuffling along.

She gasped and nearly jumped out of her skin, when she felt a strong hand grab her arm.

She spun around, prepared to cosh Swanbeck over the head with her handbag, only to find herself looking up into Victor Royce's brown eyes.

"Mr. Royce." Her voice was slightly breathless.

He smiled down at her and took a better hold of her arm. "Emmeline, what a delightful surprise." Without a backward glance at Swanbeck, he continued to propel her toward the door. His smile never faltered, but under his breath he hissed, "Let's go. You shouldn't be here. Swanbeck is on our heels."

She didn't know how to reply. Royce knew about Swanbeck?

Aloud again, he went on, "I insist that you join me for tea. My driver is waiting out front. He can take us wherever you like."

"I—I—" Her gaze strayed to Gregory, who nodded when he saw her with Royce. Then playing along with Royce, she said, "That would be lovely. Thank you."

Their progress got bogged down in the crush of people in the corridor, but Royce never let go of her arm as he politely, but determinedly, weaved a path for them toward the exit.

Royce gave her a reassuring smile.

As they set foot onto the pavement on Bruton Street, Swanbeck stepped in front of them to block their way.

His lips were twisted into a cruel grin. "Ah, I thought it was you, Victor. Spot of bad luck with the diamond. I see you haven't given up on meddling in my business." He leaned forward slightly. "But you lost this round, again. You haven't learned, have you?"

Royce drew himself up to his full height. Although he was a few inches shorter than Swanbeck, he appeared to be a giant. "Your business, Alastair? I could have sworn that I was bidding against that ugly fellow who bears a striking resemblance to a Neanderthal. You wouldn't be colluding with the chap, would you?"

Swanbeck pursed his lips. "Stay out of my way. You'll end up the loser," he spat back.

"I sincerely hope that wasn't a threat. You know it doesn't do to be over-confidant. Remember what happened to Icarus.

He flew too close to the sun, causing the wax in his wings to melt." Royce took a step forward and lowered his voice. "Then Icarus plunged into the sea. Brought down by his own hubris. That's what will happen to you. Any day now. I hope your fall is *very* hard."

He pulled Emmeline closer to his side. "You've delayed us long enough. If you'll excuse us, we're in a hurry." He tried to step around the fellow, but Swanbeck wouldn't let him get past.

Swanbeck turned his mocking smile on Emmeline, as if suddenly noticing her presence. "Yes, where are my manners? Forgive me, Emmeline." She shuddered at the sound of her name on his lips. "I must say it was an unexpected surprise to see you here today. It quite caught me off guard. I suppose Longdon, with his *vast* expertise, is the one who got you interested in jewels. How endearing. At least the two of you will have something to discuss once you're married. I hear the big day is the twenty-ninth of October."

She sucked in her breath and shrank closer to Royce. She was glad that he had his arm around her because her legs felt like water. *How did Swanbeck know about the wedding?*

"I can't tell you how much I'm looking forward to your wedding. Be sure to pop my invitation in the post." His voice dripped ice.

"There's my driver," Royce said. He gave Swanbeck a brusque shove out of the way. "We must go."

"I wouldn't dream of holding you up any further." He fixed his gaze on Emmeline again. "I won't say goodbye, but rather *adieu* because I'm certain we'll be seeing each other again *very* soon. Give my regards to Longdon."

He gave them a curt nod and pivoted on his heel. A black Mercedes drew up to the curb behind Royce's waiting Audi. The driver hustled to open the door for Swanbeck, who slipped into the back. The car merged into the afternoon traffic and was out of sight within in a few minutes.

"Bastard," Royce muttered as he and Emmeline got into his car. He had the good grace to look abashed when he caught her eye. "Sorry."

"It's perfectly understandable. Swanbeck seems to bring out the worst in people."

"Jeremy," he said to the driver, "Miss Kirby and I are in need of a restorative cup of tea. Please take us to Brown's Hotel."

"Yes, sir."

Emmeline settled back into the seat as the car pulled away from the curb. "I wanted to thank you for coming to my rescue, Mr. Royce."

He made a dismissive gesture with his hand. "Think nothing of it. I've had dealings with Alastair." A shadow crossed his face. "He's a very nasty type."

"Yes," she murmured. "I'm concerned he'll come back after Gregory."

Royce reached out and patted her hand. "Don't worry. Longdon can take care of himself. Besides, he has to—" He broke off in mid-sentence.

"Yes?" she prompted. "What *exactly* are all of you up to?"

She pinned him with a hard stare.

"All of us?" he asked innocently, although a smile quivered upon his lips. "I don't know what you mean."

Emmeline folded her arms over her chest. "At the risk of sounding impolite—I'm not going to be fobbed off by you men. I *know* you, Gregory, Philip, Superintendent Burnell, and Sergeant Finch are up to something." She held up a hand to forestall the protest that she could see was rising to his tongue. "It's no use denying it. Whatever you're plotting, it has to do with Swanbeck. I know I'm right. It's written in the furtive expression on your face. Ooh." She curled her fists into tight balls and pounded them against her thighs. "It's absolutely unforgiveable that you chose to keep me out of the loop."

Royce threw his head back. A deep, throaty chuckle rumbled forth from his lips. "Longdon was afraid that this would be your reaction, but he was most insistent."

"Hmph. I'll deal with Gregory later."

"Don't be too hard on the chap. He was merely concerned about you and wanted to keep you out of harm's way. We all did."

She relented slightly—only very slightly—at this remark. "Yes, well. Don't think I don't appreciate it, but I don't need to be coddled. I'm not a damsel in distress."

He nodded. "Right. Message received and understood. Are we forgiven?"

She couldn't help herself. She smiled. "Of course. It's the thought that counts, even if your method is misguided."

Royce wiped his forehead with the back of his hand in a dramatic gesture. "Whew. You don't know what a relief that is to hear."

"However, you can do something to redeem yourself."

His right eyebrow lifted in askance. "Oh yes?"

She gave him her most engaging smile. "Yes. You can tell me all about the scheme over tea."

"Longdon did say you were like a dog with a bone. They all shared that opinion."

She thrust her chin in the air and sniffed. "Did they? Extremely unflattering. I call it persistence. It's the only way to get to the truth."

CHAPTER 24

Gregory was grateful when Royce bundled Emmeline out of the auction house. What was she doing here? She could have ruined everything. Ah, well, crisis averted. Now to deal with today's main event.

As Symington's chief investigator, of course, he would be on hand at one of Sotheby's most prestigious sales of the year. Symington's, the auction house's insurer, had to look out for its interests and bottom line to make certain that everything was aboveboard. Gregory shook his head and sighed. Sadly, there were so many con men in the world today. You could never be too careful.

He chuckled to himself as he rapped his knuckles on the office door of the deputy director of jewel sales. Bronowski was ensconced in a chair that was clearly too small for his large frame. His head snapped up when Gregory entered the room.

"Ah, there you are, Mr. Longdon. This is Mr. Bronowski. The new owner of the Blue Angel. Mr. Bronowski, this is Mr. Longdon, Symington's chief investigator. He's here to oversee the smooth transfer of the diamond into your possession."

Bronowski gave a curt nod and shunned Gregory's extended hand altogether. "Let's get on with this. Where is my diamond?" Bronowski asked impatiently in his heavy Russian accent. He made a show of looking at his Rolex watch to indicate that his time was precious.

Naturally a Rolex, Gregory thought. *The fashionable mobster wouldn't be caught dead without one.* He beamed at the man. "You must understand, Mr. Bronowski, there are procedures that must be followed. Mere formalities, I assure you."

Bronowski made a disgusted face. "Bah. Procedures, formalities. You English like paperwork. It's very easy. I have the money." He waved a hand at his two bodyguards, who were each holding a briefcase. "All cash. I give you the money. You give me my diamond. Done." He rubbed his hands together to emphasize his point.

"I'm afraid it's not that simple. You have to certify that the item was turned over to you in perfect condition and you will hold neither Sotheby's nor Symington's liable for any future damage, theft, or other unforeseen mishap. I'm sorry, but those are the rules."

A martyred sigh escaped from Bronowski's lips. "How much longer do I have to wait? It's already been half an hour."

Gregory smiled ingratiatingly. "Not too much longer. I promise."

A tense silence descended upon the room as they stared at one another.

The deputy director of jewel sales was a soft-spoken woman with long sandy hair and slate-blue eyes. She tried smiling at Bronowski, but nothing could animate his stony countenance.

She cleared her throat. "Perhaps you gentlemen would like some tea." She reached toward a porcelain cup and the pot on the tray that her assistant had brought in shortly before.

Bronowski shook his head and examined his nails.

"There's always time for tea. I'll have a cup," Gregory said as he crossed to the desk.

She threw him a grateful smile. "Yes, of course, Mr. Longdon. Milk or lemon?"

"Milk, please."

"Right. There are biscuits too." She nodded with her chin at a plate with a selection of biscuits.

"No, thanks. Just the tea will be fine."

He accepted the cup from her. An exceedingly becoming rose blush spread across her cheeks as his fingers brushed against hers.

Bronowski exploded to his feet. "This is outrageous. Am I to be kept waiting here all day? I want my diamond."

Gregory placed his cup with deliberate care on the desk and

smoothed down the corners of his mustache. In a gentle tone that was calculated to infuriate Bronowski further, he replied, "Really, Mr. Bronowski. There's no need to raise your voice. I've just explained—"

"I know what you told me," Bronowski snarled. His body trembled and his nostrils flared. "But you will get on that phone right *now* and call whoever you have to and order them to bring my diamond to me. If it's not here in the next five minutes, I'll—"

He was interrupted in mid-tirade by a light tapping on the door. All eyes turned to the two men who entered the office. One was middle-aged with a ruddy oval face and laughing brown eyes. The second chap was younger. Gregory guessed he must be in his thirties. He was heavier and much more serious than his colleague.

"Ah, there you, Albert and Luke. Mr. Bronowski was getting anxious about his diamond," the deputy director said. "We don't want to inconvenience him any further."

Bronowski snorted. "Ha. Inconvenience. You English are masters of understatement. Just give me the papers you want me to sign and let me get out of here."

"As you wish," the deputy director replied apologetically.

The older fellow crossed to Bronowski and reverently handed him a black velvet box. Bronowski snatched it, but he sucked in his breath when he flipped open the lid. The Blue Angel's flawless facets reflected the overhead light and winked back at him.

He remained speechless for several seconds.

"Do you certify that you received the Blue Angel?" Gregory asked.

"What?" Bronowski tore his eyes away from the diamond to scowl at him. "Yes, yes."

He closed the box and snapped his fingers. His two men dutifully handed the briefcases over to the deputy director of jewel sales.

"There's no need to count it. One of your people has already done so. Now, give me the papers I have to sign."

"Of course." The deputy director nodded to Luke, the

younger fellow, who handed two sets of documents to Bronowski.

Bronowski leaned on the desk and scrawled his name or his initials in several places. "Is that it?"

"Almost. We just need Mr. Longdon's initials. Right here." The deputy director pointed to the relevant section at the end of the document.

Gregory initialed the page with a flourish where he was told and handed one set to Bronowski. "I congratulate you on your new acquisition, Mr. Bronowski. May it bring you good fortune."

Bronowski's brow furrowed as if he was trying to gauge whether Gregory was being facetious. It was apparent that he didn't trust Gregory—or anyone else for that matter—but he couldn't seem to put his finger on what bothered him so much. And Gregory could see that it was driving him mad.

Gregory offered him one of his most engaging smiles and extended a hand. Bronowski stared down his nose at the hand with disdain and turned his back on him.

Frightfully bad manners, old chap, Gregory thought as he mentally clucked his tongue at him. *Ah, well,* l'homme propose, Dieu dispose, *as the saying goes. I'm certain God will take great pleasure in disposing of you.*

He wanted to chuckle as the door closed behind Bronowski and his thugs, but he refrained from doing so. It would be poor taste to rub salt in the wound. Deliciously satisfying, but poor taste nonetheless. He shot his cuffs. A gentleman had to be above such things.

∽∾∽

Superintendent Burnell, his hands thrust deep in his pockets, was pacing back and forth in the foyer. He reminded Sergeant Finch of a caged tiger that was becoming more ill-tempered by the minute because he hadn't eaten in days. God help the unfortunate prey that crossed his path.

Burnell halted in his restless perambulations and checked his watch. "Where the devil is he?"

"Longdon did say—"

The superintendent rolled his eyes and threw his hands up in the air cutting Finch off. "Longdon, Longdon. It was madness to agree to this scheme. We're playing with fire. You do realize that, Finch, don't you?"

"Yes, sir. But I believe Mr. Acheson and Longdon felt that desperate times call for desperate measures."

This remark was rewarded with a furious scowl.

"Surely, there was a better way to draw out both Swanbeck and Bronowski than to give Longdon our blessing to—" He lowered his voice and shot a glance to his right and left at the few people milling about nearby. "—to steal the bloody diamond."

Finch held his tongue this time. He could sympathize with his boss's point of view. He was certain that the diamond would never see the light of day again.

"He's laughing his head off and taking great delight in making us his accomplices," Burnell grumbled. "After thirty years on the police force, I've become a hardened criminal."

Finch tried to bite back a smile. "Sir, that's a bit extreme. I'm sure things will come out all right in the end."

"How can you be so sanguine about it? We have Swanbeck and Bronowski on the left, and Longdon on the right. It's a nightmare. We—" He broke off when Bronowski stalked past them with his men close on his heels.

Bang on cue, Longdon hurried after him. "Mr. Bronowski. Mr. Bronowski."

Bronowski groaned and muttered something in Russian. He spun around so quickly that he nearly knocked down a Sotheby's employee who happened to be crossing the foyer. He glared at her. "Stupid woman. Watch where you're going."

Finch took a step forward to intervene, but Burnell put out a hand to restrain him. He gave a curt shake of his head.

The woman gave Bronowski a dirty look, but chose not to make a scene.

"Mr. Bronowski," Longdon called again.

"What do you want?" Bronowski's voice was laced with irritation.

Longdon's mouth curved into an ingratiating smile. "I'm so glad that I caught you. There's just one more document we need you to sign. It will only take a moment. I promise."

He held up two pages and a pen.

The Russian's hand trembled as he grabbed the pen and the papers. He jerked his chin at one of his men, who promptly turned around and offered his back.

Bronowski signed both sheets. "There. I hope that is it. You people have wasted my whole afternoon. I'm beginning to feel like a prisoner in this place." The sweep of his arm encompassed the entire foyer.

"Oh, no, no. Not a bit of it. I'm sorry you've been inconvenienced, but as I said earlier procedures must be followed." Longdon smiled again. "Here allow me. We can't have you looking disheveled."

He smoothed out some wrinkles on the Russian's suit jacket and straightened his lapels.

"Hey." Bronowski swatted at Longdon's hands. His bodyguards immediately stepped forward. Each grabbed an arm and pulled Longdon away.

Several heads turned in their direction.

Bronowski mumbled something in Russian and Longdon was released.

"Terribly sorry, old chap. No harm was intended."

Bronowski stared at him for several seconds without uttering a word. Then his eyebrows shot up.

"Anything wrong, Mr. Bronowski?" Longdon asked innocently.

Bronowski ignored him. He patted himself down. His shoulders sagged forward and his body visibly relaxed, when he felt the box in his inside pocket. He pulled it out and opened the lid. The Blue Angel was still nestled in its bed of black velvet.

He snapped the lid shut and shoved Longdon out of the way. He flew out the door without a backward glance. His lackeys glared at Longdon, but followed suit.

"And pleasant afternoon to you too," Longdon murmured. He came to join Burnell and Finch, whose jaws hung open.

"Oliver, if you're not careful you'll swallow a swarm of flies. It is summer, after all."

Burnell clamped his mouth shut, but remained speechless. When he found his voice again, it was a hoarse whisper. "The diamond...I thought you were going to steal it."

Longdon clucked his tongue and put a hand to his chest. "Me? I would never do such a thing. It's against the law."

Burnell scratched his head in confusion.

"So what was the point of this afternoon's little drama?" Finch picked up the slack for his stunned boss.

"Well," Longdon replied patiently, as if he were speaking to an imbecile child, "Bronowski was forced to pay far more than he had intended to get the Blue Angel. That's a bit of justice, isn't it?" He elbowed Burnell in the ribs. "He must want Swanbeck's arms awfully badly."

"Justice?" Burnell exploded. "How are we going to catch them? Bronowski has the diamond."

One of Longdon's eyebrows arched upward. "Does he?"

Burnell blinked and then fixed his stony blue stare on his face. "What do you mean?"

Longdon put an arm around the superintendent's shoulders. "Oliver, as a man of the world, you should know that looks can be deceiving. Don't you remember your Scott? 'Oh, what a tangled web we weave, when first we practice to deceive.'"

Burnell shook off Longdon's arm. "Where you're concerned, things are always tangled."

CHAPTER 25

After the confrontation with Swanbeck, Emmeline was still feeling a bit shaky and couldn't face tea at Brown's. Royce had a better idea. He told his chauffeur to drive them to his house in Cheyne Walk.

"We'll have tea in the garden. It will be just the thing. There's nothing like lingering over a nice cuppa with a gentle breeze blowing and the birds singing in the trees. You can give me some suggestions about what I should plant."

It sounded tempting, but Emmeline hesitated. She remembered the cool reception she had received from his wife. "What about Mrs. Royce? I don't think she'll be very pleased to have an unexpected guest in the middle of the afternoon."

He gave dismissive wave of his hand. "Don't worry about Lily. She's still at the office. She oversees the pharmaceutical division. She's lightened her workload over the last year or so, but she still goes in a few days a week. Lily's staying abreast of the latest research. She won't be home for several more hours. Besides, she likes nothing better than having guests."

Emmeline's mind flew back to Lily Royce's parting words at the party. *"The only reason you haven't been tossed out on your ear tonight is that I don't want a scene. But if you ever dare to darken my doorstep again, I will have you arrested for trespassing."*

"No more arguments," Royce was saying. "It's tea at the house and that's final."

Emmeline managed a weak smile, but prayed that she was long gone before Mrs. Royce returned.

⁂

They had been chatting amiably for about a quarter of an hour when they heard footsteps on the flagstones.

Royce rubbed his hands together. "Ah, tea at last. I hope Mrs. Mellet has baked scones today. They're absolutely heavenly."

Emmeline chuckled at his boyish enthusiasm.

"I'm afraid there aren't any scones. But there's some freshly made apple tarts, shortbread, and chocolate biscuits."

They both were surprised to find Adam, and not the maid, strolling out with the tea tray.

"Adam, what are you doing here?" Royce asked, when his son set the tray down on the table and lowered himself into a chair between his father and Emmeline.

Adam nodded to Emmeline. "Hello, again. It's a nice surprise to see you." Then to Royce he said, "I wanted to discuss something about the North Sea oil lease. Muldair rang me. Jason is making a nuisance of himself. Delia told me that you had taken the afternoon off. She said that most likely I would find you at home by now. However, we can discuss things later. It's time for tea."

Royce clapped him on the shoulder. "Emmeline, you know this son of mine has the senses of a bloodhound. Growing up, he always managed to be in the kitchen at the precise moment that something was coming out of the oven. That's why he's turned into such a strapping lad."

Adam gave her a sheepish grin and shrugged his shoulders. She chuckled. The love between father and son was abundantly evident in their lighthearted banter. Her throat constricted. The loss of her own parents hit her forcibly in that instant, choking off her breathing. She tried to swallow down the sadness. She was no closer to finding out who had murdered them. Philip had been unable to find out anything, although he promised that he would keep trying. A tear stung her eyelid and she lowered her head. She pretended to look for something in her handbag so that Royce and Adam wouldn't see that anything was amiss. She discreetly wiped away the tear with her finger. Right.

She straightened her spine and thrust her shoulders back.

She was not going to give up. But the past would have to wait a bit longer.

Adam did the honors and handed round the tea. They each helped themselves to tarts and biscuits. The conversation fell into an easy rhythm as they discussed politics and history and then meandered to art and music. They had quite lost track of time, as they sipped and munched, and refilled their cups until the pot was empty.

"How very cozy."

The trio froze when Lily's voice drifted to their ears.

Emmeline looked up to find herself in the crosshairs of Mrs. Royce's glacial stare as she closed the distance between the French doors and the table.

"What is that woman doing here again?" She didn't raise her voice, but each word flew through the air like a bullet.

Emmeline quickly rose and gathered up her handbag. "Hello, Mrs. Royce. Your husband was very kind to invite me to tea. But I'm afraid I've overstayed my welcome."

Lily had reached the table by now and loomed over her.

"You were never welcome here." Emmeline felt each word sear her skin, so palpable was the other woman's hatred.

Royce and Adam immediately jumped to their feet. Her husband slammed his open palm on the table. "Lily, what's gotten into you?"

Lily rounded on him. "I don't like you entertaining the gutter press in my house behind my back."

Adam took his mother by the elbow. "Mum, nobody was doing anything behind your back. We were simply having tea. That's all."

"I think I should go," Emmeline murmured. She extended a hand to Royce and inclined her head to Adam. "Thank you, Mr. Royce, Adam. It was a pleasant afternoon. I don't want to disrupt things any further. I'll find my own way out."

She avoided Mrs. Royce's gaze and started to walk toward the French doors.

She stiffened when Mrs. Royce called after her, "Mind that you don't nick anything along the way." However, she didn't turn around.

"This is ludicrous," Royce said as he caught up to her and grabbed her arm. "Wait a few minutes. I'll have my chauffeur drive you home."

"Oh, no, Mr. Royce. That's not necessary. Really. I've caused enough trouble."

"Never mind, Dad. I'll take Emmeline home."

Royce shot a grateful look at his son and relinquished her arm.

Emmeline's gaze strayed to Mrs. Royce, who was standing stiffly with her hands clasped so tightly at her waist that her knuckles showed white. "No, Adam, please."

"You seem to attract quite the coterie of male admirers, don't you?"

"Mum, that's uncalled for," Adam said over his shoulder. "Come on. Let's go," he told Emmeline and gave her gentle nudge.

Once she was out of earshot, Royce hissed, "Adam."

His son turned around and came to his father's side. "What is it?"

"Don't leave until Emmeline is safely inside her house."

Adam's brow puckered. "Of course, Dad. Is anything wrong?"

Royce lowered his voice further. "There was some unpleasantness earlier with Swanbeck. For my peace of mind, I'd like to know that she's all right."

Adam's eyes widened. "Swanbeck? Is he circling around again? I thought he had given up on a takeover."

They heard Lily's heels clicking on the flagstones.

"Now's not the time. We'll talk later. Go on." Royce jerked his chin toward the French doors.

Adam nodded and gave his father's arm a reassuring squeeze. He didn't want to keep Emmeline waiting any longer.

"Why am I not surprised? That woman is a magnet for 'unpleasantness' as you so quaintly put it," Lily sneered.

Royce thrust his hands deep in his pockets. His body trembled slightly as he slowly pivoted on his heel to face his wife across the terrace.

"I don't even recognize you anymore. What do you have

against Emmeline Kirby? She's an intelligent and capable young woman. She's extremely amiable. Admirable in many ways."

A shadow chased itself across Lily's pinched features. Her eyes were ablaze with turquoise fire. "Hmph. There is nothing remotely admirable about that woman. She insinuated her way into our home so that she could dig up a scandal to splash across the front page of that rag of hers. All she had to do was to bat those dark eyes at you and you were putty in her hands. You and Adam. Like all men, you were flattered by female attention. Jason is the only one not taken in by her siren charms."

He snorted. "You're being utterly ridiculous. What scandal? There is no scandal here."

Lily closed the distance between them. They were virtually on the same eye level. She impaled him with her icy glare. Her voice dipped dangerously low. "She's trouble. I don't want to see that woman in *my* home again. She can do her muckraking somewhere else. For all we know, she was involved in that man's murder at the Dorchester. She and that fiancé were questioned by the police. And now, she's dragged Swanbeck back into our lives. Doesn't that bother you? I find it alarming. I don't want her harming the family or the company. I've worked too hard over the years to see either tarnished. Therefore, *her* name will never be mentioned again. Ever. Not even a whisper. Journalists—particularly that one—are not welcome here. This is the last time I'm going to have this conversation with you." She rubbed her temple. "I'm going upstairs to lie down. I feel a headache coming on."

As his confused brain was still trying to transmit a reply to his tongue, she swept past him.

∽∾∽

Swanbeck was standing in the center of Queen Mary's Rose Garden in Regent's Park. He bent his head to inhale the heady scent of a rose that had unfurled her delicate, ruffled petals to reveal the secrets of her deep gold heart to the sun.

"Ahem." Someone cleared his throat.

Swanbeck sighed and straightened up to his full height of six foot two inches. "Ah, there you are at last, Igor."

Bronowski appeared to squirm slightly.

Good, thought Swanbeck. He liked to keep people on edge. It was so amusing.

"Sorry, Alastair, those idiots at Sotheby's had me sign a thousand papers before they would release the diamond to me."

Swanbeck lifted an eyebrow. "Any problems?"

The Russian gave a curt shake of his head. "No problems. I have it right here." He patted his suit jacket and slowly pulled out the box. He hesitated for a second before he turned it over. "It cost me much more than we had discussed."

Swanbeck shrugged his shoulders and impatiently waggled his fingers. "That's the way things go sometimes. In business, you have to plan for contingencies."

Bronowski smiled, but it only served to make his features crease into even more unattractive lines. "Yes, but this is not the deal we negotiated."

Swanbeck's mouth curved into a lupine grin. "My dear, Igor, I was under the impression you were in a hurry to get the arms into the hot little hands of your band of hooligans. Do you want to cancel the deal? It doesn't bother me. I have a dozen other clients that would be willing to pay twice as much as you did for the diamond and would consider it a bargain for the merchandise they'd be receiving in exchange. It's up to you." He strolled to another bloom and buried his nose among its dewy apricot petals, allowing Bronowski to stew silently. He lifted his head. "Have you come to a decision, Igor?"

The Russian licked his lips. Something guttural that was a cross between a growl and snarl rumbled from his throat. "The deal stands." With a disgusted flick of his wrist, he tossed the box to Swanbeck, who caught it easily with one hand.

"Careful now. This is not a shot of vodka."

Bronowski's reply was unintelligible.

Swanbeck chuckled as he flipped open the lid. He gasped when the Blue Angel's facets trapped the strands of sunlight tumbling from the sky. He took out the diamond to admire it in the light. Then he frowned. He twisted the jewel this way and that. His palm slowly wrapped around it in a tight fist.

"I don't like games, Igor." His tone was clipped.

"What are you talking about?"

In two strides, Swanbeck was at his side. He raised his hand until it was eye level for Bronowski. Then he uncurled his fingers. The diamond winked at them. "This is a fake." Through gritted teeth, he said, "I—want—the diamond— now."

The Russian's eyes became like two huge brown saucers. "What?" he exploded. "How can it be a fake?" Then his eyes narrowed as he snatched the jewel from the other man's palm. "You're lying."

Swanbeck stiffened. "Me thinks you doth protest too much, Igor. I'm starting to lose my patience with you."

Bronowski grabbed him by the lapels. "You can go to hell, *old chap*. The diamond has never been out of my sight since I left Sotheby's."

Swanbeck swatted at the other man's hands and smoothed the wrinkles from his suit jacket. "Then the switch was made at the auction house before you left."

"That's impossible. It was brought to the deputy director of jewel sales' office by two Sotheby's employees. Aside from them, the only ones in the office when the transaction took place were the deputy director, Symington's investigator, and my two men. I signed for the diamond and we came directly here. I tell you it's impossible for a switch to have been made." He snapped his mouth shut as a thought appeared to strike him. His eyes narrowed. "Unless you planned this to make me look like a fool." He nodded his head, warming to the idea. "Yes, of course. That's the only way it could have happened. You paid someone off at Sotheby's. You've made a deal with my competitors."

Swanbeck shot his cuffs. He looked Bronowski directly in the eye. "To your dying day, you're going to regret your indiscretion. No one tries to cheat me." Out of the corner of his eye, he caught some movement. "Ah, perfect timing, gentlemen."

Two burly fellows with grim faces approached them.

"Igor, this is your lucky day. I know you must be homesick for mother Russia, so here are two of your compatriots, Yuri and Ivan. I'm sure you'll enjoy getting acquainted."

Before Bronowski had a chance to gather his wits, the newcomers each grabbed an arm and started dragging him away.

The bleak knowledge of what awaited him was reflected in his eyes. "Alastair, you can't do this. You're making a mistake."

Swanbeck chuckled. "No, old chap, you made the mistake. Besides, I'm not doing anything. I came to admire the roses." He jerked his chin and Bronowski was removed from his sight.

A low grunt floated to his ears as he turned back to the flowers. He shook his head. *Resistance is useless, Igor*, he thought. *Save face and take things like a man.*

He stared down at the fake diamond in his hand and then tucked it back into its box. He was not best pleased with the way things had turned out. He pursed his lips. All his careful plans had been upended.

What was it Igor had said? A Symington's investigator had been present when the Blue Angel changed hands. *Symington's*. Of course, it was Longdon. This was his doing. But how could he be sure that Igor's bid would be the winning one? He had to have had help. Emmeline? Swanbeck dismissed this idea. He had her in view during the entire auction and then Royce took her under his protection.

Royce, yes. He nodded. *That makes perfect sense. Victor and Longdon are working together. Victor kept bidding to boost the price, leaving Igor with little choice but to follow suit.* No wonder he had been so smug outside Sotheby's. Swanbeck heard Royce's voice again in his head.

'You know it doesn't do to be over-confidant. Remember what happened to Icarus.'

Bloody hell, Victor, you have my diamond, Swanbeck cursed to himself. *You've interfered with my plans once too often. It's time to clip your wings. Once and for all.*

Then he would deal with Longdon. And dear Emmeline. It

would be ungentlemanly to leave her out of the fun. All in good time, though.

He drew his mobile out of his pocket and pressed a pre-set number. His call was answered on the second ring.

"Jason, we need to accelerate our plans."

"Alastair, we can't move forward with the merger yet. Just give me a little bit more time. I'm sure I can bring Dad round."

Swanbeck chuckled. "You've been saying that for the last six months. I see no evidence that Victor has softened his stance. In fact, he appears even more against it. Of course, it's your choice. Either you can take the reins of Royce Global Holdings or remain in your father's shadow forever. A mere errand boy. Is that what you want?" He paused and then twisted the knife in the wound. "After all, we both know that Adam is his favorite son."

He severed the connection.

CHAPTER 26

Royce stared out the library window at the garden. The shadows were deepening as the wind chased the clouds across the indigo sky. He caught a last glimpse of the moon before her light was snuffed out. They would probably have rain overnight.

His hand let go of the drape. It fell back into place with a muffled swish. He walked over to the drinks table and poured himself a large Scotch. He took it over to the desk and lowered himself into his chair with a sigh. It was quiet in the house.

He pinched the bridge of his nose. For the first time in his life, he suddenly felt old. Every part of his body was tired, but he didn't want to go to bed. Not just yet. He sat up and rolled the tumbler between his hands. His eye fell on the manila envelope with the papers Stan had drawn up. His fingers traced a pattern across the front. The corners of his mouth twitched into a smile. It couldn't bring back all those lost years, but he had tried to atone for them.

His mind was torn from these musings when the door opened. A triangle of light from the front hall spilled onto the Persian carpet.

"Oh, you're still here," Lily said, evidently startled to find him in the library. "I thought you had gone to bed already. It's after midnight."

"Yes, I know. Did you want something?"

She hesitated on the threshold for an instant and then crossed to the desk. "No, I was on my way to the kitchen to make some hot milk. I thought you had forgotten and left the light on. You often do. I'll leave you to it." She pivoted on her heel.

"Of course," he murmured to her retreating back. "Why should you want to talk me?"

With her hand on the knob, she had half-turned toward him again. "Pardon?"

Victor leaned back in his chair and held her gaze for a long moment. "What happened to us, Lily? We used to be happy. To love each other. At the beginning. And now…" His voice trailed off.

She closed the door and pressed her back against it. "Victor, our marriage was a mistake."

He snapped his fingers. "Just like that. How detached and clinical." He paused and shook his head. "All these years. Then why go on?" His voice was a hoarse whisper.

The physical space that separated them spoke volumes about their empty lives together. The silence that engulfed the room was deafening.

Lily's eyes never left his face. The intensity of her stare was too much. He tossed back a swig of Scotch.

"Victor, really. Don't be so naïve. We had a certain image to maintain. We couldn't have your mother saying, 'I told you so.'"

He downed the rest of his Scotch. "So we lived a lie. Doesn't that bother you?"

She shrugged and pushed herself away from the door. "I stopped caring a long time ago. Nothing you do bothers me anymore. I suggest you go to bed."

Her silk dressing gown rustled faintly as she slipped from the room. And then he was alone again.

As I always have been, I suppose, he thought.

A wave of nausea roiled his stomach as he mourned his wasted life. If only…

His vision began to swim. The room rose up, teetered, and came crashing down. It spun round and round. He pressed his palms to his temples. Dizziness was crushing his brain.

His hands dropped limply onto his lap. His arms and legs felt so heavy. His muscles were going slack. He was losing control of his body. He gasped, trying desperately to draw oxygen into his lungs.

No air. *No air.* His head slumped onto the desk with a *thud.* He was grateful when the darkness finally swallowed him in its embrace.

⚙⚙⚙

Lily breezed into the dining room the next morning to find the maid checking if more toast was needed.

"Good morning, Mrs. Royce. Would you like anything in particular? Poached eggs, perhaps?"

"That would be fine, Karen. Thank you."

She glanced round, noticing her husband was not ensconced at the other end of table, enjoying his second cup of coffee and munching on toast with marmalade, with the *Financial Times* spread out before him.

"Has Mr. Royce left for the office already? I wanted to discuss something with him."

"As far as I know, he hasn't come down yet."

Lily frowned. Her eyes strayed to the clock on the mantelpiece. "That's not like him. He'll be late for work."

"Would you like me to go upstairs and knock on his door, Mrs. Royce?"

"Yes, please."

The maid hurried out of the room.

Lily crossed to the table and poured herself a cup of coffee. She took a sip, tapping her long, tapered fingers on the cloth as she waited.

Karen returned a few minutes later, two vertical lines of concern between her brows. "I knocked on Mr. Royce's door several times—rather forcefully—but he's not responding."

Lily rose to her feet, banging her cup back down on the table. She rolled her eyes to the ceiling. "How tiresome." She sighed as Karen's gaze lingered on her face. "I suppose I'd better go up and check. As if I don't have better things to do."

"Yes, ma'am. Shall I call Dr. Carruthers?"

Lily pursed her lips. "I don't want to bother him unnecessarily. It's probably nothing. Mr. Royce may have overslept. Wait until I've seen him."

"Of course."

She returned to the hall almost immediately.

Karen hadn't moved from her spot at the foot of the stairs. "Is Mr. Royce all right? Should I go ring the doctor now?" she asked anxiously.

Lily clasped her hands together at her waist, hoping that her irritation didn't show. "He wasn't in his room. I'm going to ring the office. Please go and check if Jeremy is here. If he is, bring him to me at once in the library. I want to know whether Mr. Royce asked to be driven somewhere in particular this morning."

"Yes, Mrs. Royce." Karen set off at a cross between a trot and a run in the direction of the garage.

Lily took a deep breath as she watched the maid's retreating figure. The ghost of yesterday's headache beat against her temple as she walked toward the library.

She rapped lightly on the door. "Victor?"

There was no answer, so she turned the knob and popped her head round the door. "Victor, are you—" She sucked in her breath when she saw her husband hunched over the desk. She was by his side in two strides. "*Victor*," she said, louder this time as she shook him.

He didn't move a muscle.

She went and pulled the drapes open to bring more light into the room. Then she knelt down by the desk. "Victor." Her voice was low and breathy. Nothing.

Her hand hovered near his waxen cheek. She hesitated for a second and then her fingertips confirmed what her mind already knew. Beneath his cold, cold skin, his life's blood was no longer flowing. It had stopped. Forever.

Victor was dead and she felt...*nothing.*

The door rattled on its hinges, startling her momentarily. Jeremy, the chauffeur, had flung it wide open.

"Karen told me about Mr. Royce. I didn't drive him—" He broke off when his eyes fell on his employer's immobile form.

His gaze shot to her face. "Mrs. Royce?"

"It seems that my husband is dead," she said as she crumpled to the floor.

CHAPTER 27

Superintendent Burnell's face was set in grim lines as he and Sergeant Finch entered the library in the Royce townhouse in Cheyne Walk. Burnell nodded to a couple of members of the forensic team. Someone handed them each a pair of rubber gloves.

Dr. Meadows was examining Royce. He offered his old friend a half-smile. "Oliver." Then he inclined his head toward Finch. "Here we are again. This is a bit much even for you. Three bodies within a week."

Burnell pursed his lips. "Believe me, John, my ulcer is quite put out." He shook his head as he circled the desk to observe Royce. "We just saw Royce yesterday. He looked perfectly fine. So what was it? A heart attack? A stroke?"

"I'll know more after I've done the post-mortem," Meadows replied circumspectly.

Burnell caught something in his tone. He saw that Finch had heard it too. "John, why so tight-lipped? What aren't you telling me?"

Meadows lowered his voice. "Outwardly, it appears to be a heart attack."

"But?" prompted Finch.

"You know, you're getting to be as bad as your boss." He jerked his thumb at the superintendent. "If you're not careful, you'll become as crusty as he is."

Finch's mouth curved into a smile. "I'll take that as a compliment, Dr. Meadows."

"Flattery will get you nowhere, Finch," Burnell said. Although his words were sharp, his tone was light. "John, I trust your instincts. What do you suspect?"

"I won't know for certain until the postmortem is finished, but I think this might be another case of poison."

"Just like Sabitov," Finch murmured. "It can't be a coincidence, sir."

Burnell sighed. "Not unless we have two mad poisoners on the loose in London. But how the devil can we tie them together?"

Meadows clapped him on the back. "Ah, well, there I can't help you, chaps. I'm a man of science. I'll leave the detecting business to you."

Burnell pulled a face. "Thanks very much. If you were a true friend, you'd use your scientific expertise and slip something into Cruickshank's coffee. Nothing to cause permanent damage, mind you. Just something to incapacitate him for a while to give me a little breathing room."

Meadows chuckled. "I would love to help you, Oliver. But it would go against the Hippocratic Oath."

The superintendent sniffed. "I always knew you were too honest for your own good."

Meadows peeled his rubber gloves off and extended a hand toward his friend. "Happy hunting. Can we take the body now?"

Burnell shot one last glance at Royce and nodded wordlessly.

He and Finch took a turn around the room, careful not to get in the forensics team's way.

Burnell gazed out the window at the garden. If it was foul play, no one could have gotten into the room that way.

He folded one arm across his broad chest and stroked his beard with his other hand. His practiced eye took in the desk and zeroed in on the empty tumbler that had rolled to the ground, probably when Royce passed into oblivion. *If it was poison*, he reasoned, *it had to be in his drink*.

His glance strayed to the drinks table to his left. He walked over to it. Three decanters resided on a silver tray.

He called out to one of the forensics team members and waved a hand at the tray, "Fingerprints?"

"Not yet, sir. Next on my list."

Burnell's lips were twisted in a grimace. "Good. Although I'm not holding out much hope. It would be too easy for our killer to have left fingerprints behind."

"Sir," Finch said close to his ear, "you're going on the assumption that this was murder."

The superintendent lifted an eyebrow. "Aren't you?" He pounded his fist against the open palm of his other hand. "We should never have gone along with that charade Longdon and Royce concocted at Sotheby's."

"You think that Swanbeck sussed it out and had Royce killed?"

"My bet is on him given his history with Royce. It was either him or Bronowski."

"But, sir, how could anyone have gotten into the house? Someone would have seen him. Besides, Royce had a sophisticated security system."

"It could have been a delivery man. It could have been..." He let his sentence trail off as his gaze swept the room again. "Oh, I don't know. At this stage, we're running blind. Go interview the servants. I want to know everyone who came in and out of the house yesterday. Everyone."

"Right, sir. I'll—"

He broke off when Willard, the Royces' butler tapped on the door asking to see the officer in charge.

"That would be me," Burnell said as he weaved his way to the door with Finch in tow. He extended a hand to the servant, who had to be about fifty, well-groomed, with steel-gray hair that fell diagonally across his broad forehead, above wide brown eyes flecked with gold. Clearly, the man was distressed. His square jaw was clenched in a hard line, but he appeared to be doing his best to retain an outward air of calm. "I'm Superintendent Burnell and this is Sergeant Finch. How can we help you?"

Willard dipped his head deferentially at the two detectives.

"As you can imagine, Mrs. Royce is extremely upset. She fainted when she found Mr. Royce. However, she has refused to accept the sedative Dr. Carruthers prescribed. She insists on speaking to the officer in charge."

"I see. Where is Mrs. Royce now?"

"She's upstairs in the drawing room."

"Right. Finch and I will go up to her straightaway."

Relief washed over Willard's face. "Thank you, Superintendent."

"However, my sergeant would like to interview all the servants after we speak to Mrs. Royce. Please have them make themselves available."

"Of course, sir." Then, he turned to Finch. "Sergeant, I will make sure that everyone is at your disposal whenever you're ready."

They followed him into the hall. He started to lead them toward the staircase.

"Willard, we don't want to keep you from your duties. Things have been disrupted enough as it is today. We'll find our own way to the drawing room."

The butler's brow puckered. Apparently he was not enamored of the idea of policemen tramping about the house, but there was not much he could do about it. "Very well, Superintendent. It's the first door on the left just off the landing."

Burnell nodded his thanks and they began climbing the stairs.

Out of the corner of his mouth, Finch whispered, "I can feel the chap's eyes boring a hole through my shoulder blades."

"It's the shifty look on your face. He probably thinks you're a master criminal who has wormed his way into the house under false pretenses."

"Ha. Ha. Why can't you be the one with the shifty look?"

Burnell stopped and turned to him. "Because the man is perceptive and can recognize an experienced detective when he comes face to face with one."

"I bow to your wisdom, oh mighty one," was Finch's sarcastic rejoinder.

"As well you should, my lad. Meadows was right. You're becoming too cheeky for your own good. Longdon has been a bad influence on you. We'll have to do something to remedy matters."

There was no time for more. They had arrived in front of the drawing room door. Burnell raised his hand and tapped lightly with two fingers.

"Yes," a muffled female voice came from within.

Burnell reached for the handle and opened the door.

Shafts of sunlight flooded through the bow window, bouncing off the creamy walls and Aubusson carpet to give the rectangular room a cozy air. There was an ivory silk-upholstered chaise next to one of the fireplaces, and an elegant Hepplewhite table polished to an envious gleam in the center of the room. A large porcelain urn—Ming dynasty? Burnell wondered—was positioned next to the fireplace on the opposite wall.

Mrs. Royce was perched on the window seat, half her face in shadow. She rose when they entered the room and met them halfway.

Burnell proffered his hand. "I'm Superintendent Burnell and this Sergeant Finch. We're very sorry for your loss, Mrs. Royce."

Her handshake was brisk and cool. "Thank you, Superintendent. Won't the two of you please sit down?"

She gestured toward the chairs on either side of the Hepplewhite table, while she resumed her place on the window seat.

Burnell marveled at her reserve. If he were honest with himself, he was a bit mesmerized by her. She was still a beautiful woman. Two vertical lines bracketed the sides of her mouth and her jawline had slackened with the passing of the years. But they only seemed to enhance her innate elegance. Wrinkles fanned out from the corners of her eyes. Oh those eyes, though. He had never seen eyes that shade. Turquoise. And those eyes were fixed on him at the moment.

He cleared his throat. "Your butler said that you wanted to see us."

"Yes, I was wondering why such a fuss was being made. It's obvious that my husband died of heart attack."

Finch shot a glance at him, but quickly returned his attention to his open notebook.

"We haven't spoken to his GP yet, so naturally we don't know the state of Mr. Royce's health. Did your husband suffer from a heart condition?"

She tucked back a strand of red-gold hair that come loose and then clasped her hands together in her lap again. "Not as far as I'm aware, but then Victor was a proud man and may not have wanted people to know."

Burnell raised an eyebrow. "I see. We will find out from his doctor. However, Mrs. Royce, I must let you know that the medical examiner has raised some questions about your husband's death."

She sat bolt upright. "Questions? What do you mean?"

It was always tricky trying to find the words to tell someone that their loved one may have been murdered. "Of course, tests have to be conducted, but the medical examiner suspects that Mr. Royce may not have died of natural causes." He paused. "It's very likely that he was murdered."

"*What?*" she hissed, disbelief etched on her features. Her stunned gaze raked over their faces. "You can't be serious." When neither detective answered, she went on, "Who would want to kill Victor?"

"As I said before, nothing is certain. Yet." His eyes met hers. "But the medical pathologist is an expert in his field and I trust his instincts."

Her hand went to the choker at her throat, her long fingers twining around the finely shaped pearls. "I see. I can't believe—It makes absolutely no sense. I'll never forget finding Victor dead and now to learn—" She swallowed hard. "It's all so overwhelming." She turned her head toward the window behind her. The room fell silent. The detectives waited, giving her time to regain her composure. Although her voice was low and hoarse when she faced them again, what was likely her normal demeanor of stoic aloofness was firmly back in place. "Please forgive me."

"Not at all, Mrs. Royce. It's the shock setting in."

"I suppose it must be." She pulled her shoulders back. "However, I have always prided myself that I can handle any situation."

"This is rather an unusual circumstance," Finch remarked, his tone gentle and sympathetic.

Her mouth curved into a watery smile. "You're very kind, Sergeant."

"Ahem, Mrs. Royce, do you feel strong enough to answer a few questions?" Burnell ventured tentatively. After all, they did have another dead body on their hands.

He saw her stiffen slightly. "Yes, I believe so."

"Good. Can you think of anyone who would want to harm your husband? Did he have any enemies? A business rival perhaps?"

Her eyebrows knit together in concentration. She shook her head. "The only person that I can think of off the top of my head is Alastair Swanbeck." The two detectives exchanged a surprised look at the mention of Swanbeck, but she didn't seem to notice. "There was a lot of bitterness between the two of them over a collapsed business deal a few years back. Swanbeck even made a hostile takeover bid for the company at one point, but Victor managed to stop him in his tracks. Of course, I'm not as involved in the company as I used to be. My sons would know better than I would if there was anyone else."

"Right, we had planned to speak with them in any case," Burnell said. He saw her brows knit together. "Did you think of someone else?"

"No, it's just that I thought Swanbeck was completely out of our lives. Until yesterday." Her words were measured.

"Did something particular happen yesterday?"

Her blue-green gaze locked on his face. "I came home in the afternoon to find Victor having tea with our son, Adam, and that journalist."

"Journalist? What journalist?" Finch asked, although he had a fairly good idea who it could be.

"Oh, you should know. After all, the police questioned her after that Russian fellow was poisoned at the Dorchester the other day."

Finch swallowed hard. "You mean Emmeline Kirby?"

"That's her," Mrs. Royce sneered. "She wormed her way

into my husband's good graces. I warned him not get too cozy with the press. All she's after is a story. Do you know she even used her feminine wiles to get Victor to invite her—without asking me, mind you—to our annual summer party?"

Burnell cleared his throat and sought to take control of the conversation before it devolved any further. "Right, what we're really interested in is yesterday afternoon. You said that Miss Kirby had tea with Mr. Royce and your son.

She snorted. "Yes, apparently there had been some unpleasantness earlier with Swanbeck and Victor thought the poor, little miss was in need of some protection."

Burnell felt Finch's eyes on him, but he focused his attention on Mrs. Royce. "I see," he mumbled.

"Swanbeck hadn't bothered us in years and, all of a sudden, when *she* appeared on the scene, he came out of the woodwork again. I knew she was trouble when she came to the party. She's probably conspiring with Swanbeck to destroy the company. I should have followed through on my initial instinct and had her thrown out. I'm not too sure about that fiancé of hers either."

"Of course, we'll speak to Miss Kirby—"

She cut across him. "See that you do." He felt every word slice through him.

"Yes. When was the last time you saw Mr. Royce?"

"It was last night. I couldn't sleep and went down to make myself some warm milk. I saw the light on in the library and thought that Victor had gone to bed and had forgotten to turn it off. When I walked in, he was sitting there at his desk."

"What time was this?" Finch prompted.

"I think it was a little after midnight. I told Victor that it was late and that he should go to bed."

"Excuse me, Mrs. Royce, I'd like to clarify a point," Burnell broke in. "Didn't you know that your husband wasn't in bed when you came down?"

"We sleep—slept in separate bedrooms," she replied matter-of-factly, without a trace of embarrassment.

Finch slid a sideways glance at his boss, but kept jotting down notes.

"I see," the superintendent murmured.

"We've led rather separate lives for many years," she went on.

Burnell digested this information.

I don't blame Royce. If I were married to an ice queen like you, perhaps I'd want a separate bedroom too. Even an entire wing, he told himself. Her beauty, which had so captivated him at the outset of this interview, now seemed to pale upon further acquaintance.

"...and that's when I found him in the library. You know the rest of the story."

Finch had obviously asked her about her movements this morning as Burnell's mind had drifted off.

Burnell put his hands on his thighs and pushed his bulk to his feet. Finch took his boss's cue and closed his notebook, tucking it into the inside pocket of his suit jacket as he stood too.

"Thank you, Mrs. Royce. That will be all for the moment. We'll keep you apprised of developments in the case."

She slowly rose and shook his hand. "I would appreciate that."

"I'm going to leave Finch behind to interview your servants. I already spoke to your butler about it."

"Certainly." She turned to the sergeant. "Tell Willard I said that you could use the dining room."

"Thank you, Mrs. Royce. That would be helpful."

She took a step forward. "I'll see you out, Superintendent."

Burnell put up a hand. "Please don't disturb yourself. That's not necessary. I know the way. I'm sure you have other things that you must attend to."

She hesitated for a second. "I do, actually. I have to make the arrangements for Victor's funeral." She nodded her head in dismissal. "Good day, gentlemen."

They hadn't yet reached the door and she had already forgotten their existence. Burnell saw over his shoulder that she was ensconced once again in the window seat and was talking on the phone.

A low whistle escaped Finch's lips, once they were alone

in the corridor. "Emmeline seems to have stepped on Mrs. Royce's toes."

"Yes," Burnell replied distractedly as they followed the curve of the staircase. "She and Royce must have run into Swanbeck after the auction yesterday. We both saw Swanbeck in the audience. He knew Royce was the other bidder for the Blue Angel. It must have been a nasty confrontation, if Royce felt it necessary to bring Emmeline back here at the risk of her running into his wife. We'll have to talk to her, of course."

"I'll ring Emmeline and ask her to come down to the station this afternoon."

The superintendent nodded as they reached the bottom step. "In the meantime—"

Whatever he had been about to say was interrupted by the peal of his mobile. He pulled it out of his inside pocket. "Burnell. Yes, sir."

He rolled his eyes and mouthed, "*Cruickshank.*" Finch bit back a smile.

The superintendent turned his attention back to his mobile. "Finch and I are at the Royce house now. Meadows thinks that Royce's death is not as straightforward as it at first appeared. They've removed the body and the forensics team will be finishing up soon. Finch is going to interview the servants."

"Yes, yes, Burnell."

Was that a tinge of irritation he detected in Cruickshank's tone? *What a pity. The Boy Wonder is peeved.* Aloud he said, "I just wanted to keep you in the loop, sir."

He heard the assistant commissioner groan in his ear. "You've done that. Now listen. We have another problem on our hands."

Burnell raised an eyebrow in Finch's direction. "Problem, sir?"

"Yes, they just fished Igor Bronowski out of the Thames."

CHAPTER 28

B urnell kneaded the side of his neck with his fingers as best he could. He hadn't slept well last night and there was a knot the size of what he judged must be a boulder lodged between the bottom of his collar bone and the top of his shoulder.

He entered his office, took his suit jacket off with a grunt, and hung it on the back of the door. He crossed to his desk and plunked down into his chair, which protested in displeasure at this intrusion.

It felt good to sit down. He closed his eyes and tipped his head back. He and Finch had been on the go all morning and into the afternoon. They had rushed from the Royce house to the murky, churning waters of the Thames below the golden magnificence of the Houses of Parliament and in the shadow of Westminster Bridge, where Bronowski's bloated body had decided to make its final public appearance in the most dramatic manner possible.

He let loose a string of curses and sat up straight. Never had he hated a case more than this one. It seemed to be spiraling out of control. Every time they blinked another body turned up.

He shook his head. *Damn and blast.* Royce's murder—for he had no doubt that it *was* murder—bothered him the most. He hadn't even seen it coming. He had been negligent. He had underestimated Swanbeck's audacity. And because of that a man had died.

He pounded his fist against the open palm of his other hand and silently heaped withering criticism upon his weary shoulders.

He looked up when his door opened. Finch walked in bearing a large cup of strong black coffee and something wrapped in wax paper. It was a sausage roll.

"From the canteen," he said. "I thought you might be hungry, seeing as we missed lunch on account of Bronowski."

Burnell gratefully accepted both. He flashed a smile at his sergeant. "Good thinking. Thank you. I'm ravenous." He waved a hand at the chair opposite and Finch sat down, as he unwrapped the sausage roll. After he greedily sank his teeth into it, taking a large bite to tend to the increasing demands of his hunger pangs, he was ready to listen to his sergeant. He took a sip of the scalding coffee and leaned back in his chair. "Anything on Swanbeck's or Bronowski's movements yesterday afternoon after they left Sotheby's?"

Finch flipped through his notes. "I found a witness, a Sotheby's employee, who identified Swanbeck from a photo as the man who appeared to be having a heated argument with Royce and Emmeline on the pavement after the auction. The witness couldn't hear what was being said. It was just an impression she got."

"Never mind. We'll ask Emmeline. She can fill us in on the conversation. By the way, did you ring her and tell her we'd like to speak with her?"

Finch nodded. "Yes, she said that she and Longdon would come in around four-thirty." He glanced at his watch. "Only another half-hour."

"She *and* Longdon. Terrific." He sighed. "Well, like it or not, we need to see him anyway."

"Sir, how is it that Longdon is always embroiled in our cases?"

"What do you take me for? A clairvoyant? Personally, I think someone must have placed a curse on me when I was born, condemning me to the Longdon plague. I don't know what lurks in your deep, dark past so I can't answer for you."

Finch chuckled. "I was just wondering. It doesn't seem fair somehow. There's no doubt that he's a criminal, and yet—much as I hate to admit it—he *has* helped us on our last few cases."

"Mmm," was Burnell's only response.

Longdon set the superintendent's teeth on edge. He gleefully flouted the law, and he was guilty—oh, so guilty—of so many crimes. But should he really be locked behind bars?

Has this case addled my brain? Burnell screamed silently. *Of course, Longdon has to pay for his crimes. And yet what harm has he really done?*

He was jarred from this dangerous line of thought by a soft tap on the door. The next moment, Emmeline walked in with her charming thief of a fiancé by her side.

Oh, how he wanted to wipe that cheeky grin off Longdon's face.

☙❧

"Darling," Longdon murmured and held out the one free chair for Emmeline. He put a hand in the air. "No need for you to disturb yourself, Finch," he said when the sergeant made no move to vacate the other chair. "I'm sure you need your rest."

Finch ignored the dig, inclined his head at Gregory, folded his arms over his chest, and settled back more comfortably.

"Now, then, Oliver." This opening earned Longdon a sharp glance from Burnell. "I do beg your pardon, Superintendent Burnell. Why have you summoned us to your inner sanctum? Have you learned anything new or did you simply miss us?"

"Hmph," Burnell snorted. "There's no doubt everyone misses Emmeline. She's the kind of person that lights up a room." He saw a pink flush color her cheeks. But his smile vanished when he turned back to Longdon. "You, on the other hand, are a completely different story. I try to think of you as little as possible. Out of sight, out of mind, is my policy."

Gregory sniffed. "That's a bit harsh. I always miss you terribly, *Oliver.* And you too, Finch. I wouldn't want you to feel left out."

Burnell exchanged an exasperated look with Finch. *Nothing ever changes.*

"Enough of your mindless chatter, Longdon," the superintendent snapped. "I'm not in the best of moods. The last twenty-four hours have been very active, to say the least."

Gregory arched an eyebrow in askance, while Emmeline scooted to the edge of her chair. Her dark eyes gleamed with excitement. "Oh, yes? A new development? Have you found something to link Swanbeck and Bronowski to the deaths of Melnikov and Sabitov?" she asked, her voice full of eagerness.

"Not exactly. Bronowski is out of the picture completely."

"Really? Why have you ruled him out?"

He shot a glance at Longdon who held his gaze. A wary expression was etched on his handsome features, but he held his tongue.

"Because Bronowski's body rolled in with the morning tide." He let this sink in.

"It had to be Swanbeck. Obviously, they had a falling out," she said.

"Naturally, I can't say yes. We can't prove anything at the moment. The last time anyone saw them both was at Sotheby's. We can't place them together afterward."

"It had to be something to do with the diamond Bronowski and Mr. Royce were bidding for. You were there yesterday you saw how furious the bidding was."

"Ye—es," Burnell replied carefully. His eyes strayed to Gregory again. "That diamond has caused an awful lot of trouble."

"Swanbeck cornered Mr. Royce and me outside Sotheby's," Emmeline said.

"I'm glad you brought up the confrontation. That's why we wanted to see you."

"Swanbeck was in a thoroughly foul mood. He was livid about the Blue Angel. He said that Mr. Royce had interfered with his plans once too often. He was extremely menacing. He also…" Her voice trailed off.

"He also what?" the superintendent prompted.

She swallowed hard. "He also threatened us. Gregory and me."

Longdon squeezed her shoulder. "Emmy, you didn't mention any of this when Royce's son brought you home."

She tipped her head back and offered him a weak smile.

She took his hand and pressed a kiss to his palm. "I—I knew you would be upset and I didn't want you going after him. I'm sorry."

"Bloody right, I would have gone after him."

Then it's a good thing I didn't mention that Swanbeck knows the date of our wedding, she thought. Aloud she said, "This from a man who calls *me* reckless and hot-tempered. What would that have solved? You would have been playing straight into his hands."

Burnell cleared his throat. "Ahem, Longdon, she has a point. Swanbeck wants to distract us any way he can. We can't let him. We have to play this by the book. Otherwise, we'll never get him."

"Oliver, Swanbeck's games are lethal. We can't wait until Emmy becomes his next victim."

Emmeline took his hand and pressed it against her cheek. "I'm all right. I'm just a bit nervy that's all. Swanbeck hasn't been able to do anything to us." *Yet*, her mind pointed out, but she pushed this unnerving thought aside. It wouldn't do for Gregory to see how her encounter with Swanbeck had upset her. To divert the conversation in a different direction, she said, "About the auction." Her eyes impaled each man in turn. "When we were in the car on the way to his house, Mr. Royce inadvertently let it slip that yesterday's little drama was the result of some carefully laid plan that all of you *and* Philip had hatched up to draw out Swanbeck and Bronowski. Something that you all neglected to tell me. Mr. Royce mumbled something about 'a dog with a bone' and keeping me out of harm's way. The time has come for all of you to come clean. If you know what's good for you."

Burnell bit back a smile, but a bemused expression flitted across Gregory's face. Finch was the only one who managed to look somewhat contrite.

"Oh, Emmy," Gregory murmured as he caressed her dark curls.

She shifted slightly in her chair so that his hand slipped away. "Don't 'Oh, Emmy' me. If I hadn't stepped in to cover the auction at the last minute, I would never have known about your scheme."

"Our bad luck," Gregory muttered under his breath.

"What was that?" she asked, an annoyed edge to her voice.

"Nothing, darling." He lifted her hand to his lips and grazed her knuckles with a kiss. "Mea culpa. I now see the error of my ways. Am I forgiven?"

Burnell saw her body relax as Longdon's gaze locked with hers. He marveled at the silky smoothness of the man's charm. *Was there ever a doubt that she would forgive you?* he thought.

"I suppose," Emmeline was saying, "But to atone for your transgression, all of your transgressions—" She shot a glance at the superintendent and Finch as well. "—you will now tell me everything about the Blue Angel. I know there's more to the story. It's too much of a coincidence that Bronowski wound up dead twenty-four hours after the auction"

"Actually, he's not the only one," Burnell mumbled.

Her dark eyes narrowed. "What do you mean?"

The superintendent exhaled a long, slow sigh. "Victor Royce was found dead at his home this morning. It looks like a heart attack."

He saw Emmeline shiver involuntarily. "I can't believe it." Her voice was low and hoarse. "What a lovely man. I just had tea with him yesterday. He was perfectly fine. In robust health. I can't…" Her breath caught in her throat.

Longdon's brow puckered. "You said that it 'looks like' a heart attack. Do you believe it might something else?"

Emmeline's head snapped up and she sat bolt upright. Every nerve in her body appeared alert, as she waited for the superintendent's answer.

Burnell cast a sidelong glance at the door and then met their expectant gazes. "I want it clearly understood that what I'm about to say does not leave this office. It is off record." This last remark was directed at Emmeline.

She gave a mute nod.

"Meadows thinks Royce was poisoned. He won't know for

certain until after postmortem and the toxicology results come back."

A range of emotions chased themselves across Emmeline's delicate features as she collapsed back in her chair, stunned. She shook her head. "*Poison*. Just like Sabitov. How awful. The poor man."

"Yes, well. All deaths are awful." Burnell leaned back in his chair and steepled his fingers over his ample stomach. "Death leaves a sour taste in one's mouth. Especially the violent ones. Man's inhumanity to man." He shook his head. "At the moment, I have a string of bodies piling up and no way to tie them all together." He enumerated on his fingers. "First, there was Melnikov. Then he was followed in swift succession by Sabitov, Bronowski, and Royce."

There was a sharp intake of breath from Emmeline. She leaned forward and propped her elbows on the desk. "I've been a fool. He *told* me when we first met."

"Darling, what are you on about?"

She craned her neck to look up at Longdon. "We can connect the murders. Victor Royce was Rutkovsky."

Burnell planted his feet flat on the floor with a *thud*. "What? How do you know?"

"When I first went to interview Mr. Royce at his office for my profile, he told me about his family's background. His father was a Russian Jew, who was in the Resistance during World War II and managed to escape to England with his girlfriend, who became his wife. His name was Meyer Rutkovsky. He changed his name to Martin Royce when he became a British citizen. Don't you see? Victor Royce took Rutkovsky as some sort of a code name. He had been helping Melnikov and Sabitov to bring down Swanbeck, while putting a few spokes in Putin's wheel at the same time. Sabitov said that Rutkovsky was 'someone special.' I'm right about this. I can feel it in my bones."

She met their stunned expressions with a triumphant smile.

Burnell stroked his beard, but remained silent.

"Oliver, you must admit that it all fits," Longdon remarked.

"Swanbeck somehow found out about Rutkovsky/Royce and had him murdered."

"Sir, now that we know the link, we know what to look for. The other pieces are sure to fall into place," Finch ventured, a cautious smile on his lips at the prospect that they had turned a corner in the case. "Since we've finally identified Rutkovsky, perhaps Mr. Acheson can provide some assistance from his end."

"Ye—es, I'll ring Philip later. But what bothers me is how the devil could Swanbeck have gotten access to Royce's house?"

Longdon waved a hand dismissively in the air. "That's mere child's play for a man like Swanbeck. He wouldn't have done the deed himself. He's too intelligent to get his hands dirty. But he'll want to rub your nose in it. That's the nature of the beast. He likes to taunt. Not everyone can be as charming as I am—"

Burnell rolled his eyes.

"—I say haul him in and browbeat him. You're good at playing the menacing ogre, Oliver."

"Very droll. It's easy for you to say, 'Haul him in.' I—" Burnell jerked his thumb toward his chest. "—have to have probable cause. Our judicial system likes cold, hard evidence. Not a nice theory. Swanbeck's lawyer would file a lawsuit in the blink of an eye."

Longdon gave him a vigorous clap on the shoulder. "You'll think of something. I have every confidence in you, Oliver."

Burnell sighed. "You don't know how comforting that is," he retorted sarcastically.

In response, Longdon flashed one of his dazzling—and most irritating—grins. Really, the man was insufferable.

℘℘℘

Later that evening, Swanbeck was sitting in a high-backed chair in the living room of his Mayfair flat, reading the latest thriller by one of his favorite authors. From time to time, he would take a sip from the brandy balloon on the table at his elbow. It had been a long time since had spent a quiet evening at home.

The telephone chose that precise moment to ring. *Bang goes the quiet evening.*

He sighed and crossed to a small desk in the corner. His mouth curved into a smile when he saw the number.

"I was wondering when I'd hear from you," he said, foregoing any greeting. "Now that I've helped you with your little problem, it's time you kept your end of the bargain and give me what I want. Otherwise, I promise you'll regret it for whatever time is left in your life."

CHAPTER 29

The Bronowski story was the leader in *The Clarion*, as it was in all the other papers the next day. Superintendent Burnell had no problem with giving Emmeline a few quotes for her article. Although Scotland Yard was going to handle Bronowski's murder like any other case, no one was going to shed a tear about a dead Russian mobster. Good riddance was the general consensus.

The other story on the front page, of course, was the unexpected death of Victor Royce, international businessman, philanthropist, art connoisseur, father, husband, and friend. His passing sent ripples of shock around the world. Already his loss was being deeply mourned. Naturally, there was no mention in the article about the possibility that Royce might have been poisoned. Emmeline prided herself on her journalistic integrity and scruples. She had promised Burnell that she would not write or utter a word about this sinister prospect until there was some sort of official confirmation. Likely, it would be a few more days before Dr. Meadows completed all his tests. She would wait. And then, she would not stop until Royce's killer was locked away in a dark jail cell. Although their acquaintance had been brief, he had been a kind and thoughtful man, and she had liked him. She felt she owed it to him to see that justice was served.

Emmeline stared blankly at her computer monitor. Her body shuddered slightly as a sigh rose up from deep within her lungs and was released as a long, slow breath. Victor Royce's death brought to the fore thoughts of her parents. Another murder. She had been so sure that she was finally onto something, but then her lead abruptly petered out. *Somebody, somewhere, has to know something*, she reasoned. It was a matter of finding the right key.

She sat up. She decided she would tackle Philip again about her parents and the fact that they had identified Royce as the elusive Rutkovsky. Philip's dual roles at the Foreign Office and MI5 put him in an ideal position to help her with both issues. He had so many contacts. This lifted her mood. She would get her answers. No matter how long it took.

She was about to reach for her phone to call Philip, when it rang of its own accord.

She picked up the receiver. "Hello, Emmeline Kirby."

"Ah, hello, Miss Kirby," a soft-spoken, well-modulated male voice said into her ear. "My name is Stanley Horowitz, senior partner at Horowitz, Shandwick, and Musgrove. I was Victor Royce's solicitor and his friend since we were boys."

"My condolences, Mr. Horowitz. I'm certain you feel Mr. Royce's loss keenly. I only knew him for a short time. He was very kind to me. To a close friend and his loved ones, I can only imagine how deeply caring and thoughtful he had been."

There was a brief pause. She thought she heard him sniffle. "Yes," Horowitz finally replied, his voice gruff. "There was no better man than Vic. I will miss him greatly."

"Mr. Horowitz, I'm sure you didn't ring me, a stranger, to discuss Mr. Royce. How can I help you?"

He cleared his throat and became brisk and businesslike. "Vic's funeral is Saturday. But I was wondering whether you could pop round my office on Monday afternoon at two o'clock?"

She flipped through her diary. "I'm afraid I have a meeting on Monday. What's all this about?"

"It's a rather important and delicate matter. It has to do with Vic's death. That's all that I'm prepared to say over the phone."

Emmeline's pulse started racing. Perhaps he knew something about the Rutkovsky business. Maybe Royce left some papers in his keeping. "If it's that important, I'll reschedule my meeting. I'll be there on Monday at two."

"Thank you for understanding the need for discretion. I appreciate it. The address is Fifty-Fifty-Two Chancery Lane."

She scribbled it down. "Got it. I look forward to meeting you and hearing what you have to say about Mr. Royce."

She replaced the receiver and drummed her fingers on her desk. She felt a flutter in her stomach. She just had to get through the weekend and then she would be a step closer to the truth. She could almost taste it.

☙❧

Burnell, chin tucked into his chest and hands thrust deep in his pockets, was shuffling along the corridor. His mind was full of the "chat" he had just had with Assistant Commissioner Cruickshank. He still refused to allow Burnell to speak with MI6 about Melnikov, despite what had come to light about Royce/Rutkovsky and the fact that both he and Sabitov had been poisoned.

"Bloody fool," the superintendent muttered under his breath.

"Sir," Finch hissed from somewhere behind him.

He stopped and turned around. He waited for the sergeant to catch up. He could tell that something was amiss. Finch's face was set in hard lines and his brown eyes held a look of anxious concern.

"What is it?"

Finch waved a manila envelope. "I think you should take a look at this, sir. In your office. Now."

Burnell raised an eyebrow in askance, as he took the envelope. "All right."

Neither one uttered a word until the superintendent was settled behind his desk and Finch dropped into the chair opposite him.

Burnell slipped his glasses onto the bridge of his nose. "Right. What's this?"

"Sir, I was going through all the papers we found in Royce's library." Finch paused and swallowed. He jerked his chin toward the envelope. "That was under his hand when he died. He must have just finished reading it."

"From the expression on your face, it has a significant bearing on the case."

Finch nodded. "I would say so, yes."

Burnell pulled out a sheaf of papers. "It's Royce's will." He shot a glance at the sergeant and then proceeded to read through the document.

Everything appeared to be fairly routine, until the last paragraph. His eyes widened in disbelief. "Good Lord."

He read it again to make sure, but there was no way to misinterpret what was there in black and white.

He took off his glasses and tossed them onto the desk.

"It can't be true, can it, sir?"

"It has to be. But my God." He sat back and stared at Finch, whose stunned expression must have mirrored his own. "It puts quite a different complexion on the case."

"Yes," Finch mumbled. "Royce changed his will only last week."

The superintendent frowned. "Did he? I see. A strong motive for murder, wouldn't you say?"

"Yes, but sir, you can't possibly think…" Finch allowed his sentence to trail off.

"Normally, I would be over moon if something like this dropped into our laps." Burnell shook his head. "Not this time." He straightened up, his gaze locking on Finch's face. "However, we have to follow *every* lead that presents itself. No matter where it takes us," he said gruffly. "This is a case like any other case."

"Respectfully, sir, you don't seriously believe that?"

Burnell pursed his lips and was quiet for a moment. When he spoke again, his voice was low and held a hard edge. "We are sworn to uphold the law. Murder goes against the natural order of a safe world. Without the law, there is chaos."

ↇↄↇↄ

Gregory had trotted along to the Savoy and spent a tedious two hours exerting his considerable charm to reassure one of Symington's newest clients, a crusty old widow who was probably born with that sour look on her face, that everything possible was being done to investigate the disappearance of her diamond necklace. No, she didn't have to remind him—but she did several times—that it was the last gift from her dear departed husband and she cherished it. He had told her to leave the matter to him. He assured her it would be his top priority. That seemed to mollify the old biddy and at last he was able to escape.

He stepped out onto the pavement outside the hotel. This making an honest living was highly overrated in his opinion. He sighed. Ah, the things he did for love. He hoped Emmy appreciated the sacrifices he was making for her. Was she worth it? His mouth curled into a smile. There was no question about it.

A black Mercedes pulled up in front of him and blocked his path. "Oi, Longdon, this is your lucky day," the driver said as he got out. He was a beefy fellow with closely cropped sandy hair. His sunglasses hid his eyes, so that their color and the expression they held were a mystery.

Well, not quite a mystery, Gregory thought when the man grabbed his arm. *I would say it was the up-to-no-good look. Rather a cheek, in fact.*

"Get in," the man ordered, making sure Gregory caught a glimpse of the bulge of a holstered gun beneath his jacket.

Gregory flashed a smile and shook off his grasp. He shot his cuffs and straightened his suit jacket. "Do be careful, old chap. Savile Row, you know. As for your gracious invitation, I'm afraid I'm going to have to decline. I don't make a habit of consorting with unsavory types." He looked the man up and down. He shook his head and clucked his tongue. "Yes, most unsavory. Have a pleasant afternoon."

He inclined his head and tried to step off the curb, but the man took hold of his arm again. Gregory felt his fingers digging into the fleshy part between the muscles of his upper arm. "None of your lip, Longdon. Get—in—the—car," he hissed in Gregory's ear. "I'm not going to ask nicely again."

Gregory's eyebrow quirked upward. "Was that nicely? I failed to catch the subtle nuance in your tone."

In lieu of a reply, the man elbowed him in the ribs.

Oof. The wind was knocked out of him for several seconds. It was enough time for the back door to swing open. He was unceremoniously shoved inside.

He landed with a plop next to Swanbeck, who sat there staring at him with a bemused gleam in his damned green eyes.

Once he got his breath back, Gregory said, "Alastair, what a surprise. It's been ages. Was this manhandling really necessary? If you had wanted to see me that badly, you could have rung me. We could have met at the pub for a pint and had a chinwag about the good old days."

Swanbeck smiled. "You always were too glib for your own good, Longdon." He glanced up at the rearview and met the driver's gaze. "Go."

As the car pulled smoothly away from the Savoy and merged into traffic on the Strand, he turned his attention back to Gregory. "You've been very lucky until now, but no man's luck lasts forever. I'd say you've just about used up your nine lives. In the end, your charm is going to be your undoing. And dear, sweet Emmeline's. She's quite a catch. I never would have thought that she was your type." He shrugged. "But then, what do I know? They say love is blind."

Gregory's jaw clenched, but he willed himself to keep his features neutral. He rested his hands lightly on his knees, although they itched to punch Swanbeck on the nose. Oh, how he wanted to hear the satisfying crunch of bone breaking. *Alas, one can't have everything in life.* And at this moment, his life and Emmy's were his only concern.

"What do you want, Alastair?" he asked. His tone was level, calm. He even managed a touch of aloofness.

Swanbeck threw his head back and laughed. "Did you hear that, Tom?" he called to the driver. "The man wants to know what I want."

"Very amusing, Mr. Swanbeck," driver replied over his shoulder.

The mirth was gone when Swanbeck's gaze pierced Gregory with its venom. "It's very simple. I want what's mine,

Longdon." His voice was low and dangerous. "I want the Blue Angel."

Gregory smoothed down the corners of his mustache. The smile that played upon his mouth was intended to provoke. It got under one's skin and wouldn't let go. "The Blue Angel?" He brushed an imaginary piece of lint from his immaculate trouser leg. "The last time I heard, your mate Bronowski bought it at Sotheby's." He leaned in closer to Swanbeck, his lips pursing into a low whistle. "And a pretty penny he paid too. I wouldn't know personally—not being the obsessive sort, you understand—but I suppose, when collectors set their mind on an object, they simply have to have it at any price."

"In this case, it was very high price indeed and nothing to show for it in the end. But you would know all about that, wouldn't you?"

Gregory put a hand to his chest. "Me? I have no idea what you're on about, old chap."

Swanbeck smiled, but it didn't touch his eyes, which were as forbidding as a roiling sea with a storm approaching fast. "It's a fake. Worthless glass."

Gregory clucked his tongue and shook his head. "How shocking. But why would you care, Alastair? It's Bronowski's problem, surely." He put a hand to his mouth. "Oh, silly me. Bronowski's left the Blue Angel and the rest of his earthly cares behind, hasn't he?"

"The Blue Angel is mine," Swanbeck said through gritted teeth.

"Let me get this straight. Bronowski bought the Blue Angel for you as a present? Nice to have such generous friends. Pity he decided to cheat you in the end, though."

"Longdon, you're beginning to wear on my nerves."

"I'll have to try harder. It's rather difficult to be at one's best in such confined quarters."

Gregory saw a blue vein in the other man's temple pulsing furiously beneath his skin.

"I want my diamond. I know you have it. It was either you or Royce and I know he doesn't have it. Poor old Victor is no longer among the living, is he?"

"Not that I'm admitting anything, but how would you know that Victor Royce didn't have the Blue Angel, if, in fact, it is missing as you contend?"

Swanbeck's mouth twisted into a lupine smile. "Let's just say a little bird told me."

"Would this happen to be the same little bird you sent to help Royce and Bronowski on their journey into the next world, whether they wanted to go willingly or not?" His voice held a steel edge.

"Me?" Swanbeck's tone was full of mock innocence. "Why would you think I had anything to do with their deaths? I'm a simple businessman, trying to eke out an honest living."

Gregory snorted. "Pull the other one, Alastair. You're your father's son. Both of you clawed your way to the top from the dark underbelly of a rock. You made your fortune by stealing and murdering. Along the way, you may have acquired a patina of respectability but, beneath the surface, you're still the same repugnant thug your father sired."

Swanbeck's hand lashed out with lightning speed to deliver a stinging blow to Gregory's unsuspecting cheek.

His skin burned and he saw stars for a second, but male ego prevented him from touching his cheek and instead triggered a brash retort. "Still thin-skinned? Really, Alastair, I'm surprised. I thought by now you would have come to terms with the fact that Walter's thoroughly rotten genes are flowing through your veins. The sooner you accept the truth, the sooner you'll be able to move on."

This earned him another slap, harder than first.

"The diamond or Emmeline. Choose wisely. You won't get a second chance."

The car stopped abruptly and the door was flung open by Tom, who yanked Gregory out by the arm.

"I told you before, Tom, have a care with the suit."

The driver smiled and punched him in the kidney. Pain radiated across his entire body as his knees buckled under him and he collapsed to the pavement. They were somewhere in the vicinity of St. Paul's Cathedral. He was vaguely aware of the car pulling away and traffic rumbling past him. Just at the moment, drawing air into his lungs was of the utmost importance.

Breathe. In, out. In, out. That's it.

Ever so carefully, he rolled onto his side. A couple of passersby rushed to help him to his feet. His legs felt like water, but he assured them that he was all right. No, he did not want to call the police. He merely needed a minute to catch his breath. This suggestion was met with skeptical glances. However, they led him to a bench in the small garden behind the church and left him alone.

He rubbed his back. The throbbing was beginning to ease.

He smiled to himself. Swanbeck was desperate to get his hands on the diamond. The little contretemps in the car proved it. "A bit frustrated, are we, Alastair?" he said aloud.

He chuckled to himself. *Desperation leads to mistakes. The desperate man is no longer thinking clearly. Caution is thrown to the wind.*

Gregory only hoped that Swanbeck was so fixated on getting his hands on the Blue Angel that he gave up any desire to go after Emmy as revenge. It was a slim hope, but the only one he could cling to at the moment.

On the other hand, Emmy never gives up. She will hammer away at it until she finds out who murdered Melnikov, Sabitov, and Royce.

Gregory ran a hand through his hair. Life was much simpler when he only had to worry about evading the police. Emmy was going to be the death of him yet.

CHAPTER 30

The adrenaline was coursing through her veins as Emmeline exited the Chancery Lane Tube station and crossed High Holborn. The prospect of finally getting some answers about Royce and his ties to Melnikov and Sabitov made her quicken her pace as she turned down Chancery Lane and walked the short distance to the red-brick building where the Horowitz, Shandwick & Musgrove offices resided.

She checked her watch as she entered the building and made her way to the lift. It was ten minutes to two. Perfect. She always liked to give herself a little cushion. Gran had instilled in her the importance of always being on time. The doors slid open, and she stepped inside the lift and pressed the button. She rocked back and forth on the balls of her feet during the short ride to the second floor, impatience urging the car to move faster.

At last, she was deposited at her destination. She walked down a short corridor to an open area, where a young woman in a cream-colored blouse and mauve skirt was typing away on her computer.

She looked up when Emmeline approached. "Good afternoon. May I help you?"

Emmeline smiled. "I'm Emmeline Kirby. I have an appointment with Mr. Horowitz."

The woman tucked a long strand of chestnut hair behind her ear and rose to her feet "Oh, yes. Mr. Horowitz is expecting you. The others are already in the conference room. This way, please." She came around the desk and waved an arm in the direction of a closed door.

Emmeline frowned. "Others? I was under the impression

that this would be a private meeting with Mr. Horowitz."

The secretary threw her a quizzical look. "It's not for me to discuss the firm's business. I'm certain Mr. Horowitz will explain everything."

"Yes, I hope so," Emmeline mumbled under breath.

The secretary tapped lightly on the door and then opened it. Emmeline stopped on the threshold when she saw Mrs. Royce, Jason, Adam, and Sabrina seated around an oval table. Adam was the only who smiled when he saw her. She inclined her head.

"What is she doing here?" Lily asked brusquely. "This is a private family matter."

A tall, slim man, whom she guessed was about sixty, with a round face, clear gray eyes, and thinning white hair rose and bustled toward her. He extended a bony hand. "Ah, Miss Kirby, thank you for coming. I'm Stanley Horowitz." His handshake was cool, dry, and efficient. He half-turned to the group around the table. "I believe you know everyone so introductions are not necessary."

Emmeline nodded her head in confusion. "Yes, but I don't understand. I thought—"

He waved a hand to forestall her questions. "Quite. I'm sorry if I misled you over the phone. I assure you everything will become clear very soon. Won't you have a seat?"

He pulled out a chair for her. She searched his gray eyes, but they were devoid of expression. She shrugged her shoulders and lowered herself into the proffered chair.

She set her handbag to one side and folded her hands in front her. She watched as Horowitz resumed his own seat at the other end of the table. Her eyes widened, when for the first time since entering the room, she noticed Superintendent Burnell and Sergeant Finch hovering in a corner just to Horowitz's right.

Her gaze shifted between the two detectives. She opened her mouth to say something, but Burnell gave an infinitesimal shake of his head. She understood. They were here in a professional capacity. It was the only thing she understood.

Why was she here? What was this all about?

"Ladies and gentlemen, we're awaiting one more person and then we can begin."

Mrs. Royce touched Horowitz's sleeve. "Stan, this is most irregular. You still haven't told me why a stranger is—"

At that moment, the door opened again. The secretary, a rose flush upon her cheeks, ushered Gregory into the room. He smiled and thanked her. Her brown gaze lingered on him until she pulled the door closed. Reluctance was written all over her face.

Emmeline rolled her eyes. *Another one who has fallen under his spell.* As this thought occurred to her, she caught a glimpse of Sabrina at the other end of the table. There was no mistaking what was trespassing that nasty little mind of hers.

Emmeline sat up straighter in her chair and threw her shoulders back. *I'll claw those green eyes right out. See if I don't*, she screamed silently.

"Good, Mr. Longdon," Horowitz said. "We're all here now."

"Another outsider, Stan?" Mrs. Royce demanded, her fingers drumming on the table.

"Lily, Mr. Longdon is here as Symington's representative because of some of Victor's bequests."

Gregory inclined his head in her direction.

She sniffed. "Hmph" was her only response.

Gregory bent down and kissed Emmeline's cheek. "Hello, darling," he whispered against her ear as he slipped into the chair beside her.

She threw a questioning look at him, but he merely offered her a smile and focused his attention on Horowitz.

"Right, we can begin." He cleared his throat and became officious. "We are gathered here today for the reading of Victor's will."

Emmeline pursed her lips. The will? Could Royce have left some papers behind for her? She could only hope that was the case.

"There are a number of minor bequests and several charitable donations that I will dispense with at the moment to concentrate on what concerns the family directly."

"Yes, please do, Mr. Horowitz," Sabrina said, checking her watch. "I have a meeting in an hour that I simply can't miss. Just tell me how much Dad left me and I'll be off."

He ignored this callous remark. "I will try to be as brief as possible. Before I begin, I would like to inform you that Victor came to me last week and requested several changes."

"What kind of changes?" Mrs. Royce asked suspiciously.

Horowitz was unfazed by the prickly edge in her tone. "If I may proceed with the reading, all your questions will be answered presently." He adjusted his glasses on the bridge of his nose, took a deep breath, and began to read. "'I, Victor Martin Royce, being of sound mind do dispense of my worldly goods as follows: To my wife, Lily, from whom I grew estranged many, many years ago to my great sadness, I leave our home in Cheyne Walk, which will remain in her possession until the end of her life when it will pass on to our three children, who will share it equally. I also leave Lily the sum of ten million pounds, which should keep her in comfort."

Jason interrupted. "Ten million pounds? And only the house? That's outrageous, Mum. It's quite despicable on Dad's part."

Mrs. Royce patted his hand. "Hush, darling. I'll be all right. I'm quite sanguine about it really. Victor probably chose to leave everything to you, as it should be." She caressed his cheek. "I'm just an old woman. You're young."

Jason snorted in disgust, but refrained from commenting further.

"May I continue?" Horowitz asked.

"Do carry on, Stan. I can hardly wait to see what else Dad has in store for us."

Horowitz adjusted his glasses and picked up where he left off. "'As for Royce Global Holdings Group, Lily will of course retain her share of the company. But day-to-day operations I leave in the joint hands of my sons Adam and Jason. Unfortunately, Jason is too unpredictable and ill-tempered to be trusted to be in sole charge. He has made unforgivable errors in judgment that could have seriously hurt the company. And I know for a fact that he was maneuvering behind the scenes to try to oust me. All decisions regarding Royce Global Holdings Group must be countersigned by both Adam and Jason. Otherwise, they should be considered null and void. I also designate Adam as the executor of my will.'"

Jason jumped to his feet. "The bloody bastard." His green-gray eyes kindling, he rounded on Adam. "This is your doing." He grabbed his brother by the lapels and shook him so hard that his teeth rattled. "You always were the golden boy in Dad's eyes. Never missed an opportunity to blacken my name, did you?" He gave Adam another violent shake.

Adam loosened Jason's fingers from his lapels and quietly rose. Emmeline marveled at his unruffled demeanor. She would have throttled Jason and enjoyed every second of it.

A hair's breadth of space separated the brothers as they glared at one another. Through gritted teeth, Adam retorted, "This is precisely why Dad didn't have any confidence in you."

"Why you—" Jason drew his hand back in a fist.

"Stop it, Jason." Mrs. Royce's voice was like a thunderbolt sent from the heavens. She tugged on his arm. "Sit down. *Both* of you. I have never been so mortified in my life." Her gaze scorched both sons in turn. "Such unseemly outbursts. Sit down." The last two words were infused with all the authority that only mothers possessed.

Adam smoothed out the wrinkles from his suit jacket. "Sorry, Mum," he murmured as he resumed his seat.

Jason dropped back into his chair with a surly grunt. He folded his arms across his chest without uttering any apology. A crimson stain appeared on each cheek. Clearly, he was fuming inwardly.

Gregory leaned his head toward Emmeline. "Brotherly affection is so endearing, don't you find?"

She elbowed him in the ribs and tossed a disapproving stare in his direction. For a second, she thought he winced as if he were in pain. But she must have imagined it because his features assumed their usual insouciant mien almost immediately. "Shh. We don't need you inflaming matters further."

He lowered his voice. "Now, would I do that?"

"Is the sky blue?"

"Actually, it's a bit cloudy at the moment. I think it might rain."

"Incorrigible," she hissed out of the corner of her mouth.

"What was that, darling? You love me terribly. That warms a chap's heart, it does."

She gave him a kick in the ankle under the table.

"Naughty, naughty. You'll do me an injury." This was accompanied by an impish grin.

She rolled her eyes. "What am I going to do with you?"

He raised one eyebrow suggestively. "Anything you like, as far as I'm concerned."

Emmeline felt her cheeks burning. She tore her gaze from his handsome face and made a supreme effort to concentrate on what the solicitor was saying.

"'...I leave the bulk of my estate to my daughter—'"

Jason cut him off. "What? Now, I know Dad was gaga. Of all people. *Sabrina*." He threw his hands up in the air in frustration. "The same Sabrina who went through two husbands in three years and whose interior design business is in a shambles."

All heads turned to Sabrina, whose jaw was gaping open.

Horowitz cleared his throat and went on as if he hadn't been interrupted. "'—I leave the bulk of my estate to my daughter, Emmeline Kirby.'"

CHAPTER 31

Blood thundered in Emmeline's ears and her mouth went dry. She exchanged a startled look with Gregory and then turned back to Horowitz. She couldn't have heard him properly.

Her voice was a rasping croak when she found it at last. "I don't understand. There must be some mistake."

Jason was already on his feet. "It's more than that, it's a bloody lie." He wildly waved an accusatory finger in her direction. "You're not going to get away with this. I don't know what story you told Dad, but you're not going to get your hands on our money, you bloody gold digger. I'm going to hire the best lawyers in the country. Once they get finished with you, you're going to wish that you never heard the name Royce."

Quietly but firmly, Horowitz ordered Jason to sit down. "You're making a spectacle of yourself." His tone was tinged with irritation.

Jason glared at him, but he resumed his seat. Beside him, Mrs. Royce, lips pressed together in a tight line, held her body stiffly and her hands clasped together on the table in front of her. Adam sagged back in his chair, his brow puckered in confusion.

And Sabrina, well, she was still in a daze. One minute she thought she was queen bee and in the next instant she slipped back into insignificance. However, she found her voice at last. "Wait a minute, Stan," she said. Her mouth was twisted into the pout of the spoiled child she always had been. "What about me? Surely Dad must have left me something. The boys got the company."

Horowitz looked her directly in the eye. Whatever his personal opinion of her was, he kept it veiled. "Victor didn't forget you, Sabrina. I was about to get to your bequest when I was interrupted." He glanced back down at the will. "I leave my older daughter, Sabrina, an annuity of three million pounds." Her eyes glittered with delight. "To be placed in a trust administered by Adam because money runs through her fingers like water."

Sabrina scowled. "The old devil. Of all the nerve."

Horowitz ignored her outburst and went on. "I also leave the villa in Cap Ferrat to Sabrina because of all the family, she is the one who loves it best."

In the blink of an eye, her good humor was restored. "Well, that's more like it." She sat back, a smile curling round her lips. She appeared oblivious to the lingering tension in the room.

Horowitz turned his attention back to Emmeline. "Now, Miss Kirby, to answer your question, there is absolutely no mistake. I repeat—" The solicitor threw a warning look at Jason. "—no mistake whatsoever. Victor had a DNA tested performed."

"But how? I never agreed to one and I didn't give him a sample."

"Do you remember the day you first came to Victor's office to interview him?"

She nodded.

"You had tea together. Victor had the DNA from your cup tested."

Emmeline's eyes widened in disbelief. She put a hand up to her mouth and shook her head. Her words came out muffled. "It can't be true. He never said...But how?"

Horowitz pulled an envelope out and held it in the air. "Victor left a letter for you. He knew it would be a shock and wanted to explain things himself. He felt that you deserved that much."

The room fell silent. All eyes followed the solicitor as he solemnly stood up and walked over to her.

Her hands were trembling when she accepted it from him.

There was only one word across the front. Emmeline. It was scrawled in a bold, confident hand. She was vaguely conscious of Gregory murmuring something in her ear, but her brain couldn't make out the words.

She just went on staring at the envelope. She didn't know how long she sat there like that.

When she finally lifted her head, she found herself in the crosshairs of Mrs. Royce's frosty stare. The sheer, naked hatred in those turquoise eyes sliced her to pieces and penetrated deep into her bones.

A frisson slithered down Emmeline's spine. In the space of half an hour, her safe world had been tossed upside down. Nothing was as it seemed. Mummy and Daddy. A sob lodged itself in her throat. Or rather, she should say Aaron Kirby, the man she *thought* was her father was not. How could this be? It didn't make any sense. Mummy and Daddy loved each other. She knew it. She saw it in their eyes. That was the truth. Her gaze fell on the envelope again. And yet, somehow it seemed it wasn't the truth. Her jaw clenched. For the first time in her life, she hated the truth.

Tears blurring her vision, she stumbled to her feet. "I—" She glanced at Gregory helplessly.

He rose and placed his hand on her elbow to steady her. She was grateful for that because she wasn't sure if her legs would hold her up.

"Mr. Horowitz, if there's nothing else you need from Emmy at the moment, I really think she could do with some air."

"Of course. I'll be in touch in a few days. As you can imagine, there are a number of things that I must go over with you, Miss Kirby. But they can wait."

She swallowed hard. "Thank you, Mr. Horowitz."

Gregory slipped his arm around her waist and she gathered up her handbag without casting another look in the direction of the Royces. They only made it as far as the door.

"Is that it, Stan?" Jason's acerbic tone cut through the air. "Are you simply going to let that woman waltz out of here with our money? She's a thief and a liar."

Emmeline stiffened and slowly pivoted around. She

squared her shoulders. "This comes as much of a surprise to me as it does to you. Probably even more so."

Jason snorted. "I very much doubt it. I must admit you've mastered the role of innocent ingénue. The tears, the catch in your voice, the stunned look. It's quite convincing." He raised his hands in the air and clapped. "But you don't fool me. You picked the wrong family for your sordid little scheme."

Mrs. Royce piped up. "Jason, you're only upsetting yourself. Superintendent Burnell—" She turned to the detective, whom Emmeline had completely forgotten about in the wake of the revelations a few minutes earlier. "It occurs to me that if this…this…" She rolled her eyes in disgust at Emmeline. "Miss Kirby knew that my husband had changed his will in her favor then she could very well have been the one who murdered him. Frankly, I'm surprised that this thought did not strike you. After all, wasn't she also on the scene when that Russian was poisoned at the Dorchester? Another poisoning, *just like my husband.* It's rather suspicious, if you ask me. Perhaps, I should take the matter up with your superior."

Emmeline drew in a sharp breath as Burnell's deep blue gaze settled on her face. What she saw there shook her to her core. His eyes held a mixture of sympathy, annoyance, and apology. Apology? Apology for what? For thinking that she could have killed Victor Royce? Could he really believe that?

She shot a glance at Sergeant Finch. He had the good grace to blush under her intense scrutiny. But to her chagrin, the same thoughts were mirrored in his brown eyes.

Had the entire world suddenly gone mad?

"This is utterly ridiculous," Gregory snapped. "Emmy is no more capable of murder than a woolly rabbit. Surely you realize that, Superintendent Burnell?"

Superintendent Burnell? Not *Oliver. Good God, I never thought anything could unfaze Gregory. He must be afraid too.* This sent a shudder through her body.

Burnell's cheeks were flushed beneath his beard. His jaw was set in a hard line. Through gritted teeth, he said, "Mrs. Royce, I assure you that we are doing our utmost to find out who killed Mr. Royce?"

"Hmph. It seems to me that you've been remiss, or simply derelict in your duty—" Burnell stiffened at this slur on his professionalism. "—if you haven't interrogated this woman at the very least. Although I must say, it seems rather curious. Or perhaps it isn't." Her eyes raked his face. "Maybe you're shielding her. That must be it. Aren't you a friend of *hers*?" This last word was imbued with contempt.

Burnell curled his fists into tight balls at his sides. He swayed on the balls of his feet, as if trying to contain the rage that was bubbling through his veins. There was a slight tremor in his voice when he spoke. "Mrs. Royce, there is no one who has a deeper and more abiding respect for the law than I do." He paused to take a breath. Not once did his eyes leave her face. "I take my job extremely seriously. Therefore, I follow all leads, no matter where they take me. Sometimes the truth is ugly and inconvenient, but I am here to uphold the law. Nothing more, nothing less."

Mrs. Royce placed her hands on the table and pushed herself to her feet. "A very pretty speech, Superintendent," she scoffed. Her head whirled round and found its target in Emmeline. "But I am not satisfied." Then to Burnell again, she said, "Expect to hear from my solicitor."

Horowitz opened his mouth to protest, but she cut across him.

"No, not you, Stan. Someone with a little more backbone." She rubbed her temple. "I've had quite enough of this unpleasantness. I feel a migraine coming on and I'd like to go home."

Jason jumped up and took his mother by the elbow. "Mum, I'll take you."

She winced as she shook her head. "No, that's all right, darling. Jeremy is waiting downstairs with the car."

Jason frowned. "Are you sure, Mum?"

Her mouth curled into a lopsided smile and she patted his arm. "Yes, I'll be fine."

Jason appeared unconvinced. By this time, Adam and Sabrina were standing as well. "Stop fussing, Jason," Adam said. "Just give Mum some space."

Jason rounded on him. "When I want your opinion, I'll ask

for it. Until then, keep your mouth shut. And by the way, I've never needed your opinion."

"Boys, really." Sabrina stepped between her brothers, placing a manicured hand with slick red nail polish on each chest. "Haven't we had enough drama for one afternoon?"

A tense silence fell. Not a muscle twitched as they eyed each other, a lifetime's worth of pent up brotherly rivalry and hostility was exchanged, straining in the small space between them.

Adam was the first to look away. He straightened his tie and turned to his sister. "Right. Sabrina, can I drop you anywhere? I'm parked just round the corner."

Sabrina smiled and gave him a peck on the cheek, making sure to wipe away the lipstick smudge with her thumb. "You are an angel, Adam. I'll just be able to make my meeting."

She looped her arm through her twin's elbow and propelled him toward the door, before Jason could hurl another verbal volley.

At the door, Sabrina halted in front of Emmeline and Gregory, who had stood apart. "So we're one big happy family. I always wondered what it would be like to have a sister. And now, here you are." She looked Emmeline up and down as she had done at the party. "I must say I'm not impressed. But then, you come with fringe benefits." Her feline gaze shifted to Gregory. "I'm going to enjoy getting to know *you* better."

She actually had the nerve to wink at him.

A white-hot jolt of fury shot through Emmeline's body. Her hands quivered at her sides. She sorely wanted to wrap her fingers around Sabrina's swanlike throat and squeeze until all the breath was choked out of her body. It took all of her self-control not to lunge for the witch.

Adam gave his sister a not-so-gentle-shove out the door. "Sorry" he mouthed. His eyes searched Emmeline's face, a jumble of thoughts were reflected in their dark depths. Confusion, irritation—that had to be directed at his brother—but what took Emmeline by surprise was that there was a glimmer of happiness too. Perhaps in all this mess she had gained an ally. It would be nice.

Adam lowered his voice. "I'll give you a ring in a few days—" He slid a sideways glance at Jason and Mrs. Royce. "—when all the dust settles." He inclined his head toward Gregory and slipped out of the conference room.

When the dust settles, indeed. Her life was never going to be the same again.

Her gaze dropped to the letter that was burning a hole in the palms of her hands. The letter from Victor Royce. The letter from...*her father.*

Tears pricked her eyelids. She had to get out of here. It felt as if the walls of the solicitor's office were closing in on her.

She clutched at Gregory's sleeve. "I have to leave. I need some air."

"Of course, darling. We'll—"

She cut him off. "No, not we. Just me. I need some time...to think...to...I don't know..." Her voice trailed off. Her head was reeling in confusion.

She brushed past him before he could utter another word. Her clumsy fingers fumbled with the door for a few seconds. And then, she was free.

Somehow her feet had carried her out of Horowitz, Shandwick & Musgrove's office, down the lift, and out of the building. She was taking deep gulps of air out on the pavement as the traffic trundled down Chancery Lane. Everything around her appeared normal. But nothing was normal. Not anymore.

Little rivulets were trickling from the corner of her eyes. She swiped at the tears impatiently with the back of one hand.

The other hand gripped Royce's letter to her chest. She had to read it. No use putting it off. But she couldn't go back upstairs to the solicitor's office. She hurried up the block past the London Silver Vaults; snaked her way along some of the small side streets; around the imposing Lincoln's Inn, one of the four Inns of Court, which faced Lincoln's Inn Fields, the verdant and quiet park in the square.

Emmeline plunked down on an empty bench under an imposing oak tree with sturdy limbs. A whisper of a breeze dandled the leaves above her head.

She simply stared at the letter in her lap. She fingered the edge of the envelope. She couldn't bring herself to open it. And yet, she had to. She had to know.

She tipped her head back and drew air into her lungs. She exhaled a long breath. Right. She was ready. She snatched up the letter, lifted a corner, and stuck her finger along the edge, listening to the muted hiss of tearing paper as the envelope opened. *Like Moses parting the Red Sea. Or Pandora opening her dreaded box*, she told herself grimly.

She shook her head as if to rid herself of this line of thought. What's done is done. She couldn't undo the past.

She was annoyed to see her fingers trembling as she unfolded the letter. For a second, all the words blurred together. Then, Royce's bold, elegant hand came into sharp focus.

Dear Emmeline,

If you are reading this, then I am cold in my grave and now you know the truth about me. I wanted you to know that you warmed my heart in the short time I had the privilege to know you. I am so very proud of you, my daughter. How I wish I could have told you in person. But I suppose I was a coward.

We lost so many years. I know this has come as a great shock to you, as it has to me. That's why I wanted to explain. I knew from the first day you walked into my office. I knew instinctively that you were my daughter. I could feel it in my blood. And, of course, I saw Jacqueline—my dearest, darling Jacqui—in you. You have my father's dark coloring like Adam, but your face, your precious face is the mirror image of Jacqui.

Do you remember the night of the party, when we were sitting together in the garden? I told you our story, mine and Jacqui's. She was the love of my life. You must believe that. But then she went away. Now, I understand why. She was pregnant with you and was afraid that I would be angry. She wrote me a letter begging me not to search for her. That it wouldn't change things. That everything was over and there was nothing left to say. I was completely shattered. Numb. Life stopped for me that day.

I want you to know that I would have been happy, so very happy, by the news of a baby. Our baby. I would have done anything and everything to get a divorce from Lily. As it was, I was left an empty shell of a man just going through the motions. Not a day has gone by that I haven't thought about Jacqui. I never forgot her. Never.

And then, you appeared in my life. It was as if I was given a reprieve for my sins. I wish we could have had more time together. But I'm thankful for the precious moments that we did have. I died with you in my heart.

Your loving father,
Victor Royce

CHAPTER 32

When Gregory found Emmeline, she was sitting on a bench staring blankly at some invisible spot across the square. The letter dangled from her hand and was in danger of being carried away on the breeze. She looked smaller and fragile—oh so, fragile.

"Emmy," he murmured in a soft undertone, not wishing to startle her.

Not a muscle moved. Her gaze remained fixed in the distance.

"Emmy," he ventured again and lowered himself onto the bench beside her.

He slipped an arm around her shoulders and gently pried the letter from her fingers. He could see her face was moist with tears.

Without turning, she said, "You can read it if you like." Her voice cracked. It was husky from crying.

"Only if you want me too, darling," he replied, his tone low and soothing.

She turned to face him. "I don't really care."

He drew her closer to him and pressed a kiss against her temple. "Of course, you do. It's just the shock talking. Everything will be all right."

She pulled away, her dark gaze sweeping over his face. She lifted a hand and pressed it to his cheek. He held it there for a moment, before turning it over to kiss her palm. He heard a tiny sigh escape her lips.

Her finger traced his jawline and then her hand dropped into her lap.

She swallowed hard. "I can't marry you, Gregory."

He stiffened. "I beg your pardon?"

"Please don't make this more difficult than it already is." She twisted her pink sapphire engagement ring off her finger and held it out to him, her hand trembling.

He stared down at the ring in confusion.

She waved it impatiently at him. "Go on. Take it."

His head snapped up. "I will not take it. Emmy, you're not thinking clearly."

She laughed. It was a hollow, empty sound devoid of joy. "You're wrong there. I've had plenty of time to think. And I've come to the conclusion that I can't marry you..." Her sentence faded away.

He could see she was struggling to regain her composure. A sheen of unshed tears glistened upon her eyelashes.

"Don't you see? My life has been a tissue of lies from the beginning. Everything I thought was the truth was a lie." She banged her small fist against her chest. "I'm a living, breathing lie." She snorted. "I used to believe the truth was so important. I don't even know what that word means anymore. Therefore, I can't enter a marriage when my past—" She choked back a sob. "—and present are a lie."

Gregory jumped to his feet and stood in front of her. "You stupid woman. Do you think I care about any of this?" He waved the letter in the air. "None of it makes a bloody bit of difference. It's 2010, not 1910. Who your parents were has nothing—absolutely nothing—to do with *our* relationship. I don't love your parents. I love *you*. Only you."

She rose to her feet and placed her hands on his chest. The sad smile on her lips made his heart shudder. She stood on tiptoe to brush a tender kiss against his cheek. A goodbye kiss. "It matters to me. My parents are a part of me. I can't marry you."

He grabbed her by the shoulders and shook her. "You're being utterly ridiculous."

"No." Her tone was quiet and matter-of-fact. "I'm the only one who is being realistic. No marriage can survive when it starts with a lie. Now, please let me go. Prolonging this will only make it more painful."

Through clenched teeth, he hissed, "Good. I want it to be bloody excruciating. I'm in love with a mad woman." Then in milder tone, he said, "Look, darling, why don't you go down to Swaley for a few days. It would do you good to see Helen. Goodness knows your grandmother is the only one who can knock some sense into you."

Emmeline opened her mouth to reply, but was prevented from doing so.

"I'm afraid Emmeline can't go anywhere."

They both swung round to find Superintendent Burnell and Sergeant Finch approaching. Their faces were etched in grim lines.

"Oliver? What are you on about?" Gregory's voice was laced with irritation.

When the two detectives came level with them, Burnell addressed Emmeline. "I think you understand. My hands are tied. I'm sorry."

She nodded. "It's not your fault."

Turning to Gregory, he said, "Royce's will makes Emmeline a prime suspect—*the* prime suspect—in his murder. Dr. Meadows confirmed this morning that he was poisoned. Emmeline was at the house day before he died. You must see how it looks."

Gregory, his body a coil of tension and barely controlled anger, spluttered, "Oliver, you can't be bloody serious?" When the superintendent remained silent, he pressed, "You *know* it isn't true. Where would Emmy get her hands on poison? She didn't go to the corner chemist's and pick up a packet of whatever it was."

"I must do my duty according to the law—"

"Stuff the law. I never thought I'd see the day when you, of all people, would hide behind duty. I thought you had a bit more backbone than that."

A muscle convulsed along Burnell's jaw. "Longdon, I'd have a care if I were you. Your past is far from lily-white."

Gregory's mouth curved into a malicious grin. "Is that a threat? Because I'd love to file charges for police harassment."

Emmeline drew in a ragged breath. She touched his arm.

"Gregory, that is completely unfair. Superintendent Burnell is only doing his job." She inclined her head in Burnell's direction and offered him a conciliatory smile. "I'm sorry. As you can see, he's upset. He doesn't mean it."

Gregory shook off her hand. "Emmy, you don't speak for me." His gaze shifted to Burnell's face once more. "I meant every word. I think Oliver and I understand each other perfectly."

"Gregory, please. This is not how I wanted to remember our—" A sob caught in her throat. "—to remember our last meeting."

She averted her face from the three pairs of male eyes. A tear was trickling down her cheek. After a second, she straightened her back, squared her shoulders, and took a deep breath. She thrust her chin in the air and faced them again.

"Emmy—"

She shook her head and put up a hand. "No, Gregory. There's nothing left to say. Goodbye." She brushed past him. "Superintendent Burnell, I promise I won't leave London."

Burnell gave her a lopsided smile. "Yes, I know you won't. We'll need to interview you again."

"Of course, I can come down to the station now if you like."

"Emmy, you don't have to do this." Gregory took a half-step toward her.

She continued to hold the superintendent's gaze. She couldn't look at Gregory. She didn't dare. Otherwise, she would lose her nerve.

The superintendent seemed to sense her need to leave immediately. "That's not necessary, Emmeline. It can wait until tomorrow. You should go home. You've had a shock—"

"Huh." She sniffed. "That's putting it mildly. But thank you. Ring me whenever you'd like to speak to me."

"Finch, take Emmeline home. I'll make my own way back to the Yard."

"Yes, sir."

"Really, Superintendent, I'm perfectly fine," she protested.

"Humor me, Emmeline," Burnell said, his voice gentle. A faint smile touching his lips.

Finch took her elbow. "Yes, come on. The guv's right. You shouldn't be alone right now."

"My sentiments exactly. If anyone's going to take Emmy home, it's going to be me."

Burnell stepped in front of Gregory and put a restraining hand on his arm. He jerked his head at Finch. "Go on."

The sergeant nodded. Without another word, he led Emmeline across the square.

"Emmy," Gregory called after her. "Emmy, you can't do this."

They saw her stiffen. Although her step faltered for a moment, she kept walking. There was no backward glance. No wave of her hand. Nothing.

Gregory and Burnell stood there rooted to the spot until Emmeline and Finch had disappeared around the corner of Lincoln's Inn.

Burnell cleared his throat and thrust his hands in his pockets. The toe of one foot made circles in the gravel path. "For what it's worth, Longdon, I'm sorry how things have turned out with you and Emmeline." He lifted his eyes until they met Gregory's gaze. "I know you love her."

Gregory was still for several seconds. Then his trademark smile tugged at the corners of his mouth. He clapped Burnell on the shoulder. "Thanks, Oliver. But I haven't lost her yet. And I have no intention of doing so ever again. This is just Emmy being noble and self-sacrificing. The mood shall pass, I quite assure you, when she comes back to her senses. I will be placing this—" He uncurled his fist, where in the center of his palm was nestled her pink sapphire engagement ring. "—on her finger again any day now. Mark my words."

Burnell stared at him open-mouthed. "But—" He swallowed. "You're either stark raving mad or supremely arrogant. Or both."

Gregory's smile widened and he nudged the superintendent in the ribs with his elbow. "You old flatterer. I accept your apology, by the way."

"*My* apology?" the detective spluttered. "Apology for what?"

"For being so heavy-handed just now. But I forgive you. I realize your job goes to your head sometimes. I suppose it's all the officialdom." He reached out and proceeded to straighten Burnell's tie.

The superintendent swatted his hand away. "Get away with you. You're going to be the death of me yet, Longdon."

"How can you say that, Oliver? Two such bosom mates as us? Oh no, we'll live forever."

Burnell rolled his eyes heavenward. "God, for once, help me," he implored. He waited, but no reply was forthcoming.

"Come now, Oliver. You don't need divine intervention when you have me. I'm going to help you catch this killer."

The superintendent let loose a string of silent curses to register his displeasure with the Lord Almighty. Instead of peace on Earth, he was plunged into purgatory—with Longdon.

CHAPTER 33

Emmeline had taken an early lunch the next day and obediently trotted down to Scotland Yard when Superintendent Burnell had summoned her. She went over every detail of her movements the day of the auction and afterward when Victor Royce had invited her to his house for tea. Burnell and Sergeant Finch had asked her the same questions over and over. In the end, the two detectives realized that there was no new information she could offer and allowed her to leave.

Although Burnell and Finch had been their usual pleasant selves, the entire interview had been unnerving. She was actually considered a murder suspect. It was inconceivable. It was horrifying. And yet, it was true. She shuddered. But what was the truth? She was so rattled by the revelations about Royce—*my father*, she reminded herself—that she couldn't concentrate on her work and had ended up going home.

Gregory must have spoken to Brian Sanborn, the chairman and managing director of Sanborn Enterprises which owned *The Clarion*, and his brother Nigel, the corporate counsel, because both brothers were hovering in her doorway that morning to make sure she was all right. They told her to take some time off if she needed it. It was touching to see the worry etched on their faces. After all, if she had married Gregory she would have been one of the family since he was their cousin. They had been estranged for many years and only recently was Gregory welcomed back into the fold. But that was a long story. And no longer her concern since she *wasn't* going to marry Gregory, she scolded herself.

A weary sigh escaped her lips. *Gregory*. Every part of her

body ached for him. But it had been the right decision to break off the engagement. She sighed again. She would simply have to get used to the idea of not having him around.

"Some things are easier said than done," she murmured under breath as she snatched up the defenseless pillow beside her on the sofa and gave it a good punch.

She shook her head and stood up with renewed determination. "No, no, no. I was perfectly all right when Gregory disappeared before and I'll be all right again. All I need to do is to work. I'm good at my job. My work is rewarding and fulfilling."

A sadistic little voice whispered in her ear, *Who are you kidding?*

She groaned and threw her hands up in the air. Everything was so muddled in her mind. What she had to do was to focus on Melnikov, Sabitov, Swanbeck, and...and Victor Royce...her father. Nothing else. There had to be something she was missing. The key that would unlock Pandora's Box.

Let's face it, Pandora had already let loose her plagues on the world. It's my job to clean up the mess she left in her wake.

When in doubt, make tea. A nice cuppa always seemed to clear the fog.

As the kettle came to a boil, an idea suddenly struck her. Sabitov's notebook. She still had it. She couldn't make heads or tails of it because it was in Russian, but Philip could. He was fluent. She was an idiot to have kept the notebook a secret. She supposed it was ego. She had wanted to be the one to crack the case and have the scoop. Fool. Perhaps this had cost Victor Royce his life.

She shivered involuntarily as this thought crossed her mind. She sincerely hoped not.

After the tea had steeped to her satisfaction, she took the tea tray out to the living room. She set it down on the coffee table and crossed to the desk where she worked, overlooking the garden. She rooted around in her handbag. Why was it when you were looking for something invariably it was at the bottom of your handbag? At last, she unearthed Sabitov's notebook and took it over to the sofa.

With her legs tucked under her, she flipped through it as she sipped her tea. No, it was no use. It was the equivalent of reading hieroglyphics. She fumbled with one hand for the phone on the table behind the sofa.

She glanced at her watch and punched in the number. She crossed her fingers that Philip was still at the office.

She was about to give up and try him at home, when his breathless voice answered on the third ring, "Acheson."

"Philip, it's Emmeline."

"You just caught me. Are you all right? Burnell told me about Royce...and everything."

"It depends on your definition of all right, but that's a discussion for another time. For the moment, I'm doing the best I can. But I don't want to keep you long because Maggie will murder both of us."

Philip chuckled. "True. Very true. I'm already in the dog house. I was late home all of last week."

"Right. In the spirit of self-preservation, I'll come straight to the point. I have Sabitov's notebook—"

"You what?" he exploded. She had to hold the phone away from her ear. "You've had it all this time and only *now* you've seen fit to mention it."

"Guilty as charged. All I can say is I'm sorry. I don't really want to argue. Look, it's all in Russian. The only thing I can understand is Melnikov and Rutkovsky in a couple of places. I was wondering if I could pop round your office in the morning and show it to you."

He muttered something unintelligible.

"Is that a yes?" she asked eagerly.

"You already knew the answer. However, I'm afraid I can't get away until eleven-thirty. I think it's best if you don't come by the office. We don't want to draw any attention. Let's meet on neutral territory. How about the Tower Hotel in St. Katharine Docks? That's a stone's throw from *The Clarion*. We could have coffee and you can unburden your soul. Let me rephrase that. You had better unburden your soul, if you know what's good for you."

She smiled, although he couldn't see her. "I promise to tell you everything I know."

"Good. This is not a game, Emmeline. Swanbeck is a ruthless killer, even if he doesn't sully his hands with actual deed himself."

Her mind flew to the image of Swanbeck standing outside Sotheby's. Those intense sea-green eyes chilled her to the bone. She licked her lips. "Yes, I know Swanbeck is dangerous. I'll be careful."

"I hope so. Now, I must dash or else my darling wife will lock me out of the house."

She laughed. "I very much doubt that. Thanks, Philip. Give my love to Maggie. Tell her I'll ring her in a few days."

"I think you better, if you know what's good for you. By the way, I haven't said anything to her about you and Longdon. It's not my place. A friendly word of warning, though. You can't keep something like that secret for very long. Maggie *will* find out. And there will be hell to pay if she doesn't hear it from you. Actually, there will be fireworks either way."

She sighed. "Yes, I know. But I can't talk about it right now. It's still too raw."

There was a long pause. Then, Philip said, his voice laced with sympathy, "You know Longdon and I don't see eye to eye on a lot of things, but I do know that he loves you. That's his one saving grace. No chance of a reconciliation?"

"Philip, I—" She couldn't finish her sentence. She bit back the tears that threatened to undo her resolve.

He became brisk. "Sorry. I shouldn't have said anything. I'll see you tomorrow at eleven-thirty."

With that, he rang off and Emmeline was left staring at the phone in her hand.

She was about to pour herself another cup of tea, when the doorbell rang. She grunted. Why couldn't people just leave her alone?

"Go away. I'm not at home," she said to the empty room.

She sat still and waited. Perhaps whoever it was had taken the hint.

No such luck. After several seconds, the ringing started

again. *Persistent devil*, she mumbled as she uncurled herself and rose to her feet.

"All right, I'm coming," she called as she entered the corridor and unbolted the door.

Her jaw dropped at the sight of Gregory and...*Gran* on her doorstep. Her eyes darted from one to the other.

"Hello is the usual form of greeting," her grandmother said in a crisp, clipped tone. Her brown eyes narrowed and two vertical lines formed between her eyebrows.

Emmeline recognized that scowl all too well. She took a step forward and reached up to brush a kiss against the feathery skin of Helen's cheek. "Hello, Gran. What a lovely surprise."

"Hmph," was her grandmother's reply.

Emmeline's gaze strayed to Gregory. Purely as an act of self-preservation, she had avoided drinking in every plane and contour of his handsome face.

"Don't worry. I'm not staying. I just thought you needed to see Helen and as Oliver had forbidden you to leave London, well—" He shrugged his shoulders and favored her with a lopsided smile.

She thought she was going to melt as his cinnamon gaze scoured her face. Her lips parted slightly. For a second, she thought he was going to kiss her. But then he seemed to change his mind and took a step backward, putting space between them.

"I'll be off now." He leaned down and gave Helen a peck on the cheek instead. "Goodbye."

Helen patted his arm and pressed her cheek against his. "Goodbye. Thank you for taking care of my thankless granddaughter." She shot a disapproving look at Emmeline.

Gregory gave Helen a conspiratorial wink. He turned on his heel without another word.

She waved to him until his blue-gray Jaguar disappeared from view. Then she stepped into the corridor and rounded on her granddaughter. "Now, what's all this nonsense that you've broken the engagement?"

Emmeline rolled her eyes toward the ceiling and willed

herself to remain calm. She shut the door and slipped the bolt back into place. She took a deep breath and plastered a smile on her lips. "Gran, come into the living room. I have a pot of tea and some shortbread biscuits."

She stood aside and allowed Helen to bustle past.

"I won't say no to tea," her grandmother said grudgingly. However, she turned so swiftly that Emmeline nearly bumped into her. "But don't think for one instant that you can fob me off. Do I make myself clear?"

Emmeline nodded obediently and scuttled toward the kitchen, calling over her shoulder, "Yes, Gran. I'll get another cup."

Gregory has a lot to answer for, she grumbled silently on her way back to the living room, her fingers gripped tightly around the cup and saucer.

He was an absolute beast. It was completely unfair to spring Gran on her like this. She could see that Gran had already made up her mind about who the villain was in this situation. And it was not Gregory. Yet despite the tension, she was glad that Helen was here. Gran was the one person in the whole world she desperately needed at the moment.

They each retreated to opposite ends of the sofa, tacitly agreeing to a truce as they sipped their tea. For several minutes, the only thing that could be heard was the munching of shortbread.

After Helen had devoured two cups of tea, she appeared fortified once again and the assault began. She set her cup down on the coffee table.

"I'm waiting for an explanation for your bizarre behavior." She waved an arm in the vague direction of the world outside the window. "That poor boy is beside himself."

Her granddaughter threw her head back and laughed.

"Emmy, there is nothing remotely amusing about this situation."

Emmeline sobered and sat up straighter. "No, Gran. It is not. And Gregory is not a 'poor boy.' He's a grown man of forty-two."

Helen flapped her hand dismissively in the air. "A minor

detail. Are you going to tell me the reason why you've taken leave of your senses?"

Emmeline could feel the tingle of anger in her muscles and clasped her hands together in a bid to keep her temper in check. It wouldn't do to get into a full-blown row with Gran. "Why is it that *I'm* the one who is always being unreasonable? Hmm, Gran?"

"Because no one in her right mind would throw over that handsome devil after you fought so hard to find your way back to each other."

That was too much. Emmeline pounded her open palm against her chest as one by one the tears started to drip from her eyelashes. "Do you think this is easy for me?" She jumped to her feet and began pacing back and forth. "Gran, my entire life has been a lie. I can't—I won't walk into a marriage with that hanging over my head."

"What are you on about? Your life is a lie. Rubbish. Oh, please stop rushing about and sit down. You're making me dizzy." Gran patted the sofa next to her.

Emmeline halted her restless perambulations, but she refused to sit down. She stared at her grandmother for a long moment. Then she took a deep breath and plunged in. "Aaron Kirby was not my father. Apparently—" She impatiently swiped at her moist cheek with the back of her hand. "I'm the product of Mummy's affair with Victor Royce."

Helen blinked several times. She sagged against the sofa. "I see."

"I see? *I see?*" Emmeline asked in exasperation. "Is that all you have to say?"

Her grandmother lifted her gaze to look Emmeline directly in the eye. "Are you sure? No doubts?"

"Yes, I'm sure. Royce left me a letter…to explain. By the way, he left me the bulk of his fortune. As if that would make amends." She choked on a sob. "Why aren't you upset, Gran?" Then a thought struck her. "Did you *know*?" She sucked in her breath. "You did, didn't you?"

Helen rolled her eyes heavenward. "Don't be ridiculous. Let's not look for conspiracies where there aren't any."

"Why aren't you shocked?"

"It's just that—That a lot things have fallen into place. Before Jacqui and Aaron got married, I knew there had been someone else. Someone who I could tell Jacqui was very serious about. She never brought him home to introduce him to me. Now, I understand why. He was married. It went on for about a year, I think. Then suddenly Jacqui and Aaron announced one day that they were getting married. I didn't find it strange. The Kirby and Davis families had always been close. Jacqui and Aaron knew each other since they were children. They had always been friends, so it seemed natural that they would want to get married. When you came along about seven months later...well, I like to think I have an open mind. We are not living in Victorian times after all. These things are no longer a scandal."

Emmeline dropped heavily onto the sofa at last. "But, Gran, my life has been a *lie*. Everything I believed— everything I thought—was a lie."

"Will you listen to yourself?" Irritation was wrapped around each word. "You'd think, at the very least, you were sentenced to hard labor in a Siberian gulag. Aaron and Jacqui loved you more than anything on this earth. Perhaps things were a little unsettled when they first married, but they certainly fell in love with one another. It was patently obvious. And I don't care about this Victor Royce. Aaron *was* your father from the day you were born. He was the one who picked you up when you fell down and scraped your knee. He stayed up and read story after story to you when you were ill. If that's not a father, I don't know what is. No one could have loved you more. No one. He is to be greatly admired. So I don't want to hear any more silliness about your life being a lie. I want you to ring Gregory this instant and tell him you've been a complete and utter fool. Beg him to take you back."

Emmeline snuggled against her grandmother like she used to do when she was little. "Gran, I can't do that. Too much has happened. Gregory would never take me back."

Helen pushed her away and held her face tenderly between

her hands. "Of course he will, my precious girl. He loves you. Besides, he knows all your faults—"

"Hey, there aren't *that* many."

Helen went on as if she hadn't spoken. "—and he's already accepted the fact that you're a bit of a nutter."

Emmeline's mouth broke into a grin. "Well, thank you very much for that. With such a sterling character reference, I'm a prize catch."

Once their giggles had petered out, Helen softly coaxed, "Go on. Ring Gregory." She jerked her thumb at the phone on the table behind the sofa.

Emmeline sat up and exhaled a long breath. "I'll ring him. I promise. But there's a bit more that you need to know."

Helen's brow puckered. "Oh, yes? Well, no use dithering. Out with it."

"It seems…because Victor Royce decided to make me the primary beneficiary of his will—which came as complete shock to me—I am…that is…the police strongly believe that I'm his murderer."

With the agility of a teenager, rather than a woman of seventy-eight, Helen leaped to her feet. "What? Are the police mad? *You.* Who's in charge of this case? I'd like to have a word with him. It has to be a *him* because only a man would be so stupid."

Emmeline had to stifle a laugh. "Gran, please sit down. It's not Superintendent Burnell's fault. I can't really blame him. The evidence, though circumstantial, appears to point to me. I was at the Royce house the day before the murder."

Helen's eyes widened in disbelief. "*Burnell*? Is this the same Burnell that you're always going on about what a nice fellow he is under his gruff exterior?"

Emmeline nodded and felt a stab of guilt. She knew that the superintendent was doing all that was in his power to shield her. Gran didn't know him and, therefore, it was unfair to pass judgment on him.

Helen snorted and snatched up the phone. "Right, what's this Superintendent Burnell's number?"

Emmeline bit her lip and sent a silent apology to Burnell. The wrath of God was nothing compared to that of Gran.

CHAPTER 34

Burnell's stomach rumbled as he waited for Assistant Commissioner Cruickshank to finish his conference call. *Damn the man*. Sally had said to drop everything he was doing because the Boy Wonder had wanted to see him *at once*. And here he was, fifteen minutes later, still waiting for an audience. He had more important things to do with his time. His stomach growled again. Like eat. Not a single crumb had passed his lips all day what with one thing and another. If he had known it was going to take this long, he would have nipped down to the canteen to grab something. Anything to quell the gnawing in his belly.

He slid a sideways glance at Sally who was pretending to concentrate on the report she was typing but whom he could tell was making a mental note of his every movement.

He cleared his throat and ventured, "Sally, if the assistant commissioner is too busy. I can come back another time. I'm actually in the middle of—"

Without turning around, she replied in a clipped tone, "Don't even think about leaving. You will wait until Assistant Commissioner Cruickshank is ready to see you. It shouldn't be long now."

"That's what you said ten minutes ago," Burnell groused through gritted teeth.

Her mouth twisted into an unpleasant smirk. Apparently, she had used up her quota of words for the day because she didn't deign to respond.

One day she would pay for her sins on Earth, Burnell mused. Until then he would have to keep praying to God for the strength not to give in to the urge to strangle her.

Her phone buzzed to life. With a languid movement of her left hand, she reached out and picked up the receiver. "Yes, sir. Superintendent Burnell is here. Yes, of course."

She replaced the receiver and beamed at Burnell. "Assistant Commissioner Cruickshank says that you can go in."

"Aren't I the lucky one?" Burnell mumbled under his breath.

She eyed him suspiciously. "What was that, Superintendent Burnell?"

He plastered a smile on his lips. "I feel so honored to be one of the chosen few able to bask in his presence. It gives me a warm glow all over."

"Hmph." She jerked her head toward Cruickshank's door. "See that you don't detain him too long. He's a busy man."

Indeed, Cruickshank is busy. Busy driving hardworking policemen mad, Burnell thought as he twisted the doorknob and entered his superior's office.

Although he thought his face would crack from the strain, he kept the smile firmly in place. "Sir, you wanted to see me?"

Cruickshank flicked a glance at Burnell who noticed that the smile was not reciprocated.

"Ah, there you are. Sit down, Burnell." He flapped a hand impatiently at the chair opposite him.

The superintendent crossed the room in two strides and heavily lowered himself into the uncomfortable chair.

Cruickshank leaned back and steepled his fingers over his lean stomach. "Burnell, I must tell you that I am extremely disappointed in the way you are handling the Royce murder. I've just spent the last two hours with Jason Royce."

"Ah," Burnell murmured. "Sir, you see—"

Cruickshank cut him off. "I don't want to hear any excuses. It is an utter disgrace. Mr. Royce told me that his mother is quite beside herself since the reading of the will. She said that you were rude and insolent and went out of your way to defend Miss Kirby. She complained about Sergeant Finch too, although in less harsh terms. She seems to understand that Finch must defer to his superior."

Burnell gripped his knees so hard the skin across his

knuckles turned white. "Sir, I conducted myself, as always, in a completely professional manner. Naturally, this is a difficult situation for everyone involved."

The assistant commissioner sniffed. "We'll leave that point for the moment. What really concerns me is Mr. Royce's allegations that you are shielding Miss Kirby."

The chair creaked as Burnell shifted his position. "Again, sir, that is untrue. I—"

"Need I remind you that she was on the scene of both the Royce and Sabitov murders? I've read your reports. You seem to gloss over these facts."

Burnell's hands curled into tight balls. "First of all, sir, Miss Kirby was *not* on the scene when Royce's body was discovered."

Cruickshank made dismissive gesture with his hand. "A technicality. She was at the house the afternoon before the murder and had ample opportunity. By the way, Meadows has confirmed that it was the Scotch that was poisoned." He pulled a file toward him and leafed through a few pages. "Ah, yes, here it is. According to the toxicology tests, it was something called gelsemium. It's a rare plant poison and hard to detect, but Meadows said he had suspected it was a case of poisoning from the outset, especially coming on the heels of Sabitov's murder. Where again we find that Emmeline Kirby had been on the spot."

Burnell cleared his throat. "I've seen the reports. They were two different poisons. Sabitov was given atropine."

"That makes no difference. Two poisonings and one common denominator—Emmeline Kirby. It's a bit too much of a coincidence for my liking. I hope you're not allowing a pretty face to cloud your judgment." Cruickshank gave a disapproving shake of his head and clucked his tongue.

Burnell's blood was racing, but he clamped down on his outrage and persevered, "Sir, if I may draw your attention to a note Dr. Meadows made in his report. Russian assassins have long turned to gelsemium as their weapon of choice. If you will recall, Sabitov was a well-known opposition journalist and had been in the midst of an investigative piece on a money laundering scheme that involved the Russian mafia and high-ranking members of the Russian government. Alastair Swanbeck, an Englishman with dubious business dealings, seems to be involved as well. The source of this information was Pavel Melnikov who was murdered the day before Sabitov but was spirited away by our friends at MI-Six as if he were a ghost. Only he wasn't. He was a living, breathing man until someone decided to throw him off a building in Mayfair.

"In my humble view, all of this is highly suspicious." He lifted a hand to forestall whatever foolish thing was rising to the assistant commissioner's lips. "And another point, Sabitov and Melnikov appear to have been working with a certain Rutkovsky to expose the truth. We have since learned that Rutkovsky was none other than Victor Royce. All three men were directly tied together. Therefore, the only plausible conclusion that Finch and I can come to is that someone in the Kremlin desperately wanted to silence them before they caused any more damage. Sir, I hardly think that Emmeline Kirby fits the profile of a Russian assassin. But someone certainly appears to be going to great lengths to implicate her. To my mind, that seems to indicate that she's touched a raw nerve with her reporting. That means she's considered a threat and must be gotten rid of at all costs. I don't know about you, sir, but that terrifies me." He put his hands on his knees and pushed himself to his feet. "If there's nothing else, sir, I'll be getting on with the job at hand. We still have a lot of ground to cover."

Cruickshank opened his mouth to reply, thought better of it, and snapped it shut again. The phone chose that moment to scream to life. Relief washed over Cruickshank's face at the distraction. The conversation had become distinctly prickly.

"Excuse me."

Burnell inclined his head and turned toward the door.

"Yes, Sally," the assistant commissioner said. There was silence for a few seconds as he listened. "Did they now? Thank you very much. Have them bring it directly to Meadows. This is top priority." He replaced the receiver. "Oh, Burnell."

With his hand on the doorknob, the superintendent glanced back at his superior. "Sir?"

A faint smile played at the corners of Cruickshank's mouth. "I think you'll find this interesting. I obtained a warrant this morning from the magistrate to have Emmeline Kirby's office searched."

"You what?" Burnell exploded. Then he attempted to soften his tone. He was unsuccessful because his anger kept intruding. "Without informing me? This is *my* case, sir."

Cruickshank's smile only grew wider. "Since I am your superior, I am ultimately in charge of all cases. The team I sent out to conduct the search has just returned. They found a vial of something tucked in the back of one of her drawers. How much would you like to wager that it contains gelsemium?"

Burnell felt the blood drain from his face. Emmeline was in graver danger than he had believed. Those pulling strings from the shadows were not content with merely discrediting her. They wanted to destroy her.

છ૭ન૭

The door rattled on its hinges as Burnell stormed into his office. Every muscle in his body was coiled with tension and seething with rage. The gloves were off. If the law could be twisted around to carry out a vendetta against an innocent woman, he would plunge into the muck to drag out the truth and scream it at the top of his lungs regardless of the damage it caused. The only way to catch these Russian thugs and Swanbeck was to identify their weaknesses and then hit them where it hurt the most. Fortunately, he knew someone who could provide an intimate insight into the criminal mind. Longdon.

He plunked down into his chair and snatched up his receiver. He punched in the number for Longdon's mobile.

Within seconds of the connection going through, he heard his nemesis's plummy tones spilling into his ear. "Oliver, old chap, what a lovely surprise. You can't get enough of me can you?"

Burnell drummed his fingers on his desk. He reminded himself that Emmeline's future—her very life—was at stake. He would not rise to the bait. "Put a cork in it, Longdon, and listen. Our friend Swanbeck and his Russian cronies are trying to stitch Emmeline up for Royce's murder and Sabitov's too."

That caught Longdon's attention. Burnell went on to detail his conversation with Assistant Commissioner Cruickshank. "As you can see," he concluded, "Emmeline has become a liability. I have no doubt whatsoever that the lab results will reveal that the vial found in her office contains gelsemium. I've done what I could for her, but I have a feeling that Cruickshank is preparing to tie my hands." He paused and took a deep breath. He lowered his voice and hunched his shoulders over his desk. "This is your world, Longdon. You know how these people think. You can move among them undetected. I am giving you carte blanche—*unofficially*, you understand—to do whatever is necessary to get these bloody bastards. If you run into trouble, I promise I will back you up, even if it means sacrificing my career. Just keep me informed about what you find out. That's all I ask."

After a brief silence, Longdon replied, "Oliver, you are a prince among men. I knew there was a reason we are such mates."

"We are not now, nor will we ever be 'mates.' I'm only doing this for Emmeline and because I despise how these brutes are making a mockery of the law."

"Emmy has a soft spot for you too."

Burnell felt a flush rise to his cheeks.

"Thank you," Longdon continued without a trace of his usual teasing tone, "I'll check in tomorrow. I know a chap who might be able to steer us in the right direction."

"Somehow I thought you might. One last thing."

"Yes, Oliver?"

"It would raise eyebrows if I rang Nigel Sanborn, but since you're his cousin, no would think twice if you did. Emmeline is going to need a good solicitor. Someone who has her interests at heart. Someone she can trust."

CHAPTER 35

The automatic glass sliding doors parted with a muted *swish* as Emmeline stepped into the lobby of the Tower Hotel at precisely eleven twenty-five. She was a few minutes early.

Dear Gran, she thought as she crossed the gleaming cream-colored marble floor to the seating area to her right. *I would be lost without you. I can face anything with you—and Gregory.*

She lowered herself into one of the beige leather chairs where she would be able to see Philip the minute he set foot across the threshold.

Her mind wandered back to Gregory as she waited. She felt the heat rising to her cheeks as she remembered their conversation last night when she had asked him to pop round to her house so that she could prostrate herself before him. She told him that she had been an absolute fool, pure and simple. That she would always love him. And could he ever forgive her. She had held her breath for his answer. But she needn't have worried.

In typical Gregory fashion, he had pulled her into his arms, pressed the most delicious kiss upon her lips, and replied, "Darling, I knew it was only a passing phase. Nobility stands no chance against my considerable charms." He had accompanied this with one of his roguish grins.

Oh, his ego. But she wouldn't have him any other way. She sighed. No, Fate had deemed long ago that their lives would be bound together. For better or worse. She bit her lip. If she could only get through this rough patch, then perhaps the rest of their days would be one glorious, heady dream.

If she could get out of this mess.

She frowned and the hairs on the back of her neck prickled. Things appeared rather bleak. She had spent an hour this morning closeted with Nigel. He had explained that if the lab results came back positive, the police would likely arrest her for Victor Royce's murder. Nigel had tried to reassure her. He said it was not a time to panic. He stressed that Sanborn Enterprises would stand by her to the bitter end. He said no one at the company—from Brian to the mailroom clerks—believed she was guilty. Since criminal law was not Nigel's specialty, Sanborn would hire a top flight lawyer. She was not to worry.

Not worry? That was easy for Nigel to say. He wasn't the one the police were accusing of murder. A murder she did not commit.

"I'd give you a penny for your thoughts, but I have rather a good idea what they are."

Philip's voice startled her. She looked up and saw the shadow of concern reflected in his eyes.

She managed a half-smile. "Hello, Philip. I suppose Gregory rang you to tell you about what the police found in my office."

"Actually, it was Burnell. He blames himself. He asked if I could do anything to help since Assistant Commissioner Cruickshank is watching him like a hawk."

She frowned. "Well, that's silly. None of this is Superintendent Burnell's fault. Obviously with things the way they are at the moment, I can't ring him. Please tell him that I appreciate everything that he has done, but I don't want him to get into any more trouble on my behalf. I would feel awful if he was sacked because of me."

Philip leaned down and lifted her to her feet. "Let's go up to the bar in the upper foyer. We can have a coffee." He lowered his voice and shot a glance around the lobby. Then, he gave her a pointed look. "And you can show me Sabitov's notebook. Finally."

She patted her handbag. "Yes, I'm hoping there's something in it that can clear me."

They didn't utter a word until they were settled at a corner table that afforded them a marvelous view of Tower Bridge.

The Thames's surface gathered up the burning embers of sunlight tumbling from the sky and tossed cheeky winks at the passing tugboats, tour boats and other vessels gliding through its waters.

The bar was virtually empty except for two businessmen at a nearby table who appeared to be poring over some papers. Philip casually studied them for several minutes to make certain they were who they purported to be. Once he was satisfied, he gave Emmeline a slight nod.

While they waited for their double espressos, they chatted about anything except the matter at hand.

Philip cleared his throat. "Ahem. Since you mentioned Longdon earlier, I take it that the two of you are back together?"

Emmeline felt herself blush. "Yes," she replied sheepishly.

"You may not believe me, but I'm glad. Don't get me wrong. I still have deep reservations about him. But if he makes you happy, then that's what counts. I mean that sincerely."

Emmeline reached out and touched his hand. "Thank you. That means a lot to me. And yes, he does make me happy. I know there are still many things I don't know—may never know—about him, but I'd rather have Gregory in my life than be miserable without him."

Philip covered her hand with his larger one and squeezed it. "Longdon is a lucky man. I hope he realizes that."

"I think it works both ways," she said as the barman placed their coffees before them.

Philip dropped a cube of sugar in his cup and stirred. "Mind you, another reason I'm tremendously relieved that you've worked things out with Longdon is that Maggie would have made my life a living hell if the two of you had broken off the engagement for good."

Emmeline laughed.

"I am deadly serious. Maggie would have been brooding and plotting to get the two of you back together. The boys and I would have been invisible to her. She would have been on the phone every day with your grandmother. Speaking of Helen, Maggie was pleased as punch to find out that she was in London. She told me she was taking the day off so that the two of them could exchange notes on your wedding."

Emmeline nodded. "Yes, Maggie came by this morning to collect Gran. They barely noticed when I left the house to go to *The Clarion*. They had the whole day planned out."

He took a long swallow of his espresso. "Mmm. I bet they did. When the two of them get their heads together, the rest of us better get out their way. I hope you're prepared never to see Helen again. Maggie might kidnap her. The boys already consider her an honorary grandmother. She spoils them almost as much as you do. That's why they're so fond of Auntie Emmeline."

Emmeline giggled and set down her demitasse cup in mock indignation. "I never spoil them."

Philip lifted one blond eyebrow. "Oh, no?"

"No, I simply give them little treats and try to think of lovely outings," she replied matter-of-factly.

He wagged his finger at her. "Well, young lady, less treats. Henry and Andrew have to learn the meaning of deprivation—at least every now and then."

They both smiled and fell silent. All too soon the ugliness of the present pressed in on them and the lighthearted mood evaporated.

Philip downed the remainder of his coffee in one gulp. He waggled his fingers. "The notebook."

"Right." Emmeline drew it out of her handbag and slipped it across the table to him. She watched him over the rim of her cup as he flipped it open. He was meticulous. His gaze lingered on each page. Sometimes his brows knit together, while in other instances his eyes widened in surprise.

Finally, he turned the last page and set the notebook face down on the table. He sat back in his chair. He appeared to be digesting what he had just read. A thousand different thoughts appeared to be chasing themselves across his face.

Emmeline leaned forward and hissed, "Well, don't keep me in suspense."

He tapped the notebook with his forefinger. "Melnikov was

a gold mine of information. But he was too clever for his own good."

"Sabitov said as much the day I met him at the Dorchester."

"Melnikov was playing Putin against the Russian mafia, Bronowski against Swanbeck, and all the while dangling a carrot in front of MI-Six. It was only a matter of time before his enemies caught with him."

"I see," Emmeline murmured. "How does any of it help me? And what about Rutkovsky/Victor Royce?"

"Rutkovsky is mentioned in connection with Melnikov, but Sabitov doesn't appear to know his real identity. He suspects it's an alias. Hence, the name in bold in the margin. Apparently, Melnikov and Rutkovsky were in the midst of trying to unravel a complex money-laundering scheme that involved a series of wire transfers from Vnesheconombank, known as VEB, to over two dozen accounts held in a Cypriot bank. Do you know what VEB is?"

Emmeline held his gaze and gave a solemn shake of her head.

"VEB is a Russian state-owned development bank. It's well known to us—us being the intelligence services. VEB's chief is a graduate of the training school for the FSB, the successor of the KGB. The bank carries out Putin's pet projects. It's considered a 'quasi-ministry' in view of the fact that Putin reportedly takes personal charge of major decisions. VEB has a history of coming to the rescue of the Kremlin's favored oligarchs. Russian spies and VEB have long moved money through Cyprus."

"So Melnikov and Royce were killed because they must have found evidence tying the bank accounts to Bronowski and Swanbeck. And poor Sabitov was murdered because he threatened to expose the scheme."

Philip leaned back in his chair and tapped his steepled fingers to his pursed lips. "It looks that way."

Emmeline took a thoughtful swallow of her espresso. "But where's the evidence?"

He shrugged his shoulders and pursed his lips. "Obviously

Sabitov didn't have it. MI-Five, MI-Six, and Burnell's men scoured Sabitov's flat." He shook his head. "Nothing. It's possible Bronowski or Swanbeck could have gotten there before us. I doubt it, though. They appear to have been as desperate as we are to find it. Bronowski is out of the picture now, therefore the only one left is Swanbeck. I don't want to frighten you, but I think he believes Sabitov passed the evidence to you. That's why he's trying to frame you for the murders. To get you out of the way and muddy the waters to give him time to erase its existence before it falls into the wrong hands."

"Unfortunately, the only thing I have is that." She motioned with her chin toward the notebook. She pounded her fist against her open palm. "Ooh. I wish—" She scooted to the edge of her seat and leaned forward. Her voice was low and cajoling. "Philip, is there a way that—perhaps with your connections—you can get me into Melinikov's flat?"

His brows knit together. He gave a curt shake of his head. "Absolutely not."

"Come on," she murmured. "It may be our only chance to get them. Don't you want that?"

"Yes, I want to get the bastards."

Her spirits rose.

"But it's out of the question. Categorically. Emphatically. Unequivocally. *No.* " This took the wind out of her sails.

"Why are men so closed-minded?"

"Why are you so impetuous?" he countered. "Emmeline, Scotland Yard is on the verge of arresting you for two murders. How much more trouble do you want on your plate? No story is worth it."

Her nostrils flared and she tossed her chin in the air. "The truth is always worth it."

He groaned, propping his elbows on the table and dropping his head between his hands. "I am not the enemy. I only have your best interests at heart."

She touched his sleeve, relenting slightly. Her tone softened. "I know and I appreciate it enormously. But, Philip, the only way I can clear myself is if we can find the evidence. And the place to start is Melnikov's flat."

He lifted his head and fixed his gaze on her face. An internal debate appeared to be taking place in his mind. For a second, it looked as if he was wavering.

"The answer is still no."

Emmeline folded her arms over her chest mutinously. "Hmph. And you call yourself a friend."

"Yes, that is precisely why, in good conscience, I can't permit you to put yourself in that sort of situation."

She held her tongue, seething with a mixture of anger, annoyance, and frustration.

"Promise me not to go anywhere near Melinikov's flat, or Swanbeck for that matter. Let Burnell and Finch handle it. I'll look into it on my end as well. There are dozens of other stories you can work on. You're the editorial director, after all. Be selective. Chose a different story."

She remained silent, her foot tapping ominously under the table.

"Emmeline, promise me." It was not a friendly request.

She opened her mouth to unleash a blistering rejoinder, but was forestalled.

Gregory, in all his dashing aplomb, suddenly materialized.

"Hello, darling." She caught a whiff of his spicy cologne as he bent down to brush her cheek with a kiss. He inclined his head toward Philip. "Acheson."

"How did you know where to find me?" she asked.

"It was a brilliant piece of detective work. I think Oliver would have been proud. I dropped by *The Clarion* and ran into Nigel. He told me where to find you. And here I am."

"Longdon, talk to your stubborn fiancée. Make her see sense."

Gregory smiled down at her. "Emmy is eminently sensible."

She returned his smile. "Why, thank you, darling."

"When she wants to be, that is."

"This is not one of those times," Philip said.

Emmeline made a moue at both of them.

"Acheson, consider yourself relieved from your present misery. I came to take Emmy to lunch."

He touched her elbow and she allowed him to help to her feet. She reached up and kissed his cheek. "Thank you, darling, but I'm going back to the office. I have a story to work on."

Philip shot her a pointed look. "Emmeline." There was a note of warning in his tone, which she ignored.

"Philip, instinct tells me that all the information you just disclosed about Melnikov, Royce, and what they uncovered about VEB and the Cyprus bank accounts is the link we've been looking for to bring down Swanbeck. I must follow up on it. Surely you can understand that. I have to find out the truth. It's my only chance to clear myself."

Philip threw his hands up in resignation. "As long as you don't go anywhere near Melnikov's flat."

Gregory's brow furrowed and he tightened his grip on her elbow. "Melnikov's flat?"

Emmeline gave an airy wave of her hand. "Never mind. It was an idea I had. I'll tell you about it later. Tonight. But now, you must let me get back to *The Clarion*."

She tried to push past him, but he wouldn't let go of her arm.

"Woman does not live on journalism alone. You must eat. Trust me, darling. I think you'll find lunch fascinating. Besides, it would be frightfully bad manners to keep my friend waiting."

She eyed him suspiciously. "What friend? Does this have anything to do with Swanbeck or the murders?"

One brow arched upward and there was a glint of mischief in his cinnamon eyes. "You'll never know if you linger about here."

Philip rose and tossed some money on the table. "I'll leave you two to work this out amongst yourselves." He tucked Sabitov's notebook into the inside pocket of his suit jacket. "I'll hang on to this," he told Emmeline. "I want to talk to a couple of chaps. I also want to make Burnell aware of the notebook."

She touched his arm. "You'll ring me the instant you find out anything?"

His mouth curved into a crooked smile and he bent down to give her a peck on the cheek. "I can't promise 'the instant,' but I'll let you know. No one's secret is safe when you're lurking in the background."

"First of all, I don't lurk. Besides, haven't you learned that secrets always come out, one way or another?"

CHAPTER 36

Since it was such a glorious summer day—not too warm and with a gentle breeze off the Thames—Gregory left his Jaguar at the Tower Hotel and they walked across Tower Bridge toward Le Pont de la Tour restaurant on the South Bank. Along the way, Emmeline told Gregory about her sobering discussion with Nigel and the prospect that she could be charged with murder any day now.

He slipped his arm around her shoulders and pulled her close. "It won't come to that, darling. I promise."

She stopped and searched the well-loved contours of his face. "You can't make such a promise. No one can. Not even Superintendent Burnell and Sergeant Finch. They are bound to uphold the law and—"

He smothered the rest of her sentence with a kiss. When they broke apart, he said, "Trust me. Swanbeck will pay for everything."

She nodded mutely, but, deep in her heart, she didn't share his confidence. Look at how Swanbeck had already managed to turn their lives upside down.

Come on. Buck up. Worrying never helps anything, she told herself. *All's not lost yet.*

Hadn't she and Philip just discovered the VEB link? Well, almost link. It was a solid lead at any rate. This thought put a smile on her lips. A strong lead, indeed.

By this time, they had reached the other bank. Le Pont de la Tour was only a few steps from the bridge and had a marvel-ous view of the Thames. Emmeline had never been to the res-taurant before and was disappointed to see that all the tables outside were taken. It would have been delightful to dine *al fresco*.

"Who is this mystery friend of yours?" she asked over her shoulder as Gregory held the door open and allowed her to enter the restaurant ahead of him.

"All in good time."

Emmeline gritted her teeth in frustration. "Fine."

"Ah, there he is."

She followed his gaze and saw a good-looking man in a double-breasted navy suit and claret-colored silk tie sitting at a corner table by the window.

Gregory waved off the maître d', explaining that his host had already arrived. He guided Emmeline by the elbow across the room. His friend rose and smiled, displaying a perfect set of white teeth.

"Emmy, this is Rupert Cardew. Rupert, this is my fiancée, Emmeline Kirby."

Rupert inclined his head and proffered a large, elegant hand. His hand shake was cool, firm, and confident.

"How do you do," she murmured politely.

"A pleasure to finally meet the woman who snared this disreputable fellow." He jerked his thumb at Gregory.

Emmeline slid a sideways glance at Gregory.

"Now, now, Rupe, I will not have you sullying my good name."

Rupert scoffed. "What good name?"

"I know how you operate. You stand no chance with Emmy."

Rupert stared at him. His caramel eyes flecked with gold held an expression of mock innocence. "Me? Would I really do that to a friend?"

"In a word, yes."

They both burst out laughing. Rupert clapped him on the shoulder. "It's good to see you, Greg. It's been a while."

"Yes, well. You know how it is. One thing leads to another."

Rupert searched his face but didn't press for more. Instead, he said, "Please sit down."

He held out a chair for Emmeline, while Gregory took the seat on her opposite side.

"Before we get down to business, I'd like to know, when are the impending nuptials going to take place?" Rupert asked as they began to peruse their menus.

Gregory reached out and grasped Emmeline's fingertips. They smiled at one another.

"I had the devil of a time pinning her down to a specific date," Gregory replied.

Rupert nodded knowingly, an impish glint in his eye. "That's not surprising. Any woman would have to think twice before taking the plunge into matrimony with you."

"Very droll." Then, to Emmeline Gregory said, "Darling, you see before you a man consumed by envy at my good fortune." He brought her hand to his lips and brushed her knuckles with a kiss.

Emmeline giggled as her glance flitted between the two friends. She decided that she liked Rupert tremendously. He was affable and charming. There was an intensity about him. She caught the spark of intelligence in the depths of his eyes. "To answer your question, we settled on the twenty-ninth of October for the wedding."

Rupert rubbed his chin. "Autumn, a lovely time of year to get married. I hope I'm invited to the wedding."

"Naturally, that goes without saying. I will personally send you an invitation." She beamed at him. "I know so few of Gregory's friends."

"Really. Well, Greg always was a dark one. Thank you for the invitation. I will eagerly be anticipating its arrival in the post. Now, I think we should order. Personally, I recommend the wild rock oysters as a starter. They are superb."

The next few minutes were taken up with their selections.

When the wine arrived, a crisp, golden Riesling, Rupert lifted his glass. "All joking aside, I want to offer you both my sincere congratulations. May you have a long and happy marriage, and an entire rugby team of children to fill your days."

Emmeline felt herself blush. "Thank you for your good wishes," she murmured.

"Steady on, old chap. We'll have to talk about the rugby team."

"I suppose you're right," Rupert mused. "It would be a bit much."

The rest of lunch passed in this lighthearted vein. They discussed anything and everything, from the latest hit play in the West End to the state of the economy, often going off on tangents.

When their coffees arrived, Rupert cleared his throat. "I'm sorry to mar such a delightful lunch, but I'm afraid it's time to discuss unpleasant topics."

Gregory stopped stirring his cappuccino and put his spoon down on the saucer. He raised an eyebrow in askance. "Were you able to discover anything?"

Rupert leaned back in his chair, a Cheshire cat grin upon his lips. "Really, old chap. I should be insulted, but I will give you a reprieve for Emmeline's sake."

"Is anyone going to tell me what is going on, or are the two of you going to talk in code for the rest of the afternoon?" she asked.

Rupert inclined his head. "My apologies. Let me explain. Greg rang me yesterday because of my contacts in the City. I run a hedge fund of sorts and I make it my business to know everything that happens in the financial world. Who is merging with whom; who is preparing to make the jump to a rival firm; and all the dirty laundry in between. You get the idea. Alastair Swanbeck's name always swirls about when something's not kosher—" He smiled at her surprise. "—Perfect word isn't it? Greg told me you're from that noble race so you completely understand my meaning—As I said, when any deal doesn't smell right you can bet Swanbeck is behind it."

"I see. Did Gregory tell you about the murders of two Russians named Pavel Melnikov and Yevgeny Sabitov—and of course, Victor Royce? We think they're all connected and the line seems to point to Swanbeck. We just haven't found the proof."

Rupert's smile broadened. "That's because you didn't follow the money. I did."

"Don't torture us, old chap. Spill what you know."

Rupert's gaze shifted to Gregory. "It took some doing to

sift through all the wire transfers to the various bank accounts in Cyprus."

Excitement set the adrenaline singing in Emmeline's veins. She leaned forward, one elbow on the table and her chin resting on her hand. "Cyprus bank accounts? These wouldn't happen to be transfers from a Russian bank called VEB would they?"

One eyebrow quirked upward. "Greg, are you certain you needed me? Emmeline seems to be a step ahead of us."

"I'm as much in the dark as you, Rupe. Emmy, this is no time to play lone wolf."

She waved a hand at him. "No, no. It's just information I stumbled across about an hour ago. Truly." She turned to Gregory. "It's what Philip and I were discussing."

Gregory nodded. "All right. Go on, Rupe. Let's see what we can piece together."

"I don't mind telling you that Swanbeck and Jason Royce are cunning bastards."

Emmeline sucked in her breath and shot a glance at Gregory.

Jason Royce. Her newfound half-brother. He was mixed up in this? "Jason Royce?" Her tongue stumbled over the name. "What—what does he have to do with Swanbeck?"

"They're as thick as proverbial thieves. Why, do you know him?"

She swallowed hard and licked her lips. "In a way. Please—please go on."

"It's no secret in the City that Jason badly wanted to push his father out and take control of Royce Global Holdings. However, there was never anyone as shrewd as Victor Royce. He was not blind to his son's faults. Jason's problem is that he's arrogant and lacks judgment, both personal and professional. Dear old papa had to keep a *very* tight leash on Jason. He nearly brought the company to its knees on more than one occasion. That's why Victor kept Jason on the fringes most of the time. He put Adam, Jason's brother, in charge of the really important deals. As you can imagine, there is no love lost between the two brothers. They're like night and day."

"Don't we know it," Emmeline mumbled.

"Meanwhile," Rupert went on, "If this weren't enough, it's also common knowledge that Jason gambles, heavily. And he has a mistress. One with *very* expensive tastes. Enter Alastair Swanbeck. Whispers on the grapevine have it that Jason made a deal with the devil. Swanbeck offered to pay off all of Jason's gambling debts, if he helped Swanbeck take over Royce Global Holdings. It would be Swanbeck's revenge against Victor for a deal that collapsed several years back. Swanbeck also dangled the added incentive of making Jason chairman and managing director. How could Jason resist? In one fell swoop, his debts would be cleared and, at last, he would be in charge of the company. He started sabotaging deals to make it easier for Swanbeck to launch a hostile takeover bid. In return, Swanbeck saw to it that regular monthly wire transfers were made to several accounts in Cyprus. After thoroughly rooting around in the accounts, I've been able to trace the transfers. Money would flow in from a mysterious firm through the bank in Cyprus. The money would leave the account the same day, split into several smaller disbursements to accounts with no obvious owner. There is no doubt the filthy lucre was coming from VEB to Swanbeck and then to others with less than honorable intentions. And I've got the electronic fingerprints to prove every transaction."

Emmeline's jaw dropped. "My God. How—How could Jason betray his own family like that?"

Gregory extended a hand across the table to Rupert. "Brilliant. If anyone could do it, I knew it would be you."

Rupert buffed his nails against his suit jacket and preened like a peacock. "One does one's best to please."

Emmeline recovered her senses somewhat and clutched Gregory's arm. "Do you think Jason killed his father and the two Russians to cover his tracks?"

"It appears so."

"How horrible. No wonder Jason was so furious with his father's will. He knew Adam would never agree to a takeover."

Concern was etched in every line of Gregory's face. "And

then there's you, Emmy. With Royce making you his primary beneficiary, the bulk of his fortune now comes to you. This was likely the worst blow for Jason. However, if it's proven that you murdered his father, you cannot inherit."

The espresso made her feel queasy. She shook her head, stunned. It was all so hard to fathom. Could Jason hate her that much? He didn't even know her. She didn't want Victor Royce's money. She was silent as a host of disturbing thoughts raced through her mind.

Rupert cleared his throat. "I shouldn't worry if I were you, Emmeline. I told you before, I have proof that Jason was in league with Swanbeck. Enough proof to shift scrutiny from you to him. I also took the liberty of teaching Jason and Swanbeck a lesson."

Gregory smoothed down the corners of his mustache and met his friend's gaze. "A lesson? Do tell."

"Let's just say that the next time Swanbeck and Jason decide to check their Cyprus accounts they'll find that the balance in each one is zero. On the other hand, a number of charitable organizations this morning received very generous donations from an anonymous benefactor."

The corners of Gregory's eyes crinkled and a smile spread across his face. "Pure genius. A master stroke. And they say nothing good ever comes of evil."

Rupert gave a nonchalant shrug of his shoulders. "I wouldn't know. I'm not a religious man."

They all laughed at the sheer audacity of what Rupert had done.

"If I didn't know you're a financier," Emmeline said, "I would swear that you were a criminal of the highest order."

At this remark, she caught an exchange of looks between Rupert and Gregory. And in that instant, she knew. Rupert was a con man. A successful one if outward appearances were anything to go by, but a con man nonetheless. She should be shocked, but to her surprise she realized that she wasn't. Well, well, well, wonders never ceased.

"Rupert, it's been entertaining, as always. But we have to go," Gregory mumbled hastily. "Don't we, Emmy?"

They all rose.

"Yes, of course. I have to get back to *The Clarion*. I have a story to write for tomorrow's paper." She extended a hand toward Rupert. "It was delightful meeting you."

He pressed her hand between both of his. "I assure you the pleasure was all mine. I will look for your wedding invitation in the post."

She smiled up at him. "I won't forget. Perhaps you'll tell me some stories about what you and Gregory got up to in the past."

Gregory shot her a warning look. "Emmy, there's nothing to tell. I've lived an exemplary life without a blemish to my name."

She snorted. "Hmph. And pigs fly, right?"

Rupert laughed. "I'd watch my step, if I were you, Greg."

Gregory sighed melodramatically. "It seems I don't have much choice. But seriously, Rupe, thanks for everything."

Rupert flapped his hands. "Think nothing of it. Men like Jason Royce and Swanbeck leave a bad taste in one's mouth. I'll have a messenger deliver the USB drive with evidence of the wire transfers. It was too risky for me to bring it here today."

"Thanks. I understand." A shadow of concern clouded Gregory's eyes as he scanned his friend's face. "But you're certain there's no way to trace anything back to you?"

Rupert clapped him on the shoulder and smiled. "Greg, I'm not an amateur. I don't leave fingerprints, electronic or otherwise."

"No, of course not. It was a silly question."

ᘓᘓᘓ

Rupert walked with Emmeline and Gregory to the foot of Tower Bridge, where they all parted ways. Emmeline continued straight on along the river toward the office, while Gregory climbed the stairs to cross back over the bridge to get his car.

Rupert wended his way back to his Audi, which was

parked on Gainsford Street at the intersection with Lafone Street.

He slipped in behind the wheel and checked the messages on his mobile. Nothing that couldn't wait until he got home tonight.

He smiled as he clicked his seatbelt into place. He had truly enjoyed meeting Emmeline. What a wonderful girl. Greg was a lucky man. He made a mental note to start looking for a wedding present for the happy couple.

Rupert slipped the key in the ignition. It made a sputtering, guttural noise. Damn. It had just been to the garage for a tune-up.

He turned the key again. This time the engine turned over.

The hot rush of the explosion seared the air, shattering the windows of nearby buildings.

A giant, invisible hand reached down from the sky to scoop up the car and drop it back with a sickening *thud*. Greedy, crackling tongues of orange-red flame licked at the crumpled heap of mangled metal. And all the while, the acrid, choking smell of death clung with ferocious tenacity to what had been a lovely summer afternoon.

CHAPTER 37

By the time Superintendent Burnell and Sergeant Finch had arrived, the fire had been put out and the gruesome scene was cordoned off with yellow *DO NOT CROSS* tape. Burnell and Finch were handed gloves, and blue plastic suits and booties to slip over their clothes so that they wouldn't contaminate any evidence.

Uniformed constables had managed to clear the site. Panic had rippled through the area earlier sending people running and screaming in different directions. It was not surprising after the infamous July 2005 bombings in the Underground. Everyone thought it had been another terrorist attack.

As his practiced eye surveyed the detritus and damage, Burnell was not so sure. Murder, yes. Most definitely. But terrorist attack? That remained to be determined.

"Finch, find out if they've identified the poor sod and whatever else they've come up with so far."

Finch nodded. "Right, sir." He strode off toward a pair of officers from the Yard's counterterrorism unit. Their heads were bent together, dour expressions on their weary faces.

Burnell sighed. Such a tragic waste. Even after thirty years on the force, he would never get used to death. Every fiber of his being rebelled against the idea of taking another life. It was an anathema. Only someone with evil lodged deep in his black heart could even contemplate something that would be so repugnant to a sane mind.

He made a circle of what had once been a sleek, beautiful, top-of-the-range Audi that now was reduced to a charred, twisted metal tomb.

Dr. Meadows's voice drifted to his ears. "Here we are again, Oliver."

Burnell turned and gave his old friend a half-hearted smile. "Yes, here we are again, John."

"The whole world has gone mad. Absolutely crackers. Why can't people get along anymore?"

Burnell pursed his lips and gave a disgusted shake of his head. "No idea." He exhaled a long, slow breath and mumbled, "No idea at all. There's too much hatred. Or maybe it's just me. Maybe I'm too old for this job."

Meadows snorted and waved his hands impatiently in the air. "Stuff and nonsense. Your mind is razor-sharp. You can run rings around these chaps and ladies." The sweep of his arm encompassed all the constables and members of the forensics team who were going about their jobs.

The superintendent pulled himself up to his full height and shook his head to clear his mind of this depressing train of thought. "Right. What can you tell me?"

"Thankfully, the explosion killed him almost instantly. The ensuing fire burnt the body beyond recognition." Burnell winced at this remark. "We'll have to try to identify him from dental records. After my preliminary examination, I'd have to say he was around thirty-five to forty. More than that I can't tell you."

"I understand." Burnell's stomach turned over several times as he took one last tour around the wreck. "Off you go then, John. Take him away."

Meadows nodded. "I'll see you Friday for our usual pint?"

"What?" The superintendent shot him a quizzical look, his mind was mulling over the few facts that they were able to piece together. "Oh, yes, right. Friday. As usual. Wouldn't miss it."

Meadows signaled to one of his team and then turned back to Burnell. "It may sound trite and you wouldn't be human otherwise, but don't let the violence get to you. Then the baddies will have won, and we can't have that."

The superintendent clapped him between the shoulder blades. "No, we can't have that. I'll be fine."

Meadows favored him with a half-smile. "You think I don't know that? I'll have the report to you as soon as I can."

He drifted off and Burnell shuffled down the block to see what Finch had been able to discover.

"Thanks," Finch murmured to a constable as Burnell drew level with him.

The sergeant tapped his notebook with his pen. "Sir, they've run the license plate. Our victim is a Rupert Cardew. I had them do a check. He doesn't have a criminal record. He seems to be—he was some sort of financial genius. He ran a hedge fund in the City. Divorced. No children. She kept the house in Belsize Park. He has a flat near Sloane Square."

"It's a start. As soon as we're finished here, I want you to pay a visit to the ex-Mrs. Cardew. Find out if he had any enemies. Girlfriends. Money troubles. The usual thing."

"Right, sir. I'd already planned to do so."

Burnell cocked an eyebrow. "Can you read minds now too? Already know my next step, before I take it?"

Finch chuckled. "Hardly, sir. It's just that you're such a wealth of knowledge, I simply absorb your wisdom through osmosis."

The superintendent snorted. "Hmph. That's doing it a bit too brown. Don't think flattery will get you that pay rise." But this was said without any rancor.

"No, sir, it never even crossed my mind."

"Uh. Huh. What else can you tell me? Have you found out what Cardew was doing in the area?"

"Yes, I've spoken to a few witnesses. Apparently, he had lunch at the Le Pont de la Tour just along the river." He waved a hand vaguely in the direction to his right.

"Did he dine alone?"

"No. He had two luncheon companions. A man and a woman."

Burnell's eyes narrowed. He had caught a change of inflexion in Finch's tone. "What is it? Something wrong?"

"Well," the sergeant hedged. "You're not going to like it."

The superintendent threw his hands up in the air in exasperation. "I don't like murder. So out with it, before I have you back in uniform walking a beat again."

Finch took a deep breath. "Cardew had lunch with Emmeline and Longdon."

Burnell's eyes widened in surprise. "Bloody hell," he exploded.

"Yes. Succinct, to the point. You always get to the crux of the matter. I couldn't have put it better myself, sir. I suppose that's why you're superintendent and I'm still a lowly sergeant."

The superintendent impaled him with a frosty glare.

Finch swallowed hard. "Sorry, sir. I was just trying to lighten the mood."

"You failed," Burnell replied through gritted teeth, "*miserably.*"

The sergeant dipped his head, suitably chastened, and mumbled, "Sorry. It looks bad, but we *know* Longdon and Emmeline couldn't have had anything to do with this."

The superintendent sighed wearily. "I wish I had never gotten out of bed this morning." This was said more to himself than the sergeant. He shook his head. "No, of course, Emmeline and Longdon were not involved. I'm not senile yet. But someone is going to great lengths to incriminate them."

They both fell into a troubled silence for a moment as they watched the activity taking place around them.

Finch's brow puckered. "Sir, in view of his financial background, do you think that Cardew could have had anything to do with those wire transfers Mr. Acheson told us about from that Russian bank to Swanbeck and those accounts in Cyprus? Could Cardew have been the go-between and gotten greedy? Or perhaps he killed Melnikov and then he was a liability to Swanbeck because he knew too much."

Burnell folded an arm over his chest and stroked his beard with his other hand. "It's possible. All of it fits. I'll have a private word with Philip. Before you speak with Cardew's ex-wife, I want you to take a team and scour his flat from top to bottom."

"On it, sir." The sergeant started to walk away and then pivoted on his heel. He cleared his throat. "What are we going to do about Emmeline and Longdon?"

Burnell grimaced. "What choice do we have? We'll have to question them. Again we have a dead body and again they were among the last people to see the victim alive. Why do they insist on making our lives so complicated?"

Finch couldn't think of a suitable answer to this question.

∽∾∿

Burnell was in a thoroughly foul mood later that afternoon when Finch tapped on his door with Emmeline and Gregory in tow.

"Sir, Emmeline and Longdon are here," the sergeant said needlessly.

"I do have eyes, Finch." He pointed at the chairs opposite. "Well, don't stand there gawping. Come in and sit down."

Emmeline and Gregory did as they were bid, while Finch quietly pressed the door closed behind them.

He crossed over to the desk and hovered just behind Burnell.

The silence loomed heavy and disquieting. Emmeline attempted a watery smile, but it was quickly smothered by the superintendent's fixed scrutiny.

Gregory was the first one to speak, naturally. "It's extremely flattering, Oliver, to know that you miss us so much."

Burnell folded his hands, fingers interlaced, on his desk. "Longdon, if I never see you again it will be too soon. I want none of your lip."

Gregory pressed a hand to his chest. "It hurts right here to hear you say that. I'm a shy, sensitive soul you know."

"*Longdon*," Burnell roared.

Emmeline touched Gregory's sleeve and gave a disapproving shake of her head. Gregory merely smiled and turned his attention back to the superintendent.

"Forgive me. I am yours to command," he said, but the bemused gleam in his eyes belied the words.

"Do you know why I've called you down here? *Again*."

"Absolutely no idea. We're all ears waiting for you to enlighten us."

"Hmph. I'm sure you've heard about the explosion that took place earlier this afternoon on the South Bank."

This finally wiped the grin off Gregory's lips. By his side, a troubled expression clouded Emmeline's dark eyes.

"Yes," she replied in a hushed tone. "I've sent one of my chaps to cover the story. From the initial reports, it was a car bomb, right?"

Burnell nodded grimly. "That's correct."

"I was nearly back at *The Clarion*, when I heard the explosion."

"And I was halfway across Tower Bridge," Gregory replied. "I saw the plume of black smoke rise in the air."

Always the reporter, Emmeline couldn't help firing questions at the superintendent. "Was anyone hurt? Do you think it was a terrorist attack? Has anyone claimed responsibility?"

Burnell lifted his hands in the air. "Just a moment, I want to make something perfectly clear. I didn't call you down here to give an interview."

She nodded solemnly.

"Good. Now then, our preliminary investigation seems to rule out a terrorist attack. However, it *was* murder. And it appears that the two of you—" His glance trailed from Emmeline to Gregory. "—are involved up to your necks. Again."

Emmeline turned to Gregory and raised a brow in askance.

He shrugged, for once baffled as much as she was. "Respectfully, Oliver, you've been out in the sun too long if you think that we had anything to do with this."

"Ha. There isn't an ounce of respect in your body, Longdon. But let's get back to the matter at hand. A little bird told me that the two of you just so happened to have had lunch with the victim."

He heard a sharp intake of breath from Emmeline. Her hand flew to her mouth. "*No.*" It was an anguished cry ripped from her throat.

A sheen of tears glistened upon her eyelashes as her head whipped round to look at Gregory, whose complexion took on a sickly, grayish hue. His mouth went slack. The sparkle had been extinguished in the depths of his eyes. For a second, it was replaced by a dull sadness, then a shadow fell and his face became a mask of inscrutability. He was so still. He simply sat there, ramrod straight, hands on his knees, staring at Burnell.

Emmeline exchanged a worried glance with the superintendent, who shook his head and shrugged.

She tentatively reached out to touch Gregory's arm. "Darling," she whispered.

At the sound of her voice, he turned to face her. His lips curved into a crooked smile. He patted her small hand. "I'm all right." This was a hoarse croak." I didn't expect—I can't believe—We were with him only a few hours ago."

She laced her fingers through his. "I know. It's a shock for me and I only just met Rupert. Such a lovely man. But for you, my darling, it must be devastating because he was your friend."

Burnell noisily cleared his throat. This was too much emotion for him. "Umm, Longdon. For what it's worth, I'm sorry."

Finch dipped his head and mumbled, "My condolences as well."

"Thanks, Oliver. Finch. Rupert was a first-rate fellow. A loyal friend. He didn't deserve this."

"No, I agree with you there. No one deserves to die that way," Burnell replied. "I'm sorry to have to be blunt, but we're conducting a murder investigation. There's no time for dilly-dallying. We've ruled out terrorism. Cardew appears to have been the sole target. The bomb—" He paused, fixing his gaze on Longdon. He saw the other man tense when he uttered the latter word. Well, best get it over with. "The bomb was rigged to explode when he turned the key. There would have been no chance to escape. Likely he was killed instantly."

"That's cold comfort," Longdon muttered.

"Do you have any idea who could have done this? Did Cardew have any enemies?" Finch asked.

The muscle in Longdon's jaw started to pulse furiously beneath his skin. When he spoke, his voice was low and infused with venom. "You mean you haven't guessed, Oliver? Shame on you." His eyes were alight with cinnamon fire. "Look no farther than Swanbeck and Jason Royce."

CHAPTER 38

*J*ason *Royce*? You can't be serious," Burnell roared. Longdon shook off Emmeline's hand and leaned across the desk, his face only inches from the superintendent. "I'm deadly serious," he hissed. "Royce likely killed his father to get his greedy hands on the company. All he cares about is money and power. Just like Swanbeck. The dirty, miserable swine."

"Shh, Gregory," Emmeline murmured soothingly. Then to Burnell, she said, "You can see that he's upset. Let me explain."

Without embellishments, she proceeded to apprise the two detectives about everything Rupert had divulged over lunch about VEB, the wire transfers, Swanbeck, the accounts in Cyprus, and Jason Royce's gambling debts.

A low whistle escaped Finch's lips when she came to the end of her story. "Royce has been a busy boy. The hypocrite," he spat in disgust.

"What do you say now, Oliver?" Gregory pressed.

Burnell leaned back in his chair and stroked his beard. "I say this puts a different complexion on the case. However—"

"Ha," Gregory snorted in triumph.

"—however," Burnell went on, "we need proof. Royce has powerful friends. I can't just go out and accuse him of skullduggery and murder. Where's the USB drive?"

Gregory's jaw hardened. "I don't have it. Rupert said he was going to send it by messenger. He didn't want to risk bringing it with him this afternoon. It must still be in his flat."

Finch coughed. "Sir."

Three pairs of eyes shifted toward him. Burnell didn't like

the look on the sergeant's face. What else could go wrong to-day?

"What is it, Finch?" he retorted tetchily.

"Sir, this is the first opportunity I've had to speak to you since I returned to the station. Your mobile was off for some reason."

Burnell drummed his fingers on the desk impatiently. "Well, tell me *now* for Christ's sake and stop making a meal of it."

Finch nodded. "We found Cardew's flat ransacked. Some-one appeared to be in a great hurry." His gaze flitted to Grego-ry. "If there was a USB drive, we'll never know. The team catalogued and photographed everything. I've sealed the flat, but it will take days to sift through the mess."

The superintendent slammed his open palm against the desk, making his telephone and everything that was loose jump. "Damn and blast."

"Oliver, it doesn't matter. Bring Royce and Swanbeck in for questioning. Rattle their cages." Gregory held Burnell's gaze. "You *know* they're guilty as sin. You know it."

"Bring Royce in? Have you taken leave of your senses? I already have him and his mother breathing down my neck about Emmeline. They've found a very sympathetic ear in Cruickshank. He's taken to cooing like a dove. The spineless weasel. He'll have my guts for garters if he hears that I've brought Royce in for questioning. Unless you find that USB drive, we have no proof. Just circumstantial evidence. There's nothing I can do."

Gregory surged to his feet. "So you're simply going to give up?"

"Now look here, Longdon, there are procedures that must be followed. *Laws* that must be followed. I didn't say I liked it, but I'm bound to uphold the law."

Gregory sneered derisively. "I see. Far be it from me to in-terfere with your duty." He pivoted on his heel and looked down at Emmeline. "Oliver, can you see that Emmy gets home all right?"

Burnell nodded in confusion. "Of course. Finch will take her home."

Emmeline started to protest, but Gregory ignored her. "Good."

He crossed to the door in two strides, his shoulders rigid with determination.

"Where are you going?" Burnell called after him.

Gregory tossed a backward glance over his shoulder. A roguish glint flashed in his eyes. "Nowhere in particular. I just felt a sudden urge to stretch my legs."

The door opened and closed before the superintendent could utter another word.

Burnell's gaze locked on Emmeline's face. "Where's he going?"

She shrugged and spread her hands wide.

"I hope he's not going to do anything foolish."

Her mouth curved into an enchanting smile. She was learning from Longdon, Burnell thought.

"Certainly not. Gregory's never foolish." She rose and hitched her handbag over her shoulder. "He knows exactly what he's doing." Then to Finch she said, "There's no need for you to drive me home. I have a lot of work to do. I'm going back to the office."

"Emmeline." Burnell's tone held a note of warning.

"Yes, Superintendent Burnell?" she asked sweetly as she took a few steps backward, inching closer to the door in preparation to flee.

"You could get hurt antagonizing men like Swanbeck and Royce."

She put a hand to her chest, her dark eyes all wide with innocence. "I wouldn't dream of it. Now, I must dash."

And dash she did.

Burnell exhaled a weary breath. "Finch, why do I have an uneasy feeling in the pit of my stomach? I always thought Longdon and Emmeline were completely mismatched. I was wrong. They're like two peas in pod. I don't know who is more of a bad influence."

❧❧❧

The rain was pelting the windows of the cab from all angles. Mother Nature had unleashed her anger on the poor hapless citizens of London and its environs for the last two hours. She, too, was unsatisfied with the pace of justice and was expressing her displeasure in the only way she knew how.

Gregory checked his watch. It was a few minutes before ten. The play should be letting out soon.

The driver swiveled round to peer at him through the shadows. "It's your money, guv. But wouldn't you rather have me take you somewhere to get out of this filthy night?"

"It won't be long now. My friend should—Ah, there he is."

Gregory easily picked out Jason Royce and a blonde woman, presumably his mistress, among the crowd exiting the Duke of York's Theatre. Both were huddled under the marquis. The woman had her hand clamped through Jason's elbow. Royce ducked his head and whispered something in her ear, before he prized his arm free of her grip. He went to the curb to hail a cab.

"I won't be a minute," Gregory told the driver. "I'm just going to run across the road to get my friend."

"Suit yourself," the driver replied and turned back to gaze out the windscreen, his fingers tapping a tattoo on the steering wheel.

In one graceful movement, Gregory unfurled his umbrella and sprinted across the road. He came up behind Jason.

"Hello, Jason old chap,"

Royce whirled round at the sound of his voice. "Longdon? What the devil are you doing here? I thought you'd be tucked up at home trying to find a good lawyer for your fiancée. She's going to need one." His mouth curled into a smug smile.

Gregory held himself in check. As tempting as it would be to loosen all of Royce's teeth with a single blow to his cruel mouth, he had to remain in control. For Emmeline. And for Rupert. Royce and Swanbeck had to pay for all their sins. That meant doing it the legal way—well, almost legal. After all, the law could do with a little bending here and there. Just to keep things interesting.

He took a step closer and plastered a smile on his lips. He

lowered his voice so that only Royce could hear him. "I know about VEB and the Cyprus accounts, which are now suddenly devoid of funds. Poor Jason."

Royce stiffened. "I have no idea what you're talking about." But he made no move to leave.

Gregory clapped him on the shoulder and drew him closer. "Your mouth says no, but your eyes betray you. I have the evidence. Dates, wire transfers, account numbers. Everything. A nice straight line that ties you to Swanbeck and the Russians."

"Jason, what are you doing?" His mistress had sidled up to them.

"I—I—" Royce stammered.

Gregory filled the breach. "Forgive me, dear lady. It is entirely my fault." He favored her with a smile that brought a blush to her face, as it was intended to do. "Unfortunately, Jason is needed back at the office. Urgent business, you understand."

"What? At this time of night?" she asked incredulously.

Royce started to protest, but Gregory stomped on his foot and hissed out of the side of his mouth, "Get rid of her unless you want the world to know your dirty secrets."

Royce cleared his throat. "Yes, I'm sorry, Anabelle. I'm afraid it can't be helped." He fumbled in his pocket and shoved a fistful of money at her. "Take a cab home. I'll ring you in the morning."

"Bloody cheek. Don't bother to ring. I won't be home."

She tossed her chin in air and moved off, at last. She disappeared into a cab half a minute later and was gone.

"That was very good, Jason. Perhaps you should consider a new career in acting."

"What do you want, Longdon?" Royce griped through gritted teeth.

"It's very simple. You and Swanbeck have been very naughty boys. Rupert Cardew was my friend. And you killed him." There was a tremor in his tone, but he went on. "Blew him to bits this afternoon because he was about to expose you. That was a mistake. I'm going to make sure you remember Rupert's name for what's left of your miserable life."

"*Murder?*" Royce's voice rose an octave. "I didn't kill anyone. I'm an innocent man."

Gregory tossed his head back and laughed. It was a harsh, bitter sound that grated on the ears. "Oh, Jason." He patted the other man's face, hard. "You are so far from innocent that you make a black sheep look like a snowy swan. Remember I have the evidence. I haven't *quite* decided how I'll use the proof of your treachery." He flashed a malicious grin at the other man. "I think I'll surprise you. But rest assured, you and Swanbeck are going down. Give my regards to Swanbeck. I'll be in touch."

He gave Royce a shove toward the curb, where a cab had just pulled alongside. "Look there's your cab. Off you go home to your wife. You can tell her all about your night out with Annabelle."

He turned his back and left Royce standing there, his mouth hanging open, his Adam's apple working up and down furiously, and fear etched in every crevice of his pinched face.

CHAPTER 39

The next morning, Jason was still reeling from his encounter with Longdon. Sleep had eluded him and now he felt drained of energy.

What did the scoundrel want? He was going to ruin everything.

Jason pushed his plate away in disgust. He couldn't even contemplate breakfast. His stomach was a churning sea. Instead, he reached for *The Clarion* and cast his eye over the front page as he lifted his coffee cup to his lips with a hand that was not quite steady. He burned his tongue and nearly went into apoplexy when he saw Emmeline's leader. Her story was about suspicious wire transfers from Vnesheconombank, or VEB, a Russian development bank to accounts in Cyprus.

Jason dropped his head into his hands and shook it from side to side. All his carefully laid plans were tumbling about his ears. *What am I going to do?* he screamed inwardly. The money was gone, thanks to Longdon and his bloody fiancée, and now they wanted to fit him up for murder.

He got to his feet so quickly that he nearly toppled his chair over as he fled the dining room of his South Kensington townhouse. He barely registered his wife as he barreled past her in the corridor in his haste to shut himself up in his study.

He dropped heavily into the chair behind his desk and immediately reached for the phone. He bloody well wasn't going to be sacrificed to the wolves alone.

His fingers drummed on the desk. "Pick up the damn phone," he roared at the receiver.

He was on the verge of giving up, when the call was answered on the fourth ring. A languid voice, distorted mid-yawn, murmured in his ear, "Ahh. To what do I owe a call at this hour?"

"It's eight-thirty for Christ's sake, Alastair, not the crack of dawn."

"It might as well be dawn. What do you want? I haven't had my coffee yet."

"You and your coffee can go to the devil for all I care. We have a problem."

"Do we?"

Swanbeck's nonchalance irked Jason. "Ye—es. Longdon ambushed me last night when I came out of the theater. He knows all about VEB and the accounts in Cyprus."

"Don't get your knickers in a twist, Jason. Longdon's bluffing. He knows nothing. He was simply trying to scare you. And from the frantic tone of this call, he appears to have succeeded. Relax."

"I can't relax. He told me he has evidence. He got it from Rupert Cardew. The chap who died in that explosion yesterday. Apparently, Cardew was Longdon's friend. He said that he was going to see to it that we get the blame for Cardew's murder. Alastair, tell me that you had nothing to do with this? Tell me." Jason hated the plaintive tremor he heard in his own voice.

Swanbeck was silent so long that Jason wondered whether he had severed the connection. "Alastair?"

"Yes, I'm here," he replied, his tone tinged with irritation. "I was waiting for you to finish with your tantrum."

"Don't you dare patronize me. Just tell me you didn't murder this Cardew fellow," he insisted.

Swanbeck's husky laugh grated on his nerves, pulling them taut. "Don't be naïve, Jason. Sometimes you have to get your hands dirty to get what you want. Besides, Cardew had to be punished for wiping out the Cyprus accounts. It's bad manners to touch other people's property."

Jason drew in a ragged breath. "My God, you're mad. I never agreed to murder. All I wanted was Royce Global Holdings. Nothing more. The company is mine by right. Our deal was that I was going to help you secure enough stock to get on the board. In exchange, you were going to persuade the rest of the board to give Dad the elbow and put me in charge. That was our deal."

"Things change. I was getting tired of waiting for you to deliver on your promises, so I took matters into my own hands. And now, you've become irrelevant."

Jason shook his head in disbelief. "What—what do you mean?" he stammered.

"As of yesterday morning, I own twenty-five percent of the stock in Royce Global Holdings. That automatically makes me a full board member with all privileges. I've had a quiet word with a majority of my fellow members and have persuaded them to vote you out of the company at the board's meeting next month. It's nothing personal. Just sound business sense. You're unreliable, Jason. If you're left in control, you're going to bankrupt the company. I have to protect my investment."

"You conniving bastard. This was your plan from the outset. You were simply stringing me along so that you could get your foot in the door. Who sold you the stock?"

"Does it really matter?"

"Yes," Jason bellowed, slamming his palm on the desk. "It bloody well does."

"Your mother. It was your mother."

Jason nearly dropped the receiver. *Mum?* Mum wouldn't do this to him. He must have misunderstood. "I beg your pardon," he croaked.

Swanbeck chuckled. "You heard me. It's all legal. Airtight, in fact. Your mother sold me her stock. There's absolutely nothing you can do about it."

"You took advantage of a grieving widow."

"You're entitled to your opinion. This conversation has become tedious. Don't ring me again."

The line went dead.

CHAPTER 40

Burnell grunted as he perused Emmeline's story again. Balanced though it was with credible sources cited, it didn't get better upon second reading. In fact, it fairly screamed at him. Why? Wasn't his job hard enough as it was with Cruickshank lurking about? The paper rustled indignantly as he closed it with a vicious snap and laid it face down on his desk. Out of sight, out of mind, right? Wrong. The words seemed to rise up and swirl round and round, mocking him.

Damn and blast. The story was only going to inflame an already volatile situation, especially coming on the heels of Rupert Cardew's murder. Emmeline was intentionally making herself a target, taunting Jason Royce and Swanbeck. They would come after her with a vengeance. Burnell pounded his fist against his open palm. He and Finch had to find something—fast—to prove that someone other than Emmeline had an opportunity and *motive* to kill Victor Royce. That would at least tamp down the criticism coming from Jason and Mrs. Royce, who were determined to see Emmeline arrested. Burnell got the distinct impression that they wished that hanging was still being used to mete out punishment. *Oh, how money turns people into savages.*

He exhaled a long, low breath. He snatched up his receiver and rang Finch's extension.

"Finch, pop into my office and bring all your notes as well as the formal statements from everyone you interviewed at the Royce house about their movements the day before the body was found."

"Yes, sir. I'll be there in a tick."

Burnell stroked his beard thoughtfully as he replaced the

receiver. He had the nagging feeling that they had missed something very important. Something that was right there under their noses.

As he waited for Finch, he drew out the forensic report from his drawer. He put the report to one side and methodically started to sift through the crime scene photos. His gaze lingered on every detail of the room. Victor Royce slumped facedown on his desk, his head resting on the manila folder with his new will. The empty tumbler of Scotch on the floor. The drapes drawn at the windows. Books all neatly aligned on their shelves. The two wing chairs clustered about the fireplace.

Nothing. He saw nothing. And yet, it *was* there. He knew it. He picked up the close-up of the desk and the dead man again. He squinted at it for several seconds. He shook his head and sighed. Perhaps, the report would help to jiggle loose the elusive clue that was locked in the back of his brain.

He snatched up his glasses and had only gotten through the first page, when there was a light tap at the door and then Finch entered his office.

The sergeant held up a stack of folders in the air. "These are all the statements, sir."

Burnell closed the forensic report. "Good. Bring them here. I want to go over them again. But first your notes."

Finch crossed the room and placed the files on desk, as he lowered himself into the chair opposite the superintendent. He flipped open his notebook.

"The chauffeur, Jeremy Prescott, corroborated Emmeline's story. He collected Royce and her at Sotheby's. At first, Royce asked him to take them to Brown's for tea. But he changed his mind and in the end Prescott drove them to the house in Cheyne Walk instead. He dropped them off in front and then he drove the car round the corner to the garage. Royce said that he wouldn't be needing the car that evening, so Prescott performed his daily inspection to make sure that everything was in order. Then, he nipped up to the kitchen for a quick cup of tea himself before he went home for the night. He doesn't live in. The same goes for Mrs. Mellet, the cook, Mrs. Allingdale, the housekeeper, Christopher Willard, the butler, and

Karen Nelson, the maid. Naturally, when the Royces have guests, or a party, the servants remain longer, but they still go to their separate homes at the end of the evening."

"I see. I assume all their alibis check out?"

"Yes, sir."

"And there were no deliveries that day? Or workmen at the house for any reason? No strangers?"

Finch gave a solemn shake of his head. "No, sir." He hesitated. "Emmeline was the only stranger that day. But then she was already known to the household since she and Longdon had been to the Royces' party. The only other unexpected visitor was Adam Royce. From what Mrs. Allingdale said, Royce, his son, and Emmeline were enjoying tea in the garden until Mrs. Royce returned home. Then the mood changed almost instantly. Things became distinctly strained. Royce asked Adam to drive Emmeline home. Emmeline went inside and waited in the hall, while Adam remained on the terrace for a few minutes longer to have another word with his father. Mrs. Allingdale was up and down the stairs, so it's *possible* that Emmeline could have nipped into the library to poison Royce's Scotch. But she can't believe 'that sweet girl' could do something so horrid."

Burnell gave him a crooked smile. "Well, *we* know she didn't do it. Our problem is that we have to prove it."

Finch's lips pursed. "Mmm. Her story in today's paper about Cardew and the illicit wire transfers doesn't help matters."

"No, it certainly does not," the superintendent muttered sententiously. "Anything else in your notes I should know?"

Finch glanced down and flipped through a few pages. "Not really. Mrs. Allingdale said that shortly after Adam and Emmeline left, Mrs. Royce appeared to have a heated argument with her husband. It didn't last long, though. Mrs. Allingdale was coming downstairs when Mrs. Royce came in a few minutes later. They met on the landing. Mrs. Royce said that she had a raging headache and was going straight to bed. She was not to be disturbed under any circumstances. Mrs. Allingdale asked if she'd like a tray brought up to her room. Mrs.

Royce politely refused, saying that she was too upset and wouldn't be able to swallow a single bite. She was going to take a sleeping pill. All she wanted was to be left alone.

"Mrs. Allingdale then went down to the kitchen to inform Mrs. Mellet that it would only be Mr. Royce for dinner. Before she left for the evening, she went out into the garden to see if Mr. Royce needed anything else. He said no, but as is her habit, she checked all the rooms before going home. She saw that Royce's Scotch was running low, so she topped up the decanter in the library. And that was it. Mrs. Mellet was the last of the servants to see Royce alive. She waited until he had finished dinner, did the washing up, and left at about eight o'clock. You know everyone's movements the next morning when Royce was discovered."

Burnell sat up bolt upright in his chair. "Of course, that's it. Finch, you're a genius. You've earned your pay rise."

The sergeant shot him a quizzical look. "Thank you, sir. But what exactly have I done?"

Burnell ignored his question and grabbed the forensic report again. The only sound in the room was paper crackling as he quickly leafed through to the page he wanted. He mumbled under his breath as he scanned the particular section.

"I knew it," he said with smug confidence. "It's been staring at us in the face." He pushed the file toward Finch and tapped his forefinger on the page. "Read it. Aloud."

The sergeant did as he was bid. "'The victim's fingerprints match those found on the tumbler, the desk, and the rest of the room. No fingerprints were found on the decanter.'" Finch looked up. "Sir, it makes sense that Royce's fingerprints were the only ones found. By all accounts, the library was his refuge."

Burnell leaned back in his chair and steepled his fingers over his stomach. "It's perfectly logical. But *why* weren't there any fingerprints on the decanter? Royce's should have been there, as well as Mrs. Allingdale's."

Finch's brown gaze locked on his superior's face. "But they weren't. Someone wiped it clean the next morning. In all the confusion, who would have noticed?"

Burnell's mouth curved into a Cheshire cat grin. "Precisely. Our killer is a cool and calculating bugger."

"It has to be Swanbeck."

The superintendent shook his head and shot a pityingly glance at Finch. "Swanbeck is guilty as sin. But not for the murder of Victor Royce. Melinikov, Sabitov, Bronowski, and Cardew, most definitely. Their murders have Swanbeck's signature all over them, even if he didn't commit the final act himself. From what Longdon has told us and what we've been able to piece together, Swanbeck's innate sangfroid keeps him in check. He doesn't allow himself to lose control for an instant. He's always thinking, planning. He's like a chess player in that regard. His mind is ten moves ahead of his opponents. That's why he's been able to evade the law on such a grand scale."

"But, sir, everyone can panic and make mistakes if they're angry or desperate enough."

"That's very true. In Royce's case, I think it was a mixture of blind fury and resentment."

Finch's eyes narrowed. "You know who the killer is, don't you?"

Burnell suddenly became coy. "I rather think I do. Shall I tell you my theory?"

ဢၵၱ

Theories, Emmeline groaned inwardly later that afternoon as she stared out at the Thames without really seeing it. She sighed, gripping her elbows as she hugged her arms tightly around her body. She paced back and forth in front of her desk, thoughts chasing one another across her mind.

Theories were all they had without Rupert's evidence. It was so frustrating. They knew Jason and Swanbeck were hand in glove. They knew it. And yet, the two men were still going about their nefarious business bold as brass. Ooh, she absolutely wanted to scream. How was it possible?

There had to be a way to get them. Between them, they had murdered five men. One was too many, but *five*. Gregory had told her about his "friendly" chat with Jason last night outside the theater, and she had published her story in today's paper about the wire transfers and Rupert's death. There was no reaction whatsoever. Naïve though it was, she had hoped that Jason and Swanbeck would betray themselves somehow. They hadn't. She was loath to admit it even to herself, but this frightened her. As long as they couldn't find any proof against Jason and Swanbeck, she would remain the prime suspect in Victor Royce's—she swallowed hard, *my father's*—murder. There was a real possibility she could be arrested and convicted. She shivered involuntarily. All because Victor Royce's guilty conscience prompted him to make a grand gesture at the end of his life. With the stroke of a pen, he had condemned her to suspicion, enmity, and outright contempt.

She felt a tear sting her eyelid. *Don't you dare*, she reprimanded herself. *Don't you dare cry. You can't give up now. You're so close to the truth. So close.*

She stopped in mid-stride, straightened her spine, and drew her shoulders back. "Yes," she said aloud. "I *am* close to finding all the answers. I can almost taste it."

The strident peal of the telephone jarred her from her thoughts. She lunged for the receiver. "Hello, Emmeline Kirby."

A gravelly male voice hissed in her ear. "You know you're lucky. Your granny looks like she's jolly good fun. I'm standing here watching her right now. She's chatting with a couple of young chaps at the Caffè Nero here in Charing Cross. If she's not careful, she'll miss her train back to Swaley."

Emmeline sucked in her breath. She pressed the receiver closer to her ear. "Who is this?"

The stranger chuckled. "Never mind, love. What you should really be worrying about is your granny. I'd hate to have to her hurt, or worse—I mean that with all sincerity—simply because you couldn't keep your nose out of things that are none of your bloody business."

Her hand trembled and she nearly dropped the receiver. "Touch a single hair on Gran's head and I'll—"

That irritating laugh echoed down the line again. "You're

funny. Issuing ultimatums." Another laugh. Then the man's tone changed. It was laced with menace. "You're in no position to be issuing ultimatums. Now, listen. I'm going to give you a little friendly advice. If you'd like to see dear old granny again in one piece, I suggest you develop amnesia about several topics you've been writing at length about lately." He paused for an interminable moment. "And one final thing, a mere trifle to ensure granny's continued well-being, you're going to pop along to Charing Cross and bring the Blue Angel and Cardew's USB drive with you."

Emmeline gripped the edge of her desk to keep herself from collapsing to the floor. "I—I don't have them."

"Come, come, Emmeline." She hated the sound of her name on this fiend's tongue. "Do you think we're stupid? We checked Longdon's flat. They weren't there. So that only leaves you. It's your choice. Isn't granny's life worth more than a diamond and a tiny piece of plastic?"

The vein in her temple throbbed mercilessly beneath her skin. Her mouth went dry. "I'm on my way," she croaked.

"That's a good girl. I knew you would see sense. Granny's train leaves in just under an hour and a half. I suggest you get a move on. If you're not here by three-thirty, granny will miss her train. And you'll miss granny. Forever. We have a close eye on her. Oh, look she's popped into WH Smith for some magazines on the journey back to Swaley. By the way, I shouldn't try to ring granny to warn her. I took the liberty of lifting her mobile from her handbag when she entered the station. It's snug in my pocket."

Damn, Emmeline thought. It was as if he had read her mind. And there was more than one of them. Whoever *they* are. Probably Swanbeck's lackeys.

"Of course," he went on, "I needn't have to remind you to come alone. The first whiff I get of a copper and granny will be merely a memory. Remember, I'll see you before you see me. I'll be standing under rail timetable in the main concourse. I'll have a copy of *The Clarion* tucked under my arm in your honor."

There was a soft click and then nothing.

Emmeline stood there for several seconds staring at the receiver after she had replaced it in the cradle. What was she going to do? How was she going to produce a priceless diamond and a USB drive with explosive evidence about an international money-laundering scheme? On the other hand, if she showed up at Charing Cross empty-handed she had no doubt that both she and Gran would find themselves permanently sleeping six feet underground.

She stood up and grabbed her handbag. She had to go. She'd have to take her chances. And yet, she had promised Gregory and Superintendent Burnell, not to mention Philip, that she wouldn't go haring off on her own. But they were talking about Gran's life now. She couldn't risk anything happening to her.

'If you're not here by three-thirty...'

She hesitated, bit her lip, and with a heavy sigh reached for the phone again. Her fingers fumbled as she punched in the number.

He answered on the first ring. "Gregory," she said in a harried, slightly breathless voice. "I'm in trouble."

CHAPTER 41

Emmeline drew a deep breath as she passed the replica of the Eleanor Cross in the forecourt as she headed for the doors of Charing Cross Station. After her conversation with Gregory, she had run out of *The Clarion* and hailed a taxi. She hadn't wanted to get stuck in the Underground in case there were delays with the trains.

Gregory had told her not worry. He was going to ring Superintendent Burnell. He assured her the police would be at the station by the time she arrived. Gregory said that he was on his way too. They wouldn't let anything happen to her or Gran.

'*Remember, I'll see you before you see me.*' The man's chilling words hurtled around her head.

She swallowed hard. Her step faltered for a moment. She had to pull herself together. Gran's life depended on her. Right. She straightened her spine, hitched her handbag higher on her shoulder, and entered the station.

Everything's going to fine, she muttered to herself as her fingers bit into the handbag's strap. *Everything's going to be fine.*

With a confidence she did not feel, she crossed the concourse. Natural light rained down from the barrel-vault roof. She dared to flick what she hoped was a casual glance around. The station appeared normal. The people wandering back and forth chatting with each other or checking their mobiles appeared normal. The ones stopping to get a coffee or to buy a paper appeared normal. But nothing was normal, not for her at least.

There was a short queue at the ticket office. Her eyes shot to the clock above. Three-twenty. Gran's train was supposed to leave at three thirty-five. Her gaze shifted to the timetable. The train was on time and leaving from Platform 5.

So where was her mystery stranger? She wondered if the police and Gregory had already caught him. She wished she could communicate with them, but Gregory had said it would be too risky for her to wear a wire. As a result, she knew nothing. And it gnawed at her. Her nerves were straining because they were stretched taut. She was isolated and alone, despite being surrounded by dozens of people. She self-consciously fingered the bracelet Gregory had given her, seeking to draw on his strength from a distance.

Her eyes flew to the clock again. The minute hand had moved an excruciating fraction of an inch. It was now three twenty-two. *Well come on already*, her brain screamed. *When is something going to happen?*

ϵгϵг

Superintendent Burnell and Gregory, who had been given special dispensation, were in the control room with the station's security personnel staring at the CCTV. Their attention was riveted on the screen that was providing a live feed of the main concourse. Emmeline was in the foreground. Off to the left, they could see Sergeant Finch, dressed in jeans, a black T-shirt, and trainers, a backpack slung over his shoulder, walking away from the Upper Crust. He was munching nonchalantly on a croissant.

Burnell spoke into his radio receiver. "Anything, Finch?"

Finch stopped in the middle of the concourse and took another bite of his croissant. "No, sir," his voice was loud and clear. "Emmeline's clean. No tail. If he's here, I can't see him."

"Hmph," Burnell grunted. "Count on it. He's here. I can smell him. Whatever you do, don't lose sight of her."

"Don't worry, sir. I'll stick like glue, but at a safe distance."

PC Hawkins, who was undercover and roaming about the station, also reported nothing suspicious on the concourse.

The radio crackled to life again. This time WPC Rawlings's voice came over the air. "I have visual contact with Mrs. Davis. She's boarding the train right now. No one has tried to approach her."

"Stick with her, Rawlings. Do not leave your post until the train pulls out of the station. Where's PC O'Neill?"

"He's already on the train, sir. He's sitting opposite Mrs. Davis. If anyone makes a move, they will live to regret it."

For the first time that afternoon, the superintendent permitted himself a smile. PC O'Neill could incapacitate a suspect without breaking a sweat. Now, if only the damn train would leave. It was due to pull out in five minutes. An eternity for a policeman.

He slid a sidelong glance at Gregory, who was leaning forward, palms flat on the desk. His brow was puckered as he concentrated on Emmeline's image.

"She's all right, Longdon. It will all be over in a few minutes."

He felt the full force of Longdon's cinnamon gaze. "I don't like it, Oliver."

Burnell cleared his throat noisily and gave a disapproving shake of his head.

Gregory rolled his eyes toward the ceiling. "Very well then, Superintendent Burnell. I don't like it. Something's wrong. It's too quiet. Swanbeck is up to something."

"Whatever it is, he's in for a rude awakening. There's an invisible police ring around the station. There's no way he can get through."

PC O'Neill's voice boomed in the room. "On my way to Swaley. Gran's made a new friend and is chuntering away about gardening. I'll make sure Gran is safely tucked up at home and then I'll catch the first train back to London."

Burnell spread his hands wide. "There you see, Longdon. Everything's fine."

An alarm suddenly went off and they saw people running on the concourse.

"What the devil is going on?" Burnell exploded as he jumped to his feet.

The station's security men surged forward and out the door. Hayes, their chief, none-too-gently elbowed Burnell away from the screen as he spoke into his radio. "Evacuate the station. Everyone. *Now.*"

Burnell and Gregory exchanged a wary look.

Without glancing at either of them, Hayes said out of the side of his mouth, "Bomb scare. Anonymous call." He then became oblivious to them and focused on his own job.

"Bloody hell," Gregory cursed. "Where's Emmy?"

His gaze darted to all the CCTV screens. It was a mass panic. People running in all different directions, some stumbling in their haste to flee. Terrified screams. Pushing and shoving.

"Where's Emmy?" he demanded again, urgency mingled with fear in his tone. He glanced over his shoulder at Burnell. "Oliver, I can't see her."

A knot twisted in the pit of Burnell's stomach. However, he calmly flicked the switch on his radio. "Finch, do you see Emmeline?"

There was a long pause. Finally, Finch's voice came over the line, "She's fine. I saw Hawkins leading her outside."

Burnell squeezed his eyes shut for an instant. Thank God for that.

"Sir, I'm going to see if there's anything I can do."

"Right, go ahead. Report back every ten minutes. Do I make myself clear?"

"Loud and clear."

"And Finch."

"Yes, sir?"

"Watch yourself. No heroics. Get the hell out if gets too dangerous. That's an order."

"Message received and understood." He signed off.

"It's time for you gentleman to leave the building as well," Hayes said, the contours of his face set in grim, implacable lines. "Particularly you, Mr. Longdon. You're a civilian."

Gregory's gaze locked on the superintendent. "Oliver?"

Burnell jerked his chin toward the door. "Go, Longdon. There's nothing that you can do here. It's not safe. Emmeline's outside and she's probably beside herself with worry about you."

Gregory clapped Burnell briefly on the arm and then left the room without another word.

Burnell exhaled a weary breath after he was gone and lowered his bulk into the chair next to Hayes. "I'm staying," he said, his tone brooking no arguments.

The other man gave a curt nod. "Welcome to bedlam."

❧❧❧

Half an hour later, Finch checked in for the third time. "Sir, I'm outside in the forecourt. I'm with Longdon. It appears to have been a false alarm."

Burnell slumped back in his chair and glanced over at Hayes, who was on his mobile but gave him a thumbs up sign and what passed for a smile.

Finch was talking again, "Sir, there's a problem."

Burnell went very still, waiting for the other shoe to drop.

"Sir, we can't find Emmeline. No one has seen her. She's disappeared."

The other shoe dropped and his heart sank with it.

CHAPTER 42

The black Mercedes slowly rolled to a stop in front of the four-story, red-brick Victorian mansion block in Mayfair.

Emmeline was still groggy. The last thing she remembered was being jostled in the crowd outside Charing Cross Station, a hand clamping over her mouth and then the blackness swallowed her into its embrace. It must have been chloroform.

She blinked and shifted her position as she tried to get her bearings. She shrank back into the corner when her eyes alighted on Alastair Swanbeck's smug, smiling face.

"Emmeline, Emmeline." He pursed his lips and gave a melancholy shake of his head. "I don't think you realize what an awful lot of trouble you and Longdon have caused me."

Her eyes flickered from his face to the building. "W—Where—" Her voice cracked. She licked her lips and tried again. "Where are we?"

Swanbeck chuckled. "I thought you would have recognized the place instantly. This is where Pavel Melnikov made his home." His index finger tapped the window. "There in the duplex penthouse. Do you see it?" He turned back to face her, a malicious gleam in his sea-green eyes. "Since you've exhibited such an extraordinary interest in Pavel, I thought you might like to see where he lived—and died. I'll give you a tour. Come." He waggled his hand at her.

Emmeline huddled deeper into her corner, although there was nowhere else to go.

Swanbeck sighed. "Don't make this more difficult than it has to be. Now, come on."

She folded her arms across her chest and thrust her chin in

the air with bravado, although her intestines were a terrified mass of jelly. "Go to the devil."

He wagged his forefinger at her. "That was a mistake." He shifted his head. "Tom," he said to a hulking brute of a man who seemed to have materialized out of thin air, but who in reality must have been there the entire time.

The door was flung open and she nearly tumbled backward out of the car, but Tom caught her with one massive hand that must have been made of iron. Emmeline thought the circulation was going to stop in her arm.

Tom dragged her out of the car and onto her feet in one fluid motion. He didn't break his hold for an instant. In fact, his fingers only bit deeper into the soft fleshy inside of her upper arm. She contemplated stomping on his instep to teach him a lesson, but one glance up and down told her it would be useless.

He gave her a rough shove. "Move."

She glared up at him. It made no impression. His features merely creased into a bemused smile.

"Emmeline, you've wasted enough of my valuable time already," Swanbeck called from the front door, which he held open for them.

Another push from Tom nearly sent her sprawling to the ground, but she managed to stay on her feet. Her heart was in her mouth. Inch by inch, step by step, she was getting closer to the mansion block and Swanbeck. Once she was inside, she would scream to raise a hue and cry. It was late afternoon. One of Melnikov's neighbors had to be home from work. Someone would surely run out to see what the commotion was about and she could beg for help.

The minute they crossed the threshold, Tom dug his fingers into her curls and yanked her head back viciously, making her eyes water. He put his head close to her ear and whispered, "Open your mouth just once and your brains will be decorating the wall."

She heard the muted click of the safety catch being drawn back and felt the cold muzzle of a gun trace a line along her jaw.

He pulled her hair again, even harder this time. "Understand?"

"Ye—es," she croaked.

"Good," he grunted and mercifully let go of her hair.

Swanbeck slipped his arm through hers. Now, she was sandwiched between them. The blood raced through her veins as her mind desperately scrambled for a way out of this death trap.

With fear paralyzing her senses, Emmeline was completely unaware of the fact that someone had witnessed everything that had occurred that afternoon from the moment she had been snatched at Charing Cross. Even now, he was watching from a Lexus across the road.

He pressed his forehead against the steering wheel as the trio disappeared into the mansion block. What should he do? Emmeline didn't deserve his help. None of this would have happened if it hadn't been for her stirring up things that were better left alone.

He exhaled a pitiful sigh. On the other hand, Swanbeck was a lying, contemptible swine.

Right. His head snapped up. He made his decision. There was no going back now.

He pulled out his mobile and reluctantly punched in a number. He was surprised when it was answered on the first ring. He cleared his throat. "Longdon, it's Jason Royce."

"*Royce?* What do you want?" Gregory growled. "I have more important things to contend with at the moment."

"I know. Swanbeck has your fiancée. He's going to kill her. Like he did all the others, even Dad."

Gregory's voice boomed in his ear. "Where's Emmy?"

"I want a deal first."

"I don't make deals. Damn it, man, Emmy's life is at stake."

"Then stop wasting time. Tell Burnell I will give him everything on Swanbeck, in exchange for leniency. I think that's fair."

"Fair? You cold-blooded bastard—" Gregory broke off and Jason heard a muffled conversation in the background for several seconds. Then Gregory came back on the line. "You've got your deal, Royce. Where's Emmy?"

"Melnikov's penthouse. Swanbeck's not alone. He has Tom, his driver-cum-bodyguard, with him."

"Ah, yes, dear old Tom." Gregory's tone was laced with venom. "I owe him a token of my affection. The police are on the way. Royce, if this is a game and anything happens to Emmy, I will kill you myself. Just so that there are no misunderstandings."

"Honesty deserves honesty. I despise her and everything she's done to my family. I still intend to file a lawsuit against her when this is all over. But no one can hate Alastair more than I do. I want the satisfaction of seeing him burn in hell."

∽∾∽

"Why are we here?" Emmeline asked, her eyes curiously roaming around Melnikov's penthouse.

It was pristine, ultra-modern, and utterly graceless. Although strands of summer sunshine streamed in through the two sets of French doors in the reception room, the flat lacked warmth and the feeling of home. The utilitarian furniture was done in varying shades of white and gray. The walls were a lifeless ash. The only nod to color was a rectangular painting, which took up most of one wall and looked as if the artist had closed his eyes and thrown whatever color came to hand at the canvas.

It was definitely not to Emmeline's taste. She preferred the soft, gentle lines and subjects of the Impressionists.

Tom tugged her toward the middle of the room and unceremoniously dumped her on the sofa as Swanbeck closed the door in the corridor without sliding the bolt back into place.

"You haven't answered my question," she said as Swanbeck circled round the sofa to stand before her.

"You were dead keen—forgive the pun—to see where Pavel spent his sad, final moments in this world. So your wish has been granted. I hope the flat meets with your expectations." His silky smooth voice twined itself around her heart and filled her with a cold dread that was more palpable than if he had shouted at her.

He lowered himself onto the sofa next to her and casually stretched his arm along the back as if they were old chums having a cozy natter. "Now, Emmeline," He paused, his sea green stare locking on her face. "The Blue Angel and the money Cardew stole when he decided to play detective. I want them back."

Emmeline snorted. "Is that all? You don't think you're being just a tad greedy?" She squeezed her forefinger and thumb together leaving only an infinitesimal sliver of space between them as she settled back against the cushions.

God knew she shouldn't antagonize him, but she couldn't help it. The fear was ebbing and her temper was starting to kindle.

Swanbeck laughed. "Oh, Emmeline, sometimes you're your own worst enemy. That tongue of yours and your snooping is how you've ended up in this untenable situation."

She licked her lips. The malevolent gleam in his eye sent a frisson slithering down her spine. "I don't have the diamond nor the evidence Rupert uncovered, more's the pity. Believe me, if I did, your name would be splashed all over the pages of *The Clarion* and you'd be rotting in jail."

Swanbeck pursed his lips and shook his head. "I see you've picked up several of Longdon's bad habits. Habits that can get you killed."

She did her best to ignore the ugly latter comment. She clasped her hands tightly together in her lap to keep them from trembling. From the expressions on their faces, they could smell her fear beneath her brazen ripostes.

She sniffed. "Believe what you like. I can't give you what I don't have. Search me. You won't find anything."

Swanbeck's mouth curved into a lupine smile. "My dear, Emmeline—"

She cut across him. "I'm not your *dear* anything," she spat back.

"I'd have a care if I were you. You're beginning to grate on my nerves."

"Am I really? And I wasn't even trying. Wait until you see what I can do if I make a concerted effort." She beamed at him.

She had the satisfaction of seeing his jaw clamp down and his teeth grind together.

He shot his cuff and glanced at his watch. "They say patience is a virtue." He lifted his gaze to meet hers again. "I know you have what I want. Longdon doesn't have them so that only leaves you. At this moment, I have some of my chaps searching your home." He leaned in closer, his warm breath brushing her cheek. "They *will* find the Blue Angel and the USB drive. Then, you will cease to be useful. Not much longer now."

His words echoed in her ears as a knot formed in the pit of her stomach. She scooted away from him, but she was already wedged into the corner of the sofa.

Swanbeck suddenly jumped to his feet and extended a hand toward her. "I have an idea how we can *kill* the time—oh, there I go again." He chuckled. "Kill the time. I'm too witty for my own good."

Emmeline sat there stone-faced. She was not amused in the least.

"Tom, why don't we show Emmeline the exact spot from where Pavel took his fatal leap? She'd love the view."

Tom grabbed her arm, his eyes twinkling with sadistic glee. "That's a brilliant idea."

Emmeline could not bring herself to regard the suggestion with quite the same enthusiasm. In fact, the window from which Melnikov was thrown to his death was the last place on Earth that she wanted to see.

CHAPTER 43

Jason Royce tapped an angry tattoo on the steering wheel. He was getting restless. He had remained in his car, eyes glued to the mansion block. He checked his watch for hundredth time since his call to Longdon. If the police didn't hurry, Alastair would slip through their fingers. What the devil was taking them so long?

He tipped his head back against the headrest. He squeezed his eyes shut and excoriated himself once again for ever getting involved with Alastair Swanbeck.

His eyes popped open when he heard a car heading toward him and pull into a spot about a hundred feet down the block. At last, the bloody police.

But it was not the police.

He sat up straighter and craned his neck to look over his shoulder. "It can't be," he mumbled.

But it was. He saw the driver get out of the car, shoot a glance up and down the road, and then hurry toward Melnikov's building.

He shook his head in disbelief as he watched the newcomer calmly slip a key into the front door and disappear inside.

He sat for several minutes enveloped in a cloud of confusion. He couldn't make any sense of it. In the end, curiosity got the better of him. He unfastened his seatbelt and got out of the car. He knew he should stay out of the way and let the police handle it, but he couldn't. The appearance of the newcomer disturbed him profoundly. He had to find out what was going on.

❧❧❧

Gregory practically leaped out of the car before Sergeant Finch brought it to a halt in front of Melinikov's building.

"Steady on, Longdon," Burnell said over his shoulder. "You're likely to get yourself, as well as Emmeline, killed if you rush in without thinking."

Gregory was already on the pavement. "Just get a move on, Oliver."

Burnell, however, took his time getting out of the car. His gaze swept over their surroundings. Although he didn't see them, he knew at that moment Special Branch and Metropolitan Police Hostage Unit officers were streaming into the building across the road through the rear and would soon be taking up positions. Unmarked police cars were sealing off both ends of the block. And finally, Sergeant Denholm and PC MacBride were coming toward them at a run.

"What's the situation, Denholm?"

"Swanbeck, his driver, and Miss Kirby arrived about half an hour ago. We heeded your order and stayed well back."

Burnell clapped him on the shoulder. "Good. I don't want to frighten off Swanbeck. The other team is in place here?"

"Yes, sir," MacBride replied. "Everyone's in position and out of sight. They're ready to move when you give the nod."

Burnell glanced round. "Where's Royce? I thought you were keeping your eye on him until we got here."

"He nipped into the building not more than ten minutes ago," Denholm replied.

"What?" The superintendent growled. "Why? This isn't a party."

Denholm cleared his throat. "No, sir. It's because he saw someone else arrive."

"Someone else? This gets worse. Who?"

"His father's murderer."

Burnell frowned. "You're sure?"

"Oh, yes. No doubt about it."

The superintendent pursed his lips and sighed wearily. "Oliver."

Burnell whipped his head around to give Gregory a withering look.

"Superintendent Burnell," Gregory hurriedly corrected himself. "What's wrong?" The eyes that stared back at him were full of concern.

Burnell was silent for several seconds as his mind tried to come up with the words to convey to Longdon that the woman he loved was in far graver danger than they had imagined and extricating her would pose a challenge. If, that is, they could extricate her alive.

He cleared his throat. "Let's just say that this news does not bring joy to my heart."

⫷⫸

Emmeline's heart hammered against her chest and her heels made scuff marks on the parquet floor as Tom took cruel pleasure in dragging her across to the French door. He pressed her against the railing on the south facing balcony. She could feel his fingers making deep impressions in the nape of her neck as he forced her to look down at the pavement. Her eyes locked with horror on the lethal railings below, where Melnikov had become impaled. That's where she was going to end her life.

Oh, God. She felt giddy. A wave of nausea roiled her stomach. Her legs were beginning to buckle under her. She was going to fall. Down, down, down. *Dead.*

Just as she was about to lose consciousness, Swanbeck's voice floated to her ears. "Not yet, Tom. Not quite yet."

"Hmph," Tom grunted in disappointment.

Emmeline began to draw deep, greedy gulps of air into her lungs, when she realized that Tom was pulling her back inside. A reprieve. But for how long?

Swanbeck spread his arm in a wide arc that encompassed the reception room and the world outside the French door. "Do you like the view?"

She simply held his gaze without uttering a word.

He leaned in closer, his face only inches from hers. "What's the matter, Emmeline? You usually have an opinion on everything."

"You—" Terror had momentarily robbed her of her voice. She tried again. "You are nothing but a cold-blooded brute."

He gave a disapproving shake of his head. "Emmeline, that's not very flattering."

She took a step toward him and flashed a smile. "Then why don't you crawl back under the rock from where you came and tend to your bruised ego."

She was gratified to see a spark of anger ignite in his eyes. Good.

"It's unwise to continue irritating me in this manner."

She surprised him by tossing her head back and daring to laugh in his face. "What do I care? You're going to kill me anyway."

His mouth broke into a malicious grin. "Oh, no. I'm not going to kill you. I'm merely a spectator," he hissed. "I'm going to leave that pleasure to someone who hates you even more than I do."

They heard muffled footfalls coming from the corridor behind him. He threw a glance over his shoulder and spun her around as the door opened. "Ah, speaking of your executioner. The guest of honor has arrived."

Emmeline felt the blood drain from her face when she saw who it was.

∾∾∾

"Arrest me, if you like, Oliver," Gregory murmured out of the corner of his mouth as he shook off Finch's restraining hand on his arm and followed close on Burnell's heels into the foyer. A team had already been sent ahead to evacuate the building floor by floor.

The superintendent rounded on him at the base of the stairs next to the lift. "I'd like nothing better, Longdon." His tone was low and urgent. "But just at the moment I have more important things to think about. Namely your fiancée. Now stop making a nuisance of yourself and go back outside."

"Let us handle the situation," Finch intoned as he tried to elbow him out of the way.

Gregory scowled at him and focused his attention on the superintendent again. "Oliver," he implored. Then seeing the pink flush spreading beneath the other man's beard, he coaxed, "Superintendent Burnell, you *know* I can be of some use."

"The answer is no. You're a civilian. Cruickshank will go into a fit of apoplexy if he found out."

Gregory favored him with an impish smile. "It'll be our little secret. I won't tell, if you don't."

Burnell and Finch exchanged a wary look.

"Sir, it's ill-advised."

Several precious seconds ticked by as Burnell's gaze latched on Gregory. Finally, he sighed. "I know I'm going to regret this, but get a move on. We've wasted enough time already."

Without another word, he turned his back on them and started up the stairs. Halfway up, he stopped abruptly. "Longdon, there's one condition." He raised his forefinger and whispered, "If things get too dangerous and I tell you to leave, you *go*. At once. Do I make myself clear? I don't want any lip from you. You just go."

Gregory winked and gave him a cheeky little salute. "*Avec plaisir, mon colonel.*"

Burnell rolled his eyes heavenward. *God give me strength*, he pleaded silently.

⌘⌘⌘

Emmeline's mouth went dry when she saw Mrs. Royce getting closer. Step by step. She was as chic and elegant as ever in an aquamarine silk wrap-around dress and matching pumps with a slight heel that set off her shapely calves. A vibrant, pear-shaped blue topaz pendant dangled from her throat. The only thing that marred the effect was the pistol she held in her hand. A pistol that was trained on Emmeline's heart.

"M—Mrs. Royce," Emmeline stammered in shock. "*You?*"

Lily permitted herself a vindictive smile. "The look on your face at this moment is priceless. I can't tell you how long I've waited for this day."

Emmeline shook her head in confusion. "You and

Swanbeck murdered Mr. Royce? And tried to put the blame on me? Why?"

"Because I wanted you destroyed." Mrs. Royce's voice dripped acid. "I would have made a deal with the devil, if it wiped you off the face of the earth."

"But I didn't know about Mr. Royce being my father or the money. It was as much of a surprise to me as it was to you." Emmeline was in awe of the other woman's vehemence.

Lily snorted as she circled around Emmeline, gun waving about in the air. "You're the spitting image of your mother, except for the dark hair." She tilted her head to one side and studied Emmeline's face. "Mmm, yes, exactly the same. All coy innocence on the outside and a calculating gold digger on the inside."

Emmeline couldn't have heard her correctly. "My...*mother*?"

Lily laughed. It was an ugly sound. She leaned in close and hissed, "Yes, it all circles back to *her*. You think I didn't I know about your mother and Victor? I hired a private detective. I had dates and photos. I knew all their favorite meeting places. They thought they were being so discreet. The fools," she scoffed. "He wanted to leave me for her. Can you imagine? For some little chit of a photojournalist."

Emmeline licked her lips. "But—but Mr. Royce told me that the two of you hadn't been happy for years. Why not just give him a divorce?"

"Divorce? You must be joking," she sneered. "A divorce was out of the question. I was not going to become the subject of gossip. Oh, no. I worked too hard to get us our place in society. I wasn't going to allow your mother to destroy everything I had achieved for the family. I cornered her as she was leaving the paper one day. I warned her to stay away from Victor or I would make both their lives hell. She was so terrified, she broke it off with him. She wrote him a goodbye letter. It was nauseating."

Emmeline's eyes widened. "You read my mother's letter to Mr. Royce?" Was there nothing that this woman wouldn't stoop to? Apparently not.

"Of course, I read it. Victor had tucked it away in his desk drawer, but I found it. However—" She came to a halt right in front of Emmeline, her eyes alight with fire. "—there was no mention of you in the letter. I found out about you later. Otherwise, I would have made sure you died with them."

In that instant between heartbeats, her world stopped. The blood in her veins turned to ice. Her breath caught in her lungs as she rasped, "With them? What—what do you mean?"

But she was afraid she already knew the answer.

Silvery laughter rumbled from Lily's throat. "I mean you should have died with your mother and father. Oops—" She put a hand to her mouth in mock embarrassment. "—how silly of me. I mean Aaron Kirby. Meanwhile, there was Victor pining away for your mother. After *five* years, the silly fool still couldn't get that woman out of his head. It was only a matter of time before he decided to search for her. Naturally, I couldn't allow that to happen. Once again, I had to take matters into my own hands." She rolled her eyes dramatically. "Very tiresome I can tell you.

"I hired a detective to find her. And the clever man did. Then it was merely a matter of settling old scores. It helps when you have money. Such a wonderful thing. And I had pots of it. It can buy you anything you desire, even an assassin. The transaction was made through a third party. I never saw him. He never knew who I was. It was so easy. All neat and tidy. Until the day you turned up at my house. The minute Victor laid eyes on you, he knew. I could see it on his face. His final insult was his will. He decided to rub my nose it one last time. Well, he's not laughing now, is he?"

Emmeline felt the sour taste of bile rise to her throat. Blood thundered in her ears. She couldn't believe that this woman was calmly standing there reveling in the fact that she had murdered her parents. *Mummy and Daddy gone.* She blinked back the tears burning against her eyelids. How can someone take another person's life?

Raw, hot anger and revulsion suddenly surged through her body. Her nerves and muscles tingled with its electric force. "You're sick."

She lunged at Lily, heedless of the gun or Swanbeck or Tom. Nothing else mattered except hurting this woman. She wanted to hurt Lily Royce for leaving an aching hole in her heart all these years.

Lily was taken off guard. Emmeline's shoulder caught her mid-chest, knocking the wind from her lungs. They both tumbled to the floor and scrambled about as Swanbeck and Tom stared, mesmerized.

Emmeline had the upper hand at first, driven by her blinding rage. But Lily quickly regained her wits and began lashing out with her nails. Emmeline ducked her head at the last second to narrowly miss a blow from one of the woman's vicious claws. Their grunts were the only sound that echoed off the walls.

"Mum, enough. It's over."

They all stopped and turned as one. In all the commotion, no one had noticed Jason slip into the penthouse.

"Enough," Jason bellowed again. A muscle in his jaw convulsed and his Adam's apple fretted up and down.

Emmeline didn't like the wild gleam in his bloodshot eyes, especially since he held the gun in an extremely unsteady hand. Out of the frying and into the fire.

"Get up," he shouted.

She hastily got to her feet. "Listen, Jason—"

"Shut up." She felt the *whoosh* of the air as he waved the gun in front of her nose. "None of this would have happened if it hadn't been for you."

"That's right, darling," Lily murmured as she rose and smoothed the wrinkles from her dress. "She tried to destroy our family. We can't allow that. Give me the gun." She extended a manicured hand to her son. "Give me the gun. Let me take care of things as I had planned. Let me make things right. No more worries. I promise."

His gaze locked on his mother for an agonizingly long moment. An internal debate must have been rattling around in his brain because he appeared to be wavering.

"Jason, don't do it," Emmeline pleaded. "She killed three

people. How do you know she won't turn on you if you cross her?"

He flicked a glance at Emmeline, a crooked smile tugging at the corners of his mouth. He pulled back the safety catch and raised the gun. He stopped when it was level with her forehead. "You couldn't keep your bloody snout out of our business, could you?"

Lily hovered behind her shoulder. "Go ahead, darling," she coaxed again.

Emmeline sucked in her breath and squeezed her eyes shut, steeling herself for the shot. *Please let it be quick*, she prayed.

CHAPTER 44

Jason pivoted swiftly on his heel. The first bullet caught Tom in the upper thigh.

Emmeline's eyes popped open when she realized that she wasn't the one who had been hit. She watched transfixed as Tom collapsed with a heavy thud onto the floor. He was reduced to a mewling heap. By the expression on his face, he was startled to see his own blood seeping through his fingers and dripping onto the highly polished wood.

The next shot whizzed past Swanbeck's head to lodge itself in the wall behind him. His eyes widened in disbelief at his narrow escape. He'd stooped to pick up Tom's gun, which had landed at his feet. But he didn't wait for Jason to try a second time. He bolted up the stairs to the roof terrace.

Jason let him go. Gun dangling from his fingers, he collapsed into an armchair like a wilted flower. The fight appeared to have gone out of him.

The same could not be said of his mother.

In one fluid motion, Lily snatched the gun from her son's grasp and set her sights on Emmeline. Again.

"Now that these puerile male displays are at an end, I can take care of unfinished business." She gave an angry flick of her wrist. "Move."

Emmeline remained rooted to the spot. She stared her down, unblinking.

"I said *move*," Lily snarled through clenched teeth.

Emmeline felt the sharp jab of the pistol in her rib cage. Her heart was in her mouth. Her death was reflected in the other woman's frosty turquoise gaze.

"No." Something in her tone must have transmitted her determination because Lily raised her eyebrows in surprise. Did she also detect a spark of admiration in that glance? She wasn't sure. "You want to kill me. Well, go ahead. You've had enough practice. But I'm certainly not going to make it easy for you."

Lily's lips curled back exposing her perfect teeth. "I have no intention of soiling my hands with your blood." She thrust the gun deeper into Emmeline's rib. She grabbed one shoulder and shoved her forward. "You were distraught. You saw the writing on the wall and knew your arrest for my dear Victor's murder was only a matter of days."

Another push. Emmeline tried to resist by dragging her feet along the parquet floor but Lily was set on her mission. A step closer to the French door. Then they were suddenly out on the balcony.

Lily snatched a handful of Emmeline's curls between her fingers. She held Emmeline's head against her own. "You're going to commit suicide. You were plunged into the depths of black despair and decided to emulate Melnikov. That's why you broke into his flat."

Tears dripped from her lashes and trailed down her cheeks.

"It's so easy," Lily's husky voice murmured in her ear. "Climb over the railing. And *jump*."

Emmeline was right up against the iron railing. She was having difficulty drawing air into her lungs. She was trapped. It was either a bullet in the back of the head or—

She caught a flutter of movement out of the corner of her eye.

"Down, Emmeline. *Now*." A male voice roared from inside the flat.

There was no time to think. Pure adrenaline took control. She dropped to her knees. Primal instinct made her body curl into a fetal position, one hand protectively over her head.

Vaguely, as if from a long distance away, she registered the sniper's bullet grazing the air as it sought its target. Screams were ripped from her throat when the weight of Lily's body landed on top of her.

She was being suffocated by the screams. Every sinew,

limb, and nerve in her body convulsed with shock.

"Hush. It's all over now, Emmeline," Burnell's voice was gentle as Finch and another policeman swiftly lifted Lily off her.

Emmeline scrambled out, her chest heaving, desperate for air. She saw Burnell and threw her arms around his neck. She squeezed tight, needing reassurance that she was still alive.

She felt one of his arms awkwardly go around her waist. "It's all right." He patted her back. "You're fine. She can't hurt you anymore."

They remained that way for a couple of minutes. Then Emmeline jerked out of his embrace and held his gaze. "Gregory." The single word was a question and a demand all at once.

"Bloody hell," Burnell snapped as he struggled to get to his feet. "He went after Swanbeck alone. Finch, take a couple of men and go to the roof terrace."

The hairs on the back of Emmeline's neck prickled. She was on her feet too. "What?" She clutched his arm. "Why did you let him go? Swanbeck's going to kill him."

Lily was suddenly forgotten as she elbowed her way past Finch and dashed toward the stairs to the roof.

"Emmeline," Burnell called.

But nothing was going to stop her. She had to get to Gregory. She was not going to let Swanbeck take him from her.

⌘⌘⌘

Gregory caught up with Swanbeck at the top of the stairs. He reached out a hand and grabbed the other's man ankle, propelling them both forward. They landed on the wooden deck together. The fall jarred all the bones in his body, stunning him briefly.

Swanbeck quickly swiveled onto his side, but Gregory rolled out of the way of a savage kick. Had his reactions been a fraction slower, Swanbeck's foot would have made contact with his jaw. The other man grunted in frustration at his missed opportunity to cause severe damage. His features were flushed crimson and contorted with his exertions.

They both froze when the shot rang out. The next second Emmeline's screams floated to their ears.

Emmy. Gregory's chest tightened. If anything happened to her—

That instant of distraction was enough for Swanbeck.

A gun seemed to materialize out of nowhere and was now pointed directly at Gregory.

"Checkmate, I think, Longdon," Swanbeck said. His voice held a note of amusement. He jerked the gun up and down. "On your feet."

Gregory moved slowly. First to his knees, then to his feet, all the while willing his body to relax. His eyes never left the barrel of the gun until he was completely upright.

His gaze travelled to Swanbeck's face. He clucked his tongue and gave a disapproving shake of his head. "Alastair, it would be awfully bad manners for you to shoot me. What would the neighbors think?"

Swanbeck's mouth broke into a grin, but there was no trace of mirth in it. His eyes were clouded with undisguised hatred. "Always flippant. Always interfering." He drew the safety catch back. "I'm going to savor this moment. I'm just disappointed that Emmeline couldn't be here to watch you in your death throes. That would have made the tableau complete. Pity." He shrugged.

Gregory stiffened at the sound of Emmeline's name on the other man's tongue, but he plastered one of his most charming smiles on his lips. "There, there, Alastair. We can't have everything we want in life. By the way, I'm curious. How do you intend to explain my untimely demise to the stout fellows from Scotland Yard, especially since I'm unarmed?"

Swanbeck chuckled. "I think you'll like the story. You might get a good laugh out of it."

I rather doubt it, old chap, Gregory thought. Aloud, he said, "I'm all ears. Please go on. I always like a good yarn."

Swanbeck waved the gun carelessly in the air. "Well, you see, Tom and I happened to be driving by the building. The French doors were open and we heard raised voices coming from within. I thought I caught a glimpse of a man with a gun. I ordered Tom to stop the car at once. We dashed into the building without a second thought for our safety, good citizens that we are."

"Naturally," Gregory murmured.

Swanbeck paced back and forth, the gun bouncing against one palm. "Of course, we're human beings after all—"

Gregory cut across him. "Are you really? Fascinating. You learn something new every day."

Swanbeck went on as if Gregory hadn't spoken. "—we quickly determined the flat where the disturbance was occurring. Tom, as my bodyguard, always carries a gun so we had some protection. We burst into Pavel's flat and found dear Emmeline confronted by Lily and Jason Royce. It appears killing is a family affair. Before we could react, Jason took a shot at Tom, wounding him badly. Then, horror of horrors, I was left exposed and Jason, in his crazed state, let loose a shot at me. The bullet missed, thankfully. But I didn't hang about to give him a second chance. I scooped up Tom's gun and darted up the stairs to where I thought I could find refuge from the savage things going on in the flat. And here is where you found me. However, I was thoroughly unnerved by what had just happened that I panicked and I thought you were Jason. Of course, I had to shoot you. It was a pure case of self-defense."

Gregory snorted. "Alastair, nothing about you is pure. Mind you, you lie with such panache that you could make a career as a writer."

Swanbeck inclined his head. "I'll keep that in mind. I was always fond of literature in school. Now that I've satisfied your curiosity, it is time for the *coup de grace*."

Gregory snapped his fingers. "And just when I was warming to your engaging narrative style." He sighed melodramatically. "I suppose all good things must come to an end."

"First, you're going to tell me where the diamond is or I shoot your left knee cap."

Gregory's smile grew wider. "What diamond?"

"The Blue Angel. It's obvious that Emmeline is completely in the dark. So that means you have it."

"They say the mind is the first thing to go as we age. Your memory appears to be failing you. If you'll recall, your mate Bronowski is the one who purchased the Blue Angel in an auction room full of people. I suggest you take the matter up with him." He hit his palm against his forehead. "Oh, I forgot. Igor died a few days ago. Alas, there is nothing I can do to help you. Perhaps, you should take the matter up with his next of kin."

Swanbeck's jaw clenched and a vein in his temple shuddered with anger. He lowered the gun and aimed it at Gregory's leg.

"No," Emmeline shrieked as she burst onto the terrace and jumped in front of Gregory.

Her eyes were glazed and her hair was tousled, but to his tremendous relief she seemed to be unhurt. There was no time to share sweet-nothings, though. He put his arm around her waist and firmly drew her aside, out of the line of fire.

"Ah, Emmeline," Swanbeck said. "I'm so glad that you could join us. I must say it does a heart good to see two lovers together." He cocked his head to one side. "You make such a lovely couple. It seemed rather cruel to part the two of you at the end, but you've solved that problem for me. Together in life and together in death. It's so comforting." He raised the gun. "Would you like to toss a coin to see who goes first?"

Gregory tightened his grip on her arm. "I thought you wanted the Blue Angel."

The corner of Swanbeck's mouth quirked upward. "I thought you said you didn't have it."

Gregory leaned in closer, his dazzling smile held a challenge. "If you shoot us, you'll go to your grave wondering."

Suddenly, heavy footsteps clattered on the stairs. The next second Finch emerged onto the terrace followed by several officers armed with automatic machine guns held aloft.

Swanbeck carefully clicked the safety catch back into place and lifted his hands in the air. "Oh, thank God you arrived, officers. You just prevented a tragedy. I nearly shot Mr. Longdon and Miss Kirby *by accident*. I was terribly frightened after witnessing what happened downstairs. I ran up here to get away. My nerves are so shattered that I mistook them for Jason."

"Save it, Swanbeck," Finch spat back as he roughly spun him around and slapped handcuffs on his wrists with a satisfying snap. "You're under arrest. You do not have to say anything that might prejudice your case in a court of law later. You have the right—"

Swanbeck cut him off. "You've got it all wrong, Sergeant. I'm an innocent man."

"And I'm the Queen of Sheba," Burnell snarled from the doorway. "Get him out of here, Finch."

"Yes, sir. Come on." He gave Swanbeck a not-so-gentle nudge.

Swanbeck stopped in front of Burnell and grinned. "You have nothing, Superintendent Burnell. My solicitor will have me out by dinnertime. And I will see to it that he files a complaint against you for false arrest."

Burnell's mouth stretched into an exaggerated yawn. "You bore me, Swanbeck. I've heard it all before." He took a step closer, his deep blue gaze impaling the other man. He pitched his voice low, but it held a dangerous edge to it. "You're dirty. So dirty it seeps out of your pores. But then, you learned at the knee of a master. Your dear, old papa would be proud."

"This is a clear case of harassment," Swanbeck tossed back at him. "I'd have a care, if I were you. In fact, I'd start looking for a new job."

Burnell's mouth curved into a smile, but it failed to reach his eyes. "Threatening a police officer in front of witnesses?" He clucked his tongue. "That's a serious offense."

"I wouldn't dream of it." Then Swanbeck dropped his voice so only Burnell could hear him. "You've made a mistake you're going to regret."

Burnell stared back at him, face implacable. He jerked his chin at Finch without uttering another word.

They heard Finch informing Swanbeck of his rights as they

descended the stairs. The Special Branch officers and the Met's hostage unit team followed close behind.

When they were alone, Gregory pulled Emmeline close against his body and extended a hand to Burnell. "Thanks, Oliver, for taking care of Emmy."

Burnell inclined his head, but made a dismissive gesture in the air. "All in a day's work."

CHAPTER 45

Burnell was whistling a tuneless song as he banged away at his keyboard to write up his report on the case the following morning. He had reason to be in a jolly mood. Not ten minutes earlier, Philip had rung to say that he and a tech expert at MI5 had spent the past thirty-six hours trying to find the trail that Rupert Cardew had uncovered that tied Swanbeck and Jason Royce to the Cyprus bank accounts and the Russian bank VEB. And they found it. Everything.

There was no way Swanbeck was going to escape justice this time. He had him dead to rights for the murders of Melnikov, Sabitov, Bronowski, and Cardew, as well as providing the gelsemium to Lily Royce to kill her husband.

Burnell stopped typing and leaned back in his chair. He steepled his hands over his stomach and permitted himself a self-satisfied chuckle.

There was a tap at his door. Before he could say anything, Assistant Commissioner Cruickshank was strolling into his office.

Burnell frowned and quickly rose. "Sir, how—how can I help you?"

Cruickshank waved him back down and took the chair opposite him. He held the superintendent's gaze for a moment then folded his hands on the desk. "Burnell, first I'd like to say that you did a brilliant job on this case."

Burnell's brows shot up. *Praise from a superior officer*. It was a good thing he was sitting down. "Thank you, sir. We always strive to do our best."

Cruickshank's forehead puckered. "That's the devil of it." He exhaled a long breath. "There's no easy way to tell you this. All I'll say is that I'm just as upset."

The hairs on the back of Burnell's neck stood on end.

"I don't know whether you heard. Swanbeck was released last night. A magistrate felt that we didn't have enough evidence to hold, let alone charge him."

Burnell slammed his open palm against the desk. "What? Sir, we have him for the murders."

"All circumstantial apparently."

"What more do they want?"

Cruickshank spread his hands wide. "What can I say? He has a good lawyer."

"But, sir, I just spoke with Philip Acheson at the Foreign Office. MI-Five has been able to trace all of Swanbeck's shady financial dealings. It ties him directly to *everything*."

The assistant commissioner pursed his lips. "You're sure?"

Burnell didn't trust his voice. He gave a curt nod.

"Bloody hell."

Burnell's eyes widened. He didn't think the Boy Wonder cursed.

"That makes things even worse. Swanbeck's gone."

Burnell choked back his fury. "*Gone*?"

"Swanbeck did a runner this morning. His Mayfair flat is empty. He's left London. For all I know, he's halfway to Argentina by now."

Bloody hell, indeed.

∽∾∽

An hour later, Finch found Burnell hunched over in his chair, staring out the window. Although the superintendent was still, Finch could feel the heat of his rage wafting upon the air.

He hesitated before taking a step into the office. "Sir, I—"

The superintendent swiveled his chair around. "Save your breath. I already know. Cruickshank told me."

"Oh, right. I see."

An awkward silence hovered in the space between them.

Burnell was the first one to break it. "This case is not closed." He lifted his gaze to Finch's face. "I'm not going to let it go until Swanbeck is behind bars."

The sergeant nodded heartily. "Yes, sir. We'll get him. It may take a little longer than we had anticipated. But we'll get him."

Burnell smiled. "We will indeed."

"I must say it's nice to see you in such a good mood, Oliver."

Burnell and Finch turned to find Gregory leaning against the door frame, his arms crossed over his chest.

The superintendent clenched his fist and let loose a string of silent curses. Aloud, he said, "I'm not in a good mood, Longdon. Far from it, in fact. Go away."

Gregory pushed away from the door and strode into the office. "I can't possibly do that. I'm on a mission from Emmy."

"How is she?" Burnell asked, his voice tinged with concern.

Gregory's face softened and he became serious. "She's still a little shaken, but she's fine. Really. She wanted to thank both of you for everything that you did. She sent me along with a gift." He handed each detective an elegantly wrapped box. "It's no good asking me what they are. She wouldn't tell me. She would have delivered them in person, but she had to go up to Edinburgh to cover a story. She'll be back in a couple of days."

The superintendent stared down at the box in his hands. "That was quite unnecessary." He looked up. "We were simply doing our jobs."

"I know. I wanted to thank you from the bottom of my heart, Oliver. If you hadn't been so good at your job and realized that Lily Royce was the only one who could have wiped the fingerprints off the Scotch decanter, Emmy might not be here today."

He extended a hand to the superintendent. Their eyes met and held. The smile they exchanged spoke volumes. Then the moment was gone.

Gregory turned to Finch. "I owe you a debt of thanks too."

The sergeant accepted his hand and returned the pressure.

"Well, I must be off, chaps. I have to see a client about her diamond necklace."

He was halfway to the door when Burnell called, "Certainly, I won't detain Symington's chief investigator. But speaking of diamonds, I wonder what happened to the Blue Angel. Any ideas?"

Gregory pivoted on his heel. His cinnamon eyes gleamed with mischief. "Your memory must be going in your old age, Oliver. You were at Sotheby's when Bronowski bought the diamond."

"Swanbeck claimed it was a fake. Where's the diamond?"

"We all know Swanbeck is a professional liar. I should think Bronowski's next of kin has it. Even a disreputable fellow like him must have a next of kin."

Burnell's mouth curved into a smile. "Next of kin, of course. And here I was thinking you were back in the game."

Gregory's eyes widened in mock innocence. "What game would that be, Oliver?"

"Hmph," the superintendent snorted. "Goodbye, Longdon. Give our best to Emmeline."

Gregory gave a little salute and slipped out of the office with all the grace of a cat who has swallowed the cream.

After the door had closed behind him, Finch said, "Sir, we know he stole the diamond. He's the only one who could have made the switch. How, I'm not certain, but—"

Burnell cut him off. "Let's look at this philosophically. Bronowski's dead. It's not surprising that his unsavory life resulted in his untimely demise."

Finch nodded. "True. After all, what goes around comes around."

"Exactly," Burnell agreed, warming to his topic. "Was a crime committed? I have my doubts. The taxpayer did not suffer one iota. Bronowski paid for the diamond. In cash, in full. Sotheby's received its commission. If you think about it, Swanbeck is the only real loser. And does anyone care about him?"

Finch's mouth broke into a broad grin. "No, sir. I suppose not. So we turn a blind eye to Longdon's sleight of hand?"

Burnell leaned back, his chair groaning under his weight. "I prefer to view it as our wedding present, but God help Longdon if he's honing skills for a return engagement."

Finch nodded knowingly. "Shouldn't you have told him that Swanbeck has scarpered?"

Burnell sighed. "He'll find out soon enough. After everything that's happened, let's just give him and Emmeline a couple of days' peace. They deserve that."

℮⌒℮⌒℮

Emmeline crossed the lobby of the Roxburghe Hotel in Edinburgh. She stopped at the reception desk to request a wakeup call and to settle her bill. At nine-thirty the next morning, Alex Salmond, the first minister, was going to hold a press conference at his official residence directly opposite the hotel in Princess Charlotte Square. Then at eleven, Salmond was going to host the second and final day of the international trade conference at Edinburgh Castle. It was going to close with a lavish lunch, but Emmeline wasn't going to stay for that. She was going to catch the three-thirty train from Waverly Station, which was supposed to arrive back in London at seven-fifty tomorrow evening.

The young man on duty behind the reception desk was friendly and efficient. All the administrative tasks were dealt with in fifteen minutes. He even left a note for the morning staff to have Emmeline's bags stored with the concierge, so that she could get them quickly the next day and be on her way to the station with a minimum of fuss.

Emmeline checked her watch. It was seven. She would pop up to her room and take a shower, before having dinner in the hotel restaurant tonight. She felt drained and didn't want to go out. Perhaps she would take a short walk afterward, before going to bed.

Impatient for her shower to loosen her knotted muscles, she opted to take the stairs at the back near the restaurant rather than waiting for the lifts, which were slow.

The minute she walked into her room, she kicked off her shoes and wiggled her toes. She plunked her handbag down on the table between the door and the bathroom, and flopped onto the bed. She would give Gregory a ring before she went down to dinner. But her shower first.

It was only after she came out of the bathroom, wrapped in a towel, her skin still warm and moist, that she noticed the little gold box tied with a bow sitting on the desk. An envelope without anything written on it was propped up against the phone.

She crossed to the desk and picked up the box. Inside was a small black velvet bag. She loosened the drawstring and out tumbled an exquisite heart-shaped silver filigree locket.

Gregory, she thought as a smile touched her lips. How she loved him. Was it possible that in three months she was going to be wife?

She reached for the envelope, stuck her thumb under the corner of the flap, and tore it open. She pulled out the buff card. Her smile soon faded and the words blurred before her eyes.

My dearest Emmeline,

A small token to remember me by. I have to go away for a while. Think of this as adieu, rather than goodbye. I will never forget you. Or Longdon.

All my love,
Alastair

About the Author

Daniella Bernett is a member of the Mystery Writers of America New York Chapter. She graduated summa cum laude with a BS in Journalism from St. John's University. *Lead Me Into Danger, Deadly Legacy, From Beyond The Grave,* and *A Checkered Past* are the first four books in the Emmeline Kirby/Gregory Longdon mystery series. She also is the author of two poetry collections, *Timeless Allure* and *Silken Reflections.* In her professional life, she is the research manager for a nationally prominent engineering, architectural, and construction management firm. Bernett is currently working on Emmeline and Gregory's next adventure. Visit www.daniellabernett.com or follow her on Facebook and Goodreads.